NIGHT UNTO NIGHT

NIGHT UNTO NIGHT

by PHILIP WYLIE

FARRAR & RINEHART, INC.

New York   Toronto

This book has been manufactured in
accordance with paper conservation
orders of the War Production Board

Dedicated with love
to my wife
FREDERICA BALLARD WYLIE

TABLE OF CONTENTS

The heavens declare the glory of God: and the firmament sheweth his handywork.

Day unto day uttereth speech, and night unto night sheweth knowledge.

There is no speech nor language, where their voice is not heard.

Their line is gone out through all the earth, and their words to the end of the world. In them hath he set a tabernacle for the sun.

Which is as a bridegroom coming out of his chamber, and rejoiceth as a strong man to run a race.

His going forth is from the end of the heaven, and his circuit unto the ends of it: and there is nothing hid from the heat thereof.

Psalm 19.

Our revels now are ended. These our actors,
As I foretold you, were all spirits, and
Are melted into air, into thin air;
And, like the baseless fabric of this vision,
The cloud-capp'd towers, the gorgeous palaces,
The solemn temples, the great globe itself,
Yea, all which it inherit, shall dissolve;
And, like this insubstantial pageant faded,
Leave not a rack behind. We are such stuff
As dreams are made on, and our little life
Is rounded with a sleep.

The Tempest, Act IV, Scene 1.

PREFACE

HERE is a novel about death—a novel, that is, about the living and their thoughts of death. In human life two absolutes exist: birth and death. Of the two, we can anticipate only our end. Life is a struggle against ever-nearing death. But in it, as Sigmund Freud has found, there is a wish for death.

Part of the business of the living is to learn the meaning of that strange wish. Most existence on this planet is so primitive, alas, that it concerns itself with an effort to escape the inevitable doom of every man and even the naked thought of doom.

For this futility we struggle. Materialism is man's defiant attempt to overshadow destiny with the panoply of cities, the hurtling activity of his body, the absorption of his five senses through ceaseless compulsion—with toys and furnishings, games, stone jewelry, and fine processions—with listening and looking and smelling and touching and tasting —with all and everything that serves to stave off introspection for a minute, an hour, a lifetime. . . .

Peace is not the perquisite of nations. Individuals, alone, can savor peace. The peace of the world will come only when the people who compose it have found the way to inner peace. Materialism offers no such way—and cannot offer it. As long as we are wholly extraverted—yes, as long as we ascribe "rights" to property or defer to a "right" of possession or consider nations "righteous"—we shall have no peace. That is not an economic statement but a description of a far-off attitude few living men can guess at—and a measure of its distance from us, nowadays.

The shimmering constructions of our postwar world will someday lead us back—through envy and inhumanity, through greed, and through the lust for expressing lust without first examining it—to more wars. Wars are a collective fulfillment of the death wish; they are made necessary by the failure of individuals to reckon with themselves. Wars are a response to the orderliness of nature.

We are governed by laws which lie wholly outside the cognition of most of us—and need not. Our ignorance makes us lawless and the laws compel us to turn upon each other. They need not.

Churchly law cannot suffice for us, any longer. Our churches have studied politics instead of virtue; they have accumulated property instead of wisdom. Meanwhile, each church has dragged into these hopeful days its neolithic ritual and the medieval shabbiness of its dogma. Each has become the mother of darkness. Each now cunningly promulgates darkness to retain adherents so that they, in turn, will hold its power and its property. Christ repudiated the churches of his time with raging eloquence; they were guiltless compared to our own—naïve perforce, where later churches could be clean.

The laws—the truths—which govern man abide nowhere in churches.

Agnosticism will solve the dilemma of an individual—and leave him with half a life: the half he chooses by deciding he knows so much he is unable to know anything. Such a man may be moral; busyness will replace his spirit. He will learn no more about life than a sparrow learns.

In *Night Unto Night,* I have concerned myself with these matters—not with the laws, so much, because in the finding of them lies the source of spiritual strength, but in a description of certain avenues of search. This book contains a few small ways to begin to think rather than the thoughts. Here are attitudes, lines for investigation, and statements of common problems which are too often either shuffled off for mundane affairs or flatly rejected as valid subjects for study.

This is, then, a religious book—even when it attacks organized religion. For the "organization" of a religion is, again, an individual task and not a public work. As in *Generation of Vipers,* I have borrowed freely from the brooding of others so that the reader will not have to depend entirely upon the workings of my own most ordinary mind for his entertainment or his interest. But I have written this book as a novel rather than as a sermon because, while much of what I say here belongs to logic, much more belongs to

x

experience. I want my readers to explore human values even more than to take inventory of our collective predicament.

One or two credits should be added to this introduction— and one explanation.

Night Unto Night was not my idea. A year and a half ago, at the home of my friend, Milton MacKaye, in Washington, I was talking about that vast portion of American civilization which has been unwittingly erected as a sanctuary from, or a concealment of, human death. Our conversation led thence to immortality, and to ghosts. We also discussed the phenomenon of man's evolution in two billion painful years; and we considered consciousness—which has, I believe, a relation to space and time different from the one momentarily in acceptance among university pedants.

Mrs. MacKaye, who writes stories under the name of Dorothy Cameron Disney, suggested that my argument had made the theme for a novel; forthwith she outlined its principal characters, its setting, and its central problem. The evening's talk was thereby personalized. I thought about that kernel of commencement for a month or two—and spent the best part of a year writing this book.

Those not used to the kind of books I write to my private specifications may feel that I have taken some undue advantages here. Two of my characters are unusually disquisitious; but this whole novel is a kind of monologue. As in *Finnley Wren,* I have set one fable and half of a second in the story. They are allegories for changes of mood. And among the pages ahead will be found a section from "another" book— fragments of a chapter in a make-believe work by William Percival Gaunt. These bits are set in a different type; they may be skipped by all who are allergic to themes and concerned with surfaces alone. The altering of the type-style will make it easy for such persons to find their places again.

The title is taken, of course, from the Nineteenth Psalm, the second half of the second verse: ". . . night unto night sheweth knowledge." But it is intended to suggest, also, the thought expressed in a phrase from *The Tempest:* ". . . our little life is rounded with a sleep." Part of the psalm and the speech by Prospero are quoted on the page immediately preceding this note.

Since I believe that life and death also are parts of something else and since I believe the meaning of that otherness is different for each individual, I am made arbitrary by my own definitions. The content limits here are my own; the principal discipline is an effort not to seem obscure in *Night Unto Night*.

Its readers will doubtless wonder if I have ever seen a ghost. I have not. But most of the "supernatural" events in this book have been witnessed by me and I have set them down as I observed them, exactly—though in other contexts and situations. All are as true as I can make any description —the description, say, of my desk, or yesterday's street accident, or of an autumn-clad hill. The black, amœboid shape— the abnormal tide—premonition—the dream of "unknowable" event—are experiences with which I have had to cope as intelligently as I could.

The story of the bowl of marigolds is my story also. The scene of that astonishing occurrence was carefully examined by my friend, Dr. William A. Gardner, a well-known New York medical man and a brilliant physical scientist. In no other way or sense, incidentally, does William Gardner resemble my character Maddox—who makes the investigation in the book. Whereas I have had Maddox take a skeptical view of the affair, Gardner, for all his empiricism, came to the conclusion that a knowable explanation did not exist for what had happened to my marigold bouquet.

For the rest, I shall let the book speak and the reader think, if he cares to.

PART I

THE BEACH

NOTHING was wrong. The phrase spoke in Ann's mind. Nothing was wrong. She repeated it so that she could savor its comfort. He would come back. His ship would turn in between the brown boulders that formed the jetties. Canvas would shroud the outpointed guns. The metal canisters of TNT would be neatly ranged astern, like barrels in a grocery store, painted gray and laid horizontal. They would be places to sit in the sunshine again, not bombs. Nothing was wrong. The gulls would yaw like little angels, flying—talk like demons—and dive at the garbage. Small craft would dip in the bow's spreading corrugation. The men would be tired— some pale, some burned by the sun—all furred with a week's beard. They'd come in smartly, back water hard, foam it, annoy the pelicans, and lean the subchaser against the pier.

At the wooden gate, gray like the ship, gray as the bombs, the women would wait. The yeoman's wife with the baby and the tart with tourmaline eyes. Ann, too. They'd all be there. They'd represent hot coffee, cold beer, cocktails, perfume, music, clean sheets, low lights, love-abed.

Ann sat down in the sand. She had walked only a little way along the beach.

Perhaps the depth charges would be gone, this time. Perhaps the forward gun would hang like a broken finger. There might be a toothy hole amidships. The ship would come in grim and faster still, throw fish with her propellers, crackle against the dock. Besides the women, there would be ambulances. White-clad men running aboard with stretchers. They'd carry off Bill. He'd be smoking a cigarette. He'd see her among the women and wink. They'd pretend that they were casual about it, too, until they were alone together after the shrapnel had been successfully removed. She'd wink back. She'd chuck the yeoman's baby under the chin and smile at the girl with lovely eyes.

When Bill was well again, a small but fiercely proud swastika would be worn by his ship.

Nothing wrong about a subchaser, four days overdue.

The edge of the moon showed like a slit in the door of a white-hot furnace. It dissolved the radiant mist that had preceded it, welled, shouldered up, cast from its face a small cloud, shredded it, and shone upon the frail fragments. These, for a little while, took color, pale and prismatic. For a little while they made a rainbow against the blue night; but its phosphorescent tones resembled the spectrum of sunless plants; they were pallid; they profused a rainbow without promise, detached and lunar, like the unseen rainbows in the frosted gases of Uranus.

The moon soon floated cleanly above the roof of cumulus. Below, the sea displayed its track—the thousand-spangled broad highway that leads from every beholder to nowhere. On the beach, dimpled depressions of human feet took rims of shadow. Encroaching palms rattled, green and glistening. The onshore breeze was warm.

Ann ran sand through her fingers, feeling the day-long heat in it. South, toward the lighthouse, miles away, the underbelly of a cloud burnt briefly with orchid fire. Lightning. A gunflash. Or the wet flame in the core of a depth-charge blast. She held her grains of sand tensely, unable to know. She had seen burning tankers. But she could not tell storms on the marine backdrop from naval action—and Bill always shrugged.

Lieutenant Dodge had been—how?—over the phone: "No, Ann. No report. That is—nothing for dissemination. He told you, didn't he, that the regulation period could stretch out? That he might be on his way someplace? Iceland? England? That's how we go, you know. We can't inform the wives—not even new and beautiful ones. It's war, gal. You'll have a whole lot of this sort of thumb-twiddling to do. Bridge, maybe? Mrs. D. and I would like to have you— and the candidate list for a fourth would be as long as the Navy roster—"

She took apart each sentence. Did he know anything he could not tell? Did he sound worried? Did he flatter her too much? Was the invitation to play bridge an attempt to maneuver her into a position from which she could be bolstered against shock?

There were widows' walks around the tops of some of the houses in the New England town where she had been born. They would show you, in one, an exposed timber worn saddle-shaped by the shoe leather of a wife who had watched there—in the moonlight, in the rain, in the feathery snow of winter—for the topmast of a homebound whaler.

Steel whales, she thought.

There were no widows' walks in Florida.

She turned.

Bill's uncle's house looked at the moon with its unlighted windows. These glassy eyes, and the mouths of separate porch roofs, grimaced. She tried to read their expressions. The effort caused her to see the house itself and not its character in the dark. It was three stories high. Its weathered wood and rusted steel had survived hurricanes, but the buffer dunes had been gouged and flattened by great waves. Three stories of porches—balconies on the sides—gables on top, steep, shingled slopes—and, wreathing every edge, the scroll-work Bill's uncle had cherished. It festooned the house like blanched seaweed.

She could not see the need of paint, but remembered it, only, for the coiling frets glowed as if in fresh white lead. That was the dew, she decided. But there were boards— beams and clapboards—paint-stripped by the scouring sand and bleached by the salty wind which, on close inspection, were so warped, so gullied, and so nude as to belie ax, saw, plane and brush. These boards, rather, were suggestive of nature—of the weathered stumps of fallen trees and branches desiccating on bare mountaintops; they matched exactly the pale lumber discarded by the sea.

The house seemed entirely dark. Because of its situation, that seemingness of utter dark was a response to military regulation—a defense against the foe that cruised offshore and used the lights on land for silhouetting targets. Targets, Ann thought, are always people.

But there was illumination in the echoing intestines of the structure. She and Bill had made a blackout room of Uncle Paul's den on the ground floor—nailing worn comforters over two small windows, manufacturing a light-lock of Navajo rugs, arranging a devious corridor for ventilation, and adding to the contents of the place certain amenities against the embattled nights.

5

An ivory battery radio, "streamlined" as if it were a projectile, gleamed amid Uncle Paul's collection of walking-sticks. Under the dusty trophies—stuffed snakes and alligators, the tarpon, a turtle and a time-pecked buck's head—was a modern overspread of jacketed novels, electrical cooking appliances, stacked tins of food, tubular steel chairs with chrome plating and colored cloth seats, magazines, and—now—the white uniform coat on which she had been sewing a shining button.

Not an extensive refurbishing, considering the size of the house. They couldn't afford much.

Ann dug into cooler sand. The invisible but penetrating expression faded from her eyes. She could see parallel lines that edged the serpentine walk from the beach dunes to the steps—conch shells, set touching, all that distance. Their inner pinks and outer browns had been chalked by the decades. After each "blow" Uncle Paul had patiently re-collected them, replacing the lost shells and the broken ones, tossing his discard onto a pile in back where it stood shoulder-high, overswarmed with various vines which, on sudden mornings, were in turn buried by their own flowers—red—yellow—blue—salmon.

At the left of the house was a wooden sign, its rear supports showing from where she sat. But, as if she were facing it, she read the legend: "For Sale or Rent. Reasonable. Enquire Your Agent or Phone 5-3841."

The house was Bill's inheritance. They wished to sell or rent it—to move from the jungles and the barrens north of Miami Beach—and to settle in a smaller, more graceful abode near other young men in white coats and brass buttons, other young women with dark hair and fair hair, pretty blouses, peasant skirts and bare legs. The new development—Cinnamon Beach—would be nice, Ann thought. It was only a few miles farther up. Miles meant more minutes, and more people on the bus, but neither mattered.

She continued to gaze at the dilapidated mansion and its environs; her twisted posture was uncomfortable but she did not know that.

To the north stretched an enormous "vacant lot"—a tract of land that had been cleared during the real estate boom in 1925—but not again thereafter—so that it was thickly covered with the rankest of Florida's trees and plants. Thatch-

6

boled petticoat palms thrust up through the sea grapes. Tough creepers ran out on the sand to the spindrift margins. Saw-grass and Spanish bayonet made ragged stands. Vines laced and interlaced the underbrush. Their leaves tented over large areas, giving them a smooth external contour. To the south was genuine jungle: gumbo limbos and mahoganies lifted huge trunks, adorned, according to New England standards, with too few branches and too few leaves; around them boiled a green blur of mangrove—dense, leafy, house-high, supported by roots shaped like croquet wickets which were sunk in steaming muck and as rhymelessly interrelated as their greasy tops. At night, noises came from this Amazonian swamp. By day and night, it stank.

West of the house an eighth of a mile was the road that served the seaside—black asphalt embedded with and littered by fragments of coral as white as monument marble.

In no direction could another dwelling be seen.

The solitude of Uncle Paul's "villa"—he had once possessed enough money and effrontery to call it that—had at first enraptured its new, young tenants. Then it had palled. They had not discussed the worrisome aspects of it, but, rather, its many attendant "inconveniences." With the war—with Bill's enlistment and his graduation from the subchaser school as an ensign—the solitude had become Ann's chief possession. She had protested her satisfaction with the dwelling. But she paid for her courage with a deepening of the shadows under her eyes and a tendency to look backward in the twilight, to whistle at her work, and to start easily, even in crowds. An ensign's salary imposes such conditions—and harder ones—on many persons.

"We'll have to rent the damned Victorian pagoda—or sell it," Bill would say whenever his ship was docked in Miami. "Can you hold on till a client comes?"

And Ann would answer, "I love it. I'll miss it."

He would try to envisage the sort of person who would take the house: "A spoiled younger son of a rich mother, deceased. Somebody about sixty years old, with a scratchy housekeeper. Sinus trouble. No. Arthritis. Arthritis—and amateur archæology. He'd have a book to do. He'd have found some ruins on the one expedition his mother financed —while he was still a postgrad at Cambridge. Sodom, more than likely. Gomorroh, at the very least. Did you ever think,

7

Ann, how easy ruins are to find? That is—did you ever hear of an archæological expedition that *failed* to find ruins? World's littered with 'em. More ruins, I expect, than extant cities. Looking for ruins is no harder than looking for free public libraries. Anyhow—this old beggar would now be hunting for a place to write his book. Guys like him always think places write books—not people. He'd have a title for the tome, certainly. After all, he has had his notes for thirty-odd years, hasn't he? He's been talking about settling down in a quiet spot and doing his 'work' all that time, hasn't he? Lemme see. How about 'The Potsherds of the Stricken Infidels'?"

"It wouldn't begin with a 'The'," Ann had said. "Just—'Potsherds—' and so on. How about, 'Shards from the Hand of Jehovah,' or—wait! Why not, 'Pillar of Salt'?"

They had agreed on Pillar of Salt.

Ann smiled and became rigid. She turned her head slowly. It was only the sea. One of the small, gushing waves had pushed on the sole of her sandal. She watched it recede, swift and scintillant in the moonlight. The great track on the water was eye-confusing because of the length of time she had devoted to appraising and remembering the house standing in the low key of moonrays. Sharp reflections traveled distances on ridges of the unquiet ocean; they shimmered, flickered, and vanished into unexpected blacknesses. The sea itself was soundful. Whispers, lascivious laughter, bubblings, the gurgle of midget breakers and the indolent hiss of filtering sand formed together not a composition but the accompaniment for music there was no one to play.

The tide was very high.

Higher, Ann perceived, than it had ever been before. The moon, round, austere, imaginably tremendous and heavy, was pushing the sea ahead of its slow circumscription of the earth. Ann thought of the tide upthrust and spreading west across the Atlantic, all the way from Africa, opposite which she sat. She threw away her sand to banish the picture of tide in such dimensions.

Downtown, in Biscayne Bay, it would be seeping toward people's lawns. A tide this high would brim the canal along Dade Boulevard. Things would be killed by it—hibiscus, orchid trees, mangoes, sapadillos—and elsewhere, perhaps, golf greens. They'd have to slack off on the hawsers that held the new destroyer across the end of the Navy pier. Between the jetties—the jetties through which Bill would come home —the welling sea would flood all but the topmost stones. When the ebb came, against the breeze, there would be a maelstrom, wild with steep cones of water, sparred with darkly dashing palm fronds, aglow with churned phosphorescence. It would be nothing to a strong ship, steadily handled.

Nothing at all.

And nothing was wrong. Engine trouble had forced them to put in elsewhere. Key West, probably. Engine trouble was a military secret, these days. . . . They'd been radioed to go farther afield, to extend their regular period of submarine stalking. They'd picked up extra supplies—at Nassau, say—and hurried south or east or north to meet the onslaught of a wolf pack. PC boats were scarce and thinly spread. They'd . . .

Ann faced it.

Something was wrong.

Lieutenant Dodge had been worried.

How wrong?

How worried?

A concrete blackness materialized in the sea, in the tar and quicksilver, in the dazzling Brownian movement of it; she saw it and lost sight of it; she was afraid—and afraid of being afraid because she was so alone. It took on definition, direction—and a sound as well. In two dimensions, at an indeterminate distance from the shore, a motorboat idled across the path of the moon. Its engines simmered like a kettle. A black stencil, a property in a marionette show, it went unfalteringly through the beglamoured thoroughfare— and lost itself in the penumbra beyond.

Ann concentrated on that welcome passage. The boat represented guardianship and human company. It was the civilian patrol. She let her throat contract with the recollection of Bill's informal praise:

"Civilians, for God's sake!" (How recently he had been one!) "The butcher, the baker, the candlestick maker! A guy I met, owns a laundry. They've got those little sports cruisers —and fishing boats—and they go it all night long. Then they show up for work the next day! A few carry a depth charge —one three-hundred-pounder. They open up their motors and

9

run at surfaced subs and—so help me!—roll the damn bomb off their sterns and high-tail! Most of 'em, though, don't even have a BB gun. But the sub skippers can't chance it— they submerge. So far as I know, not one man-jack in the whole motley crowd has failed to tear dead on at every sighted sub! Can you imagine what a five-inch shell, point-blank, would do to a thirty-foot launch? I can. I've seen the pieces. Hell! Even the Minute Men had stone walls to hide behind!"

Long after the boat had passed, Ann clung to a consideration of it, proud of Bill for his pride, and proud on her own account. When its custodianship, and the vivid water, and the house behind her failed presently to divert or to transmute her thoughts, she grasped at invented straws. . . .

It was getting late, but her sister Gail might put in an appearance. She might be drunk. She would probably be accompanied by one or two other girls as explicitly turned out by nature as herself. And, men, of course. Ann tried to imagine how Gail regarded all those men—whether she saw the uniforms, or saw them without uniforms, or did not see them at all but doted on some Object, as remote as a dream of Lilith's, taking it for granted that men were part of the Object, like the small stones that make up a large idol. Gail's departures, Ann thought, left a wake of vague insatieties; but her presence was as compelling as a barbaric dance, even when she sat still and said nothing. Like such dancing, Gail-in-being drove back the little demons. But they were peripheral, always.

Then Ann remembered that Gail was going to the Country Club to help entertain some British flying students . . .

I will telephone the cleaner in the morning. I will ask him why he sent back the mauve dress without removing the spot. It was only ice cream. Mrs. Bailey's coming over to show me what to do about air raids. As if I didn't know! She'll probably wear her helmet, too. There's Red Cross, at three. I must put down ant buttons in the kitchen. They're such little ants! Like red grains of sand, a river of them, but if you step among them, you get—not wet—but bathed in fire. I should really do it tonight. Now, in fact. If I keep on scrunching back out of the way of the tide, I'll be under the trees. I wouldn't like that . . .

She had been in Florida less than a year. But the tide—this

particular night's tide—did not fit her preconceptions of its proper possibilities. It should be turning, but it was not. And it had pushed too far up on the slanted shelf of beach. There was not much wind. The waves were no more than knee-high. The sea wrack cast up by the storm three days ago should not be floating. The great, barnacle-bearing beam Bill had dragged ashore for repairs he would someday undertake should not be rolling in the silver water. But through the ground she could detect its tumbling weight. It had been hauled too high on shore to be troubled by the surge of any tranquil tide. Yet it was moving: out to sea—in again.

It might even be washed away, and Bill would be disappointed. If he knew she was watching its jeopardy, he would expect her to secure it. There was his shark line—coiled at the foot of the coconut nearest the water. Three-eighths-inch Manila, one end tied to the palm. On the other, he'd had his cable leader and his fist-sized hook, until recently. Until the subs had set loose in the sea better quarry than sharks: cartons, cases, drums, bales of raw rubber. She remembered the day she'd brought in a bale unassisted—swimming out in the warm water with the rope, making it fast, swimming back, dragging the spongy, leaden stuff as high and nearly dry as she could and tying the rope up short. Two hundred and twenty pounds of it, prime Brazilian.

"Well, baby," Bill had said when he'd come home and inspected the treasure trove, "you've put tires on a couple of bombers!"

She had only to kick off her sandals, wade in, fix a noose around the beam and snub it up when the tide finally reached its peak. She made a forward movement to rise—and could not.

Let it roll, she thought. There's an easterly breeze. It will doubtless drift in again somewhere along this beach and Bill and I can float it home. Even if it goes, it won't matter much. She thought of the circling currents that fend the Gulf Stream from the land like aquatic bearings. They could steal the hewn log. Let them. But she wondered why she lacked the energy to rise. Her eyes kept reconnoitering the moon-path. I suppose, she thought, I want to see that boat come back.

But the boat was a conscious recollection—an *excuse* . . . I'm waiting.

The notion that she was waiting—waiting patiently—in a place where nothing could be expected to happen was too unwonted to be immediately accepted. People with troubled minds, and nothing to do, probably seem to themselves to be waiting, she thought. They listen more carefully than other people, look more steadily into elemental mirrors like this mirror of the moon, and wonder more about wondering.

But I am waiting.

I came down here to wait.

She knew that for an exquisitely simple reason. Because this stretch of sand was as private as any world's end, she and Bill had used it often for their own romantic room. Always, hitherto, when she had sat here alone in the moonlight, it had been to recollect and to anticipate this passionate function of sand, sea, moon and miscellaneous stars. Tonight, she had neither remembered nor imagined.

The faint shiver transmitted through the earth from the rolling beam was rendered insensible by a quaking of her spirit. She pulled her sandal from the touching fingers of the tide. She shrank back under the star-shaped shadow of the palm. Her eyes briefly left the waves; her pupils enlarged and swept the powdery monotones of the beach. There was no one on it. The motion of distant tree and vine was too small to be discerned; the entire landscape lay frozen in the milky light.

Ann noticed that the tide did not seem to spread and respread its chrome puddles so far up on the sand, on either side of where she sat. It's the perspective, she thought; it seems strange because I feel strange. So she resolved her will against the deteriorating night.

But I am waiting, she thought.

Now, several nocturnal entities came to her assistance. A bird barked repeatedly in the mangrove swamp behind and below her. The warm fanning of the breeze was replaced for a moment by a cooler, drier overpouring of air. She looked around. Flowers, shrubs, tables, benches and winding conch shells were individually distinct in the light of the lifted moon. Implausible black shadows of Uncle Paul's scrollwork had crept down the angled façades and hung below their wooden counterparts like curly beards. On the road, the lights of a dimmed-out automobile evanescently whitewashed the branches of an Australian pine.

I'll go in, she thought; I've been silly.

The wind warmed. The bird fell silent. The car was gone. Now the tide was forcing her under the tree. She thought: It's after me. She recognized the need to make distinctions between the dark breeding of her own mind and whatever happened, or was happening. Was happening. She abandoned doubt that a process of some unrecognizable sort was already in effect. A process of which she was the center.

She fenced with it. The tide, here between the barrens and the jungle, here in front of the Victorian pagoda, did seem higher than elsewhere on the long, straight beach. Objectively, that mere seeming was the only evidence of any "process" whatever and it lent itself to explanations of perspective, refraction, distances—numberless physical criteria she could think of.

There remained the sense of waiting.

Heebie-jeebies.

Mrs. Bailey had said, "I'd get the screaming meemies in a place like this—especially at night."

Not getting them was a part of being Bill's wife. Being Bill's wife was the beginning of her life, its end, and all the meaning of it. New England women, women educated in college, women married to naval officers, don't get them. For one thing, you cannot start screaming on a great beach where nobody will hear you—but only dolphins, swimming past, and birds in the mangrove. You don't run into your house, either, looking over your shoulder all the way, and telephone someone to come and get you or to come and stay with you. You stand up. You walk slowly into the house Bill inherited. You put down the ant buttons. You pour yourself a little sherry—two or three fingers in a tumbler. You take a quarter of a grain of phenobarbital, which the doctor recommended but Bill doesn't know you possess. If you must, you finally phone somebody who wouldn't mind. The night watch down at the yard. You ask if there is any news about the PC So-and-so.

They say no.

You go to bed. By and by, you sleep. You may wake up before sunrise, in the gray light, when the birds are flying fast and trucks are bumbling on the road. You step out on the balcony and stare down at the beach and out over the sea. The east is dyed with dawn. Sand rims the indigo water. Far out, visible only because you are peering from a third story, are the hazy spars, stacks, hulls and smudges of a convoy. In it, you proudly realize, are the PCs. You see them, if the convoy is close enough inshore: if it is headed south, that is. They hurry along the sides of the ships and cut across the course; they lag astern; they stop and listen for a certain metallic beat . . .

The wind died. The ultimate respite her imagination could discover flickered and fled like the going of a homemade moving picture when the loose, last end of film whirls past the lens. The moon on the sea was the round-edged rectangle left on the wall—the radiant blank waiting for next impressions. Ann had now to cope with horror.

The night emitted it. The substance of it was palpable—but she could not name it. An uninvaded portion of her brain told her that there was a sense which could apperceive and describe it, but she thought of this sense as other-dimensional and even more dangerous to investigate than the terror she had discerned. It now swam the black night and licked the bright wave tops—real, at last. I am afraid, she thought. God help me, I am frightened. Something is going to happen. Something is happening. It has been, all evening.

Only her heart was moving. But her nervous system kept tallying her environment. It was hot, still, stuffy. There was still nobody on the beach. No sound in the house behind her. No sound around it. A cloud went across the moon. The visible landscape instantly contracted. The dancing avenue to nowhere was swept out of existence. The tide had now risen two vertical feet above any peak she had known of. She remembered that she had heard of a crocodile shot in the swamp in 1923. She turned, inch by inch, toward what seemed a lesser menace. Only the naked sand stretched back under the palm trees, faint but searchable in the wan light. There was no stretched shape, no silent forward lurch, no white snaggle. Only the stuffiness. The smell.

That was the word, the sense, for which the unpanicky part of her mind had struggled. There was a smell in the night—sweet and slight. Sweet but not sweet; slight but permeating. In the discovery, she found a momentary trifle of reassurance. The odor might have been in her nostrils for a long time. She had, indeed, endeavored to become conscious of it for minutes. She sniffed, lifted her chin, inhaled purposefully. It was the smell of carrion. Not ordinary beach carrion—not fish, acrid and repellent—but richer rot, an unknown smell that, by some immemorial instinct, she knew.

"Oh, no!" she whispered.

Her nerves wilted, veins collapsed; her hands lay palms up on the sand; she shook and twitched; she saw the pale profile of her own body with hideous humility.

The dark part of the cloud rode over the moon. Opalescent mist trailed across it. Then it shone full again. The golden road rushed in from the horizon and out to meet itself. She did not move to look there because her eyes were already fixed and statically attentive. The object on the south edge of the effulgence was so much larger than the one she had expected that she caught her breath aloud. It bobbed, wobbled, threw back glints of the moon, sailed slowly toward the center of the light, and foreshortened itself by rotating in the weak current.

It came in, over the sandbar. Part of it, near the water, was paler than the roundish attachments above; they were quite dark. Ann counted them involuntarily. Five. The wind veered and now she was directly assailed by the sticky repugnance. This was what she had awaited: these five dead men hooked onto their raft.

She was free, now, to move. She would run for it. It was a Navy raft. The Coast Guard had some. She repressed her thoughts successfully, because she could act. She would phone the Navy. They would hurry up here with a car. Or a boat. Maybe they'd notify the civilian patrol. She stood up, shaking, unaware of it. Searchlights would probe the gliscent sea. They'd throw a grapple, whatever that was—lift aboard this lush, charnel stench—and give it names. She turned toward the house, stepped, and stopped.

Would they?

The significance of that question dawned on her. If one of those five men were Bill . . .

She did not hear her own scalded sob. She faced the sea again and stared at the steady progress of the raft. It had come its long way to her beach, like the flotsam she and Bill had salvaged—in spite of the eyes of patrols. Outside, in the ocean, it would be a very small thing. It must have been in the water a long time. *Four days,* she thought.

They wouldn't turn on searchlights because of the submarines. A convoy might be passing, out there, or a lone freighter. She debated frantically. It would surely come ashore, of its own accord, farther north. But it might not. This particular bit of debris, sensed but not even yet imagined by her, might easily bob and slap and gyrate slowly, making its own way out over the edge of the horizon forever. Even now, it was approaching the far side of the moonpath. She walked a few steps to keep it in view.

These are the men of five women. She impaled that fantasy. What would they expect of me? Hope of me? The question became one with the thought of what she expected of herself.

To envision the act was different from the attempt of it— or even the beginning of the attempt. She untied the shark line from the palm tree with cold hands. The smell was diminishing. She walked several rods before she had the life raft again in sharp view. A short span of the water would be over her head in this tide. There might be sharks. She threw down the rope.

No woman, she whispered in her mind, would be expected—

No woman. No college graduate. No bachelor of arts. No girl in a playsuit. Alone. At night. No woman. It's war, gal.

No Russian woman?

No Chinese?

She ran. She caught up with the raft again. Ahead, on the bright beach, was an old log from which projected a bolt with a nut as big as her two hands amalgamated by rust to its formidable threads. She'd hung a towel on it, once or twice. She made fast her line. She kicked off her sandals. The sea felt warm on her feet; she could barely be sure when it reached her waist and her armpits; she plainly felt it splash her chin. She swam, and as she swam she wept, but she did not know that.

"Don't be afraid of sharks," Bill always said. "Mind your business. They mind theirs."

Just as if it were another bale of rubber.

She could not approach it closely from the shore side. Its reek was liquidescent—not sweet, now, not endurable. She swam out and around. Something hit her leg. She screamed thinly. She kicked. The thing rasped her leg again and she knew it was a rope—trailing from the raft. She would not have to go any closer to the suck and wallow of stretched canvas, the loll of its watching burden. She looked at the wet moonlight, spat, put her face under the surface, tied the two ropes together, and began pulling herself toward shore on the line fixed to the bolt: she could not swim any farther.

On hands and knees she crawled clear of the last rippling inches of the sea. She vomited. Then she lay on her back, shuddering paroxysmally. After a while, she saw the strewn stars. She became aware that the rope leading into the sea was pulling, irrhythmically; each time it slacked off, it touched the back of her wrist. She rose patiently and went through the same ritual she had with the bale, hauling in until her salvage grounded.

The shallows canted the five decayed bodies. One was pulled under the raft, which rubbed it, ducking the head. Three basked on their sides. The fifth floated out behind, its white face looking toward her. All five men had hooked themselves to the outside lines of the raft by snaffles in their life belts. Ann stared at this, and soon, deep within her—under audibly dripping clothes, beneath pimpling skin—she felt a perverse passion, a formidable compulsion. She, who had waited, need not wait longer. Surely, that was the true intention of this circumstance.

She went back into the water and looked. The thought of Bill, if it could have been a thought, controlled her irises, sharpening her focus. She no longer smelled anything. But she recoiled again from the new, near revelation of the moonlight: these five men had been machine-gunned. Their fungoid flesh was raddled; it lay blackly open. Waves ringed up and peeled down her thighs. This man had black hair. This man's nose was not Bill's—nor could it have been. This man was bald. That left two. This one blond, but too blond. The last—there was no hair to tell by—no nose. His strong shoulders fell forward on the canvas of the raft. One arm was wrapped, rotted—around it, the fingers interclenched with decking shrouds. There was tattooing on the arm.

Thank God.

She looked toward the shore. It was near, and she could go, now, into the house; telephone; deal with this cargo—and then commence the other, longer undertaking. Bill would come back; it might be very soon. War, he'd say. War.

She took a firm step toward shore and paused; then

17

empty of dread, she bent low and gazed at that tattooed arm.
Even as she curved her back she tried to give herself the
reason: it's a hero's arm; the subs won that one; sank his
ship; slaughtered the crew.

He died for me.

The design was sufficiently plain. Perhaps she'd had a
suspicion of its nature before she looked:

"Whitey Bates is our bosun. We couldn't run—by golly,
we couldn't dock—without him! Tough as Texas, twice as
bighearted—and he came from Vermont! Got his gal tattooed
on his arm, with wings like an angel, and he kisses her,
according to the sailors, every time he decides to take apart
some marine—or maybe a bar."

2

SHE went between the white meanders of the conches.

Bill's dead.

Like a bell that broke her brain.

I knew it.

I knew it all the time.

She thought she was running. One should run with this
word.

But she was walking, walking tediously. Halfway up
the path she stopped and faced the big, weather-beaten house.
She perceived another thing she had half understood for a
long time, as she had that Bill was dead: the malignance of
this house. Its sinuous frescoes writhed. Its antic faces looked
at her—and not at what they had seen behind her. That, to
Ann in this moment, was a part of sorrow, sorrow that over-
vaulted awfulness—left it, decrepit and sickly, to be tended
in far-off, nasty hours. Besides, she was going to enter the
house to undo the secrecy of the life raft. This house was
mindful of a different secret, one it had contained even before the sea had swallowed Bill's waxy remnants.

The realization touched her scalp, stirred it, fixed her
in the path like a drenched statue. She chattered the name
of God.

I can't go in. But it was there before, and I knew it, and
went in.

Then she could smell again, suddenly.

18

She ran.

The door banged.

Lights flared briefly in the hall. She looked at the stairs, the wooden avalanche up which she had clambered every night to bed. There was nothing on the stairs . . .

Out at sea, quartering from the house, a mile or so away, a man in a polo shirt snatched the night glasses from their place beside the radium dial of the compass, let go the wheel, and called, "Hey, Joe! Lights!" Joe woke and sat up. "On shore. Could be a signal. They've gone out! Three windows lighted up. All the shades were drawn. Might mean something!" Joe yawned. "It means some damn fool, some dame, probably, forgot her pocketbook in the living room. Dull night, hunh?" The man in the polo shirt acquiesced: "Dull as hell. I smelled something kind of funny for a while. Couldn't make out what it was. But it's gone, now." Joe yawned again and lay back on the bunk. . . .

Ann measured her way around the newel post to the tent of Navajo rugs. She had switched off the lights and gone down the long hall, trailing her finger tip on the oatmeal paper until the heavy wool fabric blocked her.

The den looked stagy: she was seeing it with eyes accustomed to the dark. Bill's coat was there, white, with brass buttons. A uniform. Like actors' uniforms in plays. She had never expected to become intimately acquainted with uniforms. The imperious telephone. Its numbers spun under the whirling holes. You're Navy; you cannot say, Something horrible has happened.

"This is Mrs. William Gracey—"

"Oh, yes, Mrs. Gracey. Anything the matter?"

The yeoman remembered her. And he heard trouble.

"Yes. Who's OD?

"Lieutenant Becker. I'll connect you—"

"Hello, Ann. Jim Becker here."

"Look, Jim. I was sitting on the beach. A Navy raft floated in. I—I was afraid it might drift out of sight and be lost—"

"*Christ!*" That was a whisper. "Spill it, gal."

"There were five men. They'd been machine-gunned—"

Urgent, now—fast, commanding. "Ann! You're trailing off! Whatever you do, don't faint till we get up there. Hear me?"

She felt her mouth make a smile, ghostly, vestigial: Jim always thought like light shooting from a mirror.

"All right, Jim. I—I recognized one of the men—"

"Not—?"

"No. But—"

"Listen. No more on the phone. Too public. Who do you want? The skipper'll come, of course—"

"Don't wake him, Jim. I mean—I know how little rest he gets."

"Look, darling. You belong to us. *He* did. Who do you want?"

"If you weren't on, tonight—"

"Twenty minutes."

Ann put the phone together.

You belong to us.

He *did*.

Official confirmation.

3

THE old man turned the old car from the road and switched off his parking lights. He drove, now, toward the sea. The two-rut track was alabastrine. Weeds mopped the drip pan. "Bright as day," he said cheerfully. "This is the best spot, and I've saved her till last."

The man at his side grunted.

The car stopped. The old man's hair, in the moonlight, was as white as the coral that glowed in the two ruts. The other man climbed out and took a surf-casting rod from the rear seat. His shoes oozed salt water noisily. "Tide's full in," he said. "Wind's cut around a little to the north'ard."

"Varying. I'll bring the bait."

They climbed over a dune, strode heavily between two more and stood before the dazzling amphitheater of moonlit ocean. The younger man admired it aloud. The old one muttered.

"Hunh?"

"I said—the tide sure is in full up here! Higher'n I've ever seen it. Well—make your cast—"

The other hesitated, looking to his right. "If the people in that house hear us—? Wouldn't it be better to go up farther?"

"Young fellow and a girl live there. Navy man. They don't mind. I talked to 'em—once. Told 'em I knew his uncle —had his permission to fish here, which I did. Peculiar old duck, Paul Gracey."

He cast. His line drew a parabola behind his flying bait. His reel bespoke the distance. They could hear the sinker splash.

The other man cast.

The wind dropped and came again from the southeast. "Something haywire in Denmark," the younger man said.

The old one reeled in slowly. He peered along the coast toward the vaporous swamp. His chamois-colored face wrinkled with the effort of far vision. "You stay here, Chuck. I'll be right back." He went down and down the beach. Chuck felt a nibble, struck, missed, waited. The old man came trudging back, his head shining. "We're gettin' out of here, Chuck."

"Suits me. We got six. What was it?"

The dunes had already closed behind the old man and his long rod before he made an answer. "Something you aren't ever going to know about, Chuck. Something that's been taken care of, and is no business of ours." He stopped, let the younger man pass, and turned to face the east. He climbed the softly sloughing sand a little way so that he could see the ocean and he screwed up his face again, as if he were trying to peer across it, and beyond.

Chuck had never heard his granddad curse before.

4

THE motorcycle cop said, "Yes, sir," and felt proud of himself for the military sound of it. He kicked his starter, turned on his crimson headlight, rolled down the drive, and put his siren on the low register. Behind him, the Navy car picked up speed.

The cop buzzed the lighted tollhouse. The night collector waved.

Islands and bridges alternated. Lieutenant Becker watched the sluicing scenery—palms, oleanders, white walls, tile roofs, empty intersections, golf courses. The tires resented the turn; springs brought back the leaning tonneau. Hotels unreeled, tenanted, dark. Estates, palatial houses, a broad canal with lawns, yachts, even gondola posts, showing striped in the moonlight. Hell of a lot of money in America, Jim Becker thought. They soared within sight of the sea, following the red aura that silhouetted the man on the brash motorcycle. Their road pushed close to the water. I said twenty minutes, Jim thought. He looked at his watch and leaned forward to see the speedometer. Seventy-five. By and by he tapped the driver. "About a mile."

They stopped under the porte-cochere, climbed out, and he saw her standing there.

"Ann."

"Hello, Jim. Captain Wilson! You needn't have come."

The skipper had her hand in his. He was looking out from under his thick brows, eyes invisible in the shadow, but she could see his mouth. "Nice going, Ann. Jim. You take her in. Which way is it?"

She pointed.

Jim looked around the den. His eyes bounced from the white coat. She was sitting on the leather sofa, swinging her leg against a spot where time and people had worn away the finish and left a rough, rust-colored patch. It was crumbling off on her bare leg. She was wearing a dress. She had several dresses that color, he thought. He'd told her the truth: "I don't know any details, Ann. It's curtains for Bill. The skipper will be able to— Can I make a drink, or anything? Cigarette?"

Her dress wasn't wet. Or her jade shoes. High heels, too. Jim was familiar with the ménage: it meant she'd gone up to the third floor—the airy one where they had slept—to change. Her dark, curly hair was damp at the nape of her neck.

Swam for it. God.

The front door thumped.

Captain Wilson was brawny, bushy, blue-eyed. Jim bent an inch. The skipper looked a fleeting command. Jim sat where he was. The Morris chair beside the sofa made an iron sound when he took it. He pulled his pipe out of his khaki pocket, loaded it, looked at Ann, and let his rumbling voice begin.

"We don't know everything about it, Ann. Naturally,

22

all we do know is—" He stopped because she had lifted her face. He grinned; Jim thought she smiled. "Your Bill's PC trailed a Dutchman—a fighting Dutchman—south of here. First night out. The Dutchman was carrying ammunition for us. The sound detector picked up a propeller. They signaled the fact, and got the PC between the enemy and the Dutchman. Headed for it—and the sub came up. That much we have from the Dutchman. Her captain began to zigzag. The sub broke fast and commenced fire immediately. The PC replied. The German's third shot got her. Part of the PC must have floated a while and some men must have escaped. The Dutchman was making off at full speed, of course, but she saw the German's machine guns spitting at the water. She broke radio silence and gave us that, almost while it was going on."

He took his pipe from his mouth and turned it in square-nailed fingers. "It's no secret to Navy wives that we have one ship where we could use fifty. One plane where we need a squadron. The sub got the Dutchman half an hour later. We had boats on the first scene of the action by that time. They left to hunt the sub. They didn't locate it. In the morning we figured the drift—it happened in the Gulf Stream—and we sent out planes and boats. Everything we could spare. Jim was out there. I was. We didn't find anything. We haven't. This is the first—probably the last. A PC is no battleship."

He stopped talking and lit his pipe, still looking at her.

She said, "I'm grateful to you, captain."

His eyes were like the ocean on a calm, clear day. "Officially, your Bill Gracey was lost in action at sea. That's probably all Washington will let us say, at present."

"It doesn't matter what—we say."

He stood suddenly. Jim stood. "I've ordered some small craft to put in here. They should arrive any minute. I'll—take care of—everything. I woke Mrs. Wilson when I barged out of the house. She asked me to ask you if you'd care to—to stay with us a few days? Would you? Mother'd like it. I would."

Tears overspilled the edges of her eyes. "Thank you—captain. I'll—I'll let you know."

"Good." He twisted his head curtly. "Lieutenant, you stand by here." He was eying her again, imprinting her on his brain. "We have a lot of brave men in the Navy," he said

23

evenly. "A lot of their women are brave. For sheer guts, though, I won't forget you, Mrs. Gracey, till the day I die."

He saluted her.

5

"I'M A good coffee and egg maker," Jim said.

Ann brushed at the particles of old leather on the calf of her leg. "Go ahead."

Eggs crackled in the small aluminum frying pan. The percolator chugged. Jim glanced away from the electric plate: she was sitting quietly, not crying. It would do—for now.

There was a new sound—outdoors. He rattled his egg turner and whistled as if absently, against it. It was a gargled whisper "purple-purple-purple": engines idling, as a small boat drifted in on the breeze to get a line ashore. He glimpsed the convulsion of Ann's shoulders; he whistled louder— stopped—and his face stiffened.

"Sorry, Ann old kid."

"It's all right."

Curse me for being a smooth whistler, he thought. Curse me for whistling, anyhow. The song he had unconsciously chosen had been "Stormy Weather."

Time slugged by. He opened a bottle of beer.

"Funny," he said. "I've known you—going on a year now. You two guys. People get to be intimate in half an hour, these days. But I really don't know much about you. I know you came from Connecticut. I know Bill went to Yale. I heard you'd met at a prom. End of biography, practically. What, for instance, do you know of equivalent value about Becker, James, lieutenant j.g.?"

"Annapolis," she said.

"Check. Practically the foot of my class."

"Eighth, weren't you?"

"Error in my superiors' judgment. I let it slip by. More?"

"For a smallish man, with a not quite straight nose and— juvenile eyes—you have a reputation among us girls—"

"Unwarranted. Pure bluster."

"Not according to Gail."

Jim flushed slightly. He tried his pockets.

"Cigarettes in that box," she said. She took one and he lighted it.

24

"What about Gail?" he asked.

"What about her?"

"You try to reach her?"

"No. No use. She was going to start out from the Country Club—"

"Oh."

"She'll be—I don't know. Upset terribly—inside, anyway. She was attached to Bill. She knew him before I did."

Jim nodded and waited; there was nothing more. "The—skipper—will ask me—certain questions tomorrow, Ann. He'll—assume—or pretend to—that I always knew the answers anyway."

"What questions?"

The coldness of the beer had condensed the night's humidity on the glass, frosting it, and making it run, like raindrops. Jim drank, put down the tumbler in a new place, and broke the surface tension of a watery ring with his finger. He drew tapered lines, so that the ring became a solar symbol. "What did you do, for instance, before you and Bill were married?"

"Nothing. Stayed at home. Father died about ten years ago. Mother insisted on my going through college, acting like an upper-class Yankee as thoroughly as possible. I didn't know how much of the insurance I had used up until I got out and Gail was set to enter. There was nothing left for Gail. So she took nursing. Mother's postmistress, now. The town's called New Lancaster. It was a little bigger in 1790 than it is today—which gives you an idea."

"You didn't work in college—or afterward?"

"Oh." He thought she was not going to answer. Her eyes were downcast. Her cigarette lay on an ash tray, its thin blue smoke sucking up into the shade of a bridge lamp. "No."

He tried again. "Bill inherited this house—"

"You're a very nice person, Jim."

"Nonsense." Since she understood, he was direct. "It's just that—if we know you aren't worrying about—dough—we won't. If you are—there's no need."

"This house." She looked at the walls and furnishings of the room. "Bill always thought the land, at least, would be worth a lot—when they build up to here. A hotel site, he said. There's no mortgage—no encumbrance. I suppose it's—mine —now. He had some insurance. We have a little money in

25

the bank. There's nothing like that to worry about. You know, I'm sure I hadn't ever thought of it but it's like so many other things." Her tone was puzzled. "It was there in my mind—organized. I hadn't thought—but I knew."

"You and Bill must have talked about it."

"Probably."

He collected her plate, his own, the empty glass; he carried them to the corner of the den which had been fitted for the preparation of light meals. He came back. "Could you go to sleep?"

"No."

"Have you got anything to take? I mean—you're probably suffering from some sort of shock, though—God knows—you don't show it."

"I'll be all right. Maybe—tomorrow—I'll get wopsy. But I'll be all right till then. That's the way most of the Chapmans are."

"Chapmans? Oh. Ann Chapman. I wonder how many girls I know whose last names I don't? Gail's one, apparently. I've heard it, I suppose—" he dropped that rumination. "You going to take up the skipper's offer? Mrs. Wilson is tops—you know that."

"No. You could explain it for me, Jim. I'm—well—I'm introverted, I guess. I'd prefer to be alone for a while—mostly."

"You can't stay here!"

"Why?" She tossed her head delicately. "Not all alone, no. Gail might come. I might take in a couple—there are plenty of wives house hunting for while their husbands are in your school. Someone like that—strangers. I haven't thought—how could I? I just know I want to stay around here awhile. I'm not—not *through* with being here. You think that's morbid."

"Yeah."

She was silent. He put out his cigarette. He looked at the room—the trophies, the canes, the moldy residue of Uncle Paul and, especially, at the new books. They were novels—the best of the new novels—and thick nonfiction books. Who read them? She? Bill? He thought of Bill—of Bill as he knew Bill. Quite likely Bill had read in them. But certainly she had bought them.

"It must be morning," she said.

26

When, at last, he started toward the road and the bus, she came outdoors with him. He'd said something about going and she had not demurred. He had added that no duty would claim him—that he could give her the day—but she had not asked for it.

The dawn was level gray, like the lighting in a professional photograph. There was no wind. The vine-wrapped palms stood sharp against the turquoise of the sea. The house hung over the two people, quietly containing its darkness. South were the grim mangroves. Overhead, low clouds proceeded—regular as fleet formations and the mud-blue color of fighting ships. Beyond them was the pearly sky. Night-blooming jasmine had fallen on the walk; the pool of tiny flowers, delicately verdant, matched the girl's dress with exactness. The air was warm. It smelled like candy.

"Thanks, Jim," she said.

He tried to assure himself that her sensibilities were exhausted. They were not.

Her skin had been tanned a rosy buff; it was not entirely pale, now. All night, her eyes had been gray. He had imagined, before then, that they were blue. In the unweird, enveloping monotone of this daybreak, they had turned hazel, with a piny undertone, a green quickening, not tropical, but northern. She was almost as tall as he. She had the unaccented figure that modern artists choose. Her profile was even-tempered; her mouth, ample and overstruck with violet-shadowed crimson. She held out her hand—small, proficient, each nail like an oval fraction of her lips.

"Thanks, Jim."

She brushed back her dark hair when they had shaken hands. He looked at that, also, as if he, like his skipper, were attempting to make her indelible in a few seconds of farewell. Hair about as long as from his wrist watch to the ends of his fingers, very curly, unmodeled, marked down one side even in this sad light of morning with diagonal nimbus of reddish gold. "Promise you'll call me later in the day."

Her throat swallowed. Her punctuating eyebrows arched. She nodded.

She was utterly stricken, he thought. At the same time, there was no syllable of surrender in her. It frightened him. He turned smartly, setting out for the road in marching strides.

27

When he had gone, Ann went around the house to the sea side.

The tide was at ebb.

6

A BINGING noise jumped Gail awake. The phone. Let it ring. The sun streamed upon her through a tipped Venetian blind, ruling her with black and white. Her head was propped high on a half dozen pastel pillows. She noted the sun's effect; it pleased her. She dug her chin in her chest and admired each grilled segment of her immaculate perfection. She became aware of the radio between blasts of the telephone; it was talking in the garrulous plush voice of an announcer she knew. It amused her to think she knew him. From the corners of her eyes she caught sight of the lemony filaments of her hair. She thrust her fingers in it and the movement caused a cloth clown doll to topple onto her brow. She seized it and held it up. In its white, laughing face, there was a vermilion smudge between the pair of polka dots for cheeks, and in the center of that, two meeting crescents that expressed the shape of her teeth.

She chuckled and hugged the clown. Damn the phone. She reached and touched, instead, a nearly full glass of flat champagne. Her voice was like a river on small rocks: "Just what the doctor ordered!" She sat up, emptied the glass, shook her hair, and found the phone. At the same time, she reached with her toe and tried to turn the dial of the radio, which sat on the floor beside the bed. Music would be better than the palaver of that gaboon.

" 'Lo."

"This is Ann, darling."

"Hell's boxes! What time is it?"

"It's just nine. But—"

"Okay! Okay, big sister! Don't apologize! It's the only unattractive thing you do! So it's nine. So you woke me up. So I am in a quandary. Is a gaboon a monkey or is it a cuspidor?"

"Is—what?" Stillness—not priggishness—made the background for the next words. "Are you very tight?"

"Not very."

"Something serious has happened, Gail. I wish you could come over."

"Lemme see. This is Sunday—isn't it?"

"Is it? I'd forgotten." The voice was honest, faintly surprised.

Gail made a face. "It must be serious! Are you all right?"

"Yes. I am. Please come over."

"Bill?"

Ann was ready for that. "It's about Bill. I can't tell you on the phone."

Gail said very quietly, "I'll be right over. Fix me some breakfast."

In her full-length mirror she saw that she had turned pale from head to foot. Wounded, she thought. Bad, Ann sounded as if. She hurried into the bathroom, paying no attention to the articles in evidence there. She wrapped her hair in a plastic bathing cap. She took her shower briskly. She came back into her bedroom and began to dress while her back still glistened. By and by she stood in the blind-slits to dry it. She had already planned to wear her new red and white gingham to the beach party in the afternoon; she put it on without further conscious thought. Red alligator shoes, red bag, red doughnut hat.

The radio had found some music of its own accord, apparently. A prune-whip voice was singing, "There'll be bluebirds over—the white cliffs of Dover—"

She unplugged the radio and set it on the vanity. The cleaning woman might trample it again.

When she turned from the vanity, her head swam for a moment, and she had to stand still to reorient herself. Her eye fell on a man's shoe, on the floor. She was momentarily startled. She reflected. A smile replaced a bothered frown. She kicked the shoe.

"Hey! Leftenant! Reveille!"

A voice came hollowly from the narrow space between the bed and the far wall. "I say!"

"Up, Toots!"

She waited long enough to make sure that the thumping scramble under the disheveled bedclothes would produce lasting activity. Then she went out, taking laughingly thoughtful care not to slam the door. Her car was in one half of the garage underneath the apartment. It was a blue and chrome

29

roadster—expensive, for a fashion model who made a hundred dollars on good weeks. She carved into Collins Avenue and headed north in a hurry—a figure known to traffic policemen, whose arrest for speeding always ended in their minor embarrassment. She was humming about the cliffs and the bluebirds.

She found Ann in the kitchen. The windows were open; sun streamed in. Ann's eyes were crying slowly now; she wiped them with sheet after sheet of pale yellow Kleenex. The rest of her was busy setting a place for Gail in the painted breakfast alcove Bill had constructed. The two sisters faced each other—alike in profile and carriage—Gail a blond replica, except for her eyes and mouth.

"He's dead, Gail."

Gail said, "Oh-my-God!" She stood there.

"Missing in action—but they know he's dead."

"I haven't seen you crying since I was a little girl!" Gail's voice was peculiar.

"Don't go into the horrors, will you? Have some coffee."

"I'd rather—"

"It's in the den."

Gail came back still shuddering. She sat down behind the big cup of coffee. "When did you hear?"

"Late last night. Captain Wilson was over. Jim Becker."

"How?"

"A sub sank the PC."

Gail put sugar in the large, heavy cup, stirred it, and drank all of the coffee, hot. "What else?"

"What else?"

Gail's voice was frailer, sharper. "What makes you look that way? What's the matter with your eyes?"

Ann felt a familiar resentment; her young sister's intuitions were invariably of the distressing sort, as if her sixth sense were not universally attuned, but concentrated upon those aspects of others they themselves regard as weaknesses and small, trying moments of near insanity. "There is nothing the matter with my eyes," Ann said reproachfully. "Bill's dead. I love him. Isn't that enough?"

"I was crazy about Bill, myself, once."

Ann made a sound not of jealousy but of weary impatience.

"I know," Gail said. "He didn't fall for me. What I call

30

play, he thinks is serious. What he calls play, I think is childish. He was a lifelong undergraduate. But I was awfully
fond of him, Ann. I adored him—for marrying you."

Ann's cheeks reddened. Sometimes she had thought the
same thing about Bill's masculine world and its immaturities.
But she did not like to hear it from Gail, who now misread
her vexed flush and said, "You don't understand. I mean—
whoever you had married, I would have adored. You know
you could have married simply hundreds of boys—practically
anybody—"

"Look, Gail. Bill's dead."

Gail held out her cup and her sister poured more. She
took off the round red ring of her hat and threw it into a
chair. "What are you going to do about it?" She amplified
that. "You can't have a funeral—"

"Thank God!"

"Are you going home?"

Ann was startled. "To New Lancaster? No!"

"You mean you're going to stay down here in Florida?"

"Certainly."

"Isn't that just sort of martyrdom?"

Ann spoke with some bitterness: "Can it be you do have
a conscience that is bothered by my being here? Didn't you
come—after Bill and I did? Do I ever, in any way, interfere
with you?"

Gail thought and answered quietly, "Don't you envy my
kind of living a little, now, Ann? You've lost everything. I—
couldn't!"

Ann knew what she was going to say and wished she
wouldn't, and said it: "Have you anything left to lose?"

Suddenly Gail's eyes filled with tears and, at the same
time, she laughed softly. "I'm sorry. I didn't mean to be
horrible." She left the table gracefully, walked to her sister,
put her arms around her, and kissed her neck where it was
beating, visibly. "I'm ashamed."

Ann sat down and shakily poured coffee for herself. "I
don't believe I can stand going on alone here—even for one
night—"

"Here! Alone! In this big haunted shambles? I should
think not! Somebody ought to burn it down! It ought to be
tabu! You pack your things! I'll drive you to a hotel."

Ann should have known that Gail would never have

come to stay. She should have known that she could not have stayed with Gail. She sagged spiritually under the prospective weight of little things that would have to be done immediately. Clothes packed. Notes left for the milkman and the eggman. Keys found. Doors locked. Luggage carried. A discussion with some limp clerk about a room in his hotel. She walked away from the table, from the inquiring expectancy in Gail's eyes. She looked out at the sea. The sun went under a cloud.

You leave a place. Most of the objects in it that belong to you flow out after you, following the magnet of their possessor. Those left behind are adopted by other people, or thrown away, or given as presents—scattered. The hieroglyphics you scribble for the milkman and the eggman are not like orders—not you, any more—but a sign that you no longer are. The things you have taken, remember for you alone; to strangers they carry no recollection of the house they once invested. Or do they? Would this dress, the cup in Gail's hand, the button I did not sew on Bill's uniform, mean, to anybody but me, in any spot but this, a once-existing person called William Clifton Gracey and a rococo wooden house that he and I had laughed at when we first walked through the tangle and came upon it?

She'd soon find out.

"I'll pack," she said.

7

IN THE Edgeport General Hospital, on the Sound, in Connecticut, two student nurses, whiling away time between a lecture on gas decontamination and the commencement of floor duties, gazed at the long, framed photographs of other nurses who had gone into training in the same institution. One girl stopped and pointed. "Look at that one!"

Both had been laughing. Now, both exclaimed.

"She's beautiful!"

"She's exactly," the first girl said, "like the female Petty is always trying to draw. But real!"

The floor superintendent, coming in behind them, blew her hair tiredly, tucked it under her cap, and stared over their shoulders. "I remember her. She was beautiful. And bright, too. She gave up a real career. Man-trouble." She said it matter-of-factly—professionally, even—as if "man-trouble" were a disease, like phlebitis.

One girl said, "No wonder!"

The other said, "Gee!"

"Her name was Gail Chapman," the superintendent added; for a space her eyes were unhappy; when she spoke, it was to give orders in a drab tone.

8

ANN finished her supper, alone. She had chosen the downtown, city hotel because Miami Beach was too expensive. A tall, square, steel-ribbed structure—with rough plaster walls, stippled colors, iron grilles, and faded tile on the main floor—half a story aboveground. This inner lining made it "Spanish." Like the omelet, Ann thought vacuously. Its furnishings were Spanish, also: iron, leather, stained wood with remarkable machined imitations of hand carving, fake tapestries, and indistinct, large-patterned upholsteries of men in helmets, carrying pikes and halberds, standing about under balconies. Maids kept it dusted. Maids could not hide its exudation of overuse, or brighten a dank brown impersonality that was intended to be serene and cool, but that ached with sordidness and gloom.

This was Ann's first meal alone—her first formal meal since she had known that Bill was dead. She sat in the dining room, listlessly eating the flaccid food, not looking at the people carefully spotted about the place by the headwaiter to give the effect of patronage. He had tried to lead her to a prominent table; she had chosen to sit alongside an iron fence, near a corner, under a fishtail palm that somehow survived in the stale, turnip-scented air.

She ate slowly from the separate little dishes. Her nerve ends were curling in her body—there was fire underneath her navel—she itched and sweated. She kept back the thought of ascending in the elevator to her single room. It was better, she repeated to herself, than "seeing people"—Gail's suggestion—or than staying on at Uncle Paul's house another night, to watch the moon rise. Her consciousness was ragged as a wind-wrecked field. Wherever she searched, there was in-

33

effable flatness; she saw the standing patches of unhurt growth not as symbols of a future but as a contrast with all that had been beaten down or swept away.

Maybe, she thought, it would have been better to have had a funeral. Better if he had been found, embalmed, viewed as remains, buried to musketry. The ritual took up the appalling slack of these hours in the lives of the survivors.

She had bought some magazines to take to her room, she remembered. As if she could read print and make out illustrations!

She tried wondering about her mother.

Her mother would get the telegram at home—after church—read it, sob through the rest of the day, think of telephoning, and decide the call would leave her daughter worse off than before—all the while mindful of the cost. Her mother would effortfully get out into the garden in the late afternoon. By then, she'd have a sick headache. She would do spring things: nip suckers from young plants, dig holes with a trowel for pansies, pick tulips—martyred by pains in her head—continuing the chores she enjoyed.

I know, Ann thought, how people feel before they kill themselves.

She wondered if she would.

Bill would despise that.

She brought her eyes up from the thick, blue-lined china and deliberately regarded the people. They were chattering and stuffing themselves, leaning forward to catch dribbling spoonfuls of food, rolling their eyes, waving their arms, whipping their napkins, wiping their tongues around their teeth, furtively removing bones from their mouths, ignoring lip-crumbs, littering the floor, mustaching themselves with milk and coffee, choking, talking in revelation of unchewed bread. A simian spectacle. She had never seen people look like that.

She said, "Check, please!" in a harsh voice and hurried out to the street.

She bumped through the crowds. They, at least, were not eating.

Eating. Carving up things with their teeth—pulling their bodies around giblets. She had never thought of teeth in that fashion—as if teeth were a separate category of thinking—and human teeth were to be envisaged with the teeth of wolves, crocodiles, tigers, snakes and fish—white, bare, ivory —all smashing and ripping and tearing and crunching—getting things ready to move up around. Everything, she thought, was teeth. Rather, teeth were the main things. Until they came, all animals were helpless; after they had teeth they were merciless. She could feel all the grinding teeth in the universe and she could actually see, in the dimly lighted streets, everywhere, the gleam and the saw edges of teeth. White biters, every man and woman and child. Gail had the whitest of all. Even the dead endlessly clung to their teeth in their tombs and at last became nothing but teeth.

She had been walking very fast.

She stopped.

Whitey Bates is our bosun.

Why, in the midst of all that crazy torment, had she thought of Whitey Bates? White biters? The similar sound?

She remembered.

Whitey Bates had been shot away clear to his lower jaw. It had hung on his hairy chest in the moonlight—a neat, glittering horseshoe of teeth.

She found a lamppost, leaned against it.

New England women do not shout or scream or grow hysterical. Not college-bred women. Not Russian women or Chinese. It was a fearsomely weak crutch, now, but it supported her.

Presently, she heard organ music. She stood quiet beside her post and listened. It came from a church across the corner, welled somberly around her and half a hundred disheartened voices trailed it. The door of the church was open. Light shone dully through its stained, autumnal window. Ann crossed the street and went into the church. I love to tell the story. It was naïve—pitiful—and she could not stay because these people, as they sang, flashed their teeth. But she went outside and half-concealed herself in the hibiscus, and she listened for a long time.

She walked back to the hotel peacefully. She went up in the elevator, trembled into a nightgown, lay in the clammy, solitary bed, and turned out the light to face down whatever hells would reach from now until dawn.

She fell asleep.

ANN spent many toilsome days in Miami before venturing back to the house on the beach. They were such days as are passed by people in hard pain—days of watching clocks, of efforts to read, of energetic discourse with other human beings which failed to distract and held in retrospect no words and no pictures more real than dreams. Mrs. Wilson invited her to dinner. She and the skipper at first carefully did not talk about Bill and then talked of him too readily, as though his flesh had not rotted and he were merely away on some longer mission. Jim Becker escorted her to a restaurant that overlooked the harbor; they drank cocktails together quietly. She saw a man at the bank, and a lawyer, a naval officer who had papers for her to sign, and a woman who was making a dress for her. They also resembled figments of imagination: they had said things and done things and she had responded with words. They had not realized the muteness of those words to Ann.

At last, however, she took the bus over the causeway and transferred to another that beetled the long route to her weedy estate. It was afternoon. Sunlight pressed upon the vegetation; butterflies vibrated over it; here and there a kind of flower she could not name had opened—each blossom the color of stigmata. The house, in spite of its bulk, seemed gaunt. Sandpipers squeaked and scurried along the curved shallow gushing of the waves. The mangrove swamp exuded sour steam. Overhead, a single airplane buzzed like a big fly, descended, and zoomed—its propeller thwacking the wooden air.

Ann cleaned the kitchen.

Afterward she carried Bill's white coat up to the third floor. Her muscles queasily responded to a leaden will; her mind was bemused. She opened a closet door and pulled out a trunk. She dragged it down the hall into the bedroom where she and Bill had slept, three stories above the sea that swished now, chuckled sometimes, and had roared, on windy nights. She folded uniforms and put them in the tray of the trunk. She set aside Bill's flannel tennis trousers for the cleaner. She opened the moothproof bags that held his civilian clothes. The room was filled with smells of camphor and benzine. She sealed the bags presently and packed them in the trunk. She took out, one by one, the shoes lined along the closet floor, and felt their heaviness. She dusted them, wrapped them in newspaper, and packed them. Then she turned to the bureau drawers.

The afternoon waned while she made neat stacks of shirts, pajamas, shorts and socks—while she set out on the candlewick bedspread the miscellaneous articles men gather in and on their bureaus: military brushes, a shoe horn made of leather, a pipe, six tarnished pennies, two boxes for cuff links, a seed like the eye of a horse which had floated ashore, a miniature gold football, lavender shells, a pocket Testament, two unpaid bills for small sums, an extra shoulder board, and a dead gardenia. She carried the gardenia across to her vanity and sat down tiredly.

Such objects bring intense recollections. She let them register in her brain but tried to keep hold on her emotions.

There were no pawn tickets on the bureau. So often, Bill had one or two. She remembered her New England horror when she had discovered his patronage of pawnshops. The ticket had been repugnant to her, shameful—itself a nastiness. It had dropped out of his pocket on the lawn in Connecticut (because he'd been doing handsprings for two little kids) and she had picked it up. She could still remember him, flushing, laughing: "It's a bad habit I got in college, Ann." She could remember her prim response: "And one you'll have to give up at once! It's revolting!" But he hadn't given up pawning things—a typewriter, his coat, a watch. She'd guessed, because she had missed such articles of his, from time to time. And she hadn't found out for many months that he had always pawned his worldly goods for one purpose only: to buy a present for her. Never for himself—but ever so often for her. If he had lived, she thought, they'd have been in debt for years, perhaps always, because of his habit of buying things for her. . . .

The gold football made her think of the time they'd had the burglar. That was before their engagement. Bill was spending the weekend, although Ann's mother disapproved of that. Mrs. Chapman woke in the night, terror-stricken: she could hear a scraping at the back door. She roused Ann who, in turn, roused Bill. He quietly removed the screen from a window, climbed barefoot up to and over the ridgepole and stared through the gloom until he made out the figure of a

37

man working on the back-door lock—and a glint that he identified as a gun. He executed a flying tackle, twelve feet across and down. The "glint" had come from a new skeleton key that didn't fit; the burglar was an amateur, a local shiftless-Sam, and drunk besides. Bill's tackle had half killed him both by direct and by spiritual shock, because even professional burglars do not keep a weather eye on the heavens and Bill seemed to have hurtled from there. The night's affray, in the end, cost Bill five dollars in cash and a moderately good suit—both of which he contritely presented to the demoralized thief.

There were things about Bill—many. His athletic training had made him the best masseur on earth (when he learned that you had to go easy on a girl) and he was never too tired, if Ann was slightly indisposed, to put his talent at her luxuriating disposal. He liked to shop, he liked to help her pick out her clothes, and he had wonderful—if too expensive—taste. He liked to rib other "guys" unmercifully—but he never teased her. He didn't tease women at all.

He could even take care of Gail. That, more than anything else, had caused Mrs. Chapman to favor Bill's suit of Ann. For a long time, Ann had known that Gail occasionally drank too much—but Ann had not known that her mother, also, was aware. Two summers ago—when Bill was again at the house—Gail had come home very late, much rumpled, and passed out in the swing in the apple orchard. Mrs. Chapman had found her in the morning and tried to carry her into the house. Bill, waking early, had seen that—and intervened, to the humiliation of Mrs. Chapman, at first. For Gail had roused and become not merely boisterous, but violent and something more than unladylike. So Bill had carried her under an ice-cold shower, shaken the epithets out of her, undressed and toweled her, brewed coffee for her—and not even mentioned the episode to Ann. Somehow, Mrs. Chapman, for all her misery and dismay, had taken an obscure, nonpuritanical solace from the proceedings: Bill, perhaps, had qualities lacking in her dead husband. Anyway, Ann's mother had ceased objecting to Bill, after that—and they had become engaged.

She looked down at the gardenia.

It was beyond doubt the flower she had worn in her hair the night he had asked her to marry him; she'd had no idea he kept it in his possession. She turned it between her thumb

38

and forefinger; one of the petals cracked away and fell on the carpet. The wave of sentiment she had feared all day now clove her mood of rigidity and blankness, brought tears, and then sobs. She watched herself cry in the mirror—unaware that she was watching. Finally she took a clean handkerchief from her own drawer and wiped her eyes. She dropped the dead gardenia into her jewel box. She shut the lid.

The room grew dusky. Above the ocean regimented clouds were absorbing the pastel colors of a sunset gaudy in the west. A sense of haste overcame her. Without forming the circumstance in words, she knew that she did not want to be caught by night alone in this house that smelled of old wood and mold—that made peculiar noises as the breeze stroked it and the day's warmth abandoned it. She placed Bill's things neatly, hurriedly in the trunk. She brought down the lid. It bulged. She sat upon it, then, and bent forward, shoving with the heel of her hand on the brass clasp.

"Ann," Bill said.

He'd fix it, she thought, as soon as he got upstairs. She kept on trying, however.

"Ann, dear!" His tone was worried.

"Yes, Bill?"

Only when she answered aloud—when her voice penetrated the corners and the door holes and the stillness—did her flesh flinch, the ends of her nerves twist in her body, and her eyes expand with horror. Bill had called to her.

"Bill!" Her throat let the syllable emerge.

There was no answer. There were no footsteps. A larger wave peeled down the beach in a running splash. The window frame trembled lightly. She sat on the trunk as though she had been carved there and did not call again. Perspiration appeared on her forehead and her upper lip. In her mind was silence. She rose through it like a swimmer coming up through deep water. Once again, she heard the ocean and the erratic ticking of the house.

Hallucination, she thought. Imagination. The idea did not relieve her fright but, for the moment, sequestered it. I'm so alone and so obsessed that, already, I've started—hearing things. Her waxy calm changed to a need to run from the house, a need that could hardly be denied. With that frantic necessity, a doubt appeared.

Surely no hallucination could be so vivid, so detached, so *uncaused*. People had symptoms of hallucination before

the event. Bill's voice certainly had been Bill's voice itself—
and not her inner echo of it. And it had contained an emotion
which she most surely would not have projected upon it—an
emotion of anxiety. He had spoken as if he were about to
introduce her to some problem or trouble. Her answer had
therefore been soothing and maternal. Yes, dear. *What is it?
What's wrong?*

She slithered from the trunk and ran on tiptoe, quietly,
so as not to alarm whatever might be standing in the narrow
stair well. She more than half expected to see a shadow there
—a shade with the contours of her husband—a wraith's smile
—and a voice that bespoke woe or peril. She saw nothing.

Now, she must contemplate going down these stairs and
the broad, bent flight below. To this urgent fact was added
the Old Fear—the instinctual one. Bill was here. Bill was
dead. But some article of his consciousness, invisible and
possessed, inhabited that dim stairway, waiting for her to
walk down upon it. She would feel the chilly mist of him. She
would be seized. She hung upon the frame of the door, biting
her lip, sweating drops that ran, and trying to cudgel herself
into not sanity but mere motion.

At last, she went—step by step, holding the banister—
slowly. When she reached the bottom of the flight she knew
that her back was turned upon it. She stopped. The hall was
murky. The newel post on the main staircase was as tall as a
person and it had a large head. She inched her eyes around
and looked back up the stairway.

Bill's voice drifted down it: she had passed him. "It's
here," he said positively.

She did not remember, afterward, the rest of the route.
She merely found herself running toward the sea along the
walk bordered by conches. The beach repelled her. She turned
at the side of the house. The oval driveway gave back whitely
the false illumination of afterglow. In a few minutes it would
be dark. But now the bowl formed by the house and the surrounding trees held a wan glitter which threw into relief
every clapboard and every vine-invaded shrub. A man was
standing at the end of the drive where locked branches made
it a tunnel mouth. Her heart stuck and surged again. She
stopped. It was another man; not as tall as Bill; not blond.
She walked toward him.

"Are you looking for somebody?"

40

PART II

THE MAN

1

SOME time before Ann came upon the stranger in her yard, he had taken up an otherness of life as burdensome as was now her own. For him, the dilemma had been born in the midst of method. His name was John Galen.

He sat—or had sat—in the office of a physician, in an armory, in Chicago. Relaxed, Galen was—feet crossed, brown eyes bright with the mere act of living, a hand in the pocket of his brown tweed jacket, in the other a cigarette; a man of vigorous complexion—his shave careless—big ears, nose, eyes; geometrical jaw; a long walker—what they once called double-jointed. Wise, full of health, informal. A professor.

The doctor examined a card, closely. He was interested in the candidate in the tweed jacket and gray slacks.

"John Galen."

The man nodded.

The doctor read from the card—aloud, but to himself: " 'Five eleven, one hundred and sixty-five pounds, mother deceased, father living and well, no siblings, mumps, measles, chickenpox, whooping cough, scarlet fever, appendicitis, peritonitis, septicemia, hernia—all okay now—drink occasionally —general condition good—migraine during childhood—tonsillectomy—unmarried'—lemme see—you're—'May, 1901'— forty-one—'psychoanalysis, 1935-6—' " He looked up—and back at the card. "Johann Altheim—good man—depression —results excellent. U'm'm. Depression and disorientation— any more of it lately?"

"Not—much." The man called John Galen took out a package of cigarettes and offered it.

"Go ahead." The doctor smiled and shook his head. "Now. You've survived all these things. *And* bubonic plague! Where'd you get that?"

"Russia," said John Galen.

The examiner nodded. "Full professor of applied biology at Langer Institute—ye gods!—why do you want to get in the Air Corps?"

"Why does any man? Freedom? To see if he's as good as every other man, maybe. To fight something tangible."

The doctor's eyebrows contracted. He looked more closely at the candidate. "Any compulsion about it?"

"Who can say that for himself? Sure."

"Good answer!" He turned over the card. "Physical all okay. Neurological examination—excellent. Patient—funny —old Shane still writes 'patient,' out of habit!—says psychoanalysis cleaned up the depression beyond the point where it interfered with work—disorientation mild, brief—" He dropped the large tan card and picked up a smaller, blue one: " 'Candidate'—that's the colonel's fist, like a tramp's foot— 'is independently well-to-do, no dependents, successful businessman—applies for majority. Recommended.' " The doctor grinned and looked again at Galen. "Successful *business*man. I thought you were a professor of applied biology?"

John laughed. "It was the business part that interested the colonel. You see, at Langer, we've been permitted to patent the results of our own research and promote them. Split the profits. I've done considerable work with hormones. I launched several products. The Officers' Training School apparently can use men with experience in medical supplies, distribution, and so on. I have it. My 'business' is pretty separate from my lab work. I've put in for the new school for ground officers, of course—"

"Yes. Miami Beach. Tell me a little bit about this so-called 'disorientation'?"

John sat in his chair, looking at his cigarette. He heard the question—thought about it. He had gone to the interview with a carefully fixed plan to be frank, relaxed, amiable—as he was anyway, most of the time. He remembered the self-admonition now, but his mind began to revolve of its own accord. The loud noises in the armory diminished and intermixed until they had the quality of thunder beyond mountains. The light from the window hazed slightly and an aureole seemed to close in and shine faintly around the doctor's head. His muscles quivered. He heard men on the street begin to drive an iron bar through asphalt with strokes that seemed separated by minutes. His heartbeats became sensible to him as soft, heavy rushes of liquid, widely spaced. He had smoked a marijuana cigarette once, years before; this was like that—not unpleasant—not especially happy—just fabulous and detached. He knew his eyes were staring a little and that his mouth had opened to answer the question, but he was not yet ready to speak. The doctor had said something about his spells of disorientation. Well. This was part of one.

He was aware of the white coat rising, leaning forward, taking out a watch. Then he imagined two watch faces, one set inside the other in an opposite plane, like a gyroscope, and both moving slowly in a clockwise direction. A bell rang. A door in his brain opened. Light streaked in—prismatic and splendid; for an instant, he felt wildly elated—but he did not move. The door slammed. The noises in the armory came back to his ears loudly. The men began pounding with rhythmic rapidity on the iron bar. The light around the doctor spread out, squared, and turned into the window again.

"Just—an exaggerated kind of absent-mindedness," John said.

The doctor looked at his watch. "Eighteen seconds."

The man's eyes were level, alert, interested. "You mean I didn't answer—for eighteen seconds? It seemed like a couple, to me. I was—thinking."

"Did Altheim—ever time you in one of those 'thinking' periods?"

He shook his head and smiled. "Not that I know of. I'm not sure I ever had one in his office. It wouldn't be noticeable. Usually. I talked—or not—as I wanted. This one was just a coincidence—suggestion, no doubt."

"I see."

John was not insensible to the doctor's surprise over his momentary abstraction. "That lapsing habit of mine is not principally what I thought of as disorientation," he said quickly. "It was something different. A sodden sort of depression that would last for hours—or days—or even months. But it's gone, pretty much."

"Like what?"

"Like—oh—a vague thing. A long echo of what I felt just now. Worrying about worries you couldn't quite place or remember. Noises being distant—sights far away—a change in the quality of perception. Dr. Altheim tracked a lot of the worries down—you're familiar with the process—and the

45

incubus got off my back. I usually could work through it, anyhow. Now, I always can. I told him—this describes it as well as anything—that I got a feeling of not belonging—not living here—having come from some other planet—being a spectator, a sort of injured, bored, depressed one—waiting for the moment of delivery back to another planet of origin."

"Have you ever had fits?"

He hesitated. "Nothing but teething fits when I was a baby. They passed. You see, I had the time and the money and the—well—perhaps hypochondria—to indulge myself— get it analyzed. No fits, really. Except—"

"Except what?"

"Except." He considered—dubiety resolving sensitively on his face. "A few times when I've had too much to drink— I've—well—frothed—had spasms. I quit, pretty much."

"What did Altheim say about all that?"

"Matter of fact, I never told him. Didn't know about the alcohol business until my analysis was finished. A friend told me."

"Just the migraine, eh?"

"What are you driving at?" Galen was unalarmed. "I was neurotic. I did something about it. Certainly these little vestiges can't affect my availability as an officer? Three-quarters of the men my age have their crotchets—their glum days—their absent-minded moments. Anybody who is fool enough to drink too much too fast is likely to give himself something that amounts to a minor convulsion."

"Is anybody?" The doctor smiled. "You're intelligent, Galen. Healthy. You look exactly like the sort of man they're asking me to send to Miami Beach to become an Air Corps major. Where'd you learn the biology?"

"Princeton. Columbia. Here."

"Ever have an electroencephalogram?"

"No."

"I'd like one of you. I'll arrange it."

2

JOHN GALEN sat in a comfortable leather chair while a woman technician shaved several small spots on his scalp. Wires were attached to the spots by glue that had acetone in it. For ten minutes, an instrument that looked like a combination radio and recording barometer registered the electrical currents in his brain. He was told to breathe heavily for five more minutes and he did that. It made him very dizzy. When he had finished, the wires were unstuck, the glue washed off, and he was given a comb. The lady technician began removing the long tracery of seismographical lines. He was nervous, now.

"What's the verdict? Moron—genius—or middle-class American?"

She laughed. He knew by her laugh that they always made a wisecrack of that ilk. He went out bleakly.

3

ELIAS POOLE, the doctor who had done the psychiatrical "check" on John Galen, stepped briskly into the Caduceus Club. It was evening and he wore a dinner jacket. His eyes journeyed over the professional domes in the library—the bald heads, the white ones, and the sleek in-betweens of practicing medical men, as well as the undertonsured heads of scientists of the purer sort. The meeting would not begin for an hour, so there was plenty of time. He spotted Altheim, sitting on a broad window sill, arguing, as usual.

Johann Altheim spoke in rolling periods, inflicting them with punctuation marks. His hands jumped like butterflies. His brown eyes shone and his head nodded sagaciously above his small, round-shouldered body. He smiled. He was on one of his favorite themes: the difference between American neuroses and those of Europeans. "Let me quote Alexander," he said earnestly.

His one-man audience, an urbane, bland, seven-foot person, edged away from the comma-shaped psychologist. "I'm afraid, Altheim, you'll never convert me to your religion—"

Altheim shrugged and laughed. "No," he said. "Alas." He observed the arrival of the new colleague and loudly addressed him. "Ass! Blithering fool! There's your modern physician, secure in his temple, sneering at psychology, making an ignorant spectacle of himself. I read a book of his, this very afternoon! To him—there are two categories of people! The ill—and those with nasty dispositions! He kept referring

47

to the symptoms of psychic disease as if it were not sickness, but criminal offense: 'She thinks she aches all over ... she is a born complainer ... an irresponsible nitwit of a person ... a self-made bundle of nerves ... a fussy, opinionated person!' Dear God! This man is a doctor and he hates half the people who are sick because he does not know how to treat them! Anybody he finds himself unable to cure with pills is not diseased, but despicable, not ill, but merely ill-mannered! Oh! *What* a contemptible doctor!" He spoke with the ornamental accent that is the property of men born with not one native tongue, but several. Dr. Altheim was a Swiss.

He thumped the window sill. He looked after the iced shoulders of the retreating physician who had been forced to overhear the diatribe. Then he shrugged, laughed, and took the arm of the other man, who grinned down at him. "Elias," he said mockingly, "if I am ever carried off in a strait jacket, it will be on account of these plausible artists of the bedside and operating table who leak a confidence that would be more acceptable in a witch doctor!"

Poole chuckled. The two men walked a little way in the library, feeling a hostility that had been added by the loud harangue to a perpetual, uneasy disdain: the Caduceus Club was old and orthodox; many members made a tiresome custom of trying to bait and discomfit the psychiatrists who belonged—persisting even though such efforts generally bounced back in their own laps from unexpected angles.

"I'm doing examining for the Air Corps," Elias Poole said, as they found a private corner. "One of your former patients came in today. John Galen."

A look of pleasure illuminated the countenance of the Swiss. "Oh! A splendid chap! And most interesting. Wants to fight, eh? I'm not surprised!"

"He has applied for a commission—a majority."

Altheim's eyebrows shot up. He chuckled. He rubbed his face with his right hand. "You want my advice—yes? I have spent a year and more analyzing him. I know every detail, every secret of his life. I know what he dreams about, what he thinks of other men and women, what symbols arise unconsciously in his mind, what his background is—his ambitions and his fears, his hopes, his repugnances, his habits, good and bad, his private fantasies, his unindulged vices and those he has indulged, his courage and his cowardices, his

48

perspectives and his faiths—what bigotry is in him, what tolerance, his humor—a ten thousand of things about one man. And you would like me to tell you if he would make a suitable major for the airmen."

Poole said, "Exactly."

Altheim restlessly inspected long distances. "There is something abnormal about John."

Poole did not respond.

"Maybe it is minor genius?" The short man turned questioningly.

"You tell me—if you want, Johann. Or tell me, only, if you think he'd make a good major. I might warn you—I've decided. This is a trap."

"Oh? Delightful!" The short man relished the thought. "You have decided that he will *not* be suitable! Otherwise— why are you sitting here? Otherwise—you would have taken the blue pencil and written 'okay-Poole' on one of those maddening cards! And he would become a major. You want to know—would I have written 'okay-Altheim'? You assume I would have. I am not so sure."

"You're doing dandy," Poole said, pleased with his warning.

"Perhaps—you have not really decided but only think you have. Perhaps you are still temporizing and do not know it. Yes, Elias Poole, that is so. You have come to the maestro. It is subtle." He shut his eyes and ad-libbed from his own records. "John Galen—to the celebrated Dr. Ass with whom I have been holding what he thinks of as a conversation—is sound of wind and limb. Younger in looks than years— vigorous—even powerful. A man of many skills—versatile beyond most people. With an intellect that, I must confess, still gives me occasional moments of bafflement, as if I, the analyst, not he, the patient, had the unresolved predicament! These so-called middle-class Americans! How many of them are timeless—how many belong to a *societas magna* that cuts across all the careful panels, frames, borders and designs of Europe! What did one say the other day—one tycoon? 'If everything went psssst! and communism came here—I would be a commissar of something in sixty days!' No European businessman would ever entertain such a mental image. Wonderful! John Galen has that interior largeness—that sense of being importantly alive. Sometimes, at least, he has it.

49

"Is he a major, though?" Altheim frowned at his own question. "He is the son of a minister. These sons of ministers in America are, again, different. Here, a minister is not a man with faults—and not a priest with privilege—but a Righteousness. His children are pushed into this Rectitude by the members of his parish and are not permitted to be as other children—an anomaly in this land of democracy, eh? Since American Protestants are not religious at all, but merely ardent cultists, the Rectitude of each minister's family is minute, Poole, and very artificial. The child in the artificial environment longs for the natural one. The youth surrounded by forced aspects of righteousness is keenly alive to sin—sin abroad and sin at home. Since a minister's sins cannot be those of common men—otherwise he would resemble them too closely to persist as the head of a cult—they must be other. The sinning public leaves him very little to choose from: occult masochisms and sadisms, the hidden revenges. That is the minister of the era of John Galen's youth. That is the father of the minister's son. There is, too, the piety of chosen poverty, the virtue of groveling, and in this the children are bound up as in all else. So—everlastingly in these ministers' families—from humiliation is born ambition; from sanctimoniousness, rebellion; from flattered impracticality, great realism that thrives without praise; from largely irrelevant and misunderstanding disciplines, a stern, productive discipline of part of the self, and from the long, psychic pain of a most unpleasant childhood, the tendency toward physical pleasure that is exaggerated and infantile. John Galen is an oral personality in that sense."

Poole helped himself to one of Altheim's proffered cigars and struck a match.

The Swiss went on, reflectively. "Pan, Puck, the Satyr—and also the detached brain in its most active, reckless manifestations. The clown, the idealist, the goat and the sage—the cynic and the mystic. Intuitions which I do not profess to understand. Which only Carl Jung understands, perhaps. Yes—these ministers' children are well explained by Carl—by Carl's law of opposites. Since, to choose ministry a generation ago took courage and heart, stamina, vision, will, intelligence, and a desperate idealism—and to become a wife of a minister took all that and, besides, patience and abnegation—the children inherit much to start with. In maturing, they become examples of those qualities, but in functions opposite to the parents. It is a most energetic and expressive situation. It almost guarantees success—and gloom."

Poole nodded. "You think the choice of the ministry today is a different choice?"

"For nearly all young men nowadays—the final recourse of a bookish weakling! Provided, now, with mail-order lessons on how to suck the last juices of emotion and funds from these sickened cults! The sons of these new ministers will have the greater incentive—and a poor heritage. Have you heard of any great and brilliant young preachers, lately? *Ah?* Maybe I am digressing. You talk to John Galen about biochemistry, if you have a chance. He is a poet of it. Talk about psychology, if you like. He is becoming a poet of *that*. I did not so much analyze him as he analyzed himself and he did that not so much from material I elicited from his subconscious mind—he has none, I'll swear it!—as assimilate the textbooks of *my* background and draw out never really concealed factors for his own inspection. He is, by turns, overtender and merciless with himself. He is by similar turns oversympathetic with others and ruthless toward them in his mind—though seldom by act. His inner person is uninhibited. The numerous inhibitions of his ego are, to him, irritants, depressants, things seen, conquered for a moment, but never wholly digested, so that they rise to plague him even though he can describe them to the outermost lengths of Oedipus phenomena or to the farthest possible imaginings of the hunger of a soul. Peculiar."

"What do you mean—he has no subconscious mind?" Poole's question was emphasized by a held-over look of surprise.

"Not in the sense others have. Why? Because he is an introvert? No. He hardly is. Because he is honest with himself, I should imagine. Perhaps I should substitute for 'honest' the word 'observant.' He has always seen clearly, in himself and in other people, the land behind the curtain of tabu, the fact behind the rationalization, the true motives of the emotional conflict. His waking fantasies are like his dreams—exactly. He has evidently been able, from childhood, to trace miles of them to their origins and to identify those origins with the usually secret elements so familiar to us—the strivings, greeds, lusts, lip hungers, animal appetites, curryings

51

for favor, rejections of unwished truth, conditioned reflexes —all such casual factors. He had not been especially interested in psychology when I met him. But in our first two or three meetings, he had told me more about what, in other patients, is hidden than I could drag and drive from most in a year of sessions. He *knew!*" Altheim puffed several times on his cigar. "It was a most interesting experience—for me."

Poole crossed his long legs and stared at his elegant black shoe. "Could there be people in whom the mere physical functioning of the mind is such that they are automatically kept in cognizance with the instinctual beat of their personalities—whether or not they try to adjust to such cognition?"

"Lunatics," said Altheim.

Poole was visibly startled. "Sane people?"

The eyebrows of the Swiss lifted. "Maybe. Maybe John Galen is one. Go on."

"It's hardly theory. Just a hunch. Most of the material hidden in the mind of the individual—most of the material hidden by society—is the result of the conscious pursuit of one wish at the expense of demands which, from their instinctual standpoint, are just as important."

"I accept that, naturally."

"But the process of the concealment—the rationalization itself—condoned by the individual and accepted by society— is equally as significant as the buried material. It is the instrument. It is the mechanism that creates a subconscious. Its nature must change and vary—in individuals, with their codes and conflicts—and, similarly, in nations. A person grows up to want to think of himself as such-and-such a sort of person—and arranges his subconscious accordingly. A nation does the same—and by the doing arranges its laws, history books, songs, and what not. Here—the ego is created: the person's sense of who he is. And the group's sense of what *it* is. All interfering facts—all opposites—all belying instincts—are shunted by this instrument behind the wall and kept there, with violence if necessary."

"My dear Poole—elementary!"

"Quite so. But suppose a person was born without the *instrument* to dispose of these *materiae*? Or—perhaps—without a *wall* to hide them behind? Suppose, for example, that some function of his brain or nervous system continually *exhibited* these elements? Or suppose some deficiency, as we could also call it, deprived him of a place to conceal them? This person would know every time he lied. When he acted from false values, he would have more than a mere suspicion of behaving wrongly—he would know the description of it. He would be able to travel at will, or against his will, all the long way back to his infancy; the origin of his Oedipus relationships, as you say, would be a direct sensation, not a horror closeted from himself. And every instinct besides the Oedipus one would surge irrhythmically in his awareness. His understanding of other people would be immense. The range of his imagination would be stupefying. This lack of barricades would give to him numberless, measureless resources that other people have denied to themselves, out of vanity, or fear —or both, if you prefer not to call them one."

Altheim had put his fingers together. "By George! That might almost be an exorbitant description of the most interesting parts of Galen's personality. Indeed, of human personality!" He sighed. "It would not explain John Galen's difficulties, however."

"No. Because this instinctual mass, the beat and impulse of it, would be expressed through the same medium we all possess—our common and human fallibility. Our little appetites and desires. Our trivial attempts, ambitions, pursuits, frustrations. The personality I describe might hold the universe between the arms of his mind—but he still might be unable to make a world of his own from it—or to pick a place on it to inhabit."

"And so?" said Altheim.

"The *amount* of unconscious—subconscious—material in the minds of people differs. The less there is—the better integrated a person should be. That is the axiom of our profession. Know thyself—which means, by implication, knowing everybody else, back to the beasts. If we grant the existence of personalities without the power to rationalize which common men possess—or else without the great pit to discard unwanted facts into, which becomes the pitfall of so many people in this world—what shall we say of those other personalities? Shall we say their minds are atavistic? That their awareness is more the awareness of the beast than of man? Or shall we say, on the contrary, that they represent the next forward step of biological consciousness? That they

53

are, not victims of a deficiency but the puzzled possessors of a rudimentary *new* organ of the psyche? Are these hypothesized persons to be regarded as throwbacks or as the results of pioneering by nature? And, if they are new, is not their personal dilemma the product of being out of gear with time —with society—with a whole species which does not think, feel, believe or behave as they feel impelled to?"

Dr. Altheim looked at his watch. "You are brilliant tonight, Poole. However, these eccentric speculations—"

"Don't go Freudian on me, Johann. I'm not through. Not quite. There is one more possibility. Disease—or what we call disease."

"John Galen is certainly not in any way diseased."

"He has epilepsy."

"What!" The word rang through the library. The short man leaped from his chair.

Poole sat still and peered up at him. "I had his electroencephalogram today."

Altheim stared and presently stomped his foot. "The presence of those broad waves proves nothing!" He glowered at his colleague and then said softly, "He had 'em, eh?" He continued with pompous irritation: "Cerebral dysrhythmia! One person in every twenty has the waves! Often—peculiarly often—those waves accompany exceptional intelligence. They are—also—invariably present in epileptics—one minor discovery of these ridiculous brain-wave measurers! To be epileptic means to have the broad waves. To have them means nothing. I am aware that there is some evidence that the mating of two people with these special waves may produce epilepsy. It does not always produce it. I am aware that people with this cerebral dysrhythmia are liable to instability. Since they are often extremely intelligent—and since this is a stupid world—there are other, more reasonable ways to account for their uneasiness. You find beta waves in my patient. You come here to tell me that he is an epileptic. You lead up to the telling with a long argument intended to prove that, perhaps, epilepsy is the by-product of a tentative extension of the psychobiological functions of man! Bah! It is charlatanism, Poole!"

The lean man was impassive. "There are a hundred kinds of what we call epilepsy, Johann. Two have been recognized for ages. Grand mal. Petit mal. There are degrees of both.

54

There is epilepsy that increases until its victim dies. There is the epilepsy of childhood or adolescence that appears to wear itself out. Five hundred thousand Americans are recognized to have this—disease—in some form. What is it?"

"Who knows?" Altheim answered. "With epileptics—I never trouble myself! It is futile!"

Poole grinned. "I've got you, old boy! That's a line from the 'eminent Dr. Ass' you were just talking to."

Altheim thought—and laughed. He sat down. "Certainly you are not asking me to believe that you accept the unsubstantiated dictum of a brain wave for a diagnosis of epilepsy! John Galen had melancholia. Disorientation—" Altheim paused, winced, and went on— "of a very occasional and ordinary nature. I treated him. He needed some mental hygiene—even he. I supplied it. For the rest, he needed new and deeper interests for his active brain. The literature of psychology supplied that. But—*epilepsy*!"

"I talked to his father on long-distance this afternoon," Poole said calmly. "There were two uncles with it. They deteriorated. Status epilepticus, finally. It was kept wholly secret—still is. You've certainly encountered *that* clinical blind alley, dozens of times. The uncles apparently suffered at first from a form of pseudepilepsy. There was a grandparent—maternal—who had fits all through his youth—and recovered entirely. Your John Galen never knew about it. However, he occasionally drank to excess."

"I have done it myself," said Altheim firmly.

"M'm'm'm. Did you know that sometimes, when he was drunk, he had spasms and frothed at the lips? You *do* know, of course, that any increase of intracranial pressure in an epileptic is likely to bring on an attack. There's no better way to build up pressure than to flood your veins with alcohol."

Altheim smacked his forehead, when Poole was silent. "He never told me! He had—something after all on his subconscious, eh?"

"He didn't know. Somebody saw him do it since he was your patient. Told him. I've taken an unfair advantage of you, Johann—in that particular. Also, he recalled for me that he'd had 'teething fits' in infancy."

"Still—I—Altheim—should have uncovered it! Deep in his memory—somewhere—no matter how passed-out he was

55

—lay the recollection of this—this convulsion and this froth! I failed to find it!"

"No need," Poole said in a kindly tone, "to go into self-castigation. You saw him for more than a year. You possibly even noticed his periods of drop-jawed, glassy-eyed inattentiveness. Possibly not. You Freudians! The darkroom! The confessional cot! However, maybe you never saw an attack. He had one in my office. I asked some questions and got the facts about his manifestations while intoxicated. New facts —to you. I'd like to know two things from you, Johann. First, do you think, from your knowledge of his medical history, that he is getting better or worse—that is, ending whatever degree of epilepsy he has—or commencing it?"

Altheim's face was pale and there were drops of perspiration on his upper lip. He thought hard. "I cannot say."

"And, second—since you understand the man—how would you recommend going about telling him? He reports back to me tomorrow. He's valuable—mighty valuable. As a scientist. As a person. Naturally, he will never be a major. Never be even a private, unless he's crazy enough to change his name and enlist. But I don't want to shock the man any more than I have to when I tell him that, from here on, everything he does and thinks and is must be to some degree conditioned by a possibly fatal set of new realities!"

"You won't have to tell him."

Poole scowled. "I must, man! Damn it—he's the kind who would insist on being told—isn't he? Besides—"

"He is the kind," Altheim answered slowly, "who will have gone to his college medical library after that encephalogram and read every word about the procedure. He will probably be able to recite to you more than you know yourself about it—tomorrow. And he will know more about his own prognosis, I daresay." Johann Altheim hopped to his feet. "Good night, Elias."

"Aren't you here for the meeting?"

"Could I go to a meeting, Elias, *now?*" he asked gently. "I have analyzed an epileptic as a mild neurotic. God! And since that time he has become my friend. My *very good* friend!"

"Then—won't *you* tell him?" Poole saw the human dread in the little man's eyes. "I'm sorry, Johann. I'll see him tomorrow." He watched Johann go—taking his coat and hat from the rack—crossing the vestibule—shambling through the door into the murky discords beyond. The street lamp momentarily lighted his white face; he had begun to weep.

4

GALEN pushed open the door when the doctor said, "Come in." Poole glanced up with what he hoped was casualness and turned back to the inspection of records on his desk. Galen was haggard, as if he had spent the night awake; doubtless he had. He knew about his condition: his eyes instantly projected the fact. He took the comfortable deskside chair and lighted his cigarette. His face was blank—waiting for the selection of a mood to express or a feeling to convey. Negligently, he rearranged his thick, reddish-brown hair with his hand. He tweaked his large nose.

Poole creaked his swivel chair around. "Well, Mr. Galen. How are you?"

Galen's face found the first act for the interview. He grinned. "You didn't call me major. And I know your name, now. I looked you up, Dr. Poole. I also read, most of the night, on the subject that is about to concern us. The subject that prevented you from greeting me as 'major'—just now."

Poole nodded several quick quarter-inches. "Johann Altheim said you'd do that."

John pursed his lips, pondered, let the flicker of amusement show and die in his large, dark eyes, and pulled his nose again. "I tried to reach Johann last night—late. He was out somewhere. I left a call, but he hasn't checked in yet. What were you doing—needling him?"

"Unfortunately, yes. I'd give a good deal to be able to alter or retract two or three things I said to him."

"I wouldn't worry. Johann's tough. He's made of bounce. I am, of course, aware—doubly aware, now I know you saw Johann—that my 'e.e.g.' was positive."

Poole thought, he's already using the technical slang for electroencephalogram. He remembered what Johann had predicted. He looked at Galen. "Yes."

"In a hurry?"

Poole had trouble following that. "Oh. Certainly not.

I am at liberty—urged, in fact—to take as much time with a candidate as I wish. The Army has the brains to realize we birds can save a good deal of breakdown, disaster—not to mention cost and trouble—" He had overtalked because he was embarrassed. The fact annoyed him. What he had said would have distressed most persons in Galen's predicament —but the man was merely nodding.

"You did an ace job—spotting me."

"It was the short, pseudepileptic attack. Coincidence."

"Do you suppose I threw that thing because, somewhere inside myself, I strongly *don't* want to be a major?"

Poole smiled. "I'd advise you not to follow that argument—under the circumstances. It's a reciprocating curve—just pushes itself round and round in a circle. Every major —somewhere inside himself—wants not to be one. The point is, there are enough physiological evidences to make your rejection automatic. Your brain-wave pattern has certain characteristics. There are those jerks and rigidities when you drink. There is your habit of suddenly becoming what you had thought of as inattentive. There is your record of peculiar disorientation. Teething convulsions. The migraine when you were young. There is—" He broke off.

"—my family history," Galen said. He chuckled as if the whole thing were a joke. "I called Dad about an hour after you did."

Poole smiled wanly. "So, Galen, the case is definite."

"The only argument being—am I getting worse or better? Shall I pick out a padded cell and get ready things to gnaw on—or shall I sit tight till it blows over?"

"Yeah."

Galen looked from under his thick eyebrows at the doctor. "A situation like that of a man being told the biopsy is uncertain and he'll have to live with the tumor a while longer before he can be sure whether it is benign, and operable, or a cancer, and hopeless. That, Dr. Poole, was the scummy little dramatization I first made of it for myself. But I'm damned if I can see any major—" he paused a bare instant after the use of the last word, then repeated it— "any major imperfection in the analogue."

"It's accurate enough." Poole's eyes were at once compassionate and hortative.

The younger man held his cigarette out in front of his

necktie and looked down at it. "The person who is told of the uncertainty of his biopsy is usually calm enough about it, I believe. A tradition. You psychiatrists have been hammering hard to make us laymen realize that the troubles in our psyches are like sicknesses. But there is a strong, latent tendency in a man that fills him with something very near to panic when he is told that he is a little bit nutty and liable to become more so."

Poole entered into this attitude of flippant analysis. "Most sorts of insanity are progressive. Yours isn't—necessarily. And most victims of insanity are insufficiently equipped with insight, by the time the doctor sees them, to be told of their condition. You can't tell a neurotic he's going crazy, because he is not. He just thinks so. And you can't tell it to a pathological personality—because the answer will be that the doctor is bats. Epilepsy is *neither* a neurosis *nor* a psychopathology. Indeed, epileptics never, apparently, suffer from the other psychopathologies—from schizophrenia, or mania, or paranoia."

"It ought to be a clue for you to work on."

"It is. The shock treatment for schizoids is merely an artificially produced fit."

"I mean—to work on theoretically."

"You're talking about something that haunts me, Galen. And a thousand other men like me. Insanity must be a simpler thing than we make it. But it's elusive. It's like trying to see far enough along a curved line to look at your own back."

"Which is theoretically possible, in a sense."

There was a silence. Finally Poole broke it. "There are certain drugs to take. When these oppressions—these idle disorientations—become plain enough to notice, you should dose yourself—"

"So I read. I won't bother you. Johann can prescribe."

"There is nothing in the world to keep you from going right along as you have been. Avoid medical fads. Some doctors forbid violent exercise—on the theory that hyperventilation is a causative factor. Some used to recommend a salt-free diet. Ignore the whole business. Do what you've felt best doing. I think I should tell you that, in my opinion, the migraine was probably the greater form of your affliction. I think in your case it will wash, as time passes."

"That's encouraging."

"Meanwhile, you can know that you are perfectly sane most of the time and however strange you may feel at other times—you are safer from true lunacy even than any normal person."

"Safer as of *now*."

"Is there any other time than now?"

"It is a question I'm interested in." Galen grinned and rose. "I think I better not keep you any longer from the war effort. I'm very grateful to you, Dr. Poole. And I'm disappointed. I had a firm picture in my mind of drilling hard for six weeks at Miami Beach—where I've never been —and then of barging off in convoy to help a hundred and thirty-five million reluctant but wonderful people—together with a lot of allies—rub out a large nastiness. I'll have to amend that picture. And I'd like to add that I'm especially grateful to you for another thing. I lost a small bet with myself on it."

"Oh?"

"For not starting with Julius Caesar and rolling off a long list of disgustingly important human beings who, like Galen, suffered from epilepsy. There was a glossary of 'em in one of the books I got yesterday. I was neither heartened nor flattered by it."

Poole laughed. A thought—quick, concrete, armed with its own assurance—rose in his mind. "Since you had this Miami project—why not carry it out? Evidently—you've done what they call getting your affairs in order. You must have arranged already to quit your lab and your office. You might be able to find some sort of war-related activity— as a civilian. The Army hires lots. Or you might just go down there and take a vacation. Miami is a fascinating projection of the American dream—revealing—and fun on its own account. You'll be at loose ends, certainly—"

"Loose ends," Galen repeated. "I shall remember that as my personal high for understatement." He saw the swift hurt in the doctor's eyes and, because he was the author of it, did his rapid best to heal it: "I apologize. I think I'm behaving in a way I despise in others. You know—that vacation idea—trip to Miami Beach—is a brainstorm." He held out his hand. "Thanks. And I hope we meet again."

"I hope so, too." Poole watched the man go with a

60

feeling that the conference had neither begun nor ended quite satisfactorily; he told himself that time would have to pass—a long time—before John Galen would relearn the conduct of himself. He rang for the next patient.

Galen trod the corridors of the armory.

Go to Miami Beach, he thought, and sit in batik bathing pants, watching better men bite into the manual of arms! What a dim idea!

Through a door at the end of the hall he saw row after row of marching men pass by. He heard a sergeant's voice bawl, "Column left, harch!"

5

IN THE late afternoon, John walked to his house, which faced Lake Michigan at a not great distance from the bunched skyscrapers of downtown Chicago. He took off his topcoat and his muffler in the hall. He dropped them on a bench, put his hat on top of them, and entered the library, in front of the house. There, he sat down wearily in a red-leather chair and stared through the big window at the boulevard, the bare trees and the gray surface of the lake. His mind, like any mind beset, moved with swift irrelevancies from object to object, plan to plan, level to level, in a partly conscious effort to sort and re-establish the whole of personal awareness so as to find, if possible, a satisfying reorientation in the center of it all.

He had walked a long way that day, through the city: through endless walls of damp brick which contained smells of ashes and carbon. He had thought of himself, all the way, as a man who might be leaving this scabrous stage setting of his life forever—or a man to whom it might soon become incomprehensible. He had expected that there would be some glamour in his response or some anticipation of Weltschmerz —some identification with wispish, hopeful signs of spring perhaps, or with the sweet-sad predicament people call living. There had been none.

Instead, his roving eye seemed more transparent than ever before, his listening ear far keener, and his nostrils extrasensitive, so that he rejected the wishful haze that breeds sentimentality and ignored every fatuous projection. The world through which he walked was sensed in a harsh defiance of impressionism—more real than any art. It stank with the things men burned to move themselves about and with the things men had killed and cooked to keep themselves alive. To the minute eye, it was powdered, sprinkled and muddied with all manner of dirt—and to the open ear, more cacophonous than hell.

Now, in his own home, the disillusioned aspect persisted. The grayness of the lake was the product of human ambition resolved inevitably to filth. Before man, the lake had been glacially clear. The color of the sky was the stipple of steel mills. The dead branches in the trees were warrants of civic irresponsibility. The droop of winter-burnt ramblers on his own porch was a testament to the laziness of the man who tended his lawn in summer and his furnace through the numb, bellowing winters. The fine Colonial furniture behind and all around him was affectation: his aunt Emma's, for treasuring the inefficient and now sleazy appurtenances of eighteenth-century North America, and his own, for accepting her heritage, installing it, and adding to it that which was congruous, for the most part, rather than that which he liked and needed. His eye fell acidly upon the bright brass bedwarmers which hung on each side of his fireplace. Rotten little things that gathered dust, had to be polished all the time, and actually served no greater human need than the mere infant's wish for sparkle. He looked away, expectantly, to the books. There, surely—

But even they had a new aspect. He recollected the books in Alexandria. The lost books of the Bible. The numberless manuscripts into which for thousands of years man had been pouring his soul and which had either disappeared or stood now in grimy libraries where only the eyes of archivists would reach them. Most books, indeed, were the tombstones of their authors rather than the instruments of their immortality. Like the grayness of the lake, they represented the transition of human ambition. Gobbets for mudpuppies or yellow pages for insect food—and purges as scarce historically as resurrections. Though they were the same things.

Mrs. Burns, his housekeeper, came from the kitchen through the dining room. "What time shall I have supper?"

"When you're ready. I'm not very hungry tonight."

"You look all used up. Are you catching a cold?"

His head shook at the faded primping. "No. Just tired."

He went upstairs to his den. It overlooked fences and back yards. A cold laundry hung across a plot of winter-browned turf. A child industriously pedaled a tricycle back and forth upon it, watching the juice ooze into his wheel tracks. John drew the curtains and switched on the light over his secretary. He sat down and took a sheet of paper. On it, he scrawled a note to the dean at Langer:

"Dear Paul—The Army rejected me—some physiological silly-business—but I am thinking strongly of carrying out part of the project—i.e., taking time off from my classes and the lab. For one thing, I feel that I've spent too many years in the same pair of ruts—the teaching rut and the rut of remunerative biochemistry. Even as I write this, it further occurs to me that a vacation—for that is what I am discussing, actually—might be more productive than the planned routines which I had already intended to abandon. That is, I think I shall get away for a while on my own—in the hope some perspective may be attained and in the possibly vainer hope that such perspective may give me new ideas about my research. This means, I presume, that, since I cannot participate in the war as a person, I should like to do so as a scientist and that I would like to get my brain on a wartime basis. What humanity has needed for better health and more efficient physical functioning is possibly different from what humanity will need as battle casualties and as invaders in a global war. At least, after I have thought of myself a bit, I shall try to do some thinking about that. I shall keep you advised of this rather capricious program. Meanwhile, I trust you will prepare the moral conscience of the Great Man for an absence of this cog in his faculty, this heretic. An absence he will not be able to reconcile with duty. He is a wonder of a college president. I am indebted to him for an understanding of pomp that has deepened with every year of his incumbency. In other words, I trust you will twist his tail with the fact that I am going to be a deliberate renegade. Truly, as you have guessed, it is rather startling to discover at my age that your mechanical innards aren't up to draft board standards and probably I am only behaving in a wounded and fugitive manner. At any rate, I'll be back in a few months, and this colic of the ego will have healed. Yours —John.

"P.S. Such, at least, is my expectation."

He put the letter in an envelope and stamped it.

For a while, he gazed at the photographs on his wall: his father and his mother—the former swathed in the folds of his black pulpit gown and the latter in a moiré dress that was streaked with highlights in the pattern of—what? An electroencephalogram. He grinned. The two faces had character—the character of faces in family albums. Modern photographs show no such stern jaw, burning eye, or disciplined configuration of line and wrinkle. He had always attributed the difference to the advance of photographic art. Could it be, he now wondered, the difference in generations?

There were two photographs of girls. Ellen—looking silly, now, in bangs and a helmet hat, short skirts and a low, lax waistline. He had not seen Ellen for a decade. Married to Bill Armstrong. John's grin waned. He had come very near to marrying Ellen himself—four—was it five?—years after Princeton. And there was the photograph of Robbie. Just as blonde, just as beautiful, just as captious now—in the Chicago-stained picture—as she had been ten years ago. He stood, remembering Robbie with pain and with relief. Too reckless—which was to say—too selfish. A short engagement broken off with double grief and double brandies. Robbie was a mother and a hostess in Forest Hills, and the look in her eyes today no longer struck the heart. It puzzled the brain—rather—for it was a look of disappointment concealed by brassy invitation. A no-good beautiful woman. Another man's dilemma.

Mrs. Burns's voice patiently climbed the stairs. He went down, through the shadows. The house was peaceful and pretty now, in the gray corners and in the halos of low lights. His table was set for himself alone.

How many students had dined here—politely, worshipfully, gaily, enchantedly—or sometimes, if their marks were low, concernedly. How many professors and their wives, how many advertising men and publicity agents and manufacturers. Robbie, too—with the candles sinking into themselves after Mrs. Burns's sniffed good night. A pageant of people. The young, trying to hurry time. The old, trying to restrain it. His friends, his guests, his acquaintances, learned visiting firemen from abroad, bright youngsters in shabby suits, the dull and the pushing—all had lived a little while in the dining room and the library, and they had gone away.

Swell host. Swell guy. Good storyteller. Bachelor. Wonder why.

John sat down and sipped his sherry. Mrs. Burns brought the soup. He realized he was exceedingly hungry.

Miami, he thought vaguely.

Well, why not? Warm weather would be a good change.

For thirty days—or fifty—Chicago would freeze and spit.

Palm trees rattled his imagination.

The soup was good.

Palms—a long beach—quietude and privacy.

He went upstairs early. His head ached and he felt restless. Feverish. Perhaps he needed to begin already—the drug that had been prescribed. He'd taken a test dose in the morning. Wearily he went down the steps. The bottle was in his overcoat pocket. He brought it back to his bedroom; he undressed. In the bathroom-door mirror he saw that he was covered with a rash.

So he was one of the few who couldn't take that drug. Allergic. That much less chance—if the main chance broke against him.

He put on his pajamas and brushed his teeth and sat on the edge of his bed, grinning at space—not sardonically, not even perplexedly. Just grinning—the way a man does.

6

When John came through the tunnel of tropical growth that served the Gracey mansion as a driveway, he stopped at its mouth and stared—the renting agent's list held folded in his hand. Her words came back to him: "This might be a possible for you. After all, the qualifications you wish are rather unusual. It's solitary enough. Not expensive. Nothing is, this time of year. I mean to say, you could take a season rental and afford to leave it if you changed your mind—without losing much. That was what you wanted, I think? I'd try it last, though. It's farthest up the beach—and it is—

well—it's maybe more solitude than you're bargaining for, Mr. Galen."

The waste of verdure was like a private sea that cut off the bleached old house from humanity. On the other side was the planetary ocean, too—so that this address was in itself a remoteness, a street number on Saturn, a place the sun and the rain and the wind could find but one that people would not discover easily and might even avoid if they chanced upon it. He drew a breath, deep and satisfied, and looked at the list to make sure he was right. For a long time he stood there.

Then he heard footsteps.

A girl hurried around the desolate house—a house which he had somehow assumed to be inhabited, in spite of its bleakness and his lack of data on the point. Her appearance, oddly enough, did not startle him. His thoughts, turned inward ever since Poole had passed judgment on him, were scarcely budged by the materialization of a human figure in this environment. He had been savoring it, drinking it in, exploring it before marching around to look at the sea side of the weird structure. With the emergence of the girl, it merely became the property of strangers. He had noticed that she had been running as if pursued and he fully expected to see the man pursuing her. Nobody appeared or called.

That, he reflected, was germane to the scene. The place was melancholy and whimsical. People here could be imagined as running suddenly, for no visible reason. The girl spoke a word of greeting in a calm voice. He had answered, "Why, yes. I was," and started toward her. It did not surprise him that she was lovely; he would have been astonished, rather, and much disappointed, if she had been anything else. That was owing to the real estate agent who had called her "attractive, nice, and a new war widow." The last phrase had been matter-of-fact at the time; it seemed heartless in her presence.

They stopped, about two paces apart. He could see now that she was pallid and that the veins in her throat were flexing swiftly. She was making an effort to repress labored breathing.

"I got this address from an agent," Galen said, showing her the penciled sheet of memorandum paper. "I'm looking for a place to rent—for a while. The agent said—"

She looked back over her shoulder. "It was—for rent."

"You've changed your mind? Withdrawn it?"

"I don't know." Her eyes came back to him, studied him, noting his clothes and his expression. "That depends."

On me, he thought. He smiled. "My name's Galen. John Galen. I'm a professor. A biochemist. I'm down here for my health." He had been wondering for a long while whether he would explain even that much—and how he would explain. Now he had his answer. "Nerves. Overwork. Need rest and quiet."

"Nerves," the girl repeated. She stared at him and her dark head shook perceptibly. "You don't look—"

His smile broadened. "Jittery? It's not that kind of nervousness."

"Oh." She held out her hand. "I'm Mrs. Gracey. This is my husband's house—mine, now, that is. He died a little while ago."

"I was told at the agent's—" He thought he had no right to add anything to that.

She seemed to be struggling with herself. "I'd planned on renting it," she finally said. "Or selling it. I suppose I should go ahead—"

"I'm not fussy. It looks like"—he rejected, then used, the platitude—"just what the doctor ordered." She stood there, not speaking. Gloom gathered. "You see," he went on, "I arrived a couple of days ago. I definitely don't like the chrome-plated, Coney Island aspect of the lower Beach. I also do not believe my doctor would approve of my sharing reveille with several thousand soldiers every morning at five-thirty. Not, at least, while I was following his orders about resting. But I am an aficionado for beaches and I want, most of all, to be by myself for—for quite a long while. Months. Months, that is, if I could have a place as secluded and wonderful as this. I'm not a really rich man but I could readily afford—"

She stirred. The very way she moved arrested his flow of words: it had to do with his inquiry—it was, indeed, the visual commencement of an answer. She, and he, looked toward the ornate old house. "It's haunted," the girl finally said.

"Haunted?" He repeated the statement without emotion, his voice searching for further information.

"I just found out."

That did startle him. "You mean—you were running from—?" Suppositions, uneasy—but possibly wounding to the girl—stopped him again.

She nodded. "I was packing up my husband's things all afternoon—and just now—he began talking to me."

His first reaction was the barest impulse to step back from her—the impulse one has when the sanity of a companion is suddenly opened to question. He stood motionless.

"It was no hallucination," the girl continued. "He said only a few words. I didn't see anything. I ran. It scared me—then. Now—"

"I understand, Mrs. Gracey."

"You don't believe in ghosts?"

"I've never met one. Or heard one. As a scientist—I'd say I didn't. But—in a place like this, with night falling—as a *person*—I'd probably yield a point. There are many things science doesn't know about—to be sententious."

She smiled slightly—he could see the turning of her mouth. "Yes. The strange part is—I don't, either. Believe in ghosts, I mean. I've always been certain that, when you die, you are gone. Like autumn leaves. Like the flame of a fire. Like anything spent and exterminated and finished. My mother's religious. The things religious people accept for the dead, and for life after death, are insults to the living, I think. But now—he did speak to me. He has a reason."

"Reason?"

"Don't they all—have a reason?"

He did not comprehend.

"A reason," she went on, "to come *back*—from wherever they are?"

"Oh." Galen shifted his feet. He felt that perhaps it would be wisest to make a graceful apology—or an ungraceful one—and depart. But the wind in his soul veered at that moment. Here was a charming girl, her veins still bursting but her voice controlled, facing for the first time an immense and terrifying uncertainty about her own mind. Here was he, enduring a similar uncertainty in another category. Yet he had been ready to doubt her, to offer her neither sympathy nor aid, to flee from her, in effect—while she had candidly admitted the nature of her dubiety to him, a stranger.

He suddenly felt toward her an intense compassion. It

68

made him assured. He began to think some of her thoughts: to realize the naked awfulness to which his abrupt departure might expose her. She was turning her handkerchief in her hands, looking at him, and letting herself tremble, now that twilight was deepening into dark. He tracked his cogitation back to the words she had set in the air.

"Did—your husband—*say* his reason for coming—back?"

"No."

"Have you had dinner?"

"No." Ann's voice was wondering. "I hadn't even connected the fact that it's dark with how late it must be! I was packing—and I didn't notice the time—and then—"

"Of course. Look, Mrs. Gracey. I don't have a car. I came on the bus. I certainly don't want to be a bother to you now, or a problem. If you want to be left alone, say so. But your actions a while ago suggest—"

"Would you? Would you come inside while I get a wrap—and take me to the bus with you?"

"Gladly. In fact—if you won't consider it presuming—I'll offer you my company at dinner. I haven't eaten, either. You aren't—staying here? Or are you?"

"No." She sighed relievedly. "No. I'm staying over in Miami. We'll go in."

The blackout room still contained some of the day's heat. His eyes moved from object to object. He was, after all, a prospective tenant. Ann had gone upstairs—rejecting his offer to accompany her after a moment of struggle. He could hear her moving about. Comfortable room, he thought. Ugly, though. And odd. What of it? He could have a woman by the day to cook and clean; spend the nights in here reading and writing—or out on the beach, in fine weather, thinking and idling; ride down on the bus in the afternoons to shoot some golf; get to know a few people—the kind he liked, if there were any—to occupy those times when a creature needs its fellows. Maybe the old monstrosity was haunted—it certainly had the look—but ghosts didn't bother unbelievers and, in any case, the shade of the naval officer had no honorable concern with him. He grinned.

Her feet came down the stairs—accurately, but as swiftly as she could move them.

7

THE RESTAURANT decoration resembled new machine parts combined with primitive Caribbean art—semi-nudes in sultry pigment. They ordered daiquiris and sipped them, listening to music emitted by no visible instrument but omnipresent and apparently eternal in the large room.

With the drink, Ann felt her new obsession draw back a little. She saw John Galen more clearly than she had seen other people in the past six days. He seemed peaceful—almost placid. Ability shone in his brown eyes; character was revealed by each of his large features. His brow was a pedant's; his reddish hair unruly and reassuring in that it represented a certain reaction to pure pedantry. His hands were small but the muscles around his palms bunched when he lifted his glass: he used his hands for harder work than their size suggested. He was friendly, intelligent, and decent, like hundreds of thousands of Americans—trying now to hide his curiosity about her so that it would not intrude upon her unhappiness.

He talked easily, purposefully: "I've never been in Miami before. The doctor who recommended it said it was an expression of the national dream. I imagine he's right. Every possible element and aspect of physical comfort—and the façades—the outer seemings—of a Maxfield Parrish paradise. Something very close, in fact, to the Moslem idea. Even Moorish architecture! I understand there's a village that actually has domes and minarets somewhere back toward the 'Glades. I suppose the American people would be insulted to know that all they can think of, when they deliberately build a Valhalla, is a sort of paste replica of something Mohammed dreamed up fourteen centuries ago. Something his followers repeatedly mimicked—and in far more durable materials. Besides, the Americans don't follow through. Nobody has a harem, here. Funny, how often you talk about Americans as though they were somebody else! Still—ninety-nine point something of our noble population would be outraged at the idea of trying openly to make anything practical out of that aspect of Mohammedanism. The stage setting is complete—but the dancing girls never walk on. It's a serious flaw. The whole thing is a flaw, as a matter of fact. Scrape away the stucco and you get railroads, drugstores, garages, pool halls, hot-dog wagons, slums, and Y.M.C.A.'s—with hardly any culture, either. No art—"

"There are some artists here."

"Artists? Sure. Wherever there are people. But I bet they send their canvases north. This place is strictly an air-brush composition—all excepting the ocean and those swamps and fields around your place. They're real enough—and probably not even very safe."

Ann smiled. "Safe? Oh. You mean—bugs—and snakes! They have their quota, all right. This isn't Minneapolis—except, as you say, where Minneapolis citizens have built their imitation Meccas. Are you interested in art, Mr. Galen?"

"Sometimes."

"I was just thinking—" She accepted a large menu from the waiter and ordered immediately. "I know an artist. I've been half meaning to see him for several days. I haven't felt up to it. Perhaps—after dinner—"

"Sure." He smiled at her as if she had made a wise prescription for their separate ailments. "Or am I included?"

"Everybody's included at Shawn's. I'll phone him." She showed an unexplained, inner eagerness. "In fact—I think I'd like to talk to Shawn very much—now."

"Last name?"

She shook her head. "First. Shawn Peecey Mullcup. He's an illustrator."

"Another cocktail? We'll have to wait for the sole."

"All right," Ann said. "An illustrator. That's how he makes his money—and he makes a lot. But he's a painter besides—a peculiar one. And I think—a good many people do—that he's really a teacher who has an unfortunate knack for painting, because he talks better, even, than he draws. Maybe he'll make you angry. He does me—often. But I get over it. He just used to make Bill embarrassed—but I've known Shawn ever since I was a child. He went to high school in my town in Connecticut. Then he went to Europe to study. I made Bill look him up, when we arrived in Miami. He lives on one of those islands in the bay. You could see it from up here, if it weren't for the blackout."

With his second cocktail, John's thoughts shifted again. He had been on the verge of taking a plane back to Chicago. His preoccupation was too barren for the flamboyant back-

grounds of the hotel-lined section of Miami Beach. He had
starved for no man's company but he had been willing to
accept any sort of companionship. He had found none. He
had been seeking surcease for the hours and the weeks of
contemplation wished upon him; but this Gilead was without
balm. It was like an unroofed and loveless Tunnel of Love,
bizarre and papier-mâché; it was pretty but unsignificant,
full of people resenting the newcome soldiers and of soldiers
resenting the civilians, of quibbles over dimout rules and
complaints about gasoline rationing. It was as if the inhabitants of purgatory had overswarmed the Seventh Heaven
and made it abhorrent by their trivial, multiplicious pres-
ences. The grandeur of sea and sky belittled the buildings
and the grandiosity of these was diminished by the unpleas-
antness of pleasure seekers.

The agent's list had represented his sworn last attempt
upon the inhospitable territory. He could not tolerate its
overblown will to appear what the people would not let it
be. He had taken the list, along with his waning recollection
of a vision of himself living in solitude on a great beach, and
he had reached the last address before he had felt any other
urge than to hurry away.

Ann watched him quietly, not minding his silence. It
was, perhaps, great good manners in a total stranger. That
she felt him to be anything but a stranger did not prevent
her from making the observation. She was sure—unshakably
and also quite unknowingly—that the timing of his arrival
in the drive and her rush around the side of the house were
no more accidental than the rising of the moon. It was
necessary for him to have been there. If he had not been
thus standing quietly in the treacherously bright last light of
evening, she would have collapsed. Her nerves would have
snapped. She might easily have gone mad. Instead, she was
here amidst the bright colors, the dulcet music, drinking a
daiquiri, and feeling that her spirit was less heavy. She had
discovered a friend when it would have been impossible to
go on alone.

Her concept of going on referred to Bill, of course.
She was scarcely conscious of the fact that John Galen was
a man; he was a person, and that sufficed. He was like one
of the friendly figures who had arrived in dire hours to
assist Pilgrim in his fearful progression.

Because she had an inkling of her future, and a companion to share it, she felt less afraid and less agonized. She could reason again. Bill was still somehow alive, or partly alive, or in death not dead; this was merely the beginning of a new understanding that held certain consolation among its other, unguessable attributes. She would have to think about it, to test it, to experience it. John Galen would be a help.

"I hope you take our house," she said.

He turned from his distant inspection. "I was about to say the same thing. That is, I was about to say I liked the house. It suits my purposes. I enjoy swimming. I don't mind doing it alone. Maybe I'll take up surf casting. There are lots of books I'd like to read. Now, I can read them."

"You won't mind—that it's haunted?"

His eyes were curious. "You're sure?"

"Sure."

"You don't object to discussing it?"

"Why—no. That is—I wouldn't want everybody—or anybody, much—to know it. They'd think I was crazy. You don't—do you?"

He shook his head. "Your expression, when you came around the house, was pretty convincing, Mrs. Gracey. I feel the way—you evidently did until this afternoon. I believe death is death. I find myself wishing it were otherwise, occasionally—and then I remind myself of all the false beliefs that have been fathered by such wishing. I am a scientist and I have no data at first hand. Put it that way. I won't challenge your experience any more than you do mine. My lack of experience, if you wish. People like me pride themselves on their open minds. We would be less than intelligent if we presumed to describe life and death exactly—when the very attempt makes us perceive how inscrutable they are. I suppose"—he hesitated thoughtfully—"that I could get a grudging assent from the less bigoted of my scientific friends to the proposition that our attitude toward life is so restricted it blinds us to the precise nature of death. Put that way, it would be defensible in some circles of erudition. Most scientists, I regret to say, would pooh-pooh it. Because what is called 'pure' science is generally a most sorry form of fanaticism, I think. Indeed, I'd even like to be convinced that your Bill was present in the old house. It would give me some

73

furious good debates when I go home—and it would make so many bores avoid me as a lunatic. I trust I don't offend you?"

She shook her head sadly. "No. You are—going to rent the house?"

The curious expression returned to his eyes. He looked at her and through her and around into himself. He was thinking, simultaneously, of abstractions that barely touched his awareness and of an actual commitment of himself to the venture. "Of course. You knew that, didn't you, when you saw me standing there?"

She swallowed. "I guess I did."

"Of course you did. I'll move in as soon as I may. Tomorrow, if that's possible. I have no real prejudice against bugles." He paused. "On the contrary." His voice had fallen; he rallied it. "But now I have a passion for solitude—great stretches of it—solitude on demand, like ice water in my hotel."

"You seem anything but—nervous. You said—"

"I'm not any more neurotic than everybody else. Or any jumpier. Or any more given to imaginary flights of alarm. My—my little difficulty—is something else. If you are afraid your old mansion will frighten me—let me put it this way: I believe my condition might tend to make me reckless rather than apprehensive."

"Oh." Ann lifted a shrimp, red with catsup. "You haven't asked me how much."

Galen laughed.

8

THE MULLCUP house was long and low and shaped like three sides of a square. The open end faced the bay. The back part, on the street side, was two stories high. A forest of ficus trees hid it partly from the rays of a dimmed street lamp. The walls were white. In the center of the house was an archway with an iron gate. The taxi stopped. Ann allowed John to help her out; she protested his payment for the ride; she went to the door ahead of him and paused before she touched the bell. There was a whacking and bumping going on inside; over it came the baritone roar of Shawn's voice

74

raised in Homeric wrath. She was in no mood to meet Shawn in one of his major tizzies. John Galen, furthermore, would hardly understand. She stood there, looking down a long corridor that bisected the house and lay open to the bay at the opposite end.

"'If thy right eye offend thee,'" Shawn bellowed, "'pluck it out.' Much less thy radio. Turn it on, Willie. See if we've got the life out of it yet!"

There was a silence. Ann held her finger on the bell, not yet pressing it; she became aware of the cab driving away and of John Galen moving on the deep St. Augustine grass to her side. Now, the voice of a radio exploded, loudly and suddenly, into the stillness:

"If you have offensive face pores, skin thickening, abnormal facial hairs, greasy nostril—"

"Greasy nostril!" Shawn thundered. "Lay on it, Willie! The damn thing's like a rattlesnake. Lucky you can pull the cord apart in the last extremity. Sour breath, eh?" The query was followed by a monstrous boom. "Vanilla Itties for Bitsy-Itsy folk, eh? Take that." Smack! "The soap that's sweet to your skin and sweet to your sweetie." Crash!

There followed a fusillade of blows and bangings over which came the shrill shout of a child. Ann still hesitated.

"Murdering his radio, I take it," John Galen said quietly at her side. "Justifiable act."

Ann pushed the bell. It pealed softly, once. The pounding went on, but a woman appeared in the corridor. She hurried toward the entrance, calling, "I'm awfully sorry, but it won't last much longer, really!" Then she saw them clearly. "Oh, Ann! I thought it was the neighbors, complaining again! Sometimes they bring cops. Ann, dear, I'm terribly glad to see you. Shawn's bound to subside in a minute or two."

They went in. The noise was coming from the left-hand section of this part of the house—a very large room, two stories high, filled with pictures, chairs, tables, divans, smoking stands, fireplace logs, cabinets, consoles, bookcases, lamps, and a host of other ameubles and impedimenta not readily identifiable in a single glimpse. John had time for one glance only because his attention was centered thereafter upon a fat, tall, bald man with a beard as red as rust. The man, and a girl about ten, in a nightie, together with a boy

75

about twelve, in shorts, were belaboring a vast, luxurious radio cabinet with baseball bats, the bill of a marlin, and pieces of firewood.

This was Shawn, his son Willie, and his daughter Willa. The woman, whom John had not yet noticed at all, was Thalia, his wife. Shawn ignored the arrival. He strode to the fireside, selected a larger log, returned to the smashed and staggering wreck of the radio, aimed, and brought down the wood with ferocity. One of the legs supporting the cabinet splintered lengthwise and the thing buckled. As it went over, the boy caught it with his baseball bat and knocked it upright. Shawn hit again, and this time the second leg broke. The cabinet went down.

"Once," Shawn said more quietly, as they all stood back and stared at the mess, "in the good old phonograph days, it was 'his master's voice.' Now, by all the potbellied gods in China, this is the voice of our master! Out with him! Down with him! To hell with him! Sweet soup and liquid sewage! Puree of nostrum and quackery, potage of flawed diamonds and veneered furniture, essence of everything awful, big, cosmic, world-wide throat of upsidedown men who have got their windpipes attached somehow to their—"

"Shawn!" said Thalia.

"—whose fluttering cheeks emit these maple syrup ejaculations night and day! Shoot the scum! Willie. Try her."

The boy knelt in the splinters, in the ripped-off imitation tapestry, and found a switch. It clicked. After a moment, the radio, as viable as a lizard, bawled in a thunderous voice that which a far-off announcer was silkily whispering: "Perhaps he has been neglecting you. No phone call. No letter. No car stopping at your gate. No swift ride through the pine-scented night. No happy stop—no ecstasy—no engagement— nothing. Yes, perhaps he has been neglecting you. But—have *you* been neglecting *yourself*? Armpit odor—"

With this last phrase, the radio condemned itself to even swifter and more horrible death. Shawn jumped on it. Now, the main part of the cabinet, like a breached inner fortress, flew apart. Shawn's brogan kicked out a whole side. The inwards of the thing, tubes still showing a faint cherry glow, were laid bare. Shawn's two majestic feet shot up above them. His knees flexed. He came down. The crash was more complex, as a sound, than any effect ever produced in a studio. Shawn stamped and kicked. Tubes, grids, knobs, wires, condensers, fuses, began to fly from the place and the children ran around the room after them, belaboring each one as it rolled, shouting with their father and behaving as if they were killing off an opened nest of tarantulas that had threatened their home.

"Try it," Shawn Mullcup finally said in a stern and skeptical tone.

"It couldn't work," Willie answered. "It just couldn't."

"Try it," the vast man repeated. "Who knows? The manufacturers may have prepared for this sort of thing. There may be a little teeny radio inside the big one, that cuts in when you trample its parent. The thing may have seeds. It may have fertile eggs of itself inside. It might grow back together at night. We'll have to dump it in the sea—with sash weights—like a body."

"I can't find the switch," Willie said earnestly.

Shawn stirred the shambles, which crunched and tinkled. He looked anxiously at his wife. "Do you think we got it, Thalia?"

She took the handkerchief out of her mouth, wiped her eyes, and nodded. She was a beautiful woman, John saw, with a straight nose and gray-blue eyes, high-piled yellow hair, and lips that had been kissed on her with generous passion.

Shawn said, "Hello, Ann." He spoke very quietly. Behind him, the two children were already commencing to collect the rubble in a large heap.

John wondered what Ann's expression would be. It was grave, he saw—grave with tension at the corners of her mouth and a dancing light in her eyes. "This is John Galen," she said. "Thalia and Shawn Mullcup. And Willie and Willa." The children ducked their heads when he turned toward them.

Shawn took a package of cigarettes from his shirt pocket. In his hand, it looked half-size. He offered the package, which was damp from his exertions. John accepted a cigarette.

Ann spoke. "Mr. Galen's going to rent my house."

Thalia said, "How wonderful!"

Shawn took John's hand, squeezed it, appreciated the returning power with a slight lift of one of his thick, shooting eyebrows, and said somberly, shaking his head, "We had to kill it. The thing was getting the best of us all. You're a witness to that, Mr. Galen? You heard that last, desperate gurgle about armpits?"

Galen looked at the kids. They were working swiftly and the floor was clearing. "I did. I'm here to testify it was treason to every sensibility of the human spirit. Loathsome, criminal, revolting, debauching and hideous."

Shawn Mullcup looked a second longer at Galen. Then he turned to the children. "You heard that, didn't you? Mr. Galen is an expert in good taste. He came here specially as a professional witness. We'll throw the thing in the ocean tomorrow. It nearly mastered us. Time is the chains it uses. Willie has three evenings a week destroyed because he has to use them to wait for a quarter of eight and nine-fifteen. Willa was losing her life on four afternoons a week. She never had time to do anything between the waits for her favorite programs. So she just listened to whatever it said or played—while she waited. Thalia was a slave to ten o'clock and half past eleven. Some people—millions—have given away most of their whole lives waiting for it to get to be a quarter to something. Waiting worriedly—for fear they'd miss. That's peonage. It is the master of America. So we killed it. And now, you kids—"

He thrust two fingers under Willie's belt. He gathered the skirt of Willa's nightdress in his hand, hiked it up to the tops of her legs, pulled it tight, swung both youngsters off the floor, and carried them out of the room, like buckets. As they disappeared, Willie waved good night. Shawn's feet moved up a flight of stairs across the hall. The children, horizontally transported, were beginning to giggle.

"It's a little drastic," Thalia said presently. "But not quite as cockeyed as it looked, Mr. Galen. For one thing, Shawn's always despised that supergadget because it was so ugly. A sister of his gave it to us. For another, the two kids really have been radio-batty, lately. It was a useful lesson. Then—Shawn's Shawn."

"My only regrets," John said, "are, first, that I didn't see the inception of this little execution. And, second, that Mr. Mullcup cannot extend the scope of his activities to every household in the land. He is a man of vision."

Shawn came back. "Galen," he said. "No relation? I

78

thought not. Now. Scotch? Rye? Bourbon? Sherry? Gin and lemonade?"

"No, thanks. Nothing."

"Ann?"

She shook her head. She smiled a little at John. "You'll be persona grata here in no time, Mr. Galen. The Mullcups don't drink."

"We merely serve it to the addicts, the bored, and those who have been lying in Alpine snow." Thalia said that.

"And the Mullcups appreciate people who are enemies of the radio, so to speak." Ann nodded toward Shawn. "Of course, his list of mortal foes is immense."

"Right now," Shawn said, "the mainsail of my aversion is a magazine called *Home and Style*. I am painting their April cover. It is to be a Waac riding a motorcycle in the mud. About a twenty-five-dollar painting, as art. But this Waac, when I get done with her, will give you what the staff calls a 'warm and welling emotional reaction of attraction and repose, not quite moistly sweet, a touch flirtatious.' I have a letter to prove it. By painting in these wet, saccharine, magnetic quanta, I shall increase the value of the opus from twenty-five dollars to twelve hundred and fifty dollars. I tackled it this morning. But how my insides boiled! The radio's a compensation, I guess. Because I finished the slightly sexy, wetsy-pantsy Waac before it was dark enough to strain these piercing eyes! What in hell do you do and is it any different?"

"I'm a biochemist," John replied, still grinning.

Shawn slapped the side of his beefy face. "I give up! I'm sunk. Scientists awe me. Maybe what they do *is* different, for all I know. Maybe it's good—even. Sometimes, I'm afraid it is."

"And sometimes, I'm afraid it's not." John moved his hand a disparaging inch. "What you say about your painting goes double for me. I make hormones that give nuisances enough energy to become dangerous pests, for example!"

Shawn's nod was quick. He walked over to the divan where Ann was sitting near Thalia. "We're glad you came," he said, in an entirely changed tone. "We—missed you."

Ann was—and had been—thinking hard. Her eyes were not distrait, but uncertain. "I know, Shawn. People are selfish with their sorrow. I wanted to get through the first

79

part—alone. Now—" Her voice hung, and stopped on that word.

"We'll talk about Bill—later—a lot," Shawn said quietly. "Wherever he is—" with the phrase, Ann looked up—"he's making a good job of it. He expects as much from you." Quite suddenly he bent down—his beard swept her cheek— and he kissed her. John looked away—inadvertently toward Thalia—and saw little tears gather in her eyes. The Mullcups liked Ann more than people usually liked one another. Shawn began speaking again. "You know what he expects of you, too."

"I hope I do, Shawn. I'm still—mixed up."

"But not as much as you thought you'd be." Shawn's tone was puzzled. "No. Well. Mr. Galen—we should explain we are old friends."

"Ann did. Since I haven't any here, at all—I think my luck is beyond reasonable expectation. I hope—"

Ann interrupted, urgently. "What do you mean—I am not as mixed up as I thought I'd be? Shawn, can you read minds? Why—?"

"I can read faces," Shawn replied gravely. "If you want to talk about it—why, of course, Ann, we want you to. There is an expression of a *happening* to you, in your face, you know."

She sat silent, looking at them, speculating still. Thalia reached over and touched her shoulder. Shawn stroked his beard.

"What makes you say that?" Ann's gray-green eyes widened slowly and looked into Shawn's. John fastened his gaze at the water glinting beyond the front yard. These were indeed old friends; he was on the point of taking his intrusion out onto the lawn. Ann perceived that while she was still looking at Shawn. "Don't leave. Why did you ask that, Shawn?"

He wrinkled his nose and squinted at her. "Because you don't look quite exactly the way I'd expected. You've got something more and something different on your mind."

That was astute, John thought.

"Shawn," she said, "I—I was there, alone, this afternoon—till half past seven, anyway. I heard him. He called to me."

"Oh." Shawn began a glance toward Galen and decided to restrain it.

"He called, 'Ann!'" she said impetuously, "and, 'Ann, dear!' and later, when I had passed the place on the stairs from where he'd spoken, he called down to me, 'It's here.'"

Shawn said, "My God," in a matter-of-fact tone. "Know what he was talking about?"

"I haven't the faintest idea. It's only that—"

"That what?"

"That he said it was *there*. In the house. And I've had a feeling for ever so long that there was *something* in the house."

"Something—what?"

"Horrible," Ann said softly.

John stretched out his hand and stared hard at the palm of it. One never knew what sorts of people held what kinds of beliefs. It was odd, though, to sit in this living room, this chamber stuffed like the display floors of a rich, eccentric department store, and hear two highly educated people introduce a ghost as though it were a neighbor. He wondered if, perhaps, Shawn Mullcup was being compassionate and no more. That supposition was short-lived. Mullcup sat down and used one thick arm to pivot his body like a hogshead, toward Galen. "And you're moving in, eh? Ever see one— hear one speak?"

"I'm afraid not." Galen felt uncomfortable. He had said all there was for him to say, at dinner.

"I have." Shawn fingered his beard. "We civilized Westerners are such asses about ourselves! We grow stupider with every generation! We are bent upon proving, as a society, that all space, all time, all energy, all awareness— are surfaces. The substance of wave motion is thought of as superficial, like a caress or a series of pats. And the anatomy of an atom is similarly conceived. We measure everything with three dimensions, plus clocks, and call the result 'consciousness of the nature of the universe.' Even the Einsteinians, who have thrust their investigations a little way beyond those outward boundaries, seem bent upon denying what they have learned by describing it in terms of sides, tops, bottoms and returning curves, balls of energy or waves of it, space that is palpable and pliable, hours and minutes. As if the meaning of reality lay wholly in texture, and the essential purpose of awareness were to measure it, like yard goods!"

John chuckled. "You seem to think mathematicians are malicious."

"But—of course they are! Most of them! *People* are! Which mathematician is not, unconsciously, engaged in working toward an a priori conclusion? Which one, confronted by enigma, does not twist it back toward superficialism in the hope of solution? And when even the greatest of them founder—or come upon a dismaying notion—which one does not hole up in his ivory tower and continue to ponder his 'problem' instead of what is so cogently and eternally implied by it: himself? Who among all the savants of science has come the full round his equations imply and stopped asking himself 'what?' in order to inquire 'why?' The very attitude is regarded as infantile. There lies the malice. It is the malice of the ego. The pedant's malice. The malice of the property owner. For the property of the mathematician is his equations and he is as unreasoningly possessive of them as any landholder—as dogmatic, as legally authoritarian. And why? It is his franchise and, therein, his earthly security. He would be wholly insecure, as an ego, if you demanded of him that he meditate outside his convictions. His attack upon reality, like all the effort of everyone else, is directed toward the attainment of the illusion of security. Suppose there were a higher morality? Suppose his security could exist only through, first, the understanding and, second, the rejection, of all the claims of his ego? What then? By attaining that condition, he would have lost his world—the world of his mathematical assurance—the world of the lot on which his house stands. But, perhaps, he would have gained himself. Somebody said as much, long ago. You find me a mathematician or a physicist who feels that his truisms are one with cooking recipes and I'll meet a chap to talk to about ghosts or death or what a human being could consist of. Not what one does consist of, mind you. What one might."

"Psychology," John said in the gap Shawn left.

The huge, red-bearded artist grunted. "The time for psychology has come. Not the psychology of conditioned reflexes alone—that's another surface. The time for introspections so deep, so timeless, so dimensional, so informed and mathematical that the student will begin to see, at the very least, how love is a flower that grows only through death, why goodness and evil are real—and, perhaps, beyond that, beyond that, beyond instinct—the dimensions his own energy, applied with value and integrity, can create around himself." Shawn shrugged. "You go and live in Bill's house. You're bright. You've got a curiosity-drawn nose. You're basting hot juice on some personal problem of your own—and that's good—because it'll sharpen your perceptions."

"It's just that I think life is a mechanical phenomenon," John answered. "Stop the brain—consciousness stops. Take the blood from a dog and it dies. Put it back, and it lives again. In between—it was dead. Protoplasm. Chemicals. An automaton. Like an automobile—which runs when you supply it with fuel and an electric spark."

Shawn's eyebrows had been lifting. "But what is the matter with this automatonism? Surely we work like mechanical toys! Surely we follow laws! Surely every choice we make is conditioned by our heredity, our environment, and the state of our livers! I am only suggesting that there are more laws and different laws, also. I would not put man outside the pattern of the universe as a willful freak—a biological anarchy. I would, rather, have him see more of his whole place within that universe! I would search out the exquisite truths that do not limit his actions, as you scientists always seem to wish to show they do, but give them their infinite extensions! Why, above all, shall the researcher choose *tawdriness* as his a priori conclusion? Because he is himself already tawdry! Why should he bend his scopes to look in and out so that he can say, 'You see? Put the blood back and the brain lives again? It is miserable mechanics! And see here! The gravity of the sun bends space itself and the light coming through it is curved by the warp! It is nothing, really, but a phenomenon in advanced arithmetic!' These discoveries are always handed down insolently to make man feel littler, less important, more helpless, more the kicked creature of certain rules written in shoddy copybooks by belching old men with beards! Oh—I know—part of the motive in this long struggle for enlightenment is to lift man out of superstition and prejudice—to make him think less of the deceitful lies in which he has so long put his faith. But the honesty of that effort does not explain all of the insolence of the chemist and the astronomer. Part of it is to conceal his disappointment, perhaps, that he has never focused his telescope on

God." Shawn snorted. "Part, though, is to hide his secret awareness that he is still a nasty little ego himself. Not every scientist is like that, either, to be honest. But enough of them are to give science that seeming. It loses touch with wisdom. It has no philosophy any longer. It exists more to show what fools we are than to reveal our limitless possibilities. And why that? Because the pipsqueaks who operate these big tools have themselves, as human creatures, only small possibilities."

Shawn stopped and beamed. "I always attack scientists to see if they can take it. I'm impressed. Still—I do more or less mean what I say. That is—over what abyss, what depth in time and space—and with what timeless quantum of energy might Bill have spoken yesterday to Ann, here, whom he loved with all his heart—a big heart—bigger than his brain, or mine maybe, or perhaps even yours?"

John did not answer immediately. The question, coming at the end of the protracted speech, struck his sensibilities in an odd manner. He looked at Ann, who was listening with shining eyes. He glanced at the artist and stared, afterward, across the tousled room until its contents no longer occupied his attention. His mind had leaped back to the instant when he had come to the end of the tunneled drive that led into the old Gracey place, and stood there, looking at the house. He had experienced a feeling akin to déjà vue—but not quite —because he had actually remembered imagining just such a situation, if not just such an abode, when he had been dining in his Chicago home—full of panicky marvel over the new fact that he might be losing his wits, with no way to ameliorate or maybe even to detect the process.

He had thought the house was tenanted, even at first. Of course, when he had heard the feet of the running girl, he had realized there was somebody near it. That was not quite it, either. He had known, for a full minute, that the house was occupied. He could remember, now, the sound of her feet on the steps inside—a distant clatter, soon ended. The wind had dropped with the setting of the sun and the open area behind the house had been still. But there seemed to be another factor—dimmer—scarcely perceived through the mood of self-consideration which had occupied him as he stood. Ann had run down the stairs. Naturally, he would have heard her—indoors. While he had compared and weighed

84

moods, while he had wondered if this faltering dowager of a house would suitably contain him and his agitated future, those stray, extraneous sensibilities which kept his body in contact with its locus had mechanically noted the hasty, descending footsteps, noted the appearance of the girl—and anticipated the emergence of the man who was chasing her.

That was the core of it. He had expected a man to round the corner behind her. There had been no heavier tread indoors, behind her. And yet, he had presupposed a man. Why? His body had grown tense as he searched back along the inadequate thread of his recollection. Now, his heart threw itself against the walls that confined it. He had known it was a man because, in that quiet, untended, rank garden he had heard, faintly but unmistakably, the urgent sound of a male voice! Not the words, but their tone. The words had been few—possibly only two or three. Words spoken by a man. Then footsteps swift on a staircase. Then a pause and the same feet running on sand. Then Ann had appeared.

He rejected that construction as soon as it had been completely established. His quick mind invented several explanations. It had been the basso creak of an ancient hinge, full of sand and mutter. He himself had grafted the idea onto the event afterward, because he was overwrought, or because some corner of him half wanted to enter into the spirit of this particular evening and these people, or because Shawn had momentarily convinced him such things were possible and he had created an example of his own as a straw man for testing. Possibly Ann, in a weird condition of self-hypnosis, not altogether improbable in view of her afternoon-long occupation, had spoken aloud to herself in a deep voice that had automatically imitated Bill's. Such an act would be a form of schizoid behavior—an example of a personality momentarily split by the wedge of despair. This last seemed likely because the more he thought the more certain he was that his peripheral consciousness had, indeed, clearly heard a masculine voice pronounce at least two words with considerable emphasis. He could very nearly identify them, now, as "It's here."

Again, he thought, it might have been telepathy, if there were such a thing. Words that burst in Ann's brain might have been echoed in his own senses, down there in the yard.

85

Ann had thought something was in the house, apparently, for a considerable while; her brain might have pretended that Bill was confirming her suspicion. Such a confirmation would tie Bill and herself to the old house and it would serve the even larger purpose of reassuring her that the man she had loved was not yet altogether blotted out in space and time.

These impressions had coursed through his mind in the space of less than a minute. He had stared, stiffened, felt his heart leap—and slowly relaxed, a frown on his face. The attention of the others was drawn toward him. He became aware of that and smiled a feeble sort of apology. He prepared to speak.

Shawn, however, struck a match and looked over its flickering light with a Mephistophelian expression. "You remembered something, eh? You recall that somewhere in your past you've left a little inexplicability. You're wondering, now, if maybe it wouldn't fit in with what I have said, rather than with what the books say. Well, you'll have time to consider that—time and plenty of it—on the beach."

John knew his answering expression was unsuccessful. He did not know, indeed, what he had wanted it to be. It had been kind of Shawn to talk so earnestly and reasonably for the girl's benefit. She had drunk in every word. Perhaps she had known of Shawn's theories and come to visit him in order to hear them again. And perhaps Shawn knew that, also. It was difficult to discern just where his accurate expectations had their ending-places. But, much as he liked and approved of Ann, John did not want to be casually included in a circle of people who were going to establish the shadowy presence of a dead man in the residence he had just rented. He wanted Ann's sorrow to be assuaged. But he did not want his own logical mind to be betrayed through an act of assuagement that involved both specious and speculative dialectic.

So he gave Shawn an inadequate look and he said with no conviction, "Of course. Plenty of time. I'll be there in the—the Gracey house." He smiled at Ann, more effectively.

"You were like a miracle," she said. "You just—materialized yourself. Oh, I was terrified. It seems silly now. Almost—unfaithful. If—well—if it *was* Bill—would I have been afraid?"

"Certainly," Shawn said.

"I know I would have been," Thalia agreed. "Even of Shawn."

A relief—a secret relaxation—momentarily comforted Ann. Her face seemed more alive. Now, her lips twitched. "Shawn," she said, "is so much more august. If it had been Shawn—I would never have recovered! You must promise, Shawn—" she thought of what she was saying; her voice trembled; but she finished it: "—never to haunt me."

This, John realized, was brave banter. It was, also, Ann's second admission of the situation in that definitive phrase. If there were a Bill anywhere now, then, indeed, he was haunting his wife. He saw Ann turn her face away.

Thalia said, "Darling, I have a wonderful idea! You move in here with us for a while. All spring—if you want. We'd love it!"

Ann's head shook. For a moment, she could not speak. Then she said to all of them, "I'd rather be alone. I almost feel that I must. Maybe none of you understand—"

Shawn said, "We do." He crossed the room and opened a drawer. "Ann," he continued, talking over his shoulder, "I've written a new one. What do you say I read it?"

She nodded—wrestling again with the rush of confusions —of embarrassments and grief and loneliness.

"Shawn," Thalia explained to John, "writes fables. Nobody knows what for. Or what they mean. He just writes them. He pastes them in scrapbooks and reads them to people whenever he has half a hope that they'll listen. Of course, as a nonpaying audience, you can walk out at any point."

John understood that Shawn was going to read for Ann's benefit. To divert her. She had plunged too deeply and too publicly into a revelation of her afternoon's experience. Now, perplexed, self-conscious—only partially reassured by Shawn—she was unable to go on with the discussion and also unable to withdraw from it. So the artist was changing the subject. John said politely that he'd enjoy hearing the fable.

Shawn was already turning leaves in a large, leather-bound book. He glanced at Ann. "You heard the one about the man who could *broadcast* radio programs from his tooth fillings. And the one about the biochemist"—he glanced at John—"who grew a single germ as big as a camel and **then** found he had to catch people to keep it fed. This is a new one—"

Ann said, "Goody!"

"—about a fellow named Snibbs. Here goes."

He read his fable:

THE SNIBBS PHENOMENON

In the village of Mudford, New York, which is situated at an altitude of two thousand four hundred and eight feet atop the rolling western foothills of the Allegheny Mountains, there appeared, on an autumn afternoon very nearly concident with the date of the commencement of the struggle now identified as World War II, a gentleman named Valentine Snibbs. This person's arrival was dealt with locally according to customs established for all such events in small rural communities. That is to say, Snibbs was both snubbed and interrogated, shunned and sought after, ignored and suspected. That is, he was made to feel very much what he actually was, a complete stranger.

Because he was uncommunicative, he soon created around himself a collection of those invented stories which provide the principal mental occupation of small-town people, especially in sections that are off main highways and winter-bound for long periods. It was said that he had been released from prison after serving a long term for some desperate crime which was variously described by the townsfolk as mayhem, arson, rape, and statutory rape, which is different. It was said that he was by way of being a retired, successful burglar who had (or had not) served his sentence and thus Paid his Debt to

Society. It was also said that he had been a bank teller who had defalcated with the funds and was now entering upon a career of consuming them quietly in this, another, place under an alias or assumed name.

One widow in the town, a Mrs. Botten, even went so far as to say that she thought his former name had been Herkimer. She had seen that name on a fragment of brown wrapping paper which the wind had blown into her back yard where it had been stuck in the oozy muck that surrounded the cover of her cesspool. Certainly there was nobody in Mudford by the name of Herkimer—which was Mrs. Botten's reason for jumping to the conclusion that Herkimer referred to the newcomer. She calmly asserted, indeed, that Snibbs *was* an alias, that he *was* an abscondant from a bank (in the deep South, she said, although he had not a trace of southern accent) and that his true name had been Herkimer.

In doing this, she completely overlooked the fact that Snibbs, if, indeed, he were living a guilty life under an assumed name, would surely not have let loose a paper with his proper cognomen upon it and would hardly have been in such a position as to have received, say, a package wrapped in brown paper upon which was the name of Herkimer. It was, in fact, extremely silly of Mrs. Botten to make such assumptions and asseverations anent Mr. Snibbs; but that is the way country people think and the way they talk—especially about strangers of whom they know nothing whatever. It was not only silly of Mrs. Botten, it was plainly atrocious. Because, for all she really knew, Mr. Snibbs might have been the soul of charity, the essence of decency, and the very spirit of humanitarianism. He was not, but the direction in which he veered from that idealistical level was not one which either had come or could come readily into the cognizance of Mrs. Botten, who was, it must be reported, not only a wretch but stupid—a very commonplace pair of qualities.

Mr. Valentine Snibbs settled in Mudford by the simple expedient of purchasing the old Heppendof farm and moving into it. He paid cash for the farm and paid in full, availing himself of no mortgage and thus furthering the dubiety of the local folk, who seemed to feel that suspicion was as natural a garment to put on a well-to-do newcomer as a hat. The first spring, Mr. Snibbs sowed thirty acres of oats, fifteen of potatoes, some rye, corn, and a little barley. He plowed a fallow meadow and left it bare to the sun for a later planting of buckwheat. Moderate comment was stirred up when it was learned that he was also growing soybeans in his kitchen garden, but no scandal followed, since the Grange had, during the past few years, introduced Mudford to several novel ideas and new crops, as well.

Snibbs also purchased, from Dr. Fellon, a local physician, an automobile in such despairful condition that the acquisition was widely regarded as his first gross error, and a bad one at that, because anybody who had ever so much as driven a car would have known that Fellon's coupé was a wreck beyond redemption. The austere medico himself unbent, for once, and amused his fellow citizens (instead of tormenting their bodies) by reciting in detail and with illustrating diagrams precisely what was wrong with the clutch, how the gears were worn, where the crack could have been discerned in the cylinder head by anyone with half an eye, how rotten the rubber tubing was, how worn the commutator points and, in short, what a miserable bargain the "foreigner" had made.

Fellon's amusement was relatively short-lived, however. It was soon reported that Mr. Snibbs had an excellent collection of tools and machinery, delivered by a truck without a name on its side, that had approached Mudford from the direction of the south. Snibbs, after he had managed to get the car towed to his home (it had broken down after running the length of Fellon's drive and some additional two blocks), had gone furiously to work upon it. Shortly thereafter, the car appeared on the streets of the village and its environs, and, although it did not look any more beautiful externally, its motor sounded like the motor of a car on its second thousand miles. It no longer left a stinking wake of half-consumed gasoline, it took the Main Street hill in high, and one and all were forced to admit that Snibbs had scored even here.

His first year's crop was a success and he had built a new and larger barn in which he stored his produce and to which he transferred his repair equipment. He purchased two piglets in the middle of the summer and by autumn they were the heaviest, for their age, to be seen in the county. He also constructed a henhouse and introduced into it some fifty fowl, mostly Rhode Island Reds but with a few Barred Rocks. There was a woodlot of modest size on his acreage which contained a small patch of good timber and this, in the later autumn, Snibbs carefully tended—felling here, trimming there, stacking the green wood to season, splitting and hauling the hard deadwood for his winter hearth.

By this time, he had also tidied and repainted his home, so that it had resumed some of the piquant charm of its original intent, which was simple, but fundamentally in good taste and proportion. Moreover, he had been called upon by no less than eight ministers from the vicinity, and the wives of four along with their husbands, and he had contributed a resounding twenty-five dollars to each of the churches represented (redoubling and quadrupling the suspicions of persons like Mrs. Botten, who smelled at once the "guilty conscience"). But he had refused to join any church whatsoever, saying that, while he believed heartily in good works, he was not what would be called a religious man in the commonly accepted sense of the term. The ministers (three of whom contrived to interpret their twenty-five-dollar benefits as personal gifts, "since they were tendered by hand and in cash") could not immediately decide whether they were glad Mr. Snibbs was a "freethinker" or sorry. Long arguments raged over the hypothesis that, were he a member of a denomination, he would have given the entire two hundred dollars to the single congregation, and the counter theory that he would have contented himself with the eighth, as a sum sufficient unto any particular sect. The majority of the people felt certain that the latter view was the likely one and that the eight ministers might therefore count themselves lucky—or seven of them, anyway—although which seven, they could never decide.

On the second of January, as if in pursuance of a New Year's Resolution, Snibbs deposited in the Mudford State Bank the staggering sum of ten thousand dollars—in ten one-thousand-dollar bills. These, of course, were rushed to the nearest big city bank (a member of the Federal Reserve) by Registered Mail, with a letter from the president of the Mudford institution which directed that the bank notes be minutely and expertly scrutinized to discover if perchance they were (a) counterfeit and (b) hot— which is to say, stolen money. The big city bank— it was in Buffalo—replied immediately that the money was genuine and, presently, that its serial numbers did not correspond to those of any thousand-dollar bills known to have been stolen. At this point, it seems fairly certain that Valentine Snibbs would slowly have settled into the life and framework of the community without further undue remark, save for one more act of his.

He was deemed to be about forty years of age. He was a person of medium height, medium coloring, medium brown hair, rather exceptional physical endurance (to judge from his summer's work on his farm), a pleasant but distinctly undramatic manner, and a number of minor accomplishments, such as his mechanical skill. He was neither handsome nor ugly—and not rude, not cruel, but not markedly sentimental, either. His church contributions could have been—and were—regarded as political gestures rather than as deeds sprung from the heart. Nobody had yet asked him to join the Grange but the matter was being discussed. He was on the verge of being invited to serve on the committee to help dig out the clay bank along the first-base line of the local baseball diamond—lazier citizens having smothered ingrained hostility in order to make use of Snibbs' stamina.

But, on a cold night in January, he was observed by several persons to pick up, at the drug-and-hardware store, a village belle—or *the* village belle—Cordelia Fulsh—and to drive with her beyond the confines of Mudford, to where, no man immediately knew. This matter raced through the village faster than any fire. Indeed, it might be said that Snibbs was no more than out of town when the fact that Cordelia was with him was all over town. So many receivers were down on party lines at once that dozens of women had to scream into their transmitters to make themselves heard at all. But, weak though the current was, the word journeyed and Mudford reacted with every known pitch of human indignation. It was not so much that Snibbs was probably about forty years old and that Cordelia, or Deelie, as they called her, was eighteen, as it was that they had known Deelie's father, grandfather, and great-grandfather—while they did not know even the name and address of a solitary living relative of Mr. Snibbs and they did not even know Snibbs himself.

Cordelia's fate, as such, was of little moment to them. A tall, heavy-busted wench with a nice profile and a heavy downfall of that curly, brass-colored hair that country girls occasionally possess, Cordelia had bloomed, and overbloomed a little, in a backwash area which most of the enterprising young men had fled at ages ranging from fifteen to twenty, according to the development of their insight and impatience. Cordelia had remained because her family had remained—helping her father operate his cheese factory and keeping a weather eye open for almost anybody who would be even vaguely suitable as a permanent answer, not to the calls, but to the categorical imperatives, of nature. In this activity, she had stumbled once or twice. The Mildens' hired boy, an uncouth lad with warts extending far up one arm, had got her with child on one occasion, but she had luckily aborted. On another, during an unnatural warm spell in the month of April, when but sixteen, she had been caught naked in the grotto formed by the ground-touching boughs of the Clibbles' side-lawn spruce in the company of a divinity student of a near-by college who also was unclad.

So the rush to the telephones that followed Snibbs' departure *en voiture* with the girl was less a defense of virtue than it was an occasion for evil speculation on virtue's further infamies. It was Snibbs' money, they all said—and how shameful of Deelie to be so obvious. Although the farm boy and the divinity student also had been obvious (not to say *conspicuous,* by being merely present within the range of Deelie's eye), her acceptance of Snibbs' offer of a ride was instantly taken as brazen behavior and near-strumpetry—while the other two matters were regarded as the lapses of a nice girl who was, after all, lonely, and a most natural little thing, to boot. Such is morality in the hinterland.

Indignation knew no bounds, however, when an informal check developed the fact that Snibbs had driven Cordelia directly and without stopping (Biggsley Meekless had followed the car that far) to the cinema theater in the near-by town of Rutshire. From Mudford to Rutshire is fifteen miles, and a small school of spoken thought developed (although it was frowned upon by most) that Snibbs had insulted Cordelia and, in some remote way, her home town also, by not so much as drawing off the road and at least trying his luck. It further became known that Snibbs and Cordelia entered the theater, sat side by side (next to the Rutshire High School algebra teacher's aunt) without holding hands—partook, after the show, of hot chocolate and saltines at the Sherrynub Pharmacy—and then went straight to Cordelia's home, which was located in the rear part of the cheese factory (followed, upon this second venture, by Pop Pooltool, who drove his Buick with the lights extinguished). Mudford was agog.

It may be seen that Snibbs was very much the underdog, socially, at this time. But the fact did not daunt him. He continued to take Cordelia to the motion pictures, and nowhere else, all winter. That next April, however, there happened to be an unusual warm spell again. Skunk cabbages and mandrake burst from earth. Violets bloomed prematurely. Fruit trees began to bud and old-timers shook their heads over the indubitable fact that it would freeze up again in a few days and things, generally, would go to pot. Meanwhile, there was a full moon. Cancey Cupple, while taking the short cut through the Pluck meadow, came upon Deelie and Snibbs and saw by the lunar light that, once again, the village belle had succumbed to nature—her own, and Snibbs'.

The day after that is one that Mudford will not soon forget. Men instead of the ladies went for the morning mail. They hung around outside the post office even after the window was open and after they had collected their second-class matter and mail-order catalogues—stamping their boots on the broad sidewalk and muttering about forming a little "party" to call on "that devil Snibbs." Old Poh Fulsh, Cordelia's father, was last to arrive, which is ritualistic in these affairs; he took the boys over to his car, lifted a horse blanket, and showed them the shotgun lying on the floor. The men nodded and spat and said they'd back him up. At that moment, word was flashed along the street by Timmie Gelpsie, a young lad whom a Fagin would have coveted in a bigger city, that Snibbs *and* Cordelia had appeared in Pellis's General Store and demanded of Mr. Pellis, who was not only proprietor but also clerk of the town, a marriage license.

This was the last time that Snibbs deflated and undercut his fellow citizens. He and Cordelia were married. In January, Cordelia bore triplets—two boys and a girl. And no further unusual circumstances were forthcoming, if minor matters be accepted.

The minor matters? For one, Valentine Snibbs was unable to produce a certificate of birth at the time of his application for a marriage license. He said he had been born in the town of Rostonona, or something of the sort, and that at the time of his birth no records were kept in the whole region. He did not mention in what state Rostonona would be found and nobody was ever able to discover it in any atlas.

Again, it was noted that Cordelia became unusually devoted and faithful to her rather determined but certainly innocuous husband. In communities such as Mudford, where the winters are long and the menfolk take all possible opportunities to leave town for conventions, to make purchases, and simply "on business," it is not exactly the custom but certainly the practice of the more comely and progressive matrons to vary the hard routine of one husband and of farm life by consorting in such brief moments as circumstances allow with other husbands and with such interesting unattached gentlemen as may be in town at the time. Cordelia never did this. She was not even tempted, in a five-month, incessant pursuit by the handsome, dashing, 4-F architect who was boarding at the Meemises while he drew plans for the new school gymnasium. The architect, Mr. Gainlet, had only to glance elsewhere to succeed. And, though Snibbs' "business" once kept him away for three solid weeks, Cordelia insisted to all who would listen that even Gainlet, from what she had heard (which was everything), would prove pale in comparison to Snibbs.

If Mr. Snibbs had a peccadillo at all, it was to lie in his side lawn on clear summer nights peering intently through a small telescope into the sky. At first, Cordelia thought he was looking at the stars, but, when she mentioned it, he corrected her sharply. "The planets," he said, and it was the only time he ever used rough speech with her; "the planets, idiot!

Who'd look at stars? They're blazing suns! If you go near one, you fry like an egg!"

Soon after the triplets, twins were on their way. Snibbs began to plan carefully and privately the exact form the education of his children would take. He was a foresighted man. And Mudford had accepted him as one of its own.

Which ends, actually, the account of Snibbs.

The rest of this tale is concerned with related phenomena and only indirectly with the commonplace farmer who invaded and won the upland village.

Snibbs, it will be recalled, arrived in Mudford in the early autumn of 1939. Nobody remarked the fact (and nobody could have remarked it except by the rarest and most improbable coincidence) that men closely resembling Snibbs in general contour, though not always in color of hair and eyes, arrived in much the same way in the various towns and villages that surrounded Mudford—in Rutshire, for instance, and in Stutz Forks—in Lizzarville, Cleet Manor, Deevis Crossings, Hoit, Popopoon Township, Paugus, Almohunk, Rectile, Barjes, Colt's Corners, Treehus, Ram Junction, Grainout, Sessing River Bridge, Alamountabing, Mable, Groin City, Tweele, Iron Forge Village, Ballop, Cussip, Four Crossings, Vistula, and Peeds—to name just a few. Men like Snibbs appeared in all the communities of the county that contained Mudford.

And they appeared in the other counties of the state of New York. By Christmas, they were also arriving in the New England States, Pennsylvania, Delaware and Maryland. By Washington's Birthday, strangers of an acceptable sort, provided in each case with ample funds, and warmed with a decent intent to marry, had reached every corner of the Union.

Thus, the first Registration for Selective Service in the United States of America showed a somewhat larger number and percentage of male American citizens in the 35-45-year age group than most statisticians had anticipated. The increase over expectancy was, it is true, a mere fraction of a per cent, a decimal point followed by a zero and a nine, but it was enough so that Forrest, in his paper, "Changes in Population Age-Sex Relationships in Decade Three of the Twentieth Century," wrote as follows: ". . . so that, while it is unquestionably certain that the ratio of females to males is increasing and will increase in the years ahead, it is of some moment to note that there appears to be almost one whole man more, to every one thousand men in the 35-45-year group, than our previous calculations had led us to expect. Unfortunately, from the viewpoint of population increase, it cannot be expected that this minor increment will make any difference, as it actually represents a mere few thousands of men in early middle age, most of whom, if they are not already married, will probably not marry at all but remain bachelors."

There, of course, Forrest erred.

Perhaps the next original observation of what might be described as the Snibbs incident (for the observations in the towns mentioned above, and all like towns, were sufficiently similar to those of Snibbs in Mudford to be here considered as unoriginal) was made by a medical man of considerable talent. His name was Melthias Whitbourne; he was a surgeon.

At the time of his discovery (or partial discovery) he was performing, free of charge, as chief surgeon for the clinic attached to the New York City-Halewell University-Presbyterian Medical Center, a towering thicket of edifices located just outside New York City. It is a pity, perhaps, that Whitbourne's large and lucrative private practice so fatigued him that he was able to devote to his charitable surgery only the more deeply inculcated lobes of his brain. That is to say, he gave the nonpaying clinic patients the full benefit of his renowned surgical cunning, pouring out his energy cheerfully and even making some rather passable wisecracks under his thick gauze masks while he operated, but he did not exert that extra swatch of energy which illumines the very highest centers of the cerebrum, while he thus worked for nothing. Free sufferers, that is, were not given the benefits of his imagination, which was glowing, or of his full critical faculties, which were immense. He carved them open, removed that which offended, sewed them up, and they got well. It was enough, in the sight of Whitbourne and probably in God's sight, too.

However that may be (and it is a philosophical point of some magnitude but of no concern to this narrative), on an afternoon of that summer during which the blitzkrieging of France was in full swing (so that, perhaps, the doctor was unusually distracted by thoughts of the material his talents were missing at Sedan) a case was put in operating room number

105 for Whitbourne's attention. The surgeon entered the theater confidently, his favorite nurses following in his wake like newspapers swirling behind a passing truck. A passing truck, indeed, had provided the occasion which turned a citizen into this particular patient. His skull was fractured, there was a clot of blood somewhere inside it, the man was barely breathing, the X rays were alarming, and Whitbourne, alone of anybody on duty that weekend, offered hope.

The surgeon, after a survey of the wound of the anaesthetized patient and a pun about the advisability of having no truck with heavy vehicles, applied himself to the shattered side wall of the skull with the tense dexterity of a player at jackstraws. Splinters, chips, clots, and a small bit of wood picked up from the street were removed. Blood was siphoned off. A large section of the cortex was laid bare and, as it emerged from the debris, the trained fingers of Dr. Whitbourne trembled for the first time in his career as a operator.

Brain surgery was his forte; this brain very nearly his undoing. It became evident upon examination of the exposed lateral area of cortex that there were unknown *divisions* in the man's head and the shock of the finding was very great. Apparently, the one partially visible hemisphere was thrice segmented, so that the man possessed six upper lobes instead of the conventional two. They were, of course, proportionately smaller, but, on the other hand, their convolutions were deeper, more highly ramified, more tortuous, and in other sensible but not rapidly describable ways, *different* from the winding valleys that furnish merit to the normal brain.

Whitbourne realized that he was dealing with an astonishing freak—that, indeed, if he had come upon this cerebrum in pickle he would not immediately have ascribed it to Homo sapiens and yet he would certainly not have attributed it to even the highest of apes. It was, he swiftly decided, a sport, one of the genetic accidents sometimes produced in nature —bizarre and structurally redundant—which, nine hundred and ninety-nine times out of a thousand, so restrict or confuse the biological processes of the individual possessing them as to lead to death at birth or in infancy, but which, in the thousandth case, owing to the adaptability of living things, permit survival and reasonably normal growth. This man, for example, was certainly a normal adult to the superficial eye and he had obviously owned sense enough to get about on the public streets or otherwise he could not have been run down.

As a pure scientist, Whitbourne would have preferred to overlook the man's extremely slight chance of recovery, allow him to perish, and preserve his brain for study. As a swearer of the Hippocratic oath, which is so often so close to a hypocritic oath, he could not do so, of course. He palpated the brain with the handle of a scalpel, noted with further perturbation that it was abnormally tough, tended to the torn dura, carefully carved a plate out of a plastic upon which he was experimenting, adroitly fitted it, sewed back the scalp as well as possible, and had the accident victim rolled to a screened ward bed.

103

There the man lay for three days. During that time Whitbourne was extremely busy and made no rounds in the ward. His telephoned inquiry elicited the fact that the curious patient lived the first day, took liquid nourishment the second, and, on the third, lifted his own water glass to drink, although his mind appeared to be utterly confused. There was an intern's note on the chart for the third day to the effect that he believed the accident victim (still unidentified) had been wide awake, conscious, and looking thoughtfully at the ceiling when he had slipped into the ward in the late afternoon. But the man, in the intern's phrase, "on seeing me had popped his peepers shut and feigned total nisi-quisi." Whitbourne had doubted the observation and made a mental memorandum to upbraid the intern for his flippancy.

There was no patient on the fourth day. Sometime during the night he had risen from his bed, eluded the slender night staff on the hard-working, undermanned floor, stolen the clothes hanging in the closet of a private patient asleep in his room on L corridor, walked down sixteen flights of stairs and so escaped. No other possible explanation could be given for his disappearance and it proved that the special officer on duty at the main entrance had seen the man, or a man like him, emerge from the edifice and depart. The officer had thought the fellow to be "one of the new doctors, going home late."

Ramifications of the "Snibbs incident," or "phenomenon," occurred everywhere in the nation in 1940 and 1941. Snibbses appeared, unbeknownst to anybody, in the Air Force, the Army, and the Navy. Some passed themselves as thirty-five. Some made themselves out as forty, and even forty-five. All carried, by that time, birth certificates, letters, and other papers which indicated that the records in their claimed places of origin had not been kept or had been destroyed by fire, hurricane, tornado, earthquake, and other acts of God—whose acts, it appears, are invariably deemed to be ruinous. An examination of the birthplaces of these Snibbses, had one such been undertaken, would have revealed that civic backwardness or elemental disaster had, indeed, adversely affected the maintenance of vital records in every one of the claimed regions. There was never such an examination, of course, because nobody got onto the fact that there were Snibbses (also individually called, of course, Smith, Brown, Jones, Green, Fergusson, Taylor, Baker, Shoemaker, Cooper, Gray, Black, Painter, Czymshlinski, Taberelli, Schultz, and so on, and resembling, in national and racial types, the norm in every case). Normalcy is, in theory, the most coveted goal of all good Americans; the fact that it is so colorless and inconspicuous as to be almost invisible when it occurs has not, evidently, entered the heads of those millions who think themselves greedy of it. But normalcy (except in trifles) covered the Snibbses like a mist—the early hundreds, the later thousands, and the eventual tens of thousands.

They were steadfast and honorable persons. They did not seem to take any unique interest in each other or hold with one another any special communication. All of them were men. They chose fertile, healthful mates and they were productive. In their wives they sought good looks, but only moderate mental equipment, as though they either disliked the prospect of domestic heckle on an intellectual plane or else were so assured of the dominance of their own chromosomes in their offspring that they could reasonably afford the contentment to be found in women who were nubile, fecund and not pushing.

Their aptitudes would have made them seem a godsend (if, again, they had been noted as a separate class) in a nation at war, a world in chaos, and a time of man when integrity, decency and zeal had once again become cogent factors in the struggle to maintain civilization on the face of the globe. Those aptitudes, indeed, *were* a godsend, and ultimately a few persons of unusual perception and intelligence came very close to identifying the Snibbses as men apart—though never quite close enough.

Feodor Van Blenkman, for example, in an address made before the Kiwanis Club of Los Dorados, had this to say in May, 1942: "It is a remarkable tribute to the American way of life that, in these days of manpower shortages, of floating populations, of dizzy labor turnovers and of terrible production pressures, there has appeared everywhere that backbone of democracy, that raison d'être of human society, the able and willing 'little guy.' He is ubiquitous. Steady, competent, learned at his craft, quiet, pipe-smoking, a family man—he comes to the factory, the shop, the mine, the laboratory, takes over a post, and *sticks*. He is the guy who will win the war!"

There was applause at this point. Van Blenkman spoke, as a matter of fact, with more accurate prophecy than he knew. His audience was an eager one because Van Blenkman occupied a high and hush-hush post as director of research on rocket propulsion for the armed forces. "This ordinary little fellow," he went on, "has the resourcefulness of the frontiersman, the ingenuity of the Yankee, and the courage and tenacity that only democracy can breed. Rocket propulsion, my field, is new and, of course, most of it is 'secret' nowadays. Nevertheless, these everyday men, these machinists from all over the land, have taken it up as if they had been familiar with it all their lives. There are dozens of such 'good Joes' working in the heart of enterprise this very day who seem not just to understand what work we have done, but to anticipate the work we, the designers, have hardly ourselves visualized. Electricians from Chillicothe, patternmakers from Maine, machinists from Montgomery—they are the unsung, talented, welded might that will wring victory from the foe and firmly implement the peace—hundreds of thousands of ordinary people, sprung up like Jason's men to meet the disaster!"

If this speech feazed the Snibbses themselves, they did not show it. They merely continued to appear in increasing numbers—lost to count in the great labor migrations of the period—snatched by employers for their skills—promoted by officers for their cold courage and intelligence in battle—fanning out through farms and villages—a gray and growing horde. They raised their families and showed a particular genius for paternity in that, from the cradle hours, they took an intense and almost secretive interest in child-training techniques. . . .

There must be a million undetected Snibbses in America at this writing. There may be—there must be—millions more, elsewhere, speaking other languages and resembling other nationals. They are, in sober truth, "good Joes." The only *real* difference between them and us—the rest of their fellow creatures—is that the Snibbses are Martians.

9

LATE that night, John lay on his bed in his hotel room. Shawn had driven him there, and Ann to Miami, afterward. The fable had served the purpose of diversion, entertainment, and transition. Ann, who had been too eager, too sensitive, too filled with excitement, hope and embarrassment, until the reading began, had gradually restored herself to what was surely her accustomed demeanor. At the story's end she had seemed entirely self-contained. The psychic condition which had made her accept his invitation to dinner, and caused her to suggest calling on the Mullcups, and which, finally, had allowed her to blurt out her "ghost" experience, was buried inside her again—perhaps to stay there. For she was certainly the kind of woman who would normally exert every effort to appear poised and impersonal to strangers—such as himself.

Shawn, John thought with a smile, was a good mental hygienist.

Nice people.

John tried to sleep. It was hot and dark in his bedroom —no lights were allowed to show on Miami Beach, so hotel guests lived without them—and John was unaccustomed to the warm Florida dampness as much as to the darkness. A great many people in Chicago, he mused, would be astonished to know how black the Florida blackout was—and for what grim reason. Most Chicagoans seemed to believe that the war was a political trick—but also that Illinois, singlehanded, would win it anyway. Fools.

John rolled in a sweat-dampened spot. Maybe he, too, was a fool. The time ahead would be a good chance to find out—if he could. Certainly he was a fool beside Shawn, who had a wife, a family, a real art and a commercial art. (Didn't he, also?) Perhaps he was even a fool to insist on thinking that reality was a matter of atoms. Maybe Shawn was right about that, also. A professor-scientist-businessman in a big American city hasn't much *time* for random speculation. Now, maybe, he had hardly any time left at all. The idea failed to chill him. . . .

He discarded it and began to reflect further upon his Chicago life.

Chicago was the core of the Middle West, the worm-fattening fat heart of the fat lands. It was a dreadful place, really, as nearly all cities are—this one more than most. A city full of vulgar people—hard-drinking, fornicatious, malodorous, juvenile smoke-breathers. Still, John thought, they were not as soddenly vulgar as the English, in comparable cities, because class distinctions had not yet frozen the pattern of vulgarity: there were no definite grades of accepted obscenity and no charnel little habits about garbage, gas fireplaces, catarrh, and the frying of leftovers, which you would invariably find in Manchester levels. Nothing like the retching British nicety about the word "bloody," for instance. That, when thoughtfully assessed, was surely man's most monumental vulgarism. But Chicago was easily as insular and self-satisfied as Britain. It, too, had long called for bombs to wake it up; it, too, was a warren of bag-bellied, gassy hypocrites sustained by prairie commerce—which is no different from empire trade. Probably Chicagoans were anti-British because of their inward resemblance to all that is acquisitive and banal in England. Snobs, in effect. Ignorant, middle-class snobs.

John didn't like Chicago, he had never liked Chicago, and he was glad to be away from there. Bad as cities were, there were better ones: nobody he ever knew who had moved to Chicago had learned to care deeply for it, which could not be said of New York, where the opposite was true. Chicago was, indeed, the big brick pap of the prairies, sucked by all, replenished by none.

He could see himself in the channel of the years, teaching college, pottering with test tubes, sitting in business conferences and, occasionally, standing at the bar behind the neon-rimmed window of Sugarboy's Saloon, drinking whisky until the roar of the elevated was softened, the hard light diluted, and he could enter into the public illusion with the rest of his fellow citizens. Then he seemed sturdy in his own eyes because he lived in a she-wolf climate; he could attribute imagination and scope to himself because of the nearness of the infinite flat landscape; and empty municipal boast (made in a city unaware of the fact that it was half a national shame, to everyone else, and half a joke) would take on the seeming of up-and-coming civic virtue—just as a belch was locally identified not with bad manners but as a declaration of independence from the seaboard and a sign of important, unfettered gusto.

When drunk, he could assume the spirit of the thing. Maybe that was why Chicagoans drank so much.

Nobody knew, in Chicago, that everybody else knew more about Chicago than he did—even those who had never been there. Everybody else knew Chicago was cuckold— you could read it in the papers daily—but the merchants and advertisers of merchandise went skidding about in their large cars unaware that the great, beating heart of the eroding grainland Mother yearned only for a gigolo who lived across the tracks. John knew it, of course, when he was sober.

His students of applied biology were, nearly all, bent upon the study in order that they might eventually profit— possibly by dealing more efficiently with waste animal products, or perhaps by finding a cheaper method for the manufacture of glycerin, or maybe by learning how to hydrogenate lard and mutton tallow, or by compounding cheaper soap, or pursuing, to its last nitrogenous molecule, the nature and substance of fertilizer. This whole project, long-ranged and avaricious, was overcast with the smells and sensations of secondhand protoplasm.

The businessmen with whom he dealt had their own grublike insatieties. They were never content that he should synthesize a hormone substance and bottle it in tidy ampules for distribution at a fair price to the medical profession. Such work was no sooner done than they were on his heels for amplifications and bastardizations of the basic process. They would want a dilute product which could be introduced in white flour, crackers, milk, tea, yeast, breakfast food and chewing gum—items that might then be nationally advertised not only as comestibles but as medicines also, curing diseases to be invented by double-doomed agency copywriters: "Noon Yawns," or, perhaps, "Intestinal Disinterest," "No-play," "Sex Repeal," and "Evening Eyesore?" Fortunes lay in such deceit.

The professors at Langer envied him his outside income—an attitude John despised because the college made such income possible to all of them in return for a little extra work. But they concerned themselves either with minutiae of their trade or with academic politics which involved the clothes their wives wore, social acquaintanceships, secret lodges, the schools their children attended, and matters so peripheral to learning as to be related thereto only through the most feeble centripetal forces. In consequence, the college spun swiftly, with the professors, assistant professors, instructors, deans, president and students all sprawled about its rim and nobody in the power-supplying center at all, so that it was a mere hoop, binding irrelevant persons and acts together—but not a wheel. And it spun in one spot without going anyplace—a monument, in weak perpetual motion, to the rich thief who had founded it. Even technical achievements, as, for instance, John's own discoveries, were flung from the outer edges of the whirling microcosm into society like pebbles and gobbets of mud, aimed at nothing and, in result, often doing more social damage than good. The college-attached males all felt the moving rim to be a sure center.

The girls in his classrooms had a certain *interchangeability*. They were lively without being alive. They reflected the fads of the passing years like stereopticon lanterns supplied with a fresh set of slides each Christmas: new views, merely, of the old things. Every year the names were different but the objects the same: a band, a crooner, a male and a female movie star, a comedian, a night club, a perfume, a race horse, a pitcher or perhaps a halfback, a slang phrase, an adverb, an adjective, a show, a little foreign restaurant, a new word for a bodily organ, a torch song, a blues, a kind of joke, a novel, a nonfiction book, nowadays a war book, a radio program, a parlor game, a quartet, a card game, a choir, an interesting engineering project, a color, a waistline, a skirt length, a shape, an adornment, a hat, a dance step, a cartoon character, a sex code-word, and so on and so on, to depths and complexities of standardization beyond imagining and dreaming and bearing.

With these, the girls mixed in standard lantern slides and occasional revivals from the near past. Thus, in an hour outside the classroom, any one of them might present three-quarters of the gamut to the various senses:

Glen-Gray-Bing-Crosby-Humphrey-Bogart-Hedy-Lamarr-Joe-Louis-Empire-Room-Russian-leather-strictly-peachy-the-Athens-White-Cliffs-know-a-moron-who-gin-rummy-They-Were-Expendable-the-Alaska-Highway-Whirl-away-costume-jewelry-conga-Li'l-Abner-wolf-etc. etc.

In the second hour, the rest of it would emerge, and nothing more. Every syllable of it was as temporal and regional as the print on a handbill, yet it was universally regarded as sufficient background for an abundant life on this earth. The attainment of it took study and memory, to be sure, but it was almost as near to nothing as a normal brain could get. There were fashions even for wooing, derived from books and movies which changed only a little more slowly, so that Patricia might say or do on Sunday when someone kissed her just what Vivian had said and done the Monday before.

John had spent a vast amount of time trying to teach these feminine stereotypes and had even been engaged to Robbie, who, doubtless, was one—or had been one. He'd remained a bachelor by accident, not choice, but there had burned within him, sometimes lambent and high, again flickering and low, a notion that it would be both a duty and a pleasure to espouse somebody someday—providing, always, a suitable woman came along. For suitability (he realized on this early morning) he had no better criterion than that he not tire of her in a few weeks. But the single condition had, in the end, sabotaged his romances. He saw, now, why. He was tired of the pattern.

These women, moreover, deteriorated rather abruptly, as wives. Robbie and Ellen were cases in point. Out in Forest Hills and Evanston they aged quickly; their skins spoiled: their flat, granulated voices notched upward; dieting and golf did not keep them in any human shape whatever; they reddened, to tell the truth, and took on an underodor of burnt hair and old sweat which nothing in a bottle could conceal. They became stocky in the legs and fat as bellows in the chest; they beefed up until they had power enough to drive a golf ball two hundred yards. They developed squint and got glasses. They bore boorish children. Their husbands soon rented quarters in town and stayed there as much as possible, free at last (since they were paying through the nose for the honorable alternative) to consort and disport themselves with doxies, who, John had found out, and all his friends had found out, were clever and satisfying, which these middle-western wives somehow could never be—your own or the other fellow's. In every club, there had been long arguments on the reason—but nobody knew. The truth was that the doxies were pretty and pliable, while the suburban dragons had no quality left of any sort. They wore the purple, true, but it was the purple stamp of government-licensed meat, which guarantees fat in the muscle tissue. They were gigantic jellies; neuter masses; corset-bursters.

John saw that he could entertain a proposition never to return to Chicago with no trace of nostalgia. Who in hell could get lonesome for it? he thought. Only natives—purblind, like natives of every color in every corner of the earth.

He had been maundering with that overconcentration which is often applied to a train of ideas so that zeal itself will hide another set. For a moment he speculated upon the possibility that he had tried to divert himself from thinking about the young widow. She certainly had nothing in common with the Illinois beeves he'd been remembering. There were plenty of women unlike them—some even in Chicago. Some of his girl students had exhibited delicacies and sensitivities, but then, they were young and youth was a trap. . . .

He turned his attention deliberately to Ann Chapman Gracey. She had an olden-time charm, oblique desires, curiosity, and courage. She had appreciated him because he was human and because he had appeared, like a djin, at the right moment and in the right place. She would, doubtless, try to rush the healing of her hurt—throw herself into war work, stir about among people to lose her recollections—and take the inevitable cycles of sorrow into her own room when they fell upon her. That is—she would behave nicely. Someday, some other good egg would get her, some egg not good enough quite to exploit her altogether, as nature had intended.

She would do all that—unless she fell under the spell of this spiritualist business—unless she started to believe her Bill was mooing about in that great, slatty old house over some forgotten horror that, granted it existed, should be encouraged to turn into history, like a mossy tombstone, and not to be poked out, like the bones beneath. It would be a temptation to her New England conscience—a temptation easily identified with a pseudo sense of honest investigation. She would try to make room for immortality in Shawn's kind of sciolisms which, God knows, were disturbing even to the orderly mind. Then, like billions, she would attempt the proof—and there would be the rub.

This notion made John feel that all people, even the best, were such puppets of emotion as to be unworthy of the time and attention they gave themselves. Why couldn't she be satisfied with the fact that, whatever had happened to Bill, she was alive and had her responsibilities here, not in the grave Bill evidently lacked? Why couldn't she use the energy of her spirit to restore her inner person to real and useful acts? Why did she seem to feel she had to go jeeping along like a weird sister in twilight after the breath that had escaped the biological ruin of what had once composed a man? Why did such a prospect elate her? Wasn't it enough to be living? Was there any necessity—any sanity—in inquiring further along the cosmic blanks we call the future?

Here, he said to himself, I am doing what Shawn does. I am hypothesizing. Let me go on calling a blank a blank— I can't think any other way.

The voice, then. Had he really heard it?

John rose, crossed the room, pulled up the heavy curtains and looked out the open window. He was tired. The old skin of a moon hung above the low clouds. On the sea, in the miasmic limelight, a little black boat throbbed vaporously toward the north. Patrol.

We are a wonderful people, John thought. We always start our wars throwing pots and bedpans, swinging pick-handles, and chucking brick-halves. Our enemies begin with Big Berthas. Yet it is they who wind up winging furniture from their windows. A good thing.

He chuckled, lay down, and slept.

10

A few days later, he moved to the Gracey house.

He had seen Ann twice: once at luncheon and again at the Mullcups'. He knew her whole story now—and was, in consequence, less surprised by her ready acceptance of the ghost than he had been on the night of their first meeting. The Mullcups had surrounded him with friendliness. All bouncing, well-adjusted families want audience approval and affection, John thought, and he freely granted it. He now had invitations for two parties which were to be given by friends of the Mullcups. He had a dinner engagement with Ann for the following Saturday. He had met Jim Becker and liked him. In his wallet was an Emerald Country Club guest card. His social future was abundantly assured: a links to play on, an acquaintance in the service, a lovely girl to dance with, parties at which to meet others, and the energetic Mullcup home where he was welcome and where the entertainment, whatever its genre, would be wonderful. These humanities made him feel rich, and he began to overlook his early purpose of discovering a near-unbroken seclusion.

This first day of residence was bright—cooler than it had been since his arrival—windy, with a salty freshness indoors as well as out, and not a soul to disturb the glittering reach of sand that marked off the green shore from the indigo and azure of the water.

He bustled into the old house gaily. While a colored woman named Josephine began cleaning and cooking for him, he settled his lares and penates where he wanted them— books, magazines, golf bag, new fishing tackle, portable typewriter, stationery, radio, cigarettes, slippers, dressing gown, medicaments, shaving things, suits, slacks, shirts, ties, topcoat. For a doomed man, if he was one, he could not have been more nearly content.

He decided to sleep in the front room on the first floor. It had been the main room of the house until the dimout. There was a piano in it and it also contained several blackleather leviathans which Paul Gracey had evidently thought of as the most elegant furniture obtainable. In addition, there was, along one wall, a large couch of more recent purchase—too wide to sit on comfortably, wide enough for a bed, with thick cushions and excellent springs. John had Josephine make up the couch for the night. He had anticipated a demurrer, or the facial counterpart of a criticism, especially when she found his suits hanging in the coat closet in the hall and his shirts in the drawers of a monstrous secretary. Instead, Josephine had concurred—with an approving smile.

"I'd sleep downstairs here, too, Mr. Galen."

This veiled intimation had displeased John so that he had considered giving up the plan to sleep downstairs (where he could hear the waves all night, where they would run and break right outside his window) and moving up to one of the bedrooms. He had instantly inquired of himself if he had unconsciously chosen this lower floor sleeping place against some fancied emergency. The nerves—the instinctual centers—were tricky, as he knew—and they would often seek out ways to avoid the commands of the more reasonable apparatus to which they were attached. He decided not. He had chosen the first floor because he liked to feel the hammer of the surf.

He proved that to himself, later in the day.

Josephine made an excellent shrimp curry which she served with grated coconut, flaked bacon, ground peanuts, onion, and chutney. With it came a big artichoke, fresh and tender. Afterward, an avocado salad, a blueberry tart and coffee. ("She'll work for you," Shawn had said, in recommending her, "about six months. She'll cook such meals as ship-wrecked epicures would dream up—and at the end of six months, if you stay that long, you'll come down to the kitchen one morning and find it palisaded with rum bottles. She'll have the butcher knife handy in the sink—she'll talk African to you—and you'll have to give her the sack. She never slit a client's throat—and she never came back to a job when she sobered up. She is a temporary wonder—just right for the bachelor on an introspective holiday.")

Josephine cooked, cleared away, washed the dishes, and sauntered off toward the sunset and her long ride home. He had offered her quarters on the premises; she had said she enjoyed the bus.

Consciousness of being alone in the house for the first time came abruptly. He stood on his back porch looking at the shadowy hole that held the driveway and at the splashed colors above it which changed like large scenery shifted by unseen, silent hands. Salmon clouds were made mauve and enlarged;

116

the crimson cumulus was altered to a dark violet and slowly torn to pieces before his gaze; luminous gold fringes were compressed into buff balls which moved off toward the northwest at an even tempo. The entire prismatic scheme finally faded, in the space of fifty seconds, and became pastel, muddy, second-rate. He walked around the house. The sea was brimming in the dusk.

He stepped up on his front porch, surveyed the water, and thought how melancholy were all seas in this unimportant, transitional period between sunset and night. He went in. He thoughtfully climbed the broad, high, turning staircase, passed the headed newel post and climbed again. He went down the little, carpetless hall. In the wan light he could see the room that Ann and Bill had occupied: bed, chairs, vanity—and the trunk which was packed with Bill's clothes and now shut firmly, hasps snapped and the straps tight. One pair of white curtains was blowing. He put down the window.

He walked back along the hall and opened the doors that led from it, three in number. Behind two were bedrooms that had been the quarters of servants. They had that look: torn wallpaper with once red roses time-dyed nearly brown, brass bedsteads demoted in another age to this service, a washstand, bowls and pitchers. The third door opened into an attic under bare beams. Here, steel showed, rusted and out of place among the wooden rafters—the steel that had saved the Gracey house in years past. Here there were barrels, boxes, old trunks, a litter of moldy-smelling clothes and draperies, odd rolls of wallpaper, a saddle mildewed green, iron lawn furniture, broken tables, and, back in the darkness, the morning-glory-shaped horn of an ancient phonograph. He closed that door and went down to the floor underneath. On it were two Victorian bathrooms and four bedrooms. He entered and inspected each, pulling the chain of one of the toilets (there was a more modern bath on the ground floor) and sitting, for a little time, on one of the several four-poster beds—a sleeping convenience for which Paul Gracey seemed to have had a preference. These rooms were ornate, somber, white with marble, dark with mahogany, and they preserved, better than the rest of the house, the reputation of Paul Gracey as a man of means and culture. John was aware that during his tour he had sweated more than was necessary—not much, but a

117

little—and that he had *listened* with unusual care. This sort of thing, he would have explained if he had noticed, would make almost anybody a trifle nervous and he was not quite himself, anyway—fagged—and harassed by a personal incubus which he had not yet managed to dispose of.

As he stood outside the last room, seeing the objects in it only because his vision had sharpened with the dying light, he had the sudden thought—a logical offspring of the inturning of his mind upon his own situation—that it was within the bounds of medical possibility, at least, that he could suddenly be seized by a fit which might throw him on his face, the helpless victim of his own muscles, biting, kicking, groaning, frothing at the mouth, eyes rolling, his gibbering teeth cutting his stiff-thrust tongue to lace. So far as he knew, or the doctors, this could happen to him if his were a developing and not a receding form of the malady. He stepped into the gray chamber to sit, for another minute, on one of the beds. This last was of mahogany also, but the old-fashioned sort known as a sleighbed. Its springs muttered; he hooked his arm over the foot.

Not only could he do himself considerable damage (in the horrid eventuality he considered) but he could also lie, in coma, after such a seizure for a long while—alone—on the floor somewhere—within this mahogany-heavy, mold-scented leper of a house.

Galen was a man of imagination. He was also one of grit. He had calmly considered this possibility elsewhere. He made himself consider it again. His previous resolution had been to accept the chance as though it were another of the many nasty ones in normal life. He had, indeed, sought out this very kind of solitude in order to reinforce his decision and become accustomed to it. Now, inching his mind along as if his will were a crowbar, he restored that determination. The peculiar condition of the house, granted that could be given the status of a factor at all, neither should nor would in the slightest alter his stand toward himself. A ghost—the grimmest ghost that ever wagged its skull and rattled its chains—was a mediocre competitor to the specter he was going to have to entertain at least for some considerable time to come: the specter of madness. He took a certain icy mirth from the idea. He heard his lips part to form a taut grin. He stood again, firmly, and left the room.

In the hall it was now dark, and he did not know where the electric switches were. He kept his smile by reasoning that he had been piling it on thick to have stayed so long upstairs without, at least, a torch. He felt for the balustrade, followed it, found the newel, and shuffled a foot forward to discover the edge of the first step. When he located it, he flexed his knee farther and farther, but his foot reached down into nothing. The circumstance was so unexpected and momentarily inexplicable that he was severely startled. He hung onto the post, however, and fished in his pocket for matches. He lighted one with fingers that visibly quivered. It was a simple thing. The steps, at the top of the flight, rotated sharply about the post and the first three, at the spot where he stood, were some two inches wide. He had stepped out too far. He had only to go to one side, which he did, and proceed in the center of the staircase—which he would have done, but the match heated his thumb and he blew it out.

He stood, for a few seconds, in the dark, touching neither the balustrade on his right nor the wall on his left. He intended to walk down, avoiding the treacherous corner and grabbing the railing at a point somewhere below, but, before he was quite ready, there came from downstairs a wail which pulled his skin and nailed him in his tracks even though he recognized it, instantly, to be the sound of a gradually opening door. The noise ended with a series of low, metallic cracks, characteristic of heavy, dry hinges. He felt the dead air of the house stir delicately against his damp brow.

His brain at that moment set up an insane inquiry: what would he do—how would he resist or balance himself—if he were *pushed*, suddenly, from the darkness behind? He had no more than encountered this reasonless idea when he felt himself actually bend at the waist, teeter, and begin to fall. Even as he pitched into the darkness, he examined the distinct impression that he had been touched between the shoulders—lightly—but enough to throw him off balance.

PART III

THE DEAD

1

GALEN's fall began as the tumble of a man in possession of his faculties; his reflexes prepared themselves before he struck the steps. He had gone over headlong. He twisted in the air and ducked his head so as to land first, not on his face, but on his shoulders. This he did. The blow knocked the wind out of him and his feet flung in a semicircle. Then he hurtled on down toward his feet. The heel of one of his shoes, his left, caught on the edge of a step and his full weight, with the inertia of a distance measured twice by his body, rammed down upon that one foot. His ankle was wrenched frighteningly; it shot free. He rolled and clattered the rest of the way.

At the bottom he sat up and grasped his shin in both hands at its narrowest point, squeezing furiously against the pain he knew was coming—the pain that soon leaked up through his flesh like cold water, set his lungs convulsing, his heart bucking, and the sweat dribbling from pores everywhere on his body. The darkness was like ink. He remained there, gasping, concentrating on his pain, and, finally, weakly aware of its first recession. Soon it let loose of enough of his attention so that he found himself turning toward the staircase in the night behind him and bawling up it, in a towering rage, "Damn you for that one, Billy-my-boy!" The action startled him at first and presently relieved him. He chuckled ruefully, cursed in the monotonous sibilants and gutturals of personal profanity, and presently began to crawl down the hall to the Navajo rug that formed the blackout curtain across the inner room. He went through it, slippery with sweat, shaking with pain, and cold to his own touch. Finally, crawling about on the floor, he found a bridge lamp and switched it on.

His ankle was swelling. He took off his shoe, shakily, and tenderly removed his sock, seizing it by the tip and the heel. He knotted the muscles in his jaw in an attempt to wriggle his toes but only the barest discernible waver rewarded an effort that very nearly made him faint. Under the skin, on the outside of his ankle, a red-blue stain crept and spread like water on a blotter. Haematoma—ruptured capillaries there— or worse. A sprain or a break—both maybe—it did not look like a dislocation, anyway. He felt thirsty. He wished he had a drink—liquor—water—anything. His mouth was sandy. A cigarette. He found one, lighted it, sat still on the floor and smoked. Occasionally, a fresh stab of pain made him wrap his shin in his hands again and squeeze till his fingers were white. When that happened, he kept his cigarette between his lips and puffed it, making the coal burn brightly.

By and by he was aware of a draft. It came from beneath the closed door to the kitchen. He crawled over and opened it, blackout or no blackout. The kitchen door had been blown wide. He'd heard that. Outside, beyond, through the screen, was the night and the smell of the trees. He came back, easing his injured foot a little way at a time. He pulled the telephone and the directory down to the floor, looked up Ann's hotel, and dialed.

He first intended to tell her everything—then, just that he'd stupidly turned his ankle. By the time she had said, "Oh! Mr. Galen. I'm so glad you phoned. Are you comfortable?" he'd changed his mind once more.

"Perfectly swell," he said. "It's beautiful up here—and quiet—just the way I'd hoped it would be. But I remembered a question I'd wanted to ask you. About doctors. Do you know a good one—anywhere around here?"

"Nothing's the *matter*?" Her voice had caught.

"Of course not. It's just—that in my—condition—I might want to see one. Call one in, even. You know. Sleeping pills—or something."

"Oh." It was a word spoken in the midst of an exhalation. "I was—worried—for a moment. Of course. Dr.—" she hesitated and said the name after what he thought of as a decision made. "Dr. Maddox. M-a-d-d-o-x. Hank. Henry. He's sort of a cold fish—but he's a whole lot of doctor as a scientist. You know. Up-to-date—last-minute theory—reads everything—a good surgeon, too."

"Sounds just right."

"I'm sure he will be. And *you're* sure *you're* all right? You sound kind of—peculiar."

He wished passionately that she'd stop talking. There was lava in his foot again. "Sure. Thanks a million. Maddox. Okay. Well—good night."

"Good night, John."

He hung up, grabbed the directory, looked, and dialed feverishly. Maddox, a nurse said, was out. Was it something important? You're damned right it's important, sister. I'm alone, on the floor, at the old Gracey place—know where that is? I see you do—with a sprained or broken ankle that's swelling like a football. My name is Galen. John Galen. Yes, I know. I rented the place from Mrs. Gracey. And tell him to hurry and tell him to push right in because I haven't a butler and I don't feel like standing even on ceremony.

She said she would find the doctor and send him.

John hauled himself over to the leather sofa, hitched up on it, and started in on a package of Chesterfields.

He did not think about his ghostly mishap.

He thought about its result: pain.

As a child, he had been "sickly," as an adolescent, "undeveloped"; as a young man, in college—and afterward, when he had been a laboratory assistant, an instructor—his thinness, his easily inflamed cheeks, his flat chest and febrile eyes had made many maternal women warn him against tuberculosis. Then, in his mid-thirties, he had gained twenty-five pounds—good pounds of muscle—and taken on the shape of a man grown. He'd caught bubonic plague in Russia, though, fallen back to a wasted, jittery creature with a cough, arthritis, and a stubborn pallor. Years of exercise, often agonizing, had gone into his restoration. And that had not lasted long. Dr. Elias Poole had peered at him, timed his fugue, and made as dire a prognosis as any including two or three by worried medicos who had said he would die utterly and within the next few hours.

All his life, John thought, not with self-pity but with a cold and angry fatalism, he kept struggling to recover from this or that shattering of his health: month after month after month of remembered debility, crawling nerves, sensitive skin, short wind, shaky muscles, watery eyes, unsteady voice —a thousand things—and forever, during those times, a will that alternately blazed and flickered wretchedly to fight on, recover, get back to work.

The afflictions themselves, the sickbeds and surgery, the

writhing, sweat, nausea and dread—the panoply of pain of every sort in every part of his body—the sheer humiliation of being horribly and helplessly ill—came back to him even in his best interludes of health, unwonted as nightmares and more bitter, because they were not the stuff of imagination. They were actual torture, re-experienceable in every inch and instant: thirst, feebleness, vomiting, probes in the belly, the warm flow of pus, stuck-shut eyes, scalding throat, cramped guts, tormented joints, fever and chill, ache, ague, the hand that could no longer reach the nurse's bell, tooth-grinding, desperate devices of looking away from clock hands and counting wallpaper patterns, tubes swallowed, enemas, needles, scissors, knives, drills and forceps, bone-scrapers, sweat-boxes, ether, chloroform, gas, drains and siphons, months, months, months.

A human body could withstand that much and survive it; one would not think the human mind could endure through it, or want to. Certainly, there had been no whelming love of life which had buoyed him over these oceans of suffering. Life had become contracted into pure pain often enough, and he would have slipped out of it willingly. Sometimes, the near prospect of extinction had not seemed sufficient recompense: then he would have died cheated.

Nevertheless, in the worst of it, he had always partially existed above, around, outside himself—now as a speck of consciousness—now as a mist—but so detached in his one province that thirst or nausea would resemble an epic being read aloud and the opening of his own mouth to groan would be a waxwork movement he could visualize as if he were a mirror held above himself—another consciousness, not stinking, not sticky, not in pain—but detachedly looking down or flowing around himself—like a little equation, everlastingly, ever satisfyingly adding two plus two plus two on into decillions, never making a mistake, never wanting more —aware arithmetic, insulting to mortal beholders, who might erase its chalked delineation on the blackboard but who would shrivel in their graves, wash into the sea with the continent that enfolded them, burn when the earth dropped at last into the sun, and fall back with the cold nebulae into the final entropic speck which, in turn, could burst and recommence— without so much as making him falter in the addition of two plus two plus two plus two plus two.

This entity that he was and that was all else, too, could hold him like a jewel and he could look out, infinitely, at the prismatic colors of its sides, or it could flow dissolved without losing its identity; in it and of it was not music, but what caused music—not art, but what that was—no time and all time—and it was nameless. It felt like two plus twos, also, because he was scientific: that was another door between this reality and the mumbling, adherent smelliness that had his name. What was it? The epitome of consciousness? The beingness of being? The crystallized counterpart of truth contemplated? His soul? The seed of individuality or the common denominator of living things? The sentient gene? The rhythm—the endless pulse—of consciousness? Did it fix the attention of horses stamping in their stalls and fishes standing in the blue abyss, or was it men alone who knew about it? Did men know? Was not this crystal the precise counterpart of every structure great and small, each atom, molecule, chemical compound, planetary system, galaxy, and of the universe itself? Did not every race of men forever repeat in ten thousand tongues, designs, melodies, this center and its surrounding elements—this mandala that described everything that was and would be? Wasn't it on Indian tents, rune stones, temples, in Persian rugs, in garden designs as old as history, in Sanskrit treatises, children's toys, machinery, architecture, Chinese embroidery, in all religious art, in every science, in the spontaneous paintings (albeit lopsidedly) of maniacs? It was, of course. Only —few realized it was all *one thing*—one single attempt at definition and expression.

John ground out his tenth cigarette. There was a car in the drive.

Whatever it was, it was. It happened to everybody, whether they knew it or not. At least, it could happen. It lay at the end of every true experience and in the foundation of every concept, a base and a zenith of all reality investigated to its outer borders—even the reality of pain. It lurked in sleep. It came in anaesthesia. You recognized it when it was present and afterward you groped for it, as he had been groping.

There were two sets of footsteps. The screen door knocked.

John's ankle was fat and taut and the color of port wine.

"Come in," he called. There would be more pain, now. His meticulous knowledge of it made him afraid. He summoned, once again, his accustomed weapon for that old enemy: his bitter rage, his academic hatred, his imprisoned fury at this necessary use of his nerves—a stoicism purchased at a cost to be paid later in the coin of blank hours. He said, "Hello, doctor."

The man was unblinking, short, fat, brown-eyed, with a stiff little pompadour, his lips bending up his small, black mustache, his skin grayish—in his hand the black bag that contained the boot, the thumbscrew, the rack, the Iron Maiden—his face amiable with expectation and reassurance, the familiar countenance of all the healing Himmlers John had known. Behind him was a girl about twenty-five, blonde as new metal. She wore a black dress that was like a sword sheath; she looked at him and at his foot and at him again. Some nurse, John thought disinterestedly.

The doctor said, "Well! Had an accident, eh?"

John grimaced invisibly at that musty old one. Would a man put his foot in a tree crotch, swing on it, and do this to himself deliberately? He chuckled. "Just a minor one. Fell on the stairs. Darned fool to try them in the dark."

The girl said, "Good Lord! Were you barging around this place in the dark?"

"I couldn't find the light switches," he replied. Like a doctor, he thought, to bring along a pretty girl. As if he needed to be kept in good order by the presence of one! As if he had not had experience, all the long way, in what was coming and in far, far worse—no matter how bad it might be! "I turned it—with my whole weight."

"This is Dr. Maddox," the girl said. She looked at him and away from John. "Don't you introduce yourself to new patients?"

Maddox laughed and opened his bag. He had merely glanced at the ankle.

"They get to know me. Calling cards aren't essential. Often, when I first meet 'em, they're unconscious, anyhow. And bills are better than engraved pasteboard as a reminder." He seemed to be pleased with the humor of these statements. He said, "Ha-*ha*! Well, Mr.—?"

"Galen."

"I'm Gail," the girl said.

John nodded quietly and lay back on his pillows. "Good evening, Gail."

She raised one delicate eyebrow. "Didn't Ann tell you about—me?"

He had been watching the doctor's hands. Now he turned in sudden perplexity. "Why, no. Gail, you said? Should she have?"

Gail sat down on a leather chair. "I like that! Decide yourself. I'm her sister. Didn't she even mention me?"

John watched the hands again as they set things on a little table. A hypodermic outfit. He was tempted—and the hate, the old bravura, made him resist. "If you're thinking I need a hypo before you examine my foot, doctor—I don't. I can take it." He turned to the girl. "Perhaps Ann did tell me about you. I suppose she did. You see—I don't know her well. She mentioned a number of people—"

"Why the 'Ann,' then?"

"Echo of your own."

Maddox had ignored John's speech about his nerve. He walked into the kitchen, carrying the syringe and a small kidney pan.

"I didn't know she'd rented the house," Gail said. "Let alone to a—"

John offered her a cigarette, held the match for her. "A what?"

"Man. A good-looking man. What are you doing down here?"

"Sunning myself. That was the idea, anyhow."

"What do you do—when you're in the shade?"

"Teach biology. I'm a professor."

"Oh."

She did not add to that. John finally said, "Exactly."

She ignored also the recognition of her mild insult. "Where?"

"In Chicago."

"I lived there awhile, once." Her blue eyes were backward-looking. "I liked it. Do you?"

"No."

"The people don't give a damn. I like that."

This was another girl, John thought, who judged everything and everybody by a simple and swift weighing in a pair of selfish scales. He was sick of such. Not much like her sister, evidently. "I do give a damn and I don't like the people," he said.

She thought that over. "Your foot hurt much?"

"Enough."

She nodded and bent over it. "Nasty," she agreed. "Hank'll fix you up, though. He's good—as a doctor. You see—" her eyes met his—"I had a date with Hank tonight. He was at my place. When your call reached him, and I heard you were here, I came along. Besides, I'm a trained nurse."

John nodded. "In that case, maybe I ought to hire you. It looks as if I'll be campused on this couch for a few weeks."

Gail laughed. "I'm not working. Not as a nurse. Sometimes, as a model. But—unless you've broken it—Hank'll have you walking by tomorrow."

"A faith healer?"

"New technique. He injects some sort of novocaine. That's why he's boiling up the hypo. Takes away the feeling —the patient can walk—I mean, right off—and the sprain heals faster. It works. If it's a break, though, that's different."

"Sounds encouraging. I was getting ready to be keel-hauled."

Her expression was interested, appraising. "He won't hurt you. Doesn't believe in it."

"Then he'll be the first one."

"Aren't you fairly bitter—for a professor?"

"I do other things, besides," John answered.

"I can imagine."

Maddox came, carrying the steaming pan in a towel. He looked at Gail intently, his mouth working, and then said, "Well, well. In about ten minutes, you'll be through suffering, Mr. Galen."

"Miss Chapman's been telling me."

The doctor painted busily with iodine. "The pain of any sprain immobilizes it. Congestion increases. Becomes atrophy, sometimes. Inject the painful region, however—remove the pain—let the patient walk—restore normal use immediately, that is—and your joint heals pronto. Simple?" He turned to witness John's nod. "Now—this will hurt, but only a little."

The needle was perceptible as a mechanical entity in flesh. Nevertheless, because that flesh was contused and sore,

John had a powerful impulse to exaggerate the sensation—to think of it as intolerable. He grinned and quenched it.

"As soon as this takes effect," Maddox continued, swiftly withdrawing the needle, "I'll put in more. You won't feel it, from now on. Then I'll make my examination. If it requires an X ray, we'll arrange for it. If not, you can start walking on it immediately. Do you drive a car?"

"I do. Haven't one here. I intend to rent one."

"Good. Then you can drive to my office, providing this is a mere sprain. I'll inject the ankle daily. In a week—it'll heal beyond the painful condition. They started this therapy in France. A logical procedure. Sort of thing you expect the French to work out." He smirked professionally, glanced at Gail, and went on: "I trust you don't mind my bringing Miss Chapman? She is—was—a nurse, after all."

John shook his head. His foot was beginning to feel wooden. The relief was weakening. "Glad of it. After all, I'm her sister's tenant."

"Precisely." His eyes ranged about the room. "Fascinating old place. Remarkable collection of walking sticks. Paul Gracey used to tell me about them. Some of them have quite a history. Paul had it catalogued and recorded, somewhere."

"He was your patient?"

Maddox nodded. "For several years. Peculiar old character. Roamed the earth. Made his money nobody knows how—spent it the same way. A lifetime of adventure—and nothing left to show it but this place—these walking sticks. Died as oddly as he lived. But I presume you know about that."

Gail said, "Hank! If he doesn't—it's not fair to mention it! Ann might lose her tenant—and, Lord knows, she needs one!"

John chuckled. "I'm hardly the sort of person, Miss Chapman, to be disturbed by the demise of a former occupant of any place I live in. I assume he died here, eh?" He noticed that Gail's eyes had swept toward Maddox with an expression that seemed almost vicious; Maddox was now blushing.

"I shouldn't have brought it up." He touched John's ankle. "Feel that? No?" He squeezed. "Still no sensation? Good. I'll go on with the injections." He painted more surface and thrust a new needle.

"What happened?" John asked.

Gail exclaimed, "You see? Now he's got to be told, Hank. And if I were Mr. Galen—sprained ankle or not— I'd walk out, when I heard." She did not wait for further questioning but began to tell him—rapidly and almost with relish. "He died in the sleigh bed in the front room upstairs. He'd told his friends—the few he had—that he was going to St. Louis. He'd closed his house and dismissed his servant. He used to leave for long periods—so that wasn't anything. But he must have missed his train and come back here for another night. Or else he must have decided to catch a train the next day. Nobody knows. His baggage was all checked— over in Miami. But he spent an extra night here—and he died—and nobody ever knew from what—because, well, because nobody ever found out that he was in here, dead, till autumn."

John was startled. But anybody, he reflected, would have been at least moderately surprised. It was not pleasant. He realized, however, that Gail was watching him for effects, so he hid his inner repugnance, tapped the ash from his cigarette and cocked an eyebrow. "Bones, eh?"

Somehow, he did not expect an affirmative answer. He had tried to make a conjecture more sinister than presumed reality. But Maddox answered, in an impatient-sounding voice: "Bones. Rats—and insects. He'd made arrangements with a house-tending firm to open the place in the fall, ahead of his return. The maid who started cleaning found the skeleton—and had near-convulsions. A colleague of mine was summoned—and he sent for me, to identify the—remains. It was difficult. Meanwhile, we kept the story out of the papers—at the request of the police. When identity was established, the bones had already been disposed of. So the matter never had any publicity."

"You mean it was hushed up?" John asked.

"Nothing of the sort. It was hardly proper news, in the journalistic sense, anyway. Young Bill Gracey agreed, himself, when he was told. The likelihood is that his uncle Paul died of heart failure. His heart was poor—as I could testify."

"At lot of reporters wouldn't agree with your ideas of what constitutes journalism," John said mildly.

Gail laughed. "Hank hates reporters!"

Maddox's flush was deeper, this time. "I don't see any reason for hauling a thing like that into view. There was no evidence of foul play. He was dead. Nothing was missing from his estate. It was just one of those flukes that turn out to be ghastly—but utterly without importance. People are better off for not knowing about them." He turned upon John a countenance regulated to a pat expression.

" 'What you don't know,' " Gail murmured, " 'won't hurt you.' Is that *ever* a lie!"

"It's very sensible, on the contrary," said the doctor. His thin fingers began to explore the feelingless ankle. Watching them made John glad of the local anaesthesia.

"What you don't know," Gail protested, "is what gets you."

"I'm inclined to agree," John grinned. "And I'm grateful for this fragment of history." He looked from one to the other. Their association was apparently of considerable depth. Gail's baiting tone, although not vehement, had the earmarks of well-worn habit. His response, too, had been that of a man resenting a familiar annoyance. John felt an antipathy toward the doctor—possibly because Ann had already spoken of him as a "cold fish." He was that. Moreover, Ann had hesitated to give his name. Probably on account of the relationship between Maddox and Gail. John did not like Gail much better than her escort. A girl so handsome should not be so forward; that was unfair. She had put herself before his eyes as deliberately as if she were displaying wares. She had done that not by words, but by gestures, looks, movements of her body. He thought, suddenly, that it would be easy to return shock for shock—to startle with his tale as they had with the record of Paul Gracey. He wondered what they would think. Impulsively, he tested his question: "I'm glad to know one of the real facts, at least, which gives this house its peculiar—aura, shall we say?"

Maddox continued to examine the ankle. Gail exhaled. "You're thinking about what happened to Ann. Wasn't it horrible?"

"It wasn't," he answered. "Though that was grim enough."

"I don't know"—Maddox twisted the foot, and John felt nothing—"that there's any *more* charnel history here. Enough is enough."

"There's the ghost," John said meekly.

Maddox let the foot slip an inch and caught it. But Gail

133

gasped. So John looked at her. She wore, evanescently, the strained and sniggering expression of a terrified person trying to smile; presently she turned her face away. "Whose ghost?" she finally asked in a troubled voice.

The doctor said, "Ghost? Surely, Galen, you're not the type of man—"

"—to believe in ghosts? Miss Chapman does, evidently."

"But I don't!" She looked at him again—and her face was under control. "Not really. It's just the idea. That scares me—always. Is there really a ghost?"

"There really is." John's experiment was an emotional success. Maddox was working again—intently. The girl was frightened—and hiding it. "A grade-A ghost."

"Whose?" she repeated.

It was, again, not the response he had expected. Now, he himself was puzzled. Suppose there was such a thing as a haunted house? Suppose this was one? Suppose he had heard a ghost and been pushed by a ghost? *Whose?* He had thought, of course, of Bill Gracey only. The fate of Bill's uncle opened up another impossible possibility. "I don't know —yet."

"What do you mean—you don't know yet?" Gail's question was quick.

"I've heard it. It pushed me down the stairs—which is how I sprained my ankle. But I haven't seen it."

"*Heard* it! What did it *say?*"

John shrugged one shoulder. "I don't know that. It was talking in a room. I was outdoors."

"Does Ann know?"

Maddox interrupted. "Gail, for heaven's sake, don't be such an easy mark. Professor Galen's kidding you."

"Not at all." John still pretended humility.

Maddox put a pillow under the foot, and turned. "You don't mean to sit there, man, and tell me you believe in spooks?"

"I don't believe or disbelieve. I just tell you that there's a ghost in the house."

"Rubbish!"

John did not like the timbre with which the word was pronounced. He did not like the word. He found himself thinking that the doctor was something of a jerk, in common campus parlance, and egoistic and ornery besides. He said,

"You have probably bought a great many Smith-Galen Biological Laboratory products, doctor. I'm that Galen. A businessman—as well as a prof. And I give you my word as a scientist that I believe I have heard voices in this house and I think I was pushed in the dark—by nobody."

Gail said, "Oh-my-God."

Maddox's eyes brightened and John wondered if it were in recognition of an important colleague or in realization of the size of the fee he could legitimately charge. The glitter was certainly of an acquisitive sort. "John Galen," the doctor said. "Why, of course. Read two or three of your papers. Using about everything you manufacture. This is really quite a pleasure. Have to come up and talk endocrines someday." He turned toward the woman. "You see, Gail. He *is* kidding."

"But I'm not!" John was suddenly indignant.

Now, for the first time, the doctor seemed to appreciate that his patient meant what he had said. He also knew who his patient was. His expression slowly grew blank. He appeared to have difficulty in finding words to express himself. "But—you can't mean it, Galen—you simply can't—you're overwrought—shock, no doubt—blow on the head—probably gave you a false retrospection—"

"Oh, the hell with it!" John was tiring of his test.

Maddox opened his mouth, closed it, and returned his attention to John's foot. "It's not broken. Bad sprain. But we'll have you around in a week, almost as good as new. In two weeks—you'll be back to normal. The X ray can wait till morning."

The phone rang. John pointed to it. Gail answered. She said, "Yes? Yes—this is Gail Chapman—he's here." She turned. "For you, Hank. It's the exchange."

Both John and Gail listened to the audible end of a short conversation: "Hello? . . . yes . . . yes . . . Smith? . . . yes . . . Collins? . . . Very well." Maddox hung up. "I've got to get along. Some kid on Collins has just been bitten by a snake—and the father killed the snake and thinks it's a coral. If it is—well, come on, Gail."

Gail sat in her chair. "Whereabouts on Collins?"

"This end." He shut his bag hurriedly.

"You run down, Hank—and pick me up afterward. The least we can do is help Mr. Galen get set for the night."

135

Maddox stopped and half straightened up. "I said, come on."

"And I said—make the call and pick me up later."

Now, his lips were working like two pink, panicky individuals. "I have no time to waste. If that kid was bitten by a coral snake—he's in great danger!"

"Okay. So you go and help him. I'll make the professor comfortable and wait for you."

"I may be an hour or two. I haven't any cobra antivenom here."

"So, all the more reason to come back for me. Do you want me to sit two hours on somebody's front porch?"

"Gail, I insist!"

Her voice came after an instant, sibilant as a whip. "Insist, you sweet thing? Insist? To me?"

Maddox now glanced furiously toward Galen. "Miss Chapman has moments of extreme irresponsibility. Sometimes I think she is—"

"Hank! That's enough! There's a kid. Snakebite. I'd rather wait here. I'm sure Mr. Galen doesn't mind."

John said quietly, "Not in the least." He was embarrassed—and even more interested. A "scene" such as this, in which he was an impotent spectator, ordinarily made him covet escape while it was going on, and left him uneasy afterward. This situation—this trivial but frenetic conflict—seemed to contain implications for the mind of the bystander rather than abuse for his emotions.

The doctor now focused his writhing attention on John, seeing him as a man, instead of as a patient. He was holding his black bag loosely, rattling his dry finger tips on its handle, and rapidly spreading and respreading his small mustache with the thumb and forefinger of his free hand. His gestures were those of a man customarily too composed to become readily aware of the physical absurdities of wrath. His dark eyes bugged slightly; his face was pumped up with blood and purplish. His anger seemed all out of proportion to the circumstance; manifestly, it referred to a history John could only surmise. Maddox thus agitated himself for several seconds, in one spot, making no attempt to conceal or change his appearance. At last he ducked his head in what may, in some remote realm of his brain, have been intended as a cold and threatening bow. "I realize," he said in a register higher than he had expected to use, "that this—incident—has happened through no fault of yours."

John allowed his features, in rejoinder, to express a moderate amazement, which he certainly felt, and he said, "I should hope you do!"

The doctor then turned to the young woman and repeated, "Come, Gail."

This, John thought, would be the signal for some formidable outbreak of answering temper. The girl's beginning reaction implied as much. She was quite pale and she had begun to tremble. She advanced a step or two and murmured in a swelling voice, "Hank, I simply will not stand for more of this insane jealousy." At that, she stopped, and very abruptly broke into laughter. It was truly amused laughter—not hearty, but direct. She pointed her long arm and the long finger ending it, at Maddox's face. "You look so silly," she said. "You look like a stepped-on bullfrog." Her laughter pealed again and she sat down in the leather chair. A deep breath lifted her chest and her face became less animated. "Hank," she went on in a more reasonable tone, "you forget about the little boy and the coral snake. You're wasting quite a lot of time."

Dr. Maddox's reaction suggested that he really had forgotten the emergency. He looked blank, then alarmed, and finally stricken. He said, "Call at my office at ten tomorrow, Galen," in a curt manner—and he ran from the room. The doors slammed in succession, a starter grated, and his car spat pebbles as it swung round the circling drive. He had gone without another glance at Gail.

The two people left behind allowed time to make a margin around the departure. Then the girl sighed. "What a fool! What a nuisance! I had the grippe a few months ago. Ann called Hank—and Hank's been calling ever since. I happened to be bored and I must have had a fever or something, because—oh, well, you know how those things are."

Her voice had dropped, in the last portion of the speech. John now regarded her intently. "In a general way, I suppose I do."

"He's so proprietary! So—not even demanding. Commanding. He's one of those puppet-men with the Napoleon complex toward women. I hardly liked him at first. Now, he's getting detestable. After all, what was so unnice or unnatural about my waiting here—or about my offering to make you comfortable?"

"Nothing."

"But you saw how he behaved?"

"Clearly."

"It's humiliating."

"I rather gathered," John said dryly, "that you and he were acting on different assumptions. That is to say, I thought he took his interest in you most seriously. And I could discern that you didn't share the feeling in the same manner or measure. It's always a disagreeable situation. If you have been indiscreet, I think I can say that you are having to pay for it."

"Nobody but Queen Victoria would say I had been indiscreet!"

"Then Maddox's emotions are somewhat exaggerated."

"Exaggerated! Why, if every man I—" She rejected that line of conjecture in the middle of it. "He's a fuddy-duddy and a fool."

"And also," John looked down at his foot, "a good doctor."

"Let's not talk about him. He makes me sick." Gail turned in the chair so that she faced him. She crossed her legs, reached for a cigarette, bent over the match he held, and tossed back her long shining hair, which had cascaded over his wrist while she had made sure of her light. "Let's talk about the ghost, for example. What did it say? Don't you know—really?"

"Really, I'd rather forget all about the ghost. Say it was a figment of my imagination. What did Maddox call it? Shock. Or say I made it up."

"You didn't!"

"I might have." He paid attention to her blonde insolence as though it were inhuman: machinery, or statuary. "Professors are whimsical and they make up things like that. Whimsey, you know, can be worked from the end opposite to charm. It is then called irony." He pulled on his cigarette, breathed smoke, exhaled it. "Frankly, I brought up the ghost because I was getting very tired of a doctor who came to my side accompanied by a bickering inamorata—or, shall we say, accompanied by a trained nurse in the role of a publicly subsiding Hecate."

"Hecate?"

"A witch. She had six arms and three faces. She carried a torch, I might add. Sometimes it was a spear." He grinned.

Gail laughed. "You're pretty good."

"I have had a classical education, Gail, and ample opportunity to learn the vernacular from those in the process of acquiring it. Now, look. In the kitchen on the sink is a flashlight. In the front room closet, downstairs, are my pajamas and my slippers. Also my robe. I would like a large pitcher of ice water and the pills marked, 'One or two at bedtime for insomnia,' in the medicine chest in the downstairs bathroom. Any other little arrangements for my comfort which you can think of would be appreciated. No doubt, being a nurse, you *can* think of one or two. Toothbrush, paste, and extra glass, for example. Maddox may wish me to walk on this rancid ankle tonight, but I rather incline to take a rain check. When you have performed these various kind offices, you will be able to get a cab by telephone, and I shall be able to rest."

Gail had listened at first with plain incredulity and presently with amusement. She now rose and procured the flashlight. As she walked toward the blackout curtain she said, "I'm scared to pieces to go in that hall."

"Good," John replied.

She scowled, faltered, and went through the Navajo barrier. She came back, shakily, with the requested articles. Then, working swiftly and efficiently, she commenced to make him ready for the night.

"See anybody in there?" he asked.

She was plumping up his pillows. She stopped for an instant. "No." She finished her duties, or very nearly.

John said, "Thanks. From here on, I can fend for myself."

Gail had not given any complete clue to her feelings about the mocking assignment until then. She leaned over and kissed him lightly on the cheek. She drew her head away slowly, however, and her long hair caressed him again. She was wearing a perfume exactly designed, he noted, for operations of that sort. She made a face at him. "You are rather a love."

"And you're rather old for teasing."

"I'll file that," she answered, "with other wrong guesses. I'm supposed to phone now?"

"Now."

"I'll come back here again."

"Be sure to bring Ann along."

Gail chuckled. She did not phone, however, because a car drove in and slid to a stop. The screen banged. Gail had time to say "Hanky-Panky" to John before Maddox appeared. He was in a clothes-dampening perspiration.

"False alarm," he said jerkily. "Kid wasn't bitten, for one thing. Just thought he had been. And it was a harlequin snake—not a coral. Damn-fool hysterical parents. Ready, Gail?"

"For anything, dearest," Gail replied.

She didn't look back when he took her right arm and fairly forced her away. But, with her left hand, she managed a little wave of farewell behind her back.

The car drove off.

It had been quite an evening, John decided. Quite a housewarming.

2

HE DROVE in a rented car to Maddox's office some days later, had his ankle injected for the fifth or sixth time, and started home. On the way, he turned from his route and went to Shawn Mullcup's. He rang the bell vainly several times and was on the point of departing when Shawn appeared in the hall, wearing a smock and carrying a brush. His Shavian eyebrows lifted with pleasure as he recognized his caller and he tugged at a beard anointed with samples from his palette. "Come in! Come in! How's the foot?"

"Fine. Maddox seems to know his stuff. You're working, though—"

"Nothing a commercial artist likes better than an interruption! If I'd been attempting art, as such, I wouldn't have answered the bell. Kids are at school—Thalia's out—and the maid's probably over with the chauffeur next door. Usually is." Shawn led him across the patio which faced the bay and the far, low coast of the Florida mainland. The ground was flagged with coral. A fountain hissed up as high as a man's head and pattered into a cement fishpond. Travelers' palms grew flatly against the walls; star jasmine climbed on them; there were holes in the flags from which grew gumbo limbo trees, ficuses, and fragipanis. They crossed this "yard"; Shawn kicked open the door of his studio.

On his easel was a canvas, nearly completed, of a girl in a red evening dress being kissed by a young man in a sergeant's uniform. Overstuffed chairs in the picture, and the visible corner of a carved mantel, indicated that the girl belonged to the upper classes. The studio itself was small and orderly. Unused canvases filled special racks; a supply cupboard bulged with materials; there were tables, two chairs, the easel—and bare walls. A solid cube of light subtended a square skylight overhead.

"I have painted that kiss," Shawn said, pointing to the picture, "at least five hundred times. Cinderella and the Prince. This girl is worth millions, in the story. The sergeant isn't worth a dime but he saved sixteen men barehanded at Bataan and got out by accidentally being cast adrift in a rubber boat. The boy and the girl merge at the end of the confection. I get eight hundred bucks for the picture. You will note, I have an especial knack for painting the legs and fannies of young women. A valuable knack.

"In the real-life sequel to this thing—which does actually happen—the sergeant will get bored with his wife's habit of cheating. Hurt, then bored. He will take unto himself somebody else's wife. Being rugged, he will eventually become the pampered buddy and/or husband of about five successive rich dames—in view of his entree into their society, here blantantly depicted. The wives will go, en suite, to Reno to be rid of him. He will end up an alcoholic. It is amazing what a rotten time of it rich people have. The ladies' magazines, you might be interested to note, do not stop at the boudoir any more, either. They go in. They carry on to Reno. They follow the second marriage, the third, the alcoholism. They even go into the john. But they always get their heroes and heroines out of it all, at last, while the people themselves never get out. Money's almost as much a treadmill as poverty; in some ways, it offers less variety, even, and less change of emotional scene."

"You'll never sell that bill of goods."

"No." Shawn had recommenced work. His hand moved rapidly, with repeated purpose which became assured when he drew back from time to time, squinted, and turned to a new line, color, or object. Watching his hand was like watching a hummingbird fly up and down a stalk of flowers. "Grand opera," Shawn said presently, "is the rich man's soap opera. No real difference. Both spectator sports. That's the point—which the rich miss. They preen themselves for admiring virtuosity—as the boob preens himself for catching onto a pun. Neither *does* anything. Doing's the point. Poverty has one magnificent advantage. It makes doing imperative—the penalty of inaction being immediate." Without changing his tone, he continued, "I hear you met the ineffable Gail the night of the accident. What do you think of her? She does *something*, anyway."

John chuckled. "So she informed me—with a minimum of indirection."

Shawn leered. "She can make a man happier for a little while than any woman in the state, maybe. And unhappier for longer than most. I found out, to the pain of my vanity. She could be very useful, though, running classes for fiancées, young girls, matrons, and other women."

"Classes in what?"

"Love." He painted. "Making love. The anatomy of ecstasy. You ever make love to anybody's wife?"

"Sure."

"A tart?"

"Yes, again."

"Which was better?"

John chuckled.

Shawn waved his brush. "There you are. The coming generation of married women—an unfaithful lot—are going to be a disappointment to their lovers. I don't say that respectable women cannot compete with professional ladies. I just say they don't. They should."

"Marie Stopes."

Shawn laughed, now. "You like to put periods to people's monologues, don't you, John? Mine, anyway. Well, look at the dames. Look at this job I'm painting in the red dress. A hot number. A rich man's daughter. Sophisticated. She has undoubtedly read such treatises on the art of love as you refer to. But she has no real talent for it. No energy. No appetite. No taste. The marriage bed'll find her inert—as it does most all the wives ever heard of. Take a consensus at a stag party. What's the answer? To be able to enjoy even love demands more practice and more effort than most ladies would dream of giving it. That's what's immortal in the lady behind the red lamp. She learns. Look at primitive dancing. Rehearsal."

"You don't give any credit to attitude."

"Sure I do! But what good is an attitude when you can't put it into effect? Why lust, why yearn, why do what the popular songs call 'dream'—if you're too flabby for anything else? Too clumsy? Too anatomically immature or atrophied? Too lazy." He looked archly at John. "Still—it's probably self-protective. A natural device. I mean—can you imagine the typical lady of this era becoming extremely proficient at making love—and then staying content with one guy? When all the damsels are exhibitionistic, anyhow? You cannot. Teach a bride to be an able houri—and your bride will possess a light she does not wish to hide under the domestic bushel. Her temptation, then, will not be merely one of the libido. It will involve pride of achievement. Was there really ever a clever woman who kept it to herself? Would one clever at love be an exception to that? No, my friend. Connubial ineptitude is the last resource of chastity— dim, but almost universal in these sorry times. What *helpless* fools these mortals be! For one reason or another, they frustrate their pleasures. And happiness, which lies beyond, is something they do not even understand."

John found that he was blushing as the result of his conscience in the matter—his awareness of ineptitude in his own amatory history. He did not mind what the artist said, but only what it caused him to think of himself. The blush, then, came from a sense of guilt for being unadept at guilt itself. Or, rather, at what was usually counted guilt.

Shawn continued. "Not that a promiscuous world is the way to every man's dolce far niente. Just that, since people are getting more promiscuous every hour, they should take some conscious thought of what they are doing and invest some values in it—if only technical ones. Whether society is profligate or ascetic doesn't matter so long as it goes at the thing wholeheartedly. But the present and growing picture of

143

a society that practices the sex morals of rabbits without any concomitant attention to training and talent is, so help me, most tedious. Most hypocritical, if I may underscore the thing. Perhaps a generation of jitterbugs will redeem a long era of debilitated cadism. Let us hope so."

"And where does this lead?"

"Not whither, whence. These are the reflections that Gail and her ilk set up in the inquiring mind. How many millions of good women have lost their husbands to wanton nitwits all because the nitwits had a better co-ordination! Because they had less sense of prissiness. You cannot talk about these things in public. You certainly daren't paint 'em! You cannot write much about them in books, because people do not wish to believe so much of them is physical. Even if convinced, they are too lazy and hence too self-conscious to improve themselves. The principal expression of sex, when you think of it, depends considerably upon calisthenics— though that's a new thought, so far as I am aware. Someday there will be classes."

"Will you send your kids?"

Shawn put down his brush. "I would, sure. But Thalia wouldn't let them go unless it became the thing to do. If the magazine I'm painting this for recommended it, Thalia would put the kids in the costume advised, and ship them off to study making love without a tremor. But she wouldn't let them pioneer. So they may grow up and make indifferent love to whatever may be the conventional number of people for their generation. Better lovers may steal their loved ones. It would all happen, of course, under the cloak of 'preferences' and 'changes of heart.' They may miss a good deal, since this world of the future will offer precious little besides physical pleasures and comforts."

John shook his head. "I can hardly imagine those two young kids winding up nonentities. Not when I saw them hammering that radio to bits! They'll never be conventional."

"Probably they will. That's every father's defeat, in a sense. His kids become, often enough, not so much people, as reactions to parents. I, for instance, am less a man and an artist than a reaction to the fact that my father was a Methodist choir director and a pipe organist. My kids may push back the pendulum, and react to a father who was a loquacious egotist and a spokesman for license."

"Teach school? Be mousy? Marry and remain both flabby and chaste?"

"Yeah. Who knows? I do my best. I try to teach them imagination and criticism—to think and then to do. I will probably fail. The world around the corner is against me." He rummaged in the cupboard. "Have a date? Fresh California."

John took a date. "You seem pretty certain about the world of the future."

Shawn sat down. The chair made a shrill utterance. He picked the stone of a date from his teeth and looked at it. "We're for it, now. We—and the world. We're going to win the war. The two wars. United States, Great Britain, Russia, China. We will have to develop the ensuing peace with the solitary advantageous symbol we commonly possess: material 'improvement'. The philosophy of democracy has become confused with the economics of socialism. They are actually parallel in no sense whatever. Democracy is a way for people to operate politically—a way to live in mutual respect. It covers everything. Socialism is merely one of many systems that refer to people as producers and consumers—a particular aspect of man. *Democracy* could be socialistic, or capitalistic, or anything between, sliced either vertically or horizontally. Democracy's *economics* are optional. But nobody is interested in that basic philosophy of democracy, any more. Nobody even understands it, any longer. Businessmen ignorantly deny the fact of it. The accent isn't on the individual and his rights, now. The attempt—in Great Britain, in Russia, or here—is not to educate the individual for his responsibility in a democracy but to instruct, coerce, buy or organize masses so that they will serve the labor requirements of machines and to finance them somehow so that they can use up the things machines produce. Democracy is an applied philosophy of man; but no government, any more, has a philosophy. They all try to run by logarithms.

"The main present tendency of man is to escape pain and produce pleasure. By following it, he has already produced the most pain in his history. But there is more to come. The machine itself exists principally, so far, to create pleasure: ease, that is, smoothness of transportation, speed, simplicity of communication. The laborsaving feature of machinery—its alleged great glory—saves labor for no known

145

or agreed *purpose*. That's nuts—if you stop to think. Why save it, if you haven't planned what to do with it? Labor-saving merely makes more room for more machines, the sole end of which will be to make physical existence softer for men. We are insane in this matter of believing that, by making our lives always easier, we can make ourselves any *better*, hence any better off."

He threw the date stone into a metal wastebasket and lighted a cigarette. He pushed out his feet. "The transatlantic airplane adds nothing to the fifteenth century but *ease*: Columbus made the same trip. The airplane makes it more simply. The electric refrigerator is an easier icebox. The radio is easier than going to the concert and the lecture—but no different therefrom—and the concert and lecture are thousands of years old. The automobile is an easy sedan chair. The oil furnace and the automatic coal stoker are easy campfires. The spinning mill and machine loom do not differ from the same operation performed on the hearth; they are just *easier* means of making cloth. You can hardly name a machine that is not merely an ease-maker of an old process.

"But what relationship has all this ease to man? To life? To the progress of the brain's evolution? To moral truth? To natural law and to biology? To instinct? To passion? To being alive? To good and evil? To kindness and cruelty? To honesty and crime? To prejudice, false conviction, hate, superstition, tabu, hope? All these machines mean *nothing*! They do not relate to what *actually* controls our private and our common destinies. We are not *changed* by them. We cannot grow through them. They become tools of our fears or our senseless ambitions as readily as they become tools of any intelligence we may have. They are only what *we* are.

"But we think them to be more. We, and the Russians, and the British—and someday soon after the war probably the Chinese, also—will think mere physical ease is the end. We will be *objective*. We will then become *objects in our own eyes*—not thinking, feeling, moral men—but mechanized per capitas. We will wean our children onto these gearboxes and electron tubes and suckle them with light metals until they are so full of machinery they are no longer able to respect one another more than they respect buttons and levers. We have, indeed, got up a whole school of psychology to prove

146

that we *are* merely buttons and levers—conditioned reflexes —not real at all. It is a school that assumes we shall evolve or progress through universal easiness. That is the philosophy of behaviorism. Like the economics of Karl Marx, it sees a few undoubted facts true of all men, without ever examining closely all the facts appertaining to any single one man. Yet this attitude is the attitude of the future!"

Shawn paused—but John was listening interestedly.

"We are trying in all our nations to get back to infancy. An infancy in which we shall cling—all two billion of us— to the tasteless streamlined breast of the factory! Then we shall be all, equally insipid, utterly dependent. Machinery will carry us in its big, clanking arms and feed us its tinned synthetic milk, knit our tiny garments, empty our daily pottie. So we shall become less able to sustain ourselves in this mathematically retributive cosmos. Our nourishment will hinge upon a factory in Zanzibar and also, although we will not know it, upon the prejudices, jealousies, hates and fears of the Zanzibaris. If they strike, we shall starve. Thus infantilism will make a full turn, and our corpses will wither and drop away from the dugs of the engines because people really were running them, not indoctrinated reflexes. This war is one such dropping-off. The great peace afterward will inaugurate the golden age of world-wide childishness. When populations shall quarrel and the machines boggle in consequence, the dependent multitudes will clamor for governmental arrangements at any cost, to *ease* things. The day of the appeaser has thus just *begun*—not ended. The day of the man who stands on principle alone is forfeit to hordes of unprincipled mechanics. So, it follows, as humanity grows infantile in groups, governments must grow more paternal— doling out candies here, punishing yonder with the headsman's ax, gas chamber, knout, and what not."

Shawn rubbed his face with his hands and pressed his beard between them. "Centuries of this madness may lie ahead, until sin is rediscovered and at last honestly defined. Until, that is, the meek take over their inheritance of the earth. Which is to say, the spiritually honest—that being a condition which automatically produces humility. There is nothing gentle enough, yet, in the common man. Suffering has not yet sufficiently tempered his vanities. We have civilized our machines instead of ourselves!

"The truth is diminishing every day. Our scientists are erudite in Ohm's law and ignorant of the events inside themselves. While we remain 'objective'—we shall lose inch by inch our insight. We Americans, who have so much, know less what we want, already, than the people of any other nation on earth!

"The rich, whom I am painting here, are individual monuments to insatiety. Their great wealth has already elevated them in possessions and ease far beyond the place where *any* communal system could *ever* hope to put them— and still they are miserable! They do not know where to look for happiness! It is peculiar that Karl Marx never noticed that! Perhaps he never knew the rich. And it is peculiar that Vilfredo Pareto, who correctly pondered what he called the 'cultural lag' of masses, invented, as an 'elite' to lead them, a company of men with the morals of jackals and the deep perceptions of crocodiles. More barbarians to create new barbaric societies!

"The 'profit motive' and the 'profitless society' actually *are one and the same thing*—society preoccupied with physical ease and only incidentally interested in certain minor aspects of inner discipline—since even these societies must have trained engineers to invent gadgets, and schooled abortionists to relieve women. All our notions of freedom have begun to turn negative and this is the sign of the finish of us.

"Once, freedom was positive. A man wanted to be free to be himself. But now he wants to be free from having to be himself, a wanting, fearing, struggling, dreaming, humble creature. He now wants to be free to be a big nobody doing nothing valuable to anybody but his body. I think we are going to strive en masse, perhaps for *several thousand more* years, to decerebrate ourselves. We are going to try to make the human psyche a mechanical specialist. It isn't. It is intended to perceive the cosmos, adjust to it, struggle in it, and achieve there an individuation of itself. But our materialism has slain man's good opinion of himself, stripped government of philosophy, taught the common people not to desire personal excellence but to barter in droves for the right to mediocrity! So it seems the least I can do, to have my children decently instructed in fornication—with that future in view. It will be about the only way left in which they can express themselves honestly and be honestly appreciated! As such, it is better than nothing. Here!"

Shawn had been searching in a wallet which he had taken from an inner pocket. He handed a key to John and pointed at a door in the wall of his studio. "I'll be finished in a few minutes. Take a look at my gallery."

John hesitated and then silently unlocked the door. He entered a small exhibition room. It was windowless. Shawn, reaching around the doorjamb, tipped a switch. Illumination was supplied by indirect lights under thirty or forty framed paintings. The door shut behind John.

A beige carpet, a black-and-chrome table with an ash tray in its center, and a chair: that, and the lighted pictures. John was thinking of what Shawn had said about the dismal future in store for men. Shawn evidently believed that national, civil and race wars were going to continue for hundreds of years. That John himself thought the tragedy possible did not mitigate a brief feeling of resentment toward Shawn. It was indecent, somehow, to be so pessimistic—to take such an arrogant and disgusted attitude toward your fellow creatures. Or was it—rather—just honest?

A sense that he had been let into Shawn's sanctum sanctorum came over him slowly. These paintings were not for public display. They represented a compensation for the five hundred girls in red dresses being kissed by five hundred young men, which Shawn had painted for the magazines. Now, looking around the room, John was vaguely startled, but his surprise came from a reason opposite to the expected one: the paintings were apparently conventional. They were, indeed, *trite*. John stood near the center of the room, searching for a canvas that would represent the departure from the norm, from the conventional, from the academic—which would parallel Shawn as a person.

John's emotions, meanwhile, kept resisting the righteousness of Shawn's long monologue. It was, of course, correct. Even the somewhat sardonic wish to teach his children sex antics as a virtuous bulwark against sterile postwar living was, in its way, justified by the behavior of multitudes of contemporary people. As Shawn had said, there was not much satisfaction or purpose in the lives of most persons— and it was true that they didn't make love very well. Still, amorous skill was hardly a better substitute for the complete

149

life than automobiles, telephones, and electric washing machines.

Shawn's paintings were beginning to compel John's attention. The artist had a dazzling sensitivity for color— for the near-likeness of landscape shades that yet did not quite match—and for sharp contrasts where the sky met a hill or a woman's chin curved in front of her dress. His drawing was faultless—his perspective so intense as to give the four walls of the room a quality of windows open, of recesses, and of other rooms. Each picture had a misty patina, very faint, at once troubled and magical, so that, in a sunny seascape, there was a feeling of moisture collecting for a coming storm and, in a lamplighted room, a sense of the shadows that would close in on the source of light were it to be permitted to falter. The subjects, on this first, cursory glance, were disappointing: a portrait of a young woman sitting in a chair, her expression uncannily startled. A man laden with several articles standing at a gate—and a large building behind him in the middle distance. Fowl and fish, hung in the Victorian manner. The interior of a cozy cottage with a lived-in, empty room and a fire in the grate. A setter taut in a point.

John wondered what the critics would think of this color-erudition, this flexibility, and above all, this determined conventionality—if Shawn ever chose to show the world more than his magazine illustrations. The detail of the roof of a New England house, the snow and the bare elm, the utter relaxation of the hand of the girl in the portrait— these—and many other unrelated trifles of accomplishment which now claimed his eye—convinced John that the art critics would place Shawn Peecey Mullcup very high among the traditionalists. There were thousands of worse paintings in the best galleries—and few better, as mere painting.

John lighted a cigarette. He speculated upon what Shawn intended to do with the collection. Leave it, doubtless, for posterity—as a monument to the fact that many an artist of great ability had painted out his heart for the proverbial fortune. A gesture—and one like Shawn. John walked to the picture of the dog. He would begin a close inspection there. The setter was as lifelike as any John had ever seen in oils. He had evidently run far—saliva dripped from his dewlap. His rigidity was stony. His eye—

Then John understood. The saliva was ropy. The rigor was not quite the freeze of a hunter's point—but something else, off line and angular. The teeth showed a little. The eyes were bloodshot—each tiny crimson vein was traced; over them was a rheum, an indecisiveness belied by a brilliant core, a glitter of the pupil possessed by no ordinary living dog. On the lips and tongue were particles of froth. The dog was not pointing. He was mad.

John recoiled inside himself, as if the dog might leap out and infect him with its disease. He moved away to the next picture and had, again, the sense of anxiety which had marked the beginning of his understanding of the first. Here was a still life: eggplant, oranges, a pineapple, pears, peaches, apples, and sea-grape leaves—the components of a million paintings that have been made in a thousand art schools—bright hues and round sides—the fuzziness of peach, waxiness of orange, roughness of pineapple, hardness of apple, smoothness of the pewter bowl which contained them, and the softness of the linen cloth upon which the bowl sat. Fruit that could be tasted and smelled. And yet—

Again, he understood. These fruits had been carelessly piled. Some jar or touch had unbalanced them. They were, now, on the very brink of collapse—about to topple, roll across the cloth, fall to the floor and burst lushly. They were separate and leaning—out of equilibrium and coming apart. They were *moving*. John looked at the still life that was not still, for a long time. It came near to making him dizzy. It held in itself the impulse—everlastingly frustrate—toward rescue before it was too late. He imagined that a woman, approaching the painting, would notice what was wrong sooner than he had, and rush up with outstretched hand to set it right before the damage could occur.

He went on. The fish and the pheasant hung as had others in an oval frame in his grandmother's dining room—trophies of the chase ready to be scaled and plucked and devoured. But here the pheasant was still alive. Its stretched neck, congested countenance, and bulged eye made plain the fact that the thong was throttling it; the bird glared with reproach at the beholder. The fish, too, was alive—thong through its gill—fins stiff with anxiety, pitiful eye aware of all that was happening and powerless to resist or to escape.

Next, was a bouquet in which all the flowers were dead.

151

John imagined that Shawn had spent weeks or even months on this work, so intricately and exquisitely painted were the folded browns, the turned yellows, the mildew-dappled creams.

Beside that was an African landscape—again, familiar. John remembered the Habitat Groups in the American Museum of Natural History. Here was another, "water hole" with the beasts of the veldt come down to drink. For a long time John looked—entranced. Here seemed to be no perversion or reversal, no imbalance or evil. He thought that it was the most beautiful picture of African animals he had ever seen. Curious-horned antelope drank. Two tall giraffes shepherded their young one toward the vital, muddied spring. Zebras wheeled in unison in the background. Around the water grew urgent, tropical foliage and overhead was a sky so warm and peaceful that it had put other creatures, dimly seen, to sleep in the shady depths of tree and flowering plant. Here, realistically painted, was what Rousseau had expressed about a realm that, to him, was pure fable. Then John saw, among the pebbles near the water, the torn-off human toe.

There was a Madonna with a halo—in agony. It appeared that this was an earlier study than other Madonnas. She was giving birth to the Child.

A large painting, moderne in technique, which might have been the master design for a mural. It showed the engine room of some sort of factory—the grimy men, the open maws of fires, the pipes and giant wheels, the conduits and gauges, steel stairways, shafts of light—and of itself, the scene roared and threw out heat. This, too, was admirable— and different in technique from the others. Shawn had put, through his own immense power, the power of engines into this painting. John knew what to look for, now, and found it instantly—the sheared and shooting rivet, the thin, flying strip of steam, the pressure gauge run above the red danger indicator but unnoticed by the card-playing crew below. The machine was about to explode.

In the picture of the cottage, at the far end of the glowing, empty room, was a staircase. Peering down it—transparent, all but invisible—was a ghost, toothy, old and evil.

The man who stood at the fence attracted John's attention next. His was a strange face, young but unhappy, eager but afraid, strong in design but unsure in character. In his right hand he held a cigarette lighter, a lemon, and a packet of bright-colored foreign postage stamps; in his left, a thistle in bloom, a Bible, and a piece of broken glass. On one arm he wore a bracelet made of gumdrops strung on a ribbon and around his neck was a horse collar. The gate through which he looked proved to be tall and strong and a part of a continuous high iron fence that vanished over the rolling hills; the building in the distance was repulsively institutional.

John drew up a chair and inspected a Cape Cod landscape, with dunes, hauled sailboats, and a fishhouse on a wharf. This assemblage, against a green and windy sea, was deserted by human beings and the viewing eye, following a telltale suggestion of smoke, could discern that the whole business was slightly on fire and would no doubt be consumed to ashes. Similarly, there was a ladies' sewing basket in which a black widow spider was building its cocoonlike lair, and a long view of the early evening crowds hustling through the chasm of Broadway.

This scene, again, when inspected at a moderate distance, was a masterpiece of lighting and arrangement, of shadows thrown from buildings, of wind-blown clothes and newspapers, mud-addled snow-heaps and depicted cold. Seen nearer, it showed that the reason for the general scurry was not the temperature or the biting wind but the fact that, every here and there, individuals in the crowd had broken out with smallpox; each person was fleeing everyone else.

The beautiful girl, in *that* portrait, wore a scarlet dress. John admired again her curiously amazed expression and the exquisite limpness of the hand in her lap. The color of her gown made it difficult, at first, to see that down one side of it fresh blood welled; the girl had just been shot through the heart.

John said, "I'll be damned," in a voice half amused and half furious. The door clicked and Shawn came in. He grinned his inquiry and tapped ashes from his cigarette.

"You can paint," John continued, in response to the grimace, "like an angel in a power dive. Why concentrate on atrocities?"

Shawn's smile faded. He sat on the corner of the table. "It was a long-term impulse. I got sick of icky. I know I can paint. Like every illustrator, I had a yen to do something for myself. About myself. To paint art instead of images for

153

other people's stories. I became obsessed by the *un*happy ending. And yet, since my urge to paint, in itself, seemed somehow a conventional thing, I had the perverse notion that it was incumbent upon me to treat the subjects other artists did—but to do them both better and differently. I had a message. It concerned the effort that disregards pain and pleasure, that transcends the slings and arrows of physical misfortune, and leads to happiness. Work, in short. Work is the only happiness there is for man. That's the answer to life: work. Without work well done, all pleasure is conscience-ridden. So I decided to work like hell on these—and I did. I thought that if they represented the opposite to a happy ending they would help people to strike a balance. To ignore *both* endings, that is, and take a look at the paintings. It didn't occur to me until I'd filled up this damned gallery that I was preoccupied here, too, with the *idea*. That is, I wasn't painting a picture for the sake of the picture. I was still *illustrating.*"

John reacted to this quiet analysis, this mild-tempered but grinding self-reproach, with a surge of warmth and a sudden feeling of admiration for the pictures. "Nevertheless, Shawn, they're terrific, as paintings! You've got to get them out of here where people can see them!"

The artist shook his head. "I don't believe so. Maybe, when I'm old, and my critical function has dried up, leaving only the vanity of my memory, I'll spring them on the public. Maybe my estate will. Maybe I'll destroy them. But, don't you see, they're the very thing I've protested against! They are boyish—even childish! They are not the work of a man who has ignored materialism, pleasure and pain, the physical aspect of life—they are the work of a man inextricably and inconsolably rooted in the flesh. Technically, I know I'm good. Excellent. Mentally, though, I'm still a brokenhearted chipmunk. Do you suppose I can outgrow that?"

John smiled with a large, unconscious benignity. "Haven't you, already?"

Shawn's left fingers clenched the wrist of the hand that loosely held his cigarette. The veins in his forehead swelled perceptibly. He lost himself for a moment in some obdurate thought. Then he said in a low, protesting tone, "I don't know. Maybe you never know. I only know how I despise what ordinary people call being 'adult.' The man of business is the modern 'grownup.' With his 'realism,' his nasty little appraisal of human greed, his piddling cynicism over the alleged purchasability of all people, the pious pigeonhole in which he files his church attendance and his prayer and his utterance of faith and his charity, his certainty about all laws and rules and codes, his assurance that he 'knows the game, inside-out'—sex, schools, child-raising, taxation, politics, and death—his rightness and his patness and his smug willingness to make a formal, final pronunciamento about everything—that's the American adult! That's what this nation mistakes for maturation. Stiffness of the mind. Closed convictions. An okay universal audit, good for a lifetime! That's the bookkeeper and that's the billionaire. That's the butcher and the National Association of Manufacturers. That's Mr. America!"

John was smiling. "*I'm* probably what you'd call a businessman. I could resent that diatribe, I suppose. It's true. But it isn't all there is to the truth."

An expression of scornful rejection came upon Shawn's face. "You? You're not a businessman. You've made money selling medicaments—sure. You've also practiced as a scientist. But—"

"But what?"

"Every man, really, at bottom, is neither a scientist nor a man of business, but an artist. You just haven't found your medium."

John shook his head. "I doubt it. I've tried writing sonnets—long since—and they were rather poor. I tried the violin—and I was terrible. I never tried painting. Maybe I should borrow some paints from you—but I feel certain—"

"By golly, you will! You'll paint!" Shawn rushed from the gallery. John followed him into the studio. "You'll start this minute! It's fun! It'll do you good! Everybody ought to paint. Kindergartens are just finding it out."

"I never had a lesson in my life."

"Lessons! What has that got to do with it? You'll paint!" Shawn began cramming tubes and brushes into a pasteboard carton. "Painting is knowing how to see, no more, but no less. Music is knowing how to hear. Writing may be either, or both, or something else—knowing how to think or to feel. You will paint!"

It occurred to John that he might enjoy trying. "All

right. I'll paint. After all, I can't play golf with this foot—"

Shawn surveyed his array of blank canvases and selected three. He piled them on his divan, together with an old, color-marbelized palette and the carton of brushes and tubes. He straightened up and smiled. "I give you the material. You pick the subject. I make only this one condition—that you let me see your pictures. Now," he continued briskly, changing his tone without any premonitory sign, "your foot. Your accident. The ghost of my late friend Bill Gracey. That's what you came here to talk about, eh?"

John took the empty seat beside his sudden gift of the materials of art. He looked, for a moment, through the open door of the studio, at the sifting fountain and the ambition-less flow of tide in the bay. With the precise voice of a lecturer explaining a difficult and detailed process, he described his first evening in the Gracey house and his mishap.

"And you were pushed," Shawn murmured at the end.

"Maybe. I thought I was pushed. Anyhow, I fell—and I don't generally fall down staircases in the dark. Especially unfamiliar ones, because I'm a cautious sort of guy."

"What's happened since? Anything?"

"Nothing. I've slept in the blackout room. I've heard no voices, though—did I tell you? I thought—after the fact, again—that I heard the voice Ann heard—the day I came to rent her house." John reported that event as he remembered it—or seemed to have remembered it. "I'm not sure of that, either."

Shawn's eyes were disquiet. "Why did you come to me?"

"Frankly, because you seem to believe in ghosts. I don't."

"What do you want me to do? Make you believe in them?"

"I want to know why a man as intelligent and composed —as analytical and honest—as you are believes in ghosts."

"I've seen them," Shawn replied. "That's why."

"Hallucinations? Errors of vision? Real people that appeared and didn't stay to identify themselves?"

"Ghosts. Real ghosts. Either I have seen them—or I am not quite sane. Either they are real—or my sensory impressions cannot be depended upon at all. The day after my mother died—I saw her. I was fourteen. Her body lay in its coffin in the parlor. I went in there to sit beside it—alone.

Father was talking to the minister about the funeral—what hymns were to be sung by the mourners, and by the soloist— all that. It was late afternoon. I'd been very fond of my mother—we all were. All my brothers and sisters—I've got six. Anyway, I was sitting there and it was light; the blinds were drawn but it was sunny outdoors and they were yellow blinds, not green. I was just sitting, numbly, the way you do when somebody dies. I had my elbow on a chair arm and my forehead in my hand. For some reason, I looked up. Mother stood there and smiled at me. Encouragingly. Then she faded away—just faded, slowly. She had on a dress I'd never seen before—not the one in the coffin, not one she'd ever owned. A beautiful dress. Of course, I raced across the hall and told Father and the minister. I thought they'd be as excited—as elated—as I was. They were indignant. The minister said I was overwrought. I hadn't been—at least, not as he meant. Father said I was lying. I argued. In the end, he took me out to the garage and licked me."

Shawn considered. "That. Others. Then—I've seen something else. Not a ghost, perhaps. Just—something else. This. I was walking, one evening, on a country road, with a cocker spaniel. It was not exactly dark but not very light. August. The road was dusty—the floury white kind of dust that country roads get in summer—the kind that feels like water on bare feet. Trees, bushes, a brook near, frogs, no fireflies yet. Up in Connecticut. Suddenly the dog stopped. His hair lifted—all over his back and down his sides, so that he looked woolly. He stood as stiff as ice. I spoke to him and he didn't budge. I put my hand on him and his muscles were rigid. My touch didn't seem to enter his awareness. And at that instant I myself became frightened. I have never again been afraid that way, or that much, in my life. I crawled with fear. My guts were filled with a cold douche of fear. I straightened up by a great exertion of will and looked where the dog was looking. If I had seen a twenty-foot demon, in that abrupt and inexplicable condition, I might have passed out with dread but I certainly would not have been more surprised. What my eyes actually beheld was almost an abstraction—a far more horrifying object than a horned man or a beast. On the edge of the white road, moving slowly toward the center, was a *blackness*. It was a blackness of such an unusual nature that it dissociated itself instantly from any and every black object I had seen before or have seen since. I think I can speak with authority upon one subject: color intensity. This was absolute black, consuming black, deadly black, the blackness of extinction. It was as if not a color, or an absence of color, had been made manifest in that road, but a hole in the three dimensions had yawned into some other dimension which seemed black because it was a dimension invisible to man. By then, I was as tranced as my dog, which did not whimper or even breathe. I could not have moved if my life had depended upon it.

"The thing was about as long as my arm and perhaps two-thirds as wide. But it was shapeless. It did not stand up above the ground and its form changed constantly. It moved forward like a quick amoeba, putting out pseudopodia into which it then poured itself—and so it progressed. When it came to the center of the road it stopped dead still. Sweat squirted from me. I had an experience of *loathsomeness* that I cannot possibly convey. The thing sat there or lay there, two dimensional and black as the essence of the horror of ages. Then, quickly, it seeped into the pulverized earth—or so it seemed. It trickled away like a liquid. In a few seconds, there was nothing. When it was gone, my dog spun around and ran away. I had the identical impulse but I controlled it. My eyes hadn't moved from the spot in the road where the object had filtered into the earth. I compelled myself to approach—a distance of four or five steps. The light was still good enough to show every roadside pebble, every tire track. I leaned down and, finally, after an exasperating struggle, I made my hand stir the dust in the place. It was dry and it bore, like the surrounding dust, the imprint of country traffic. Nothing palpable had disturbed it and certainly no liquid had been absorbed by it.

"I have thought about this event for many years, now, and I assure you I have come to no conclusion whatever as to the nature of the object or abstraction which I perceived that evening. I was several days recovering from shock and intermittent shakes; I have always entertained about the episode a feeling of near-recognition. But the most I can honestly say is that the adventure was real, my discernment normal—at least, it came upon me in no moment of distress, bereavement or difficulty—and that my dog saw it, also. The dog was in as bad a state as I for several hours, but he got over it sooner. If this was the devil himself, he is a creature to be avoided at every cost. If it was an opening of or into the Pit, then hell has been underestimated through the millennia. If it was some obscure and so far undescribed phenomenon of dimensionality, some transient slip or flaw in the architecture of the cosmos, then its explanation will have to await further generations of mathematicians—and hardier ones, also, supposing they are to repeat the thing in experiments. If, on the other hand, it represents a hallucination on my part, then two factors are certainly established: that my dog shared the experience through telepathy and that the nature of the unconscious mind of man is far subtler, far more powerful, and much more terrifying than psychological investigation has, for the most part, permitted us to suspect. In any event, the incident took place, the thing was there, whatever it may have been. And it seemed to me demonstration enough, in itself, of the inadequacy of our present-day scientific pretensions."

John listened to this account with attention and the outward seeming of complete sympathy, however impatient and contrary his feelings may have been. He now said, shaking his head, "That's a very remarkable story, Shawn. I don't doubt a word of it. Like yourself, I am inclined to doubt, rather, the sources of your sensory impressions at the time. That, or the interpretations you make. The odd part about the so-called preternatural is not only its inexplicability and its obliquity, but the fact that the apparently 'genuine' occurrences usually involve one witness only. What takes place in séances is always proved to be fake, in the end, I find. What I am inclined to believe in, however, always depends upon the single observer. In this case—you."

"And in the case of Ann's house—you."

"Exactly," John smiled.

"Perhaps, that in itself is a *rule*. I mean, perhaps the 'preternatural' is accessible to one person only, at a time—like all other images impressed upon an individual."

"But—other images can be universal. The words pronounced by a speaker, for instance, are heard and understood by thousands—"

"The words. Yes. What about a dream? Do two people have the same dream the same night? I know instances even of that—but they are rare. A thought—an idea—consciousness itself—is peculiarly *singular* in nature. That's what people are talking about when they protest the solitariness of human existence; the infinite exile of a person in himself, the lack of thought-contact, of merged personality, of a handclasp of souls. It is a condition that compels the average person into gregarious activity, however wasteful and stupid that usually may be. It is also the condition which is the essence both of life and of death—the paradox—the incentive—the wellspring of achievement and the great frustrator, too. Consciousness is surrounded by a Space, as are the stars, and each human being is as remote from others as space keeps stars apart. From the stars, only radiations of light and heat, particles of energy and waves, reach the others. None of the primary being of a star ever spans the gap but only the secondary evidences of its existence. So it is with people. Love itself cannot build a bridge. The isolation is absolute. Across it can come only the touch of bodies, reflected light, sound, scent, waves, particles—and nothing of the being itself. Yet the being is there and we recognize it as a reality while we see it. Kill the physical instrument of the entity and it vanishes. Cut off the light of a star and it, also, seems to be gone. But, if we were to consider death as a curtain, an interruption of physical processes which are measurable to physical beings, we might also logically deduce that the living being continued to exist—"

"If you killed the star—blew it up—destroyed it—" John objected.

"—you would still go on wondering what had become of the awareness of the star—providing, of course, you had been certain it was aware. Exactly my point. If the star had known itself and time, it would have established the knowledge as *fact*. Destruction of the star would not have touched the *fact*. Similarly, that part of knowingness which is a person, by recognizing itself in one time, perhaps establishes itself in all time. Whatever it discovers, outside of a material world which has only temporal values is, by very definition, *timeless*. If—"

"Damned metaphysics," John said hotly. "Theological quibble!"

"If you ever understood eternity *once*, for *one minute*, *completely*, you would, of course, realize the *meaning of immortality*. Having been immortal in that *instant*, you would, if you remembered the circumstance, understand your immortality *always*. Can you doubt that premise?"

John shrugged. "Perhaps not—as mere logic. But I have never believed in immortality. I certainly have never understood eternity—as you call it—long enough to get myself into the picture."

"Ah." Shawn rose and stared at the illustration he had so recently finished. "Simply because, no doubt, what you think of as your 'self' is not the part of you that has a claim on eternity. Your aloneness is your essential individualism. It may also be your one possible route to knowledge—beyond—well, beyond all common knowledge."

He walked to the door and peered at the flat bay. Now the sun was low; effulgent clouds masked it; and the water gleamed violet, pink, rose and pale gold. A school of mullet swam an inch below the surface, which was riffled as if it were being stroked gently. Shawn said, looking at the sunset, "That's the whole trick. The *individualism* of the thing. If you see a ghost, you alone see it. Why? Because a ghost exists in a dimension perceptible to one person at a time, alone. Maybe more on rare occasion. But a ghost is not an object like a table. It is something other—in a different category—a *meaning,* so to speak, or an aspect of dimensionality, or a substantiation of an emotion. Its observation depends upon you. And also upon that immaterial aspect of matter which we have inadequately and tentatively described on this particular planet as consciousness—the consciousness here of another being, a consciousness which, in one segment of space and time, used tangible energy and was composed of it, a consciousness that was definitely radiant, like the star we discussed. If you believe in telepathy—and I am sure you must because you are observant—why should you balk at accepting evidence of time-space functions not yet diagnosed by men in your trade?"

"Simply because even you, now, personalize these functions, as you call them. Science demands universality in a described method. A phenomenon must be repeatable, to be accepted. Repeatable at will."

"Perhaps this one is—but who understands 'will' sufficiently? And why should the personal reference frame be rejected here, when we are dealing with personality alone? Can science defend its present insistence upon treating individuals as anything *but* separate entities? Your geneticist regards you as a product of your chromosomes; your psychologist, as the result of your environment. The fact that you (and everybody) sit on top of the heap, aware to some degree of genetic capacities and shortcomings, and of the effect of past experience, is regarded as of only incidental interest—in spite of the second, equally evident fact that the degree of your awareness is the monitor of everything you the body are dong and will do.

"It should follow, logically, that scientists would take immense interest in urging each individual to extend this awareness in *every* direction possible, for the information— and hence the judgment—it would manifestly lend. But, no. At any point where awareness brings intimations of truth outside the individual scientist's own announced dogma, that scientist nonscientifically shouts his denial. Science, therefore, is still basically witchcraft or religion, in the canonistic sense. Each practitioner is a fanatic. Each has a mind open along one avenue only. Each will accept the extension or the rectification of a chemical formula, for instance, but not of a personal fiat or a philosophical corollary. In every argument relating to consciousness, he does not say, 'Prove it.' He says, ahead of time, 'You cannot prove it because I am already convinced it is not so.' This is in no sense sane, let alone reasonable. There's *fear* in it. Unconscious but livid: the hidden knowledge, perhaps, that the world of science is the child world—and the world of *thought* so long, so adult, so difficult, so full of the prospect of personal, national and racial failure, that to admit its mere presence is to describe the minuteness of all the individual scientist is, believes, works for, and dreams!"

Shawn turned from the door, exhaling slowly and smiling a little. The colored light had left the sea; the hard greens, reds, whites and blacks of the daytime tropical landscape were now a gentle gray. "Haranguing scientists is an avocation of mine. It's my fanaticism, too, maybe. I suspect that we the peepul will stay the way we are for a long while, too. We're so busy discovering what's true and what's false in the world of materials that we have temporarily banished the equally valid investigation of what is right and wrong, or good and evil—what's subjectively true and false, that is to say. Somewhere within that frame stands Bill Gracey's ghost. You ought to try to put your finger on the position, I think. Just because you *happened* to come here when you did —if you prefer to avoid the notion that it wasn't chance. Incidentally, what's the matter with you?"

"Matter?" John repeated, abruptly ill at ease.

"Yeah. Ann said you'd had some sort of nervous breakdown. You haven't had any such thing. That's simple to diagnose. A shock—sure. I never have hidden my curiosity, when people I like have been involved. Cancer?"

John shook his head. "No, Shawn. No."

"I won't ask again. Sorry." Shawn sounded delicately injured, as though his estimate of John Galen, rather than his curiosity, had suffered from the rather flat response.

"Someday—"

"Old man, you needn't!"

"Cerebral dysrhythmia. I'm either getting epilepsy—or in the middle of an emergence from a low-grade form of it. Take time to tell. And I'm allergic to the medicine—"

Shawn pursed his lips but did not whistle. In a moment, he said, "Want to stay for supper? Thalia's back."

"Thanks. Not tonight. I'd better be going." John began to gather up the art supplies Shawn had given him. "My own dinner's waiting. And Maddox is going to call again tonight." He chuckled. "I should have been tramping around on this dead limb. Doctor's orders. But I enjoyed the gallery—and the dissertation—far more."

Shawn led him across the patio and down the dark, central hall of his home. "Maddox. There's your ordinary scientist. The able doctor who reads the new literature and draws pictures of molecules for his better-educated laymen. But Gail's got him."

"So I learned."

"And Gail hates him."

"She seemed cool."

They were standing beside John's rented car. Shawn pulled open the door. "He hangs around her. Spies, almost. Masochist, I guess, because I can imagine what he finds out. Then he accuses her. Ann's told me—because Gail has complained to her. Funny behavior for the chilly man of logic."

"Common, though."

"Dangerous," Shawn said.

163

John laughed again. "I doubt that he's the suicidal type."

"I was thinking of Gail. If he bothers her long enough to make a sufficient sum total of irritation, God knows what that Gorgon would do to drive or shame him off her campus! Well—"

" 'Night."

" 'Night, John." The motor started. Shawn raised his voice. "Incidentally—I'm usually here. Phone—if—well, *if*."

3

ANN HAD THE JITTERS. She had felt them coming on for days and fought them first with resolution and then with bromides. The privacy of her hotel room no longer had a protecting aura. When she closed the door she could imagine it opening under the hand of an amused, malicious former occupant who had secretly retained its key. She searched the rough plaster for small eyeholes through which the mumbling anonymities in the adjacent rooms might be able to watch. In the dark, her chamber would seem to expand, her bed to rise up, and the walls to fall away or dissolve so that she was in danger of crashing to the floor, rolling, and falling the long distance down to the street. The people with whom she made engagements for business reasons and those she sought as solace were helpful to her condition while she anticipated their company but, realized in the flesh, they uniformly became exacerbations: voices, gestures, ideas, war rumors, ill-expressed sympathies, worse-advised attempts at diversions—people full of alarm, people nervous at the prospects of rationing and other such discomforts—noisy, restless, trivial shades in human form.

She woke in a confused recollection of nightmare. Troubling faces rushed across the retina of her mind. When she opened her eyes she saw that plaster ceiling and did not immediately recall to what room it belonged. She did not budge her eyes to find out. Knowing who she was challenged her to remember where she lay—hot, damp, distracted—on her back, staring up. The recollection jumped into being like a landscape materializing beyond a window from which the blind has rolled up of its own accord. The loss of her sense of disorientation was differently painful. Now she could think not only of her name and her address but also of her circumstance. Bill was dead. She was in a hotel.

The morning was already humid. She lifted her arm and looked at her watch: five to seven. She sat up slowly, aware again of the shimmer of multiple nerve ends that made her feel as though life itself quivered, like a neon sign. She stood and stretched, glanced at the rough walls, listened to the silences beyond, and stripped her nightdress over her head. It smelled of cologne and perspiration. She went into the bathroom and took a cool shower. After that she dressed in a white cotton frock, white shoes, white cotton socks. Her legs were shaved, and brown with the sun that used to fall in front of the Gracey house, on the beach. She brushed up her dark, curling hair, made a morning mouth with her lipstick, atomized fresh cologne on her breast and neck and arms and stood, for a moment, looking out at the harbor.

The sky was a hard, high blue; the sea the same hue; and the line of horizon obscured by haze in such a way that boats —a tanker and two PCs—seemed suspended in a luminous, steam-colored atmosphere halfway between the water and the random clouds. The brief effect of her shower vanished: perspiration had started under her arms; she would be damp all day, and trickling. She went out.

The hotel dining room would not open until seven-thirty. Ann decided to breakfast elsewhere. She bought a paper at the newsstand in the lobby and walked toward the street— past the cool gloom, the palms, the serried tables, and the dim, pungent medley of smells: frying, coffee, catsup, and immemorial turnips.

Outdoors, the heat had early heft; it stooped her shoulders, wilted her. She walked to the boulevard. By the time she reached it, her eyes did not have to squint at the illumination. It was, even now, so vivid that it burned the tawdriness out of walls, curbs, steeples, palms, fences, baked lawns, and grayed pavement—making them glare like minerals. Workers were jabbering at the bus stops. Soldiers and sailors marched among them. Horns hooted, bells rang, red and green signals alternated—dimly winking against the shine of the sunlit sky.

Salt water flickered on her right as she turned north. She saw the stranded schooner that housed Miami's aquarium and the hot green sprawl of park; on the other hand, a façade of buildings, of hotels and night clubs—the first wet-washed for diurnal trade, the second banal in a bald light that changed the appurtenances of glamour into artifacts of glass and wood, into shoddy. Everywhere, colored boys in stained uniforms were mopping and sweeping and polishing. Soldiers, sailors. Arms jerking into salutes. Now she noticed the blue-gray paint of small fighting craft and in the middle distance the loom of a Spanish tower, rosy brown—a monument to the Boom.

The loss of Bill, she thought, was akin to the loss of sensibilities within herself. Courage had been cut out of her by his going and, with it, her sense of moral direction and her feeling of life's purpose. She had become a blank meanderer, an uneasy trudger through heat and crowds, a crab walking on a sea floor amidst other shambling monstrosities—walking in the rough terrain of buildings with doors like caves—walking against the pressure of air—walking with a fatigue that could not be slept away and was like the dark downpush of sea water and the heavy crosspressure of its currents. Her imagination stayed awake but it was no longer a process that grew naturally and produced normal blossoms; it swarmed with stinging insects. It suddenly slowed to an insectile crawl, meaningless and repugnant.

This, she thought, was proof of the unity of man and woman by a negative. Absence was as real as presence; death was a psychic surgery done to the souls of the bereaved. Or was it, her mind asked tickingly, merely a withdrawal symptom, like those which fiends suffer when their morphine is denied them? Was it artificial? Was it the product of a state invented and superimposed—a state called love, or matrimony—no more germane to the nature of a woman than any other physical addiction? Was her sorrow a disease, a neurasthenia, the unreal nimbus of unreal concepts?

A hot flame of loyalty to Bill denied such compulsions. They, not grief, were the falsehoods.

She went on slowly.

But the questioning countermotif beat back into her brain. Bill was dead and beyond all feeling and all knowing. The torturing remnant of him which she kept alive in her mind had nothing to do with him; it was her own entirely, a pitiless sickness, and not even that, because there was no contagion in it. He had not spoken to her. She had only imagined it. He was forever gone. She was the victim of too much original surrender and she could not get back from death that part of herself she had so gladly bestowed in life. She could never get it back. She would never be whole. Widowhood was a spiritual amputation.

She turned into a restaurant. Flies gyrated at the screen door when she moved it and settled again after it had slapped back into place. There were servicemen here at the tables, too—and civilians without collars. She sat down and opened her paper. In a remote corner of her mind, she tried desperately to deal with geographical names and military figures which expressed the fact that the enemy was spreading everywhere on the earth, like a forest fire, like a poured acid, like a plague. Curiously, the big black headlines gave an opposite impression: the Jap had been bombed in this village, held in that one; the German had been counterattacked in some tiny, unheard-of mountain town hung on the northern slope of the Caucasus. Submarines, the biggest headline said, had sunk a Jap destroyer and two freighters. It sounded jubilant —and yet, these fronts had extended to the enemy's advantage—since yesterday.

Ann fiercely interested herself in that phenomenon for a moment. When the slovenly waitress appeared, she said, "Orange juice, toast, and coffee."

There was something so American about this newspaper and its contents, she thought. Something so small-boyish, raging—not at one outpost, but on a circle that was growing into a hemisphere. And yet, the men who wrote headlines, the self-assured reporters, the pompous publishers—without having attempted to league themselves together for public deceit—were caught here in the very act of monumental lie. The tendency to such intellectual self-abuse was universal in America. If the truth was bad, Americans did not want to hear it, to know about it, or to have it hinted.

Publishers and broadcasters did not need to form a society of liars in order to lie so consistently. They were liars before the war had come. Boosters, bellwethers, promotors— men of self-asserted "good will," men of "confidence," men who looked "upward" and "forward." Men, unfortunately, whose necks were so stiff from optimistic stretching that they could never look backward, or down. Here were the jaws of catastrophe closing upon them from meridians that spanned the globe—but they still exulted because their enemies had lost three ships, a village, a few soldiers.

Quick, rending rage possessed Ann. Already, men like Bill had died where this crushing and insensate enemy licked the shore of America. How many more would it take, before the enemy was pushed back, slaughtered in sufficient millions, stamped out, quenched, satisfied and beaten? How could so-called important people be so stupid, so unseeing, so dishonest? Widows were in the making in hundreds of thousands. The very reporters who gathered this news and put so infantile a cast upon it were, perhaps, about to die. Women—happy women—were waking up in myriads this morning all across the summer-swept continent—waking in the beds of their husbands—upon whom, already, the first shrouds invisibly congealed.

And yet, whenever a bold and decent-minded citizen pointed out this ghastly inevitability, whole organizations rose in their political might to call the man an alarmist, an agitator, a warmonger (as if we were not overmongered now in war), and a hurter of morale. Great God! Was our morale dependent nowadays upon the insubstantial stuff of these headlines? Did the soul of the American people rely for nourishment on sick deceit? Could it be kept alive only by a cloyed misrepresentation sucked like a lollypop? Someone, somewhere, had blundered—or everyone, everywhere, had blundered. Now for grimness. Now for truth. Now for holy anger. Now—if ever—for cause.

But, because there was so little truth, there could be no cause. Americans were sick, all of them, nearly. Too sick to want truth any more. They fought not for a reason but as the delirious patient fights, and struck each other as often as they struck their enemy.

Ann contemplated her own friends and acquaintances. Catholics who preferred Franco to a republic in Spain and Mussolini to liberty, Catholics who, in crooked consequence, would not believe what Hitler had done to their own church. Protestants so face-set against all war they would no longer fight even an antichrist. Women in the D.A.R. who parroted, line for obscene line, every word that had been said to madden empty heads against the Jews—every word fashioned by Hitler and Goebbels and Rosenberg. Honest, decent (once) and once-respected men in her Connecticut town—Republicans—whose voices were raised against the embattled President of the United States as if he, not Hitler, were Satan.

This was the portrait of America at the beginning of Armageddon. This was the spirit that democracy had evolved—all liberty turned to license, all happiness to pleasure, all pain to undesirability, all morals to profitable legislation, all manners to the pursuit of money, and ideals—not just of the founding fathers but of two thousand years of struggle for truth and responsibility—delegated and redelegated until they no longer reposed anywhere at all. Even the church would have none of them, either. Catholics built their secret, international establishment of property and power without a care for country; Protestants were withered and theologically split into more quibbles than the darkest ages knew. The middle classes stamped on those below and sold out to those above. No one was shoulder to shoulder in this war. The New Deal had made, in erroneous benignity, great strides toward authoritarianism and the people were used to it, already—they doted on it, so that the form was prepared for the next party—which might not be benign.

Owing to the soft character of Americans, these days. That was it. That was why it would be necessary to fight a soft war at home. No matter how many Bills were blown up, burned, drowned or buried alive, no matter how many men faced horror in far-off, lethal lands, the self-pampered at home would insist upon a pampering war. They would have to be bought off—paid for patriotism—hired to fight. The nation would resemble a nation of mercenaries—because it had not let itself be told why it was fighting and what it was fighting. In some distant year ahead this struggle might grow costly enough, or threatening enough, to waken that last, terrible resource of humanity—its sense of self-preservation. Now, though, it did not even believe it had been threatened.

Her breakfast was sitting in front of her—put there while she had been staring into space. The orange juice had separated. She drank the thin liquor and the sour sediment.

Why had Bill enlisted? Because he didn't like Nazis? Their massacres had sometimes made him swear indignantly. But that, she knew, was too far away for Bill's imagination. He had not been capable of thinking of Europeans as people like himself; he had often spoken about them as if they were animal herds—cattle, a dirty flesh breeding in dim, odious

169

places. He had not been capable of considering the attitude of—a Prussian to a Pole—as a real and raging human prejudice, like that of an unreconstructed Southerner toward a Yankee. He did not have that sort of mind. (What other sort was there?) Europeans were subhuman, unimportant, not very real. They had wars and had been having wars for millennia. Bill seemed to regard the wars of Europe as analogous, by opposites, to the American habit of *progress*. We were peace-loving and progressive. They were *warring* instead—and retrogressive.

He would admit that out of their wars had come our founding fathers and out of their conflicts, our ideals. But the admission was tempered with the thought that the good of Europe had fled from it—moved—colonized America— and left the reproducing, battling mob behind. Typical American thought. Most Americans could not understand what was happening; they could not comprehend a total war, or even economic war; they could no more conceive of global menace than of an American king. Indeed, Ann reflected bitterly, the two were equal in minds like Bill's—and it was as impossible for him to think of somebody planning the conquest of the United States as it was to think of a coronation ceremony in Washington.

She sat stiffly before her cup, remembering the long arguments they had patiently endured before their marriage. Bill—usually good-humored—sometimes irritated—always scoffing. Political arguments, social arguments, economic arguments. Her memory ranged farther—to the days before she had met Bill—to college days. She'd been "red," then. It had been fashionable. You scanned the *New Masses* and sometimes the *Daily Worker*. You went around the campus with a copy of the *Nation* sticking out of the big patch pocket on your ski suit. You were "for" the New Deal and "against" big business. If you were really "advanced"—which Ann had never been—you went to Boston or New York and helped somebody picket something. You came out of college feeling that the "liberal" position held all the rightness on earth. You were "for" the Loyalists in Spain. You were "against" Ethiopia's violation and Jap expansion. "Against" Wall Street. You believed that America should be "socialized" to some extent—and you argued about what that extent should be, even while you worried vaguely about socialism. Then came the nonaggression pact between Russia and Germany. The bottom fell out of the world—you knew that, somehow, the liberals had been mistaken, socialized Russia was less idealistic and more opportunistic, even, than theoretical communism—and you decided nobody could think any longer and nobody could be trusted.

When Russia was attacked, your heart was with the Russians, but not your moral allegiance, any longer. You expected the Soviet to be swallowed up by Germany and the prospect was terrifying. You had eschewed the old slogans about workers' rights and the brotherhood of man; you had been wholly undeceived by the liberals about the moral fiber of your own nation in its present form (excepting, of course, the fiber of New Dealers) ; now you had precious little left to stand on. Or to stand for. Roosevelt talked about quarantining aggressors but he didn't seem worried in the least. You caromed about in your allegiances. One day, you were positive that you were living in the most exciting and valuable period in the history of man. The next day, you thought you were looking at the end of Western civilization—and all civilization. The third day, you decided that science and machinery and communication were finally getting so complicated that no man and no government could make sense out of them—that the world was a muddle and no use trying to puzzle over it. The fourth day, you weren't intellectual at all: you caught a cold or burned your finger or saw a funny movie or got a letter from a boy who was interested in you— and you didn't give one thought to what was going on in the far places. Not that you rejected those events, or accepted them, either; just that you ignored them completely.

Maybe Bill had gone through all those stages before she had. Maybe he had come to the conclusion that you bet on America—went along—and hoped for the best. Somehow, she didn't think so. He had never done the mental spadework that even such understanding required. In Bill's mind, America was another planet.

But he hadn't gone to war to accomplish anything in particular for anybody especially. . . .

The slovenly waitress was standing beside her. Ann lifted her eyes.

"Your coffee's cold," the girl said. "I'll get you a hot cup."

Ann blushed. "I'm sorry. I was daydreaming."

"I know how it is." The girl's clothing was acrid with fatigue and her hair was like raveled rope ends. "You new down here?"

"I've lived here a while. My husband—" She stopped.

"In service?" The girl saw the nod. "Mine, too. He's not exactly my husband—but we're going to get married when he comes in from his next trip. He's a boatswain's mate—second class. From New London. I took this job. You can't just sit around in a rented room twiddling your thumbs."

"No." Suddenly, the girl was not slovenly, but just harried. Ann's eyes became tender.

"Yours out at sea?"

Ann nodded.

"Don't worry. He'll come roaring back. You know how sailors are. Still, you do get fidgety. I'll bring the hot coffee."

Bill had gone to war inchmeal, she thought.

When there was the first talk about a draft, he'd laughed at it. . . .

Sitting in the living room in Connecticut, with the rain falling outdoors and the wind coming along the maples on the road—wind that was like a haughty woman with a trailing skirt, making the crowd part, turning everybody in one direction, taffeta whispering, and all movement regimented. The clock ticking. Bill cracking almonds with his fingers while she did it with a hammer on a flatiron. "They're crazy! If they think we're going to get in this war—they're crazy! Do they imagine they can turn guys like me into soldiers? Boy, what a lousy Wehrmacht my college companions would make! Who'd sober 'em up?"

Then—it became reality. . . .

His poignantly masculine features drawn slightly and beclouded not so much with worry as with incomprehension. "And now they're getting set to go over Niagara Falls in a barrel! Fine thing."

They were at dinner in New York that night. In the dining room of a big hotel—a gaudy room with a floor show —the sort of place Bill had loved and she had only—liked once in a while. There was an odd element in the air: the element of war. It made men gallant and bold, then, although it made women sick at the pits of their stomachs. Later (she had thought) it would make the men gray and sick—and perhaps the women would become brassy and vindictive. The band had played "Over There"—tentatively—and several couples had stopped dancing. Three or four tables softly booed the music. "When you're this far in," Bill had said, "you're in. And it's too late to kick. I'm for the Air Corps, baby."

She hadn't said much. . . .

But the Air Corps would not have him. . . .

He had been in a thundering rage. "Eyes! I can shoot skeet with any man alive. I can pin-point a forward pass. I've already flown Buggsy Davis's Piper Cub solo. But I can't see well enough to suit the Air Corps! They were taking rotten little store clerks who have never been in condition in their lives—guys with complexions like oatmeal—but they won't take me! Dopes!"

"What are you going to do?"

They were sitting in Central Park, that day. The squirrels looked them over hopefully. Pigeons waddled near to inspect them. The sky was blue—flung bunting of a white cloud here and there, high up. There were some uniforms, already; Bill looked at one. A soldier—a private—a nobody in a khaki suit that did not fit—spectacles—red hands—big ears. A boy, just walking on the cement path, alone, thinking limply of nothing much. "One job I'm not going to do—walk in this war. Not for me. Not walking. Next to planes—I like boats. I'm going to try the Navy next."

Because he wouldn't walk. Because he liked boats. . . .

The first night he had worn his uniform, she had slept with him. She had never slept with a man before. It had just happened and there was nothing about it to regret. They were engaged. Soon afterward they were married.

She'd lain awake, under a silken puff spread cockeyed on the wide bed in a borrowed apartment. She'd heard the fog horn down on the river—a minor third—and the whistles of tugs and the quivering hoot of liners impatient to be out in the sea. She'd heard the whole murmur of Manhattan— the medley of subways and trucks, feet, elevators, doors, voices, dishes, motors, hums, roars, booms, thumps—the sounds whereof the river whistles are the obbligato. She'd smelled the smell of the city, too—smoke and mist, burned gasoline, eternal cookery, wet cement and brick—all of it, in each deep breath. She'd felt the silk beside her and Bill's body warm and relaxed. This had been her bridal night—and it was not sad, although she felt a little sad; but they could laugh honestly on the formal one—and that was something. She could not think of him, yet, as her husband. But she was sure it would endear him to her even more to have known him for that little while as her lover. She and he and all this sensual circumference of living. She had a man, now; he had a woman.

She thought of the pitfalls and the warnings, the advice and the urgent wariness of serious books written for women on the subject of what had happened that night. And all of it—for Bill and for her—had proved to be nonsense. They were just there—in the apartment he had borrowed for her to spend the night in while he stayed at the club. The table for two was reserved, and the tickets for the show were at the box office. She had bought the ingredients of cocktails— a little uncertainly because she did not drink much—and prepared them so that she could enjoy the illusion, in this apartment, of being at home with him. He had arrived early and praised the cocktails. He had kissed her—once too often—so nobody had used the table for two and nobody had called for the pink tickets and they'd phoned a delicatessen—around nine—for sandwiches and fruit and coffee.

Then they had eaten, dressed and walked out into the night. A naval officer and his girl. They'd stopped in strange bars in the Village and had cocktails twice—champagne— and come "home." By that time they were quite old, experienced lovers, they decided. And now he was asleep and she was lying there, listening, breathing, feeling, thinking slowly —sad, maybe because she thought it was wrong to be so utterly jubilant. Love was like that, always—but, not always, marriage. The circumambient city contained her and reassured her that night, although it was not trying to contain anybody in particular and its reassurance was casual, relative, and altogether insubstantial. And everything was the same the next day. Even Bill. It was strange. Even she was. She stepped from the shower and looked and looked in the full-length mirror and she was just the same. . . .

"I got plenty o' nuttin'—and nuttin's plenty for me." She used to sing it in the days immediately after that. She sang the song for Bill. She wasn't much, she thought, and she hoped he would feel like that about getting married to a girl who wasn't much. Just attractive. A dime a dozen. Plenty of nothing. It made her happy to sing the song, because she was sure that was how Bill felt about her and about the world. One night—on the train to Florida—he skinned out of the upper berth and down to her lower—his feet sticking out straight as if he were doing an acrobatic trick and all his muscles knotted and bunched.

By and by she sang it in the plural: "We got plenty o' nuttin'—and nuttin's plenty for us."

And he said, "What do you mean—nothing? Aren't you the best-looking number on the shore line? Isn't the Chapman genealogy so Mayflower that you can shake Pilgrims out of the family Bible? Haven't I got Uncle Paul's property down in Miami? Am I not an officer in the U. S. Navy? You call that nothing?"

She did—but now she didn't say so. She felt embarrassed—as though he had discovered in her a fatuousness. She never sang the song again.

Sounds of the restaurant suddenly rushed in upon her—like sounds from a noisy room when a window opens. A radio was playing. A lean, pearly-eyed Southerner at the next table was talking in a raucous drawl to an Army lieutenant. The kitchen seethed and clattered as the doors kissed. She had finished her coffee and the newspaper had fallen to the floor. The voice of the Cracker came insistently to her ears:

"Yes, sir! I went up there from West Palm right away in my car. The whole daygonned lake had been blown right off its bottom. Man, that was a hurricane! First dead I seen was a couple of buck niggers lying in the mud without a stitch on. Left my car near there and went on afoot—had to climb over a mess of palm trunks and brush. Place was wringing itself out like a sponge—wetter'n a drowned cat—and some of the water had poured back into old Okeechobee—but not all. I got put on a huntin' posse by a sheriff—men were scarce —live ones—and we went poking around on the high hammocks. Wooded spots where the ground's lifted up a bit. Was there snakes in there! Man, was there snakes! You had to go along whacking out in front of you with a stick. Them danged snakes had kind of felt the blow coming the night before and high-tailed for raised ground. Then—when the wind hit—the people had gone scrambling and staggering through the water and the dark—looking for high spots theyselves. But—of course—the rattlers and the moccasins and the corals was there ahead of them. The daygonned lake blew out like I said—sometime during the middle of the night—and the people would have been all right in the hammocks—because in some of them the water didn't get ankle-deep—in some maybe only a foot—and in the poorliest of 'em it was passable excepting for the rain. But there warn't nobody did themselves any good a-runnin' into them hammocks at night—cause the snakes got 'em. I must of seen a hundred—all twisted up—looking real bad—blue as veins all over—swollen and getting ready to stink. Because—you can imagine how it was in there—the rain falling steady—only horizontal—and the wind hitting around a hundred and twenty or so. Black as pitch and every flashlight drowned out and every lantern blowed out—and these folks—running and stumbling to high ground—carrying the little kids—and maybe leaving 'em behind if they couldn't tote 'em—and the brush cracking like bull whips all around them—and then when they hit the high ground the old snakes began a-stingin' 'em. I found some folks with three—four—five sets of little punctures in 'em—and one old man got hit eight times before it brought him down. There was a kid dead near the old gent and we figgered he'd stood up in the snakes long as he could to hold that kid out of 'em—but the kid was bit, too. Yes, sir. That was one mean night for them folks."

Ann snatched up her check and ran. She remembered the tip and returned.

Then she fled again.

The heat seemed to have increased while she had been in the restaurant. The hand of God pushed a rheostat behind the sun, intensified it, and raised it up to burn and dazzle the people.

Now, she had nowhere to go.

Nothing to do until lunchtime.

She started back toward the hotel. It would hide her so that others could not perceive she had no place to go.

She turned up a side street, seeking shade—but here among the buildings so much reflected light was thrown into the shadows by tinted stucco walls that the shade was a mere delineation rather than a respite from the sun. She turned again. Her white dress and neat coiffure looked cool. She would seem cool. Men glanced at her and held their glances in appraisal of her coolness, her composure. Her heart was coldness itself—a still, fixed, frozen spot—a deadness. But, around it, with an active and corrosive heat, her conscience, her questions, her fears, her loss, her disloyal recollections, all boiled together dismally.

Why had she been disloyal to Bill? Was some barbaric energy of her subconscious trying to throw off Bill in order to prepare her biologically to go on with the female chore? Or, had she really been in love with Bill the young male, while, all the time, her educated sensibilities had rejected the rest of what was Bill? Or was she trying to think less of him to stop her suffering? Or was a truth leaking into her mind? And what about the voice of Bill that had spoken to her? Ghosts and charnel things! That terrible Cracker with his twisty eyes and his thin telling of that ghastly story—and all the time, his face alight with pleasure! He had enjoyed his day recovering the bodies of those victims of storm, night, and deadly serpents! She shuddered.

Panic again formed in her breast. She felt, also, a unique compulsion to yield to it—to stop dead in her tracks, scream, shake, sit on the curb. The feeling grew and its very existence so scared her that it fed upon itself, swelled, and became real. There was familiarity, known pattern, in this situation. And suddenly she knew why. This was the corner where she had stopped, many nights before, and hung upon a lamppost, remembering the teeth of Whitey Bates. She had passed by here before—and in the same mood.

It's getting to be a habit, she thought. The next time, they'll probably pick me up. Men in white. I'll be yelling.

This, she said to herself, is the same lamppost. She stopped beside it and pretended she was waiting for a bus or waiting to cross the street, so that people would not stop simply because a woman had stopped and was standing still for nothing. The street was garish and nosy, busy with people cheaply dressed and wearing grimaces—not expressions, really, but tight masks of useless intent, speculation on purchase, of trivial duty repeatedly recalled, and of minute office routine. Nobody looked happy there—nobody even looked very conscious. They were all part of a repetitive dream—and dreaming in it—endlessly, ever so tediously. Only she, Ann, was awake.

Catercorner across the street was the church. Now, as

she stood there, she saw the minister mount its stone steps and unlock its side door. His clerical collar made a little, godly noose around his neck, and he seemed indifferent to the warmth of his black garments. A spare, athletic man—not very old—with a Panama hat set level on his brow. Behind the door he opened was a vestibule into which a long shaft of sunlight fell quietly. The minister lifted his hat before he entered and, once inside, turned a sort of eager, morning look upon the passers-by. He smiled softly to himself and nodded gently at a thought.

This picture was reposeful. Ann found herself continuing in the repetition of her earlier behavior in this spot. She crossed the street both ways, hoping, almost in aloud words, that the minister would not close the door before she had made the two quick traverses through traffic. He seemed to see her and he waited—perhaps because he was alarmed at the risk she took in the pathway of the trucks and buses. She hurried up the steps and confronted him. "May I come in?"

"Certainly," he said, as if he had expected her to say just that. He was still smiling a little. His next words, however, belied all personal reference in his first expression: "All are welcome here. This is God's house."

Ann stood in the vestibule, now, and he left the door open a little—as though, she thought, he were in a hotel and this was a nice precaution when there were lady guests. A foolish thought. She stamped it out of her mind. The vestibule was cooler than the outdoors—and musty—with the smell of all large, institutional rooms in Florida. Even stained glass could not mute the blaze of sunshine. It fell across the pews in a tumult of color—rose, lavender, purple, orange, saffron, and topaz.

"Would you like to meditate alone—or—?"

She looked at him. He had dark hair, pomaded and parted in the middle—kindly eyes, hooded and recessed, like his church—and light red lips that were compressed forever from reading and thinking with lips compressed. He was not smiling now. His expression was quizzical, but ready to be made impersonal at the mere sound of her voice, should the sound demand that.

"I don't know," she said. "I've got the jitters."

"We've all had them," he answered. "From worrying—

178

from being afraid—maybe from drinking too much. From fatigue and hunger—"

"Does this—" she looked meaningfully into the spangled church—"get you over them? All kinds?"

"I'm afraid not. Sometimes, perhaps, it helps."

"Oh. I thought surely you would say it was a cure."

He went on smiling—gravely, now—and shook his head. "Are you ill?"

"No. Upset." She peered at the radiant peace for another moment and then turned toward the partly closed door. Hard sunlight streamed through it and the uproar of the street curved in around it. She made a movement of going but did not go.

"Would you like to come to my office?"

"All right." She followed him. "It's rather early for a minister to be—at work. I suppose you call it that?"

"Work?" He spoke over his shoulder as he unlocked another door. "Darn hard work, most of the time. The number of Presbyterians in this city is limited, and their religious tendencies are limited also."

His desk was an ornate table, the chair behind it tall and carved, the chair in front, low-backed, carved also, and upholstered with tapestry. There were two copies of paintings of the Madonna and Child on the wall. A church flag stood out dustily from one corner. Bookcases lined two walls. A refectory table against a third held periodicals, papers, and a heap of typed, unsigned letters. In a corner, under black covers, stood a dictagraph and a multigraphing machine. The carpet was red and very worn. She sat down in the low-backed chair and he took the tall one. He seemed amiable and sympathetic.

"My name is Ann Chapman Gracey," she said.

"I'm Dr. Bates. Elisha Bates."

"How do you do?" Ann smiled at herself for this formality. "I—I hardly know why I came in. Impulse. One night— oh, several weeks ago—I was standing across the street from this church, having near-hysterics. The evening service was going on. I came in for a while. The singing made me feel better."

"You didn't stay long," the minister said.

"You noticed me!"

"Noticing people," he answered slowly, "is often all I

179

can do for them. But then, occasionally, it seems to be enough."

Ann was interested. That sounded more intelligent than the words of most ministers she had known. And the fact that he had observed her in his church (when she had not paid him the slightest attention and could remember him only as a dark ornament on the pulpit—a part of the necessary scenery, like the large Bible) took away some of her present feeling of strangeness.

We have been practically introduced, she thought, and ministers don't require formal presentations, anyway. "I come from Connecticut," she finally said. Her eyes went up to his, lowered and returned diffidently. "My husband was an officer on a subchaser down here. The Germans sank it and he was lost. I'm still having the willies over it. That's all, Dr. Bates."

He made several slow, small, sorrowful nods. "You hadn't been married long."

"Not quite a year."

Again, he waited. "Is there anything—" he smiled whimsically at the word he was going to use—"temporal—that I or my church can help you with? I mean to say—passage home? Work to do—for money, or simply to be occupied?"

"No-o-o. I have enough money, I think. I'm too—nervous—to work right at this time. I don't want to go home, especially. My mother—wouldn't understand—how I feel. She, too, is a widow." Ann added that word with astonishment; somehow, she had not once thought of her mother's widowhood as a condition in any way related to her own. She wondered about it for a moment. "She's a postmistress. New Lancaster. She's rather deeply rooted in the life of the town— its customs. She lives by habit. And in a world that stopped existing—oh—twenty or thirty years ago."

"I understand."

She had the feeling that he did. Her next words were less uncertain. "I suppose hardly any human statement, however—peculiar—would be a real surprise to you. Ministers must meet all the kinds that make a world."

"We meet them, certainly. Sometimes we don't know what to do for them. We can offer what any considerate person would. And faith—which is more difficult to accept."

"Faith." She watched him incline his head after she had spoken the word. "Faith. Do you believe in that?"

"Of course. To the best of my ability."

"I can't imagine getting help from anything that had to be taken on faith before it could assist." Abrupt, unwilled antagonism had risen in her—the same sense of irritated hopelessness which her mother's many ministers had given her.

"But it can be no other way." He was still quiet and kindly.

"I'm not sure. Anyway, it can't be that way—for me. I have too much respect for whatever logic I've learned." She realized that she was talking quarrelsomely—but now she wanted to talk—in any vein—to anyone. Especially quarrelsomely. "Does it ever occur to people that the business about 'faith' is a trick? A psychological trap? I mean—if you decide first to have faith—then, of course, you'll get the 'grace' that goes with it. And whatever else you expect to get. I've listened to lots of preachers. In Mother's church. They all made the same argument. Have faith first—then peace will follow. It used to drive me crazy even when I was a child. But not any longer. I understand it. It's what's the matter with religion. It's a mental disease. All it says, really, is: I decide to be convinced so that I can turn around and look at myself and find that I am convinced."

"You certainly do have a severe case of—no faith."

"I have a severe case of honesty, Dr. Bates. I have a hunch that what people meant, thousands of years ago, by faith, was something much more reasonable and less—less neurotic. I think it meant faith enough in the truth, always, and in nothing else, to face the truth always, and nothing else."

"Aren't you being a sort of Portia for the universe?"

Energy was pressed into her reply. "I'm judging nobody. Just an idea. It happens that I do have faith in the truth—and nothing else. It happens that I do not believe in the acceptance 'on faith' of the Holy Ghost, or the divinity of Christ, or miracles, or any such things. Why should I? Why should anybody? You compromise your integrity to save yourself emotional wear and tear—that's all."

The minister sighed—impatiently, she thought. "Faith

181

—has been the fortress and the foundation of Christianity for two thousand years."

"And that idea is what is destroying it, now. In an age of superstition, faith in a symbol like a divine Christ was useful. In an age where there was very little knowledge, faith performed instead of knowledge. But faith itself is now the very root of ignorance and the time has come for the church to put faith in truth, not folklore and tricks."

"I couldn't do very much, I'm afraid," he said, "to help anyone who took their heresy so literally and prosecuted it so—so narrowly."

Ann puzzled within herself to discover why she had engaged even momentarily in such an argument. There was a reason—an intuitive one. She suddenly found it, and smiled at him. "But the truth must be always at hand? Where each of us can find it? That's what it is—isn't it?"

"Certainly."

"Then why do you need faith? Why not, intelligence?"

"Even intelligence needs a starting point."

"Do you believe in ghosts?"

He seemed to be studying what she had said in his mind, and troubled by it—as though, in trying to discover the flaws in her argument, he had abruptly, if dimly, come upon a question concerning his own belief. So her words, at first, did not make themselves plain. When they did, he glanced at her with obvious suspicion: was she trying to transfer the measureless discomfort of the agnostic onto his shoulders? His face sagged and soured as he spurred himself into an acceptance even of that as a righteous duty. He brought forth a lame, disinterested smile. He looked like the other ministers. "Ghosts?"

"Dead people coming back from the grave and speaking to you?"

Now his smile was more real. This little stratagem he would defeat. It was meant, no doubt, as a lead into another quibble about theology, metaphysics, the interpretation of Scripture. "In that category, Mrs. Gracey, at least—you will hardly accuse me of being superstitious. This is a modern church with an enlightened attitude. We believe in the spirit —but not an earth-bound spirit. We believe in immortality as a state beyond present comprehension. Not as a haunting state."

"I see." Her voice was level, contemplative. "Because, I think the reason I came in here was to ask that question. I think, now, that's why I was having such terrible jitters. My husband has been speaking to me."

He opened a drawer, took out a pipe and tobacco—and an ash tray which he kept hidden, evidently, against sudden calls by parishioners who did not approve of smoking. His eyes were briefly disappointed: if he had chosen another tack he might have won more sympathy for himself and his creed. That notion showed and vanished and in its place came a look of sharp worry. "Suppose you tell me."

"But why? You don't believe. I have heard a ghost. I think that statement is the truth. I have 'faith' in it. Not believing in ghosts, you can have no faith in anything I might say about my husband. You see, that's your own fundamental principle—turned about."

He made up his mind, slowly, to be practical. "Mrs. Gracey. Frankly, no. I have seen no evidence of terrestrial existence after death. I do not believe in it. It does not fit my concept of the meaning of life. A great many charlatans have fooled people into thinking such things"—he saw that was an erroneous guess—"and some people have thought they heard or observed such things. They were generally unwell. In view of your statements, and the history of similar cases—and, especially, in view of your present nervousness—don't you think a good doctor—a medical man—?"

Ann rose. "Thank you, Dr. Bates. I guess I have my answer. I came in to talk about ghosts, I suppose. I did it because—I thought—a church would be the natural place to discuss death. It should be—shouldn't it—when you think about it?"

He had risen. He was angry, and feigned to be aghast. It was an unsuccessful combination of emotions. "Have I refused you?"

"Flatly. And recommended a doctor, besides. I knew that would happen, I suppose. The church has to humble the individual to the church. But you cannot do that to me. Religion ought to make a person humble within himself, I think, and not to a church. Isn't that right? I've got it straight again, though."

He followed her down an aisle, murmuring protest. The

toned polychromes from the stained-glass window swept in procession across her white dress.

She went out on the street, aware that she had been behaving rudely and even childishly—aware, also, that the shivery incubus had left her. She knew what she had to do. Rather, she knew that she would have to do—whatever it proved to be—by herself; the knowledge immunized her to chance adversities, to maudlin moods, even to random people describing grisly calamities. She had been unkind to browbeat the minister—but, in punishing him, she had chastised herself. The morning's progression had reached its goal. Nobody could help her. She would have to go on alone—to find out alone.

She hoped that Dr. Bates could stand being made a whipping boy. No doubt it had happened to him before. No doubt he could bear it—perhaps even with humility. He was all right.

4

JOHN GALEN decided to experiment. He did so with a mind that was not entirely open, he realized, but open a hairsbreadth.

The day that preceded his experiment was hot and still. . . .

All afternoon he sat on the sea-facing veranda of the moldered house reading *For Whom the Bell Tolls*. As he finished, he was called to dinner. The dining room was an oven. Minute rivers of sweat flowed down his face while he ate. Glistening streams ran down the black, anthropoid countenance of the woman who served him.

His thoughts stuck for a long while on the panorama of the war in Spain which had been the hatching place of this war everywhere. The fact filled him with distaste for his species. Here in the war-in-the-book was pure prophecy—a landscape of the future as plain as architectural plans. But nobody had paid any attention. People had "enjoyed" such books. Someday soon, for that pleasure, and all past, omitting pleasures, their enjoyment would turn to stalagmites in their bellies. They would silt up with death, calcify with it, eat the dread of it, drink the expectation—and hang the record of it in their windows. Already, indeed, they were beginning to do so.

He had a brief sense, august and indecipherable, of a balance in nature—a cosmic eye-for-an-eye arrangement—a terrible penalty lurking behind every human responsibility that went unaccepted. He lost the thought in the heat.

Josephine departed.

John watched her go and watched the ritual twilight. Fish flashed far out on the sea. A darkling shadow—a sting-ray—swam aimlessly inshore where the water lay still and pellucid over sandbar, lisping along its edge. White birds, with the haste of eventide, winged through the calm and hazy air—silent, intently homing. The insect orchestration of the swamp tuned up, tried a strophe, and swung full into its nightlong measure-and-repeat. Night came. He limped inside, held his bandaged ankle under a tepid drizzle from the shower, and tracked water to the blackout room. Cigarette smoke eddied behind him. He lay down tiredly under the glowing circle of a bridge lamp.

He began thinking about Hemingway's formula for the smell of death. This was imagination—the meeting place of beauty and repugnance. His mind was curiously impressed by it. He perceived that a certain aspect of the book would stay with him, or in him. A kind of sentience—as valid and impalpable as ancestral memory—a feeling of things known before birth and things understood to happen after death. This was a heritage of the book which the author had clearly apperceived when he gave it a title. A title to the times and a sensuous chemistry for the savor of it—death and always more death.

This was also the part of English, John thought, that people called a gift. A universal gift, since all human beings tasted it at one time or another, a gift expressed sometimes inadvertently—but sometimes through intent and a more direct knowing than was usual these days. The idea that death had an odor some could sense was unscientific—but who could say it was not a translation of a true fact about time? Who could say it was not a use of one of many guessable images, which can be comprehended, to replace a logic not yet comprehensible? Nobody. The entities beyond the narrow limits of known truth were not properties to deride or to disclaim. Even if all religions were in part compounds

185

of demonstrable psychic processes, and even if religion could in consequence be reduced to something like algebra, the whole business would not furnish a gram of evidence to dispute the existence of real quanta, not yet described, which had given rise through incomprehension to religions. Modern men called that which they could not understand "irrational" —although it was irrational of them to call it that, as they proved every day. But among such elements might be a prescience of death.

And what did he know about death? Nothing. He had been a self-determined not-knower. And yet, he reflected, to wonder about it and to try to know—to be always aware of its imminence—was singularly important. In that sense, the Egyptian's skeleton at the feast and the Christian's crucifixion were valuable symbols. What man or woman could guarantee his future for one minute? Not one. To ignore that or to decide by private edict that death was annihilation and therefore not worth a thought was to deprive life of half its significance. What man, constantly aware of his mortality, would behave like the ignoring man? None. Or few, at any rate. And yet, how could any man be more than half alive if he were not constantly aware of his mysterious limits? From such awareness came the gusto and the sublime detachment that made man different from beasts. From it came the true knowledge that enabled men to give their lives readily for enduring principles and that placed those lives, at the same time, beyond all price.

To regard death as annihilation was to put a dirty premium on life—to render it mere moving appetite—to belittle it. And a race of self-propelled agnostics would be a race without morals or ethics—not because of lack of churchly edict but because, by so belittling their own inevitable deaths, they would have belittled their living. It would also be a race sick of living, unappreciative, existing in one dimension only, like the Wandering Jew who was immortal and strove toward relief from that. A man who chose not to be aware of such meanings in death chose such a fate— the immortality of the moment, the life restricted to materials, and a vast unconsciousness of himself.

People would worry and gnaw at themselves on the other hand, whenever they considered the darkness that lay beyond their own silly personal demises; they had not one drop of passion to spend on the equally infinite blackness that lay behind the day of their birth. Here was the order of inconsistency that had to be explained, understood, and got over, to make men look like men inside—as they did outside. Or, they could sporadically yearn for and covet eternity without stopping to think if there was a person among them who had mustered the awful courage to sit out eternity in his present shape.

Such matters were stupendous for each person alive, but all men evaded them, ignored them, or—whenever they arose—hurried to a church to get a quack remedy for the condition. Churches had become solutions for problems they could no longer formulate—instead of learning places. . . .

Here, John thought, was Bill. Here was old Uncle Paul —dead many months in a bed upstairs before they found him. Besides, five men who rode in on the tide. If the odor of death existed, surely it could be smelt here.

His foot ached. He hobbled to the refrigerator and cracked out a few cubes of ice. He put them in a pan and poured the lukewarm water of the tap upon them. He carried back the basin carefully and set it on his couch. Into this, he lowered his bandaged foot.

He lay there, relieved a little, one knee up, his head propped by many pillows. His eye rested on a bowl of marigolds sent anonymously a day or two before. Ann, he had thought, or perhaps Shawn, who grew many flowers in his gardens. The marigolds fanned out stiffly from a heavy, cylindrical glass vase. Striated cigarette smoke slowly dispersed above them in the somber air. If there were a presence hereabouts, he thought, surely it would accept an invitation to express itself. No harm in trying. Let it speak. Or let it move something. Let it perform some delicate chore, suitable to its presumptive nature. The flowers, for instance. Let it disturb one—set one bobbing.

This fancy appealed to him—mostly, perhaps, because he had no other urgent occupation. He settled himself and gazed at the flowers, smiling at the picture of himself in the process, and continuing with it, afterward, somewhat doggedly. It is not, he thought, as if the Langer faculty were observing this experiment. The business was his own and, if he chose to make a foolish experiment, he had the right. Concentration, he thought. I will concentrate upon the proposition. That should be a fair contribution to this sort of business. Bill, he thought, Paul, anybody—here I lie. Go ahead and push a flower. It's easy. I'm ready to concede, if the flower moves.

Nothing happened. It will take time, he thought. His lips curved: God knows where these ghosts may have to be summoned from; they may be entertaining lamas in Tibet, or on Polaris. He considered Bill in the light of the little he knew about him. A handsome young man—a football player —and, certainly, an obliging guy. The kind who would go to all manner of trouble to fibrillate a flower, if you really wanted him to. Shawn had a picture of him in his uniform— with Ann. Fine eyes. A good jaw. Resolution. But an unlikely marriage. There were in Ann deep mines a man like Bill could never work—dreamstained pools he couldn't tap. Bill had surely been a sort of woman's-magazine husband— pleasant because he was in excellent health, kind because he had been taught kindness, a model of male physical love—but what else? A woman's-magazine mother had shaped Bill. His otherness was submerged. Whenever Ann elicited a trace of it, he would have become embarrassed or impatient. Had she wanted that? Had she deliberately or unconsciously but wisely chosen a marriage that would not intrude? Did she prefer to live as an exile within herself—a condition which had undoubtedly been forced upon her by her family? Did thoughtful women—sensitive and intelligent wives— sometimes choose such solitude in marriage? And, if so, was it because no men were interested any more in precious elements? Perhaps. Perhaps. Then they were not men, any more, either. They were American husbands. Anyway, the barrier was plain to see in this now-finished marriage.

The flowers—on long, steady scrutiny—seemed to move as a whole—to approach and recede—to waver and dip. It was as if he were looking at them through the various lenses opticians place in frames to test the eyes. The bouquet jumped about, swirled, blurred and doubled. That phenomenon, part subjective and part neurological fault, was in no way deceptive to John. By autohypnosis, he thought, I could easily translate this business, if I were emptyheaded enough, into a Sign. I could say the flowers had moved—and believe it. But they have not moved. He looked away—and looked back. Come on, Bill, his mind murmured. You are losing your audience. But he kept at it for a long time.

Finally, he gave up and closed his eyes.

His thoughts fogged and faded. He fell asleep.

Later, he roused up momentarily. The room was unchanged. His glance rested on the flowers; he smiled and switched out the light.

A sharp thump woke him. His hand shot to the chain on the bridge lamp. He raised up on an elbow. The vase of flowers was gone. It lay on the floor, now, with the flowers fallen; the water, piled by surface tension, spread over the carpet. He watched its flowing edges until they stopped and until the puddles behind them quietly settled out of sight, leaving an amoeba-shaped spot. In the first part of the first second, he forgot his experiment. His swift mind had time to wonder how this could have happened. The vase lay ten feet from his bed, and almost as far from its table, beyond. When he did remember, he was not frightened.

He studied the settling spot and began to think. There was no wind, outdoors. The night hung in warm, wet, motionless veils. He could not see it, but any breeze would have set the palm trees talking. The blue haze of smoke in the room barely stirred—he had done that by sitting up. Or the vase had done it. His foot was still in the pan—although the water was no longer cool. He glanced from his bedside to the table. There were no tracks of the wet foot—no signs of dripping. This was not the result of a waking hypnosis carried out in a dream. Moreover, the vase had not fallen and rolled. There was no wet trail.

Even if he had been the agent of this circumstance—even if some hidden, imponderable force within himself had accomplished it—the vase had been carried into the middle of the room and dropped not by his hands but by—there was a pseudo-scientific name for it—telekinesis. The power to project physical force at a distance from the body. And also, how swift (even granting that crass unlikelihood) had been his return to himself. So swift that the water was still spilling from the fallen vase when he had turned on the light.

He looked at his watch. It was about a minute after midnight. Another person in the house? he thought. A maniac joker? He felt the natural stir of gooseflesh. Why that particular prank, then? The coincidence made such a conclusion

189

preposterous. And he had a feeling he would know—know in his bones—if there were another real human being in the house. No such knowledge existed. He examined the feeling. People sometimes did know—there was no doubting that: smell unrecorded, sound uncatalogued, echo, or the mere detectable presence of another electrical mechanism like the human brain, near-by. Something of that sort. But this?

This one, he slowly thought, is going to haunt me. He chuckled at those words in his mind. The thing to do was to make a meticulous check of all imaginable possibilities—first, lying here, so that his wet foot would not mark the scene—and then going about with great attention.

He spent two hours in that endeavor and reached no other conclusion than that his first observation of the circumstance had been precise. At last, he picked up the vase. I should not touch it, he thought: fingerprints—or brain-energy prints—or, maybe, ghost prints. He replaced the flowers, put the vase back on the table, undressed, and then could not sleep. Dawn found him on his front porch, slapping mosquitoes that came under the old screens—and wondering.

5

BEFORE Josephine's return, John had showered and shaved. He ate his breakfast and drank four cups of coffee. He resisted a strong impulse to discuss the event of the previous night with her. It seemed, simply, foolish. She would probably be scared and quit. His wish to mention it came from such thoughts as that she was a more primitive organism than he, that her approach to reality would be in no sense constricted by the conditions implicit in his own education, and also that, since death had been a regular phenomenon during two billion years of evolution on the planet, her naturalistic attitude toward it might contain inklings more useful to him now than the hints, speculations and doctrines which had arisen among such comparatively recent and juvenile institutions as churches, philosophical systems, and the sciences. But he refrained.

When he had finished his fourth cup of coffee and was idly casting about in his mind for a program for the day, Maddox appeared. It was between eight and nine o'clock—

early—and John had been visiting the offices of the doctor for his therapy—so the call was a surprise.

"I was routed out at an ungodly hour," Maddox said, "for a case north of here. Passing by. I thought I'd stop in and see how you were coming along."

John, by the look of him, was not coming along very well. The morning heat had already dried his hair and the moisture of the air had crinkled it so that it stood above his head in an unsettled fashion. He had not slept after the fall of the vase and his eyes were delicately bloodshot. His skin was grayed by weariness and his fingers suffered from the minute tremor that shakes the tired, the worried, coffee drinkers, and those who smoke too much. John satisfied all those four conditions.

But Maddox merely glanced at him and went on talking. "Okay, I see. Fine. Fine. One or two more shots—proper exercise—and you'll be ready for tennis. It was a nasty sprain."

From that, John knew that the doctor's visit had nothing to do with health. Some different motive had brought Maddox to the Gracey house and John could imagine what it was. On account of that imagining, he led the medical man through the blackout room to the porch and sat down with him there, in the shade. Maddox's glances, en route, had given him away. Upon reaching the veranda, he seemed more relaxed. Josephine offered to make a fresh pot of coffee—offered as if she were mistress of the house, or as if doctors required all possible favor from everybody—and Maddox accepted.

He sat now, his face a dermatological topography in the hard light that fell from the blue sky, his small mustache sagging, and his nutlike eyes fixed on the sea.

"I had an experience with the ghost last night," John said.

"No!"

John began to talk. Maddox laughed lightly and with condescension while John described the beginning of the experiment. At the end, however, the doctor behaved as if the story were a personal challenge which he was obliged to meet. "We'll just go in and you can explain on the ground," he said. "We'll get the data—and find out what really did happen. After all, you probably overlooked something, you know. Had to have, in fact. The thing needs a fresh mind."

John lay on his couch while Maddox hopped and bustled about the room, sipping his coffee between this various activities. He made an estimate of the weight of the vase: two and a half pounds. He measured its content with the help of a cream bottle: two quarts, one skimpy pint. He emptied it and placed it where John said it had lain. He strewed the flowers according to John's directions. He procured the pan in which John had soaked his foot and put the foot in place, although he did not bother to add water. Josephine had moved the bridge lamp; Maddox set it back beside the couch. He then asked the cook for a tape measure, accepted a yardstick, and measured all the distances involved. He next made a thorough inspection of the blackout and ventilation arrangements and thereby assured himself that it would take a considerable wind, outdoors, to produce the merest current of air inside, and a virtual hurricane to set up force enough to hurl the vase from the table.

John had consented to the reconstruction with some slight interest. He wanted to see again, for his own information, the exact dimensions of the incident. But, as Maddox made his estimates and measurements, John began to cherish a concealed amusement. No matter how carefully and how much the doctor measured and weighed, he would not add one jot of new data. John could not help reflecting that this would have been his approach to the problem not long ago. Maddox was doing the scientific thing, as nearly as his implements permitted. He was assaying the scene in order to rule out, one by one, impossible conditions, so that there would be left an "only remaining possibility"—which had to be believed because it was the only remaining possibility.

"I favor," Maddox finally said, "the self-hypnosis theory. You tried to make the flower bob by concentrating. It didn't. You were frustrated. So, when you want to sleep, you fulfilled your wish. You rose and dropped the vase—"

"And hopped into bed and then allowed myself to hear the noise and woke up and switched on the light—*all* while the water was still running out? And *all* without making tracks with my wet foot?"

"Perhaps you wiped up the tracks."

"Wiped them up while the water was running out? Why not try that? The carpet can stand being wet again."

So Maddox tried that. The vase was tipped over and

Maddox counted seconds until John said, "Now!" which he did as soon as the puddle took the approximate size and state of its original. About four seconds had elapsed. "In four seconds," John said, "I could not wipe up my footprints—even if a sleepwalker is smart enough for that—and get back to bed—and so on."

"We rule you out, then," Maddox reluctantly agreed. "We have ruled out the wind. It might have been done by a self-hypnosis, though. You carry the vase to this spot and set it there, upright. You clean up your trail. Then you upset the vase and spring on one foot into bed—"

"Spring three yards?"

"You might. In that state—"

"Look, Henry. Why not say the ghost did it? It's so much easier."

"That is an idea we don't seriously entertain."

"But isn't it, also, much more reasonable? Saner? Therefore more scientific?"

"Rubbish. Why, man, if you really thought there was a ghost in this house—such a thing is a ghost—you wouldn't stay here a minute!"

John was surprised. "Why not?"

"Because—because—well, your whole sense of security would—" He snapped his fingers.

"What sense of security?"

"Oh, very well. Now, take it as an educated man. What's left? Somebody passing through the house. Unlikely—but conceivable. More so than your ghost. An elaborate sleep-walker's joke you played on yourself. Let us say you wrung out your bandages so they wouldn't drip—and hopped. Other agents? A stray pet monkey could have—"

John lay back on the couch and laughed longer and harder than was politely permissible. Maddox watched him —angry, but not wishing to show it. Presently John spoke: "I'm sorry. But there's a great deal of light breaking in on me from all sorts of sources, these days. A stray pet monkey! I don't mean to be rude. But—"

"You're not rude. Not in the least, Galen. You're just—overwrought. I don't think this lonely old house is the right place for you. It's unsettling your perspective."

"It's certainly going to unsettle somebody's perspective! The light I'm talking about is one I'd like to share, though, doctor. Here we are—you—me—everybody—fumbling through our lives, living in the full awareness of our physical environment—and nothing else. Missing, that is, the great adventure in life. The adventure inside. The adventure of and in the realm of the spirit. Imagination. Brain. Call it anything. But there's the great romance—in there. Not out here with the patients, the bank account, and the bedpan. Inside, with the history of all life and the history of the galaxies, with infinite room to roar around in, no boundary, no limit, and you can make it practical whenever it suits you, too. Do you realize that you and I have been brought up— and have brought ourselves up from there—to live like jelly-fish—unaware of what's below, above, or on land, at all— let alone the sky? We approach our internal consciousness from that one, dull, level, not-very-rewarding angle, always. You—and I. Shouldn't we quit this nonsense? Shouldn't everybody?"

"Do you want a world of dreamy philosophers?"

"You bet! Every man and woman—fifty per cent of his time to be spent on voluntary philosophizing."

"What about progress?" Maddox spoke with super-ciliousness.

"Progress? What progress? You mean the vacuum cleaner, the sewing machine, ice cubes, and the war? Oh, they'll come—when we're ready."

Maddox looked at his watch in the physician's ritual preliminary of adieu. "Well, if you feel facetious—it's a good sign. Bring that ankle in at ten, day after tomorrow."

"Okay, doctor." John's irony was lost.

"I'll probably think up some more possible explanations —logical ones—for this business."

"And no doubt I'll see the ghost, meantime."

Maddox nodded absently, looked up sharply, and forced a smile. "No doubt you will. You haven't seen Mrs. Gracey lately?"

"Nope. Not for a few days."

"Or her sister, I presume?"

John's irritation at the question—the manner of it and its timing—was intense. The doctor had shown a repugnant possessiveness of Gail. He kept trying to hide it, as well as all that appertained to it, under a semitransparent cloak of wiles, queries, allusions and stratagems. He had called at this house not to get information but to set at rest a suspicion that Gail might be here. In doing that, he had, without knowing it, submitted a patient who was also a comparative stranger to an investigation that would have mortified Paul Pry. This was the rawest form of ego—childish ego; it could deceive itself even where it was unable to hoodwink others. It was sneaky and mildly detestable and it could not arise from love or from any emotion associated with whatever constituted love.

Damn bad breeding, John thought. He said, "No, I haven't seen her sister." Then he added, to get back his milligram of flesh, "She's away now, is she?"

He watched the flush come, unbeknownst to Maddox. His voice was thicker. "Is she? I hadn't known."

"You couldn't get in touch with her recently, though—"

Maddox nodded grudgingly. "You couldn't either, eh?"

"I hadn't tried. I merely deduced that you had—without success. Well, doctor, mighty kind of you to call."

Maddox's veins swelled. John could almost see his brain printing a schoolboyish rejoinder: You're mighty clever, aren't you? Something of the sort. But the doctor said nothing. He was afraid to try. He nodded curtly and walked from the room.

Shawn, John thought. And this clinically documented juvenile delinquent! What's so unusual or disturbing about her? He had an idea, grinned, shook it off, and lay back again. Nothing to lose, he reasoned. No man could lose that. It wasn't losable, so long as you had not lost yourself, first. He went over to the phone, looked in the book, dialed Western Union, gave Gail's name and address, and dictated: "Call me instantly about a matter that is utterly trivial." He added his name and his number and hung up.

"I'm having company for dinner," he said to Josephine, later that day.

"Yes, sir. Ah know. And you had company after dinner, last night."

"How'd you know that?"

Josephine regarded him—her black face ciphered with lines, gleams, movements, a vast, hinting physiognomy. "I always know when they been places."

"Or listen at doors?"

She laughed. "Don't have to. They make their marks."

John nodded, as if in tacit agreement. "I suppose you know all those things?"

"Ah know a few. Too many."

"Like what?"

"Like who's going to die. Like that."

"Who is?"

The vivid illegibility left her face. She laughed. "Everybody. Some sooner and some later—but everybody, Mr. Galey."

She called him that. Correction had not altered a custom begun at their first meeting. Mr. Galey. Maybe, he thought, Mr. Gailey. Let it be so.

"Have something good, Josephine."

"Yes—sir!"

He went into the middle room again. The flowers stood stiff and cryptic in their vase.

6

HE SWAM out from his private beach in the early afternoon —alone, but not quite alone. The sea was pale sapphire near the shore and undisturbed; his swimming set up the largest riffles on its surface. It was warm, also—so warm that, without looking, it had been impossible for him to tell just how far out he had waded. Days of sultry stagnation—a stagnation relieved but not muddied by the outside pour of the purple Gulf Stream—had allowed every particle of heavy material to sink to the bottom. In consequence, the water had an atmospheric clearness; its smallest breaking sparkled like cut glass; its vaguely stirring calms glistened like changeable silk. He had lain in it, floating, his eyes shut against the stare of the sun, rocked by only the slow lift which came all the way into the beach from the PCs that cruised and paused and practiced turns, miles out.

He could lie there in the transparentness and feel disembodied. He could also walk, peering down at the sand underneath the water and observe small, colored fish; he could set up aquatic sandstorms with his toe. He did not need to discipline his body much, or his mind at all, while doing this. Time did not matter; it lost, indeed, its material aspect; it became a quantity which he could alter at will, like a journey; there was no such thing and there was, concomitantly, an infinite amount of it right at hand. It fitted quantum mathematics: the exact discernment of one aspect of it prohibited any equally exact determination of another; the point of view of the observer provided the only decisive factor—and one could take whichever viewpoint one chose. If one chose no viewpoint, time itself vanished.

He walked, poked with a stick, floated, and indulged himself in wordless soliloquies. Toward the middle of the afternoon, a light breeze sprang up. He went indoors to arrange for the airing of his house. Afterward he dressed and sat under a small ficus reading a book he had just received in the mail. It was Gaunt's *De Rebus Incognitis*. Finally he heard a car in the drive; he finished a paragraph which made him glance once, smiling absently, at the subchasers.

"War will end," Gaunt wrote, "when, first, a majority of the people in one nation have learned to turn their aggressive impulses in upon themselves and not out against man and the world and when, second, this enlightened majority has succeeded in transmitting that concept and that psychological practice to a majority of the people in the rest of the world. The foregoing premise, alone, satisfies the definition of that which causes war and correctly expresses the political possibility of its transmission through a world of separate states in each of which a distinct herd complex has created an ultraego. As long as this herd ego exists, the war syndrome is inevitable. Since it is the product of referred conflicts and aggressions in the individuals composing a state, it can be obliterated only after individual obliteration (or transcendence) has taken place in a majority of the citizens and only after these proselytized mankind. Various religions have undertaken to promulgate that system, but always on the shaky foundation of old dogma, which has lost even its symbological articulation for modern, Western man. It may thus be realized that several societies—or whole civilizations —will probably rise and disastrously fall before a diminution in the numbers and violences of wars will occur. Man at present is scarcely in a position to accept this relatively new function of personality. He is still animal in orientation and his instincts are put to animal pleasure-pain uses. The evolution of intellectual detachment automatically requires this different operation of the aggressive instinct. But it must be operated consciously, because of man's consciousness, and by a majority, because of his social nature. No economic plan or social reorganization will ameliorate his warlikeness because the cause lies in the imbalance of each individual of the species, and is only mirrored by states. The first step is the mere representation of this fact. The second, its teaching. As to the urge toward such steps, besides intelligence, one can only posit the negative factor of desperational degrees to which man will be driven by these myriad individual combats which, unresolved and uncomprehended, sum themselves into the great and otherwise psychobiologically senseless struggles known as war."

At that point John looked toward the diminutive warships and thought that, perhaps, man knew this, but would not admit it. Certainly, if he knew it, he had wasted centuries, fought himself to death by millions, and written libraries to escape or to deny the endless and furious subjective labor it demanded of man. John was aware, now, of Gail, on the crooked path between the conch shells. He rose. She came near—red shoes with platform heels, tanned bare legs, an undistracting, tailored seersucker suit which was light gray, a scarlet bow in her long, lemon-colored hair, eyebrows exact, mouth painted like a single word in man's most archaic vocabulary.

"It was nice of me," she said, "to break a date and come all this way to have dinner with you."

He laughed. "It was nice of me to invite you. Hello, Gail."

"Hello, John Galen."

"I was getting fed up with empty scenery. With having a sprained ankle, which is like being on a leash. And with the unbearable I.Q. of better men than I am." He held out his book.

"*De Rebus Incognitis.* 'Concerning unknown things.'" She read it correctly in Latin and translated literally. Then, still standing, she read to herself. Presently she handed back the book. "Friend of yours?"

"Gaunt? Nope. Never heard of him. Another man sent this to me. A psychoanalyst who is a friend of mine. Name of Johann Altheim."

Gail sat down where he had been. "Were you ever psychoanalyzed?"

He nodded. "I was."

"Did it help you?"

"It did."

"Does that missing link out in the kitchen produce cool, tall iced drinks on demand?"

He bellowed. "Josephine!"

Gail winced. She said, "Helped you how?"

"To get used to myself—and everybody else. It's a knack, you know. Some families don't teach it properly."

"You're telling us Chapman girls! Or—lemme see. *Me dices*. That would be Latin for you're telling me. Right?"

He grinned. "Greek, now."

"In our high school, they didn't have Greek. You'll teach me, though?"

"I don't propose to teach you a damn thing." He sat on the warm sand, beside her.

She looked out to sea. "Ann's Bill was on one of those."

"I know. How is Ann, by the way?"

"I wish you'd get her out of that hotel! She ought to take a job. Or go north and get one. Anything. She just sits around—reads magazines—"

"Slow healer. After all, it hasn't been such a long time."

"She's slow about everything—like a vegetable. Do you think she's pretty?"

"Very."

Gail sighed. "There you are. All men do. And, of course, she is pretty. That's the hell of it. But if you and I are having supper together tonight, mister—" she turned on him eyes that were bright with sarcasm—"to plot companionship hours with my sister, well—"

"Well what?"

"I'll help you plot."

Josephine came with a tray. "Rum collinses," John said.

"I like 'em this way myself!" Josephine bent ponderously to serve.

Gail drank half of hers before the colored woman was out of sight. "They are strictly on the satin side! The missing link must be a lush!"

"Periodic, I understand." His eyes rested on her, appreciating what they saw, assaying the rest. "Companionship hours with your sister was not my program. I didn't have a program. I'm a stranger stranger here, myself, than most.

You seem to have a fraction of a universal tendency—the
tendency to add one and one, whenever a bachelor occurs in
the radius of a spinster, attractive widow, debutante, heiress,
finishing school graduate, or the like. Your sister's charm
and her distress have been touched on teleologically by Shawn
and Thalia, at various times—"

"Shawn!" Gail said emotionally.

Unable to interpret the nature of her emotion, he probed
into it by the oblique method of remaining silent.

She waited for a reaction and none came. "Shawn," she
repeated, "is a complete phony."

"How?"

"He's just a talking machine. He makes up long strings
of words. He rolls them out like ticker tape. They don't mean
anything."

"I take it he said something to offend you? So you
classify him as phony."

She opened her mouth to deny it, changed her mind, and
laughed. "I'll have to brush up on my professors! He certainly did! He spent two or three afternoons dreaming up
things to say to offend me. I thought I'd got myself organized
so that it wasn't possible to offend me. I—"

"That's an interesting idea."

"I don't mean—insult me. I mean—hurt my feelings.
People kicked my feelings around for years. Maybe just life
did, too. I got sick of it. I was always like somebody doubled
and vulnerable in bridge. You can't go on forever like that.
I decided to be what I was—after taking a long look around
at other people—and just pass up anybody who didn't approve of my system. People are hypocrites—and jealous,
besides."

"You're sure of that?"

"Now you're talking like Shawn! Of course I'm sure!"
She finished her drink and set the glass on the ground.

"And you're sure you are—being whatever you are?
What's that?"

"There is only one possible motto in this world—and
people everywhere are at last getting wise to it: Have fun.
I've had plenty, since I found it out. Before that, I had nothing but grief. From the time I was a little kid. Now—
whether it's a job, or a date with somebody I like, or a date
with somebody I don't especially like but who can—well,

help me in the main things—I just ask myself if it's going to contribute to the general gaiety of one Gail Chapman—and I get the answer right off—and I say yes or no, accordingly."

"And what's fun?"

She took the question seriously. "Not to be kicked around. Not to be somebody's property. Not to have a boss. To have plenty of clothes and be healthy and independent."

"You are independent? You feel that?"

"There isn't anybody on this earth," she answered, "I can't look in the eye and tell to go to hell."

"But can you do it to everybody? That's the real test."

Her reaction was paroxysmal. She slapped the arm of her chair with her red-nailed hands and stamped her red-leather shoe on the ground. "That's the very verbatim question Shawn asked! The answer is—nobody can tell everybody, all at the same time, to go to hell. You've got to have some people. Otherwise you'd be strictly alone, wouldn't you? At which point you'd be nowhere. And precisely nobody."

John's gaze strayed away from her toward the weather-beaten house. His eyes held a satisfied amusement. He had caused her to define herself: she lived by a "system" that had turned her into nobody. The amusement became sardonic as he thought of the millions upon millions of Americans who lived, knowingly or not, by that simple-minded formula. And who were nobody. The weight of those numbers oppressed him and lowered the light in his eyes. People who were nobody inside themselves were capable of anything—because it would be, always, nobody doing it. People who had signed over their self-respect to the pursuit of pleasure and the avoidance of pain could not even let themselves respect others, who lived on a higher level, simply because the mere act of respect granted would reawaken their own consciences and start the disintegration of their vain scheme of life. All such persons, all the millions, had to believe that every man and woman alive was no loftier, inside, than they were. The welter of twisted thinking, of mob emotionalism, and of vulgar cynicism—the beatification of pipsqueaks and the vilification of decent citizens—sprang from the perquisites of this single process. Have fun. It had ground Greece into the earth, ruined Rome, written the fate of France in its moral ashes, and it was flickering and chewing like secret fire in the heart of America. The people had decided that pursuit of happiness meant the right—and not just the right, but the constitutional compulsion—to pursue pleasure.

"Well?" she asked impatiently.

"I was thinking. On account of the war, people are having less and less fun. Fun is going to dwindle down mighty thin, in America. Ann, for instance, is having a whole lot of no fun right now. And God knows how many there will be like her."

"I'm sorry for Ann," Gail answered quietly. "I used to hate her. When she was little, she was too damn nice to be human. There she was—always a couple of grades ahead of me—always getting the good marks—always raising the dahlias or baking the cake that took the prize—and me always trailing, just because I happened to be younger. Once, when I was about nine, I tried to drown her for it. Can your Gargantua repeat?"

"My Ganymede?" He bellowed, "Josephine! One more!" He turned to her. "Drown Ann?"

"Kid stuff. But I meant it!" Her lips grew taut at the recollection. "There was a rain barrel out behind our house under one corner of the barn. Mother was away. School was out; it was summer—and hot. Ann and I decided to get undressed and take a dunk in the barrel. It was full from a whole string of thunderstorms. She went first. She undressed stark-naked and she climbed in. She pinched her nose and said to see how long she could hold her breath and squatted clear down under with one hand up, the way kids do. Her pigtails floated. And I leaned over the barrel and watched her down there and all of a sudden all the times she'd showed me up rushed into my head. I didn't see red—I saw a billion sparks. I waited until I thought she'd be about out of breath and then I held her down. By both pigtails. I jumped right up on the barrel to do it. She pushed and jerked her head and tried to bend my fingers. I kept pushing her back so she couldn't get her feet under her. Bubbles came. I got scared and let go, then, and she stood up. Her face was lavender. She leaned over the edge of the barrel and was sick. And she got out, finally, and walked away. She didn't say a word. Not then and not ever. I hated her for that more than anything. For not telling on me. I hated her so much that I even hated myself for not holding her down till she drowned and then getting my clothes on and telling people I didn't know where she was. Kids are like that. But when they grow up—they forget they were like that. They pretend they never did anything mean or cruel. But they do."

"Yeah. They do."

Josephine brought the second rum collins; it was evident that she had prepared it before being called. Gail took it. "Everything was like that. I wore her clothes when she was finished with them. Did you ever wear anybody's cast-off clothes?"

"No. I can't say I ever did."

"It isn't anything that people ought to do to dogs. Secondhand skin! The kids used to mention it. 'You don't look as nice in that dress as Ann used to.' Things like that. And it kept on being that way. She went to college—and Mother found out there wasn't enough money to send me. Ann could have gone only two years—or worked her way—but she didn't. So I went to nursing school. Why? Because anything was better than sitting in the parlor when the boys called and being the uneducated sister. I stayed till I graduated and Todd came along and that was that."

"You were married?"

"I was still young enough and fool enough to be the kind that can get a lump in their throat. Todd gave it to me. He wasn't my first beau—not by plenty. I did have the satisfaction, when I was sixteen, of getting out of the gawky stage and turning into something that wasn't just a used-jalopy copy of Ann. I was blonde, for one thing, and that helped. I finally got a figure. And nurses learn a lot. I'd thought of that before I'd become a probationer. Things girls need to know. But I got lumpy about Todd—he was the impractical kind, always hoping something wonderful would happen tomorrow and not even keeping his socks up today. He had a trailer and a car and about fifteen hundred dollars and he had decided to go-west-young-man. I was sick stiff with the hospital—I'd been reprimanded three times that one week. Todd—and another date. I got that feeling that I'd do anything to get away—and when I get that, something has to pop. Maybe you've had it?"

"Sure."

"And what do you do? You—"

He interrupted. "I stick around. I don't like to have a

feeling that anything or anybody or any process inside me can drive me out of a place. So I stick."

"I'm not built that way."

She had lifted her drink and was holding it in front of her eyes. With her left forefinger she drew a design in the condensed vapor that frosted the tall glass. He saw the design and ignored it. She was drinking now, slowly, steadily, in small swallows. He thought of what she had said: I'm not built that way. The cheapest alibi in the book. But, again, millions rested their cases for themselves upon it. They wouldn't try. They wouldn't listen to their deep wants —so, finally, even the wishes that came to the surface were debilitated—and they failed, blundered, quit, sinned, hurt others. But they would never accept the facts. I'm not built that way. Individualism had to be responsible because irresponsible individualism was decadent. But you said, I'm not built that way—and you set yourself cheek by jowl with Pilate, washing his hands.

She went on. "One week I was put on night ward duty when it wasn't my turn. The superintendent was a cross between six skunks and a leper. One of those sex-crazed spinsters that is always interfering with other people because she never had any fun herself. I was sore. It was raining— and Todd was getting desperate and threatening to go west without me—and I'd been scared for a few days that I was pregnant. Oh, it was a pretty mess, any way you sliced it. Even though I was a nurse I used to be careless and I used to drink too much. So what. So we got married and started west. He had ranch ideas. I figured that once we got out on the coast I could talk him into ranching somewhere in the general vicinity of Hollywood. I had visions of either getting work as an extra or hanging around the right places and the right people until I got asked. Anyway—we went. But there was one side of Todd I hadn't figured. He was as limp as a wet cooky about doing anything that would really get him ahead in the world. But when it came to changing his ideas after we were married, I never saw or heard of such stubbornness. The first few days, we dawdled along and had a wonderful time. I like to remember it even now. It was a regular honeymoon. Then I hinted—just barely hinted— about Hollywood."

She was silent.

"No go?" he asked.

"No go? I'll say, no go. He was the everlasting red light on that. Of course, when hinting didn't work, I tried discussing, then arguing, then I even got hysterical. And he just sat there—saying I was his wife and going to have his child and he was deciding such matters. I thought it would blow over. I just couldn't believe that a mouse would have the will power of an elephant, and that's where I was crazy. We went to a place he knew of—a hole-in-the-wall in some desert mountains—and we set up the trailer and I actually had my kid there—with a doctor from forty-seven miles away who nearly missed the party. We were there a year after that." She thought about that year for several seconds. Then she shrugged. "A typhoid carrier moved into a shack up the creek from that half-horse burg—and nearly everybody got it. I didn't—because I'd had shots, being a nurse. Todd got it and the baby got it and I sat up day and night with them and they both died."

Her face, he saw, was turned stonily toward the sea.

"That's tough."

She looked around at him. Her cheeks were rosy from the two drinks. Her eyes were liquid and direct. Her mouth was a level line of suffering remembered with bitterness. "Yes. It was tough. It is tough for Ann to have a husband die—let alone a baby. I didn't even have money left for a funeral for them—not a decent one. They were buried like dead dogs. And I left there and I did go to Hollywood and I got a job. Not in pictures. They don't put hags in pictures and I was a hag then. I got a job working at steam tables in a cafeteria. Then as a waitress. And when I got a little money, and my strength came back, I started applying for work as a model. Finally, I was taken out on a road show of a line of dresses—and then I went to work in a wholesale house in New York. It took me all that time before I even had a chance at a good agency. After that, I was a showgirl in *Blackouts of 1940,* and I came down here last winter."

John said nothing.

"So—maybe you can see how come I finally adopted the theory about having fun. I hadn't had much."

"Yes. I can see."

"I don't often tell the story of my life. Not on two drinks, anyhow. But, after all, having you move in here

205

makes a difference. You're sort of a member of the family on account of it. Not a relative—but one of those adopted members that families take on. I'm sure Ann feels the same way. She said when she first saw you, she felt as though she'd known you all her life—and wished she had."

"Did she?"

"She did. But try and make her admit it. That's the sort of thing she'll say—impulsively—and deny before firing squads, if necessary. She's that sort of girl. I don't get it."

"And what sort are you?"

"What sort do you think?" She was not being coy.

He looked at her steadily—at her face and her long, lithely voluptuous body—at the unnatural loveliness of her hair and the deft parentheses above her beautiful eyes. "Why, you're a chippy."

"What!"

"Very gorgeous. Very effective. Very desirable. Very exclusive. Very modern and sophisticated and suitable and good-at-it. I didn't say there was anything wrong with chippies, did I?"

Indignation made her pale. It spoiled the relaxed composition of her face. John had always been of the opinion that men who thought that anger enhanced the appeal of women were men so undiscerning that they could not tell their own emotions apart. Such an attitude was primitive and therefore juvenile. He considered that opinion now. Anger removed Gail from the female category and made her over into a mere person—a sexless person in an ugly, repellent state. She rose, evidently with the intention of leaving, or of pretending to be leaving.

John yelled, "Josephine!" so loudly that she flinched. He added in the same jovial, roaring tone, "Two more!"

She stood still, looked down at him, tried to smile, turned back, and seated herself. "I think I will stay awhile longer. I'd like to hear the apology you owe me."

He grinned. "I was guessing, of course, Gail. But I'm a wizard at guessing. You see, I'm not a businessman, for one thing. That is, I don't have to conduct all the operations of my brain against the background of being afraid to do anything or to say anything which might offend anybody in such a way as to lessen my profits. I can always throw over trade—and experiment and teach. But, again, I'm not

206

merely a professor who has to watch out for the sacred icons of a faculty. I can always quit the classroom and the lab and manufacture something. Besides shaking the dust of either one off my feet, I can shake both—because I am also a man of independent means. And, if I lose my money, I can work. I might become a painter, for example. I've had fun trying it, lately. Or—I might manage one of these alabaster towers that Miami Beach calls hotels. That takes only rudimentary training, I imagine. Anything. Furthermore, I am a bachelor. I do not even have to consider what my wife would think, as most married men feel they have to, before stating an opinion. I—"

"Okay," she said, still annoyedly. "So where does that take us? You called me a chippy. Are you trying to explain that it won't do me any good to sue you?"

He chuckled cheerfully. "In a way, yes. I'm trying to explain that I am, by choice and effort, an individual in that position so rare in this century—though so necessary and easy to achieve—of being able to say what I think. To achieve the position, all you do is to take it—and its consequences. The results may be exceedingly perturbing to your situation but, if so, it only proves that you were in a desperately bad circumstance anyhow—and better be done with it."

"Shawn called me a chippy, too. Though I must say he was more hateful about it."

"Oh?"

"The simpering, self-righteous—" She broke off and blushed. "Go ahead. Have fun. If you trip me often enough, I may get so I enjoy the sleighride."

"I wasn't tripping you, though. Chippy means unconventional—really. It refers to a girl who is a pickup. I know. One of the young ladies in one of my classes broke an inkwell on the head of one of my gentlemen students over that very term. I became painfully familiar with it, owing to the event. It was discussed at a faculty meeting when the young man's suspension was being considered. A doxy is definitely a loose woman. A prostitute belongs to the whole world, for a price. Tart was once an expression of endearment which, somehow, has tarnished with time. There is no name for your condition as I conceive it. That is, I assume you make love to gentlemen who see to it that you do not want for the little niceties and comforts of life—hundred-dollar bills and paid-up rent. You can stop blushing, because I am being very abstract about this matter. Mere philological byplay. Yet you are also something of a priestess, a lady greatheart—and you doubtless bestow favors upon the needy. Sometimes, too, you must act as Cupid's marionette, passion's toy, the steel fragment that leaps perforce to the passing magnet. You feel you cannot help yourself in these encounters any more than the bright bit of metal that jumps from the inert dross. That 'dross' would be the more inhibited and hence less responsive womanhood."

"You put it so beautifully that I would like to bust you right on the nose!" She set her third drink on the ground without tasting it.

John eyed her solemnly. "There are hundreds of thousands of girls and women in somewhat the same category in America today. It is a group that has been increasing rapidly and steadily. Small-town girls come to big cities, learn, and enlist in it. I trust I will not add to your offense by pointing out that the population of New Lancaster is not great. A certain measurable but unmeasured percentage of divorcees falls into your interesting classification. As the number of females passes the number of males in the nation—and especially if the casualties are great in the war—the category will become enormous. It may never be a political bloc, because there is some prissiness, here, about admitting the facts of life. But it will be influential. Incidentally, I often reflect that what we call the 'facts of life' are the very data we Americans most rigidly keep secret—a curious circumstance which means in effect that we do not admit facts here, and do not live according to fact at all."

"At last you've said something."

John nodded agreeably. "I am just barely intelligent enough to realize that sex 'morals' are really not morals at all. Not ethics—but mere custom and mere manners. Within extremely wide limits, the behavior of others in this affair does not disturb my sensibilities."

"What limits?"

"That piece is on another record."

"I'd like to hear it."

"Maybe you will. You see, I was going to add that, while I trust I am not a bluenose about you and/or Jane Doe, I was brought up in such a way that every time I think of liberty in the sex department, the words 'license,' 'transgression,' and so on, appear automatically."

"You should get over it."

"Difficult. It's like trying to get over being a Methodist. Echoes of the evangelical shibboleth hide in corners of your mind to pop out at you just at the most embarrassing moments. I realize this attitude is going to date me, very soon."

"It already has dated you."

He thought a moment, and sighed. "Yes. I presume it has—though I hate to admit it. I belong to the latest lost generation. The generation of hot mammas and sugar daddies, gold diggers, the Charleston and the shimmy. The age of gilded youth and flaming youth, of John Held, Junior, and F. Scott Fitzgerald. The age of what is now nostalgically remembered by a growing few as 'the old Smart Set.' You wouldn't know—so don't ask—and don't ask about dun't esk. The shifters and the Utellems and the flappers and the finale hoppers. Greenwich Village meant free love in those days— a term now rendered obsolete by its own full flowering. Women were battling for freedom, equality, independence, the right to smoke in restaurants without being heaved into the street, the right to make up their lips in public, and the right to enter bars, in my day. They were just one short jump beyond the suffragettes. Skirts went up above knees, alcohol in that dim epoch was gin, largely Gordon's, largely synthetic, and necking parties were heavy or plain, conducted in parked Stutz Bearcats, Cole Chummy Roadsters, model T Fords, and the like. What high school girls calmly refer to as petting in these days was still mostly morbid psychopathology which we read in Havelock Ellis. There was the camel walk, and the toddle too. You wore bell-bottom trousers. You pulled a man's necktie out and when he looked down, you snapped him on the nose by raising your finger. A polite age."

He lighted her cigarette. "Go on," she said.

"That's epitaph enough. Looked back on, as yard goods, it becomes not so much an era or a generation in itself as a stage of transition. We felt that we established a separate time, that we took on a lasting color, that we were a finished expression of sorrow for the war dead and cynicism toward the Victorian viewpoint. We were wrong. We were only the early drift that is maturing swiftly now. America is about to lose another generation. And what will the next, postwar 'lost generation' be like? Isn't it obvious in surveys of the morals—so called—of soldiers? Of school children? Isn't it apparent in juvenile delinquency statistics? In the increasing public insistence upon legal birth control and the distribution of prophylactic information—not to mention the venereal disease campaigns? This was—is—total war. After it will come the total jump. The same science that has liberated man from the hand chores of all the past centuries has liberated him, potentially, from the physical penalties of promiscuity. And, in this civilization, where the physical advance always arrives before the spirit has had a chance to anticipate, evaluate and prepare for it—let alone to get accustomed to it—we are going to have a great and nation-wide despecialization of the libido."

"It's here already, I say."

"And you doubtless speak with some knowledge! But how to adjust to it is another thing. Our customs, our religious codes, our laws, and our medical practice are all out of gear with the situation. In that discrepancy the new generation will get lost by the hundreds of thousands—or millions—just as we did to a less degree in our hiatus. Their lack of 'morals' will lead them into crime and into mania, not because sex is degrading but because a long American tradition has held it to be. If you are immoral, the schools and churches insist, you will soon become a thief and a scoundrel. The impulse to make love is different from the impulse to rob, but until the difference is publicly admitted, the loving young may readily become criminal. It's a revenge mechanism of the frustrate. If some gent were to proclaim the facts as fact and insist that people catch up to them in attitude, dogma, legislative procedure and medical practice, the coming lost generation might be saved. However, the older folks, fat with jealousy, spleen—fear, would fall apart like trampled eggshells. Since they make the rules and do not, by God, intend to fall apart—there is going to be one hell of a ruckus."

"And when it is all over," Gail said, "and a sensible, decent attitude about love exists everywhere—when people aren't possessive about each other any more, in the terrible way that they are—"

"—it will be the year Nine Million."

"I don't think so! I think—sex just won't be so important in so many absurd ways and so many harmful ones. Everybody will be sexy and nobody will mind. People will have children by people they want to have them by. You'll be able to have a family if you want to—but having families won't be practically compulsory, the way it is now."

"A point."

"Did you ever hear, for instance, about the Eskimos?"

John laughed. "Only—every time this topic comes up. Yes. There are the Eskimos, lending their wives to each other, having families, and still staying happy. Psychologically, the thing is feasible. But it will take a lot of changes in our present way of thinking. That's why I give it nine million years."

"Which only shows that you don't go around with the right kind of people. I could introduce you to some—"

"Cribbage and canoodling? A collation with after-dinner concupiscence? A little theater party and let's toss coins for the girls? I'm too austere for it."

"Have you ever tried it?"

"I must admit, I haven't."

"Then you don't know anything about it. It's saved quite a lot of marriages I know of—people who were really in love, too. You can't just suddenly get married and stay perfectly ecstatic with one type of man or woman continually, forever. Not if you grew up going out with all the boys. Or girls."

He looked at her with what he imagined was a minor kind of awe. He realized, however, that the expression was not compatible with what, for her, was simple sincerity. The condition he had theoretically foretold a moment ago, she was casually explaining—and it was he, not she, who was startled by the truth.

In his mind there came a picture—ironic and perplexed —of America as a sort of enormous bawdyhouse. That wasn't right. Bawdyhouses connoted illegal lust, dark alleys, the exchange of money, the embarrassment of public choice— and haste. Rabbit warren? No. A kind of nursery—with the children all adults but wrestling together in the undifferentiated amorousness of infants. Families living in gigantic apartment houses to be near enough to—more people. Every child a foundling—and not many children, at that. Men and women working together—union hours and wages—in a hundred thousand factories that would turn out whatever gadgets these entwined child-adults wanted. Everything clean and sterile and impersonal and—yes, damn it, scientific—and lascivious. It wouldn't be vicious. It wouldn't even hurt them. Maybe it might be fun, as Gail said. No locks on doors in coeducational colleges. Come in, Joe, or is it you, Bill? No reproof. A great, new, orgiastic religion might arise in which sexuality would be used directly by the new churches as it was unconsciously, even now. Sex solved—and what new riddles were to be studied next? The libido of humanity set free. And would they be infant-adults, as he imagined, or would they be the kind of persons Huxley had imagined in his similar circumstance? Were they really bent on finding out—by doing? Had he not just said, indeed, that they were embarked upon that precise course? Was he behaving, in his own mind, like a Pharisee? Should he take not only this girl, who appeared to have accepted such conditions, but Ann also, and Thalia, Shawn's wife? Should he not object, furthermore, if the compliment were returned by Maddox? Obviously, one would hold a poor view of that. But could he tell? Were not these nebulous future people different? They simply would not be John Galens, Thalias, Maddoxes, Anns —or anybody like them. They were planetary inhabitants toward whom one felt a sort of fear, a hatred, or an envy, because they were one's bounden successors: they might live in a better world and have a better time. Preposterous!

These days, people did not try to plan any sort of stored happiness for others. They tried to squeeze out all pleasure for themselves. And the generation to come be damned. Let them pay the taxes. Let them worry about the spread of venereal disease. Let them fret about the birth rate. Let them face the problems pertinent to increasing promiscuity. Let them figure out the consequences of science and sex. The hell with them! We have troubles enough of our own. That was the popular if unexpressed attitude. And, in the sense that he was taking no intellectual responsibility for envisaging the future connoted by his appraisals, it was his present attitude. For a moment, he thought of Gail almost with admiration. Having fun. Life was not that easy. It would never be. And what unborn generations did about their sex mores was their business. What the young generation did, concerned it alone, also. He had come from a past to which, in some respects, it was necessary for him to be loyal. The trick was not to meddle—to assist when asked—but to do no ignorant and gratuitous pontificating. To make suggestions rather than to hand down laws.

"You're thinking it over," Gail said at last.

"I certainly am! The trouble is—I have to think with a mind that hasn't the proper background in experience. I can't know where I'm prejudiced—or absurd—and where I'm being honest and logical."

"You could get the background."

He shook his head. "Nope. My ideas of sex manners came out of the nineteen-twenties. Yours, from the thirties. The ideas that are going to make the next big mark will come from people who had their first kiss in the forties. Neither of us can imagine what those ideas will be: we're already too old. Different, yes. Freer, yes. But it's none of our business. Funny that people cannot see change at hand, or even the impermanence of the changes they themselves represent. Now is always right."

Josephine's voice was like a gong: "Supperrrrr!"

For a considerable while, Gail and John gave full attention to the dinner, which Josephine served with gusto and headshakes—the former owing to her relish for her own cooking of such dishes as smothered chicken, mashed potatoes, peas with lettuce and onions, and shortcake; the latter because, so far as John could determine, Josephine seemed to feel that Gail was both a too-obvious huzzy and a huzzy whom, obviously, no man could meet and let alone. She flashed white smiles at the compliments paid to her dinner; she thumped and muttered in the kitchen after every staring circuit of the table. Once, she even twitched her head communicatively at John; trouble, her eyes gleamed, but the kind you can't resist. The performance amused him. Gail did not seem to notice it.

They had their coffee on the veranda. The sun sank slowly and the clouds cast their spell—a spell like a working of a remote, natural intellect in most places, but in Florida close, intimate, seemingly touchable magic.

Gail took up her argument again, and John realized all at once that it was purposeful. Other men, other methods. As inevitable for her to do this as the rest of her functions

213

were inevitable. Yet hers was not the textual nymphomania —the psychic disease of insatiate frigidity; it was a collective attitude of certain women nowadays—an example of specific, current emotional manners—transitional, too—but unreadable, as an omen. Because she had gauged him as an articulate, thinking man, she was translating her personality into what she regarded as the suitable language. A properly selected sentence, she undoubtedly felt, would be more effective than the pasted smiles, rolling eyes, crossing legs of a whole chorus line.

That amused him. Loss of a night's sleep had largely anaesthetized his consciousness, but yet sharpened it in small, peculiar ways. When fatigue narrows the field of awareness it also implements minor knowing with novel, compensatory apperceptions. Gail was unsubtly launching upon his mind small waves of amorous monologue disguised as sociology; but he dwelt in a different place. She might have been more effective at the level on which she lived: Lilith was, first of all, a fine she-animal. That notion annoyed him. How everlastingly men like himself conjured up the pseudo-ennoblement of classic images, of Lilith and Circe, to explain in heady terms their baldest biological behavior. To hell with Lilith. Take her as she is and as nothing more. Such archetypes had disturbed men like Shawn and distracted the doctor.

"If you went around the way I do," she was saying, her husky voice modulated to the sound of thoughtfulness, "you'd know about the kids. A lot of their parents behave the same way they do. But a lot more would find their hair standing on end if they could spend about eight evening hours with their precious Charlies and Annabelles. Some parents do finally discover that they're licked. Some shut their eyes good and tight—they want their kids to keep up with the Jones kids. They hope for the best—and don't look at what they suspect. But most of them simply don't know and they wouldn't believe it if they saw it."

"Sure," he said. "At Langer—"

"You see, all the parents working on all the kids all the time can have a terrific hunk of their holy teaching undone by one high school kid. One girl goes out with an older fellow. One boy gets tangled up with maybe some sophisticated dame whose husband's at war. Then that one boy or that gal starts doing missionary work among the other kids, and pretty soon they all know all the stuff—or think they do. And if you believe that a fifteen-year-old girl doesn't want to be taken out by a college boy or maybe a first lieutenant, you're crazy. And when she finds out all it takes is just a little info, she hurries up and gets the dope and out she goes. Only—she usually doesn't get enough dope."

"I take it you're making an argument for the instruction of the young in hygiene and birth control and such."

"You bet I am! And out of the kindness of my heart, too. More than one time I've had a boy friend go soaring off with somebody sweet sixteen. Nobody can stop the soaring any more, but they at least could make it healthy. At least. I strongly disapprove of having my boy friends put out of action by dopey kids. Strongly. Unless this great republic wants to run itself as a venereal ward and an illegitimate baby hospital, it's got to face what's happened to it. You can talk church and home and school and proper environment and juvenile courts and law and morals till you're black in the face—but you're talking about something that wouldn't have worked twenty years ago and that doesn't even exist today."

"Speaking as an observant professor who has argued the same thing among horrified academicians for a long time —although in different terms—I agree."

"You do?" She seemed surprised.

"Yes. Not for me. For the future we were discussing before dinner. The future people. I have listened to a great many pedants on the matter. They seem to have a mystical conviction that what they call the 'pendulum' will 'swing the other way.' Juvenile statistics—and what goes on under their noses—have frightened them silly. So they have made the idiotic assumption that somehow, for an unknown reason, there is going to be a great, spontaneous return to chastity after the war. It is hardly worthy of them, as logic. I can see nothing to support it. I ventured to argue, several times, that all the evidence—every iota of it—pointed to the contrary situation. I suggested that the large burst of what was called 'emancipation' after World War I will be paralleled, after this one, by a revolution in sex mores which will make the flaming youth in my day seem pretty wan. That is, I gave 'em both barrels of what we discussed before dinner. I took the view that this 'pendulum' theory was wishful thinking

and decidedly nonscientific of them. I suggested that there
was no true historical precedent for the bland notion that
either promiscuity or chastity is cyclical. And I further
pointed out that man had never before possessed a technique
for both escaping and curing venereal disease or a means
to prevent conception. Now that he has it, I argued, the whole
picture of life between men and women has been changed,
forever. I pointed out that we would not know how it had
changed until it should stabilize, several generations hence.
And I suggested that, in the meanwhile, instead of hopelessly
trying to impose old and no longer pertinent codes upon a
society that was breaking them on every hand, we might at
least apply common sense, to keep ourselves well and to stop
child motherhood, until such a time as a new way of life
among men and women should emerge and mature of
itself."

"No kidding. Did you say that at your college?"

"Whenever I had a chance. I even went further. I suggested that these circumstances were more significant than
any which had arisen among human beings for several centuries. Possibly for millennia. I offered the thought that control of the biological consequences of sex relationships was
as new and different an order-of-magnitude change as the
discoveries of fire, the wheel and gunpowder. It is a measurelessly more impressive factor than, say, communism, fascism,
or such. But perspective upon it is zero. People are too familiar with it to see its immensity. It is treated as a gadget
phenomenon, like automobiles, or a public health predicament,
like measles, or a matter of modesty, like the annual diminution of bathing suit area. It is nothing like that. It is punctuation put after all human evolution to date. It is a great question mark set facing the future. It will affect the home and
the family, love and marriage, the well-being of the world,
and even the very numbers of us, from now on. It posits
problems too vast to tackle, let alone to solve, in a mere generation. It cuts through our entire psychobiological gamut—
and demands a new start. It makes vain, in a sense, all the
traditions of virginity in which we have so carefully nurtured
ourselves for so many centuries, under the impression that
the practice was civilized and altogether desirable. It separates the meaning of the word 'lover' from the meaning
of the word 'father.' It separates the meaning of the word

'mother' from the meaning of the word 'love.' It takes from the word 'child' the intellectual construction of natural consequence. It lifts physiological tabu from adolescence.

"It does this now, in effect, to millions. In a period not far from the present, when the techniques are simpler and surer and an understanding of them has become common knowledge for all people of all ages, the entire instinctual basis of love and marriage and parenthood will be subject to voluntary modification in any way and at any time that seems desirable to any one couple. From the sociological and the psychological standpoint, this is a new dimension.

"No wonder every sort of person who is imbued with old traditions, and every sort of institution which depends upon old traditions—and that is almost a definition of the word 'institution'—throw their panicky weight full force against the spread of the information which will ineluctably lead to this new state. They cannot do otherwise because to them there is no choice: they know that if they do not resist successfully, they will either wither or survive so changed that their very irrecognizability would seem tantamount to destruction. And yet the people themselves, and the people within the institutions, are covertly and swiftly taking up with the new knowledge and the new practices. They do it covertly because they do not have the courage to defy orthodoxy—but they do it. And they will never stop.

"The immediate and manifest returns to be had from this new way of life are too large to be cast aside by contemporary man. We have not evolved even distantly close to the point at which we can take a rational view of our sex instinct. Irrationality and capriciousness are the very stuff of its folklore and its song—the very substance of what we call romance. So it is impossible for us instantly to develop a reasonable and logical set of mores toward birth control and the present end of venereal disease.

"To make any such system effective, every woman would have to be a genius and every man a judge. Since they are not, we can expect no system of ideal behavior to accompany the liberation of physical love. This is the end of the line for human sociology to date. But we people on this planet will have to go on evolving new rules and new habits and enduring new trials and making new errors under this awe-striking change—learning the hard way, by doing—just as we always have. Whether we wind up, a thousand years from now, with each girl obliged by a state to have three babies, or with each girl feeling that three must be her minimal quota owing to an element of conscience put into her by the development of some new dogma not extant today, or whether we simply peter out, or whether there should arise a great abundance, a vast tolerance, a love of children and of everybody's children alike, and we people in some far-off date shall have learnt spiritual love through the proliferation of physical love—depends not upon the dicta of a person today, not on the church, or the schools, or the home of this hour—and not upon our logic—but upon what we may learn in the future by the application of our new knowledge.

"It's a half-blind or actually a ninety-nine per cent blind knowledge now. But knowledge it is and it can never be erased. We have it here among us. That's why I agree with you. Let's attack the one aspect of it where we can do some good: health. That, at least, can be done to help us get a good start. What comes next, I do not know. I will not live to see, probably. I suppose the first men who discovered how to keep fire used it to throw in each other's faces, torture enemies and sacrifice children over. We're in about that relative state in reference to our new power over birth and our new dominion over the terrors of disease." He stopped. After a moment, he laughed lightly. "I certainly got wound up. But, no kidding, that's the truth—or something much more like the truth, and more like what lies ahead, than all the magnificent puddles of bilge that flow today out of everything from the Catholic Church to the marriage and divorce manifestoes of Communist Russia."

Gail said, "Golly."

"Why 'golly'?"

She leaned back in the gathering gloom and stretched her long length. "When you want to, you can talk like a locomotive on a downgrade. It's something like Shawn—only he always talks at things. He's mad or he's amused. You just think out loud. And maybe you're right. Maybe we just imagine we know what we're doing—and never really know at all."

"We never really know at all. That is, not many of us, for much of the time."

"And you're certainly right about disease. Venereal

218

disease. Thinking of it as a nurse, you're so right it hurts.
Thinking of it as a girl—you're right enough to make me
sore."

"It's a pretty good example of people not knowing what
they're doing. Venereal disease hasn't anything to do with
sex. Not anything. That has been an established fact for a
long time. The so-called venereal diseases happen to be an
unrelated series of sicknesses which are most easily communicated by sex relations. That doesn't make them 'venereal'—a part of love and Venus—any more than sore
throat. It's a coincidence. A bacteriological accident. In that
sense, strep sore throat is as much a venereal disease as
lues—you can get it by kissing; and babies catch g.c. from
carelessness. If venereal disease were a punishment for sin,
a nifty idea our forefathers subscribed to, it would be the
most evil and dishonest punishment ever contrived—because
it never hits those who 'sin' with the healthful, and it often
afflicts those who go about doing God's work with "innocent'
spouses. Just another medieval attitude of these middle ages
we live in. An attitude like the one we used to have toward
vaccination. As soon as we got smallpox whipped, we realized what damned fools we were. We'll do it about v.d., too
—as soon as we quit calling it v.d. and think of each illness
by its right and separate name."

"Did Josephine take the rum home with her?" Gail
asked.

John apologized. "I don't drink much—very often. She
didn't take the rum. Or the sherry or the brandy or the
Scotch or the rye."

"Then I'll switch to Scotch." He rose. "I'll help. I
forgot your ankle. Sitting down, you look pretty competent."

They went in together and made drinks. When they came
out again, they had turned on the radio and pulled aside
the Navajo rug. They left the house dark to satisfy the
coastal blackout regulations. The strains of "Blues in the
Night" swung and swam in the oppressive atmosphere.

"'My mammy done tole me,'" Gail chanted. She had a
good voice for that sort of song.

The orchestra revived an old one. She sang that. He
sipped his highball.

"'Good news—you're what I've waited for—I wasn't
slated for blues! Good news is wel—come to me! Bad news

is he—ll come to me! So, Mister Good News—come right here to me, good—you're going to do me good—news!'"

He shut his eyes. The water fell gently on the beach. It was long ago. He was on a steamer, in a deck chair, going to Europe and the band was playing and the people were dancing and the ship was moving with a gentle gush like this. Good News. The air was salty—like this, and he had a highball at his side—like this. The house began to move in his imagination. Europe. The flat-faced, foreign buildings would be gray in the morning light when they docked at Le Havre. The French customs officials would bicker and bob, waiting for a small tip. The train would ramble down to Paris with the Americans singing—Good News. I wasn't slated for blues. All the taxi horns would be chiming like bells on the Paris streets. The evenings would be soft as rainbows. There'd be crowds at the Dôme and the Cupole and the Select and other crowds at the Café de la Paix, if you stayed on the Right Bank. Only, he liked the Lutetia. He liked to walk along the stilted boulevards and take his place unctuously at a chosen café for a chosen evening and smile a little when the gendarmes appeared because they were a trifle ridiculous, too, and watch the pretty girls go by, swinging their pocketbooks, wise and winsome, smell the smells, sip cherry brandy, pile up beer saucers, relax in a purely sensory enjoyment of Paris that had nothing to do with liberté, égalité, fraternité, Le Louvre or Picasso—just be there, half asleep, half dreaming from one goldly shimmering morning to the next. God, that was a long time ago—and a different way of being alive from any possible now! He squeezed his eyelids to see if there were tears behind them. Good news, he thought. And—Paris. The Germans have it.

"I think I'll go swimming. Do you mind?"

There was his nostalgia—frail and bright as a Christmas tree ball—broken that easily. Nostalgia for what? Those days—that Paris—far away—sweet and safe as life in amniotic fluid—fragrant security—a prenatal dream—no preparation for birth into this world. The Germans. His mind reiterated her words deliberately so that he could make sense of them. Their content startled him slightly and he took another necessary part of a second to overcome and so conceal his start. "Not if you don't mind. Go ahead." He supposed she had a bathing suit in her car. "I'm kind of leary

220

of wading around out there at night. Stingrays—and stuff."

"I don't mind stuff." She stood up. "It's as warm as pots of tea, anyhow." He heard a zipper. There was not much light—starlight and the pale shine that illuminates the tropical ocean at night. Her slip was white. She walked, naked, down the steps and the path. "You coming?"

"Nix." He rose and followed her. "I'll be lifeguard."

She ran into the water, dove forward, and he could see the confused commingling of light and dark where she swam. He sat in the sand. There was sun in it, still, and the odor of day. She went out to the bar and stood on bottom—the sea came to her waist—and he could make out her precise silhouette, pallidly glowing against the water. He sat with his knees up and his hands locking his wrists around them. Why not . . . ?

Suddenly he began to laugh. She heard him, turned, swam back, and lay in the water in front of him, clearly visible now, her hair as wet as seaweed and her long back underwater, whitely divided into legs. "What's funny, mister?"

"Me. I was laughing at myself. For being puritanical."

"If I understand you—goody."

"Opportunity is one thing with us puritans," John answered lightly. "Resistance comes next—automatically. Besides, you've had too much powerful publicity. Too many advance notices."

She stirred the water. "Oh."

"And we professors talk away our feelings anyhow."

"That's a savage custom."

"Isn't it? That's why we're so exquisitely savage in our minds. We can bite off a population or destroy a continent without a tremor. We can sit and realize, perfectly calmly, that some oaf in a laboratory in Columbia University fooling with the energy in atoms, could start a disintegration that would turn the earth into a nova—a little sun—in less than ten seconds."

"And there you go again. Is that it?"

"Search me. Probably."

"Listen!" she whispered tensely.

He heard the insect aria in the swamp—the distant bleat of an automobile horn—the liquid swish of the sea. Then he heard hoofbeats. He was incredulous. His incredulity became brief fear. Hoofbeats here and at this time were unthinkable—unless the rider were extrahuman. Headless, maybe. But they were horses' hoofs in a steady gallop. Their soft thud increased in volume, drew near, and he could see down the beach the rapid materialization of the steed. He sat transfixed. Gail pushed herself backward into the water, walking with her hands. The horse thundered near, loomed, charged past—its rider bent and urgent—a man—he could not say what sort. They were not seen—not suspected. The pounding shoes threw sharp sand in his face and passed— the rider dwindled bluely in the wan reaches of the littoral.

"Who was that?" he asked aloud. It was an unnatural question.

"It scared me," Gail said. She stood, now, and hurried ashore. She ran awkwardly, as naked women run, up the path and onto the porch. He followed. The shower began falling like heavy rain on its tile floor. By and by it stopped.

"Want your clothes?" he called.

"I'll be out." She came, wiping her hair. She sat down. "Be a lamb and get me another drink, hunh? That nitwit startled me. Creepy. Some jerk out for moonlight horseback ride—with so little sense he doesn't know there isn't any moon."

He came back with her drink. She was still undressed, still rubbing the damp downfall of her hair.

"I hope so."

"Hope what? Thanks for the drink."

"Hope it was a jerk."

"I don't get it."

"I've already got one ghost," he answered. "This one's okay. But, somehow, I wouldn't be crazy about the kind that rides horses."

She stopped. "I'd forgotten about the ghost. Or practically. Have you—heard any more—from him—lately?" Her tone was ever so slightly rasping. Ever so slightly—anxious.

"A calling card—last night."

She began to put on her clothes. "Tell me about it."

He did.

When he finished, she was dressed. She sat down and drank a little. She put the glass aside afterward to toss her hair. "Does Ann know about all that?"

"Ann? No. I haven't seen her."

"I wouldn't stay here alone for a million dollars!"

He chuckled. "If it's really a ghost—it would be worth a lot more than a million dollars to find out."

"Why? What would you know when you knew?"

"That's a curious question."

Her voice was unsteady. "I know. I don't quite understand it myself. I sort of mean—nobody ever got anywhere—fooling with ghosts."

"I suppose the proper answer to that is, you can't be sure until and unless you've fooled with one." He shrugged and went on. "Of course, the whole affair is disputatious. Maddox thinks a pet monkey did it—or something of that sort."

"What's Hanky-Panky got to do with it?"

He explained.

He would not have been so explicit if he had known her well enough to understand the speed and accuracy of her suspicion: "He came up here early this morning? I'll bet I can guess why, too! To see if I was here!"

"Oh, I doubt that. After all, I am a patient. You're maybe flattering yourself."

"Flattering! And you—that's why you sent that wire—and asked me up here!" Her voice was unamused.

"Now you've positively confused me."

"I have not! Do you think I don't know anything about how men's minds work? I ought to, God knows! Henry! That fool! He's nosey—but I never thought he had that much nerve! He was dreadfully jealous of you that first night I was here. Because he could see—because he's jealous of everybody I even meet! And I've been going to—parties and places—quite a good deal, lately. No doubt he's been wearing the bell off my phone! So he came up here at the crack of dawn on a little espionage mission! And then you thought, smarty-pants, that if I was like that—you might just as well ask me up and see what made the white woman tick! You've been laughing at me all the time!"

There was a considerable paradox in this reaction which John did not miss. Nevertheless, the relation between Gail's conscience and her self-esteem was her own problem and he did not like wanton uproar. In a certain sense, he had insulted her, and she had found it out. In another, much stronger sense, he had merely fallen in with a mood of his

223

own. Shawn's description of Gail, and Maddox's behavior about her, were enough to give any normally curious male a motive for a rendezvous—even though its preliminary basis was cerebral and analytical—or, at the least, just curious.

"I haven't been laughing at you at all, Gail," he answered quietly. "I think you're about the best-looking damn dame I ever knew. I think you have the rudiments of considerable intelligence. I have been fascinated by the story of your life. I took your swim in a comradely spirit—the exigencies of a night as stuffy as hell's closets. Wasn't I right?" That, he thought, ought to reduce the woman-scorned aspect of her wrath.

It did. She spoke in a mollified tone. "I know. It's that Maddox. Can you imagine a doctor being such a fool! Do you know that I caught him, once, on the garage roof, peeking through my Venetian blinds when I had company. Can you tie that? He's growing worse all the time, too. It's getting so I can't do anything or go anyplace or see anybody without having it spoiled by him."

"He's in love with you, maybe, Gail. He can't help it."

"If that's love—then all the peeping Toms and perverts are in love with their dirty dishes!"

"Figure it out for yourself. Don't you think you'd be quite a problem to any conservative guy who fell hard for you?"

"No. And even if I was—it wouldn't be my fault. Lots of guys have been in love with me. Several are—right at this minute. But they know they can't own me—and so they don't act like Henry."

"There are all degrees, I admit. Still, if you mean what you say, you could get rid of him. You're smart enough."

"At least, you might tell me just what prompted you to get cute, all of a sudden. I've been here since six o'clock—and I haven't seen any signs of cuteness, the whole time! I thought you might be interesting. And you certainly don't look mean. But all you seem to care about is brainwork, as far as I can see."

"Look, Gail. I'm Johnny Galen. Remember me? Not a cradle-bound erotic—like Henry Maddox. Not an artist—like Shawn. Not a tourist Romeo, either—something in a night club—a big, white boiled shirt behind a battery of champagne bottles. And certainly not a second lieutenant—

224

worse luck. I wish I were someone down there marching around in the heat and the dust getting ready to fight Hitler. And I wish I knew a girl like you who could answer the soldier's prayer as quick as angels—and better. Only, Gail, I'm not. I'm perfectly human. To be a bachelor and watch you swim is a memorable experience. But—lemme see. Put it this way. I'm no cinch."

She laughed, then, and suddenly she had crossed the space between them and kissed him. "I know." She stepped away. "Hanky makes me see red. I wish I'd met you ten years ago."

"People never do."

"And is that the truth! Shall I go home? Or stay?"

"You better go home."

I was tired, he thought to himself, after she had driven away; I was groggy and it muddied up my brains. You don't rent a house from a new widow and then make a pass at her sister. The Galens don't play around with neurotic showgirl blondes. There's no future in it and not much present.

A damn Jezebel, really. She has a different act for every guy—and it's always good the first time because the curtain's guaranteed—sure-fire. She's brighter than she pretends—and it's not a nice kind of brightness; it's the kind that makes you laugh at yourself for thinking of as dangerous—but it is dangerous. So pure a degree of selfishness is always a menace. It's not as if she were just a loose woman—she's a fallen-apart woman. She hasn't any values. If that's all there's going to be to the new woman—we're doomed and doomed soon. She's like that kind of man about whom women say—he thinks only of one thing. She thinks only of one—and, furthermore, she doesn't believe anybody else thinks differently. There was a time when Freud might have backed her up, in a sense. Life is sex-craving. And, because the craving is so enormous, life is sex fear. What else is it? Later, the old man found a wish for death and the fear of that. How does she think about death—now that she has made the extraversion of sex an absolute? And what fear keeps her so tense?

He went back to the porch. He sat down in the chair Gail had occupied.

There was a dull flash to the southward—lightning. Or

gunfire. The swamp throbbed raucously. The house snapped and mumbled as if it suffered stresses from the passage of time or perhaps from the turning of the earth. The perfume she had worn hung round the chair. It was on his hands. When he tried to appraise it, he lost track of it altogether, but whenever he gave up the attempt, it was there again—ethereal, impellent, quickening. What idiot idealism, what fancy vanity had stood between himself and the offering girl? Why had it stood there? Was he less a man for permitting it? Now that his emotion was futile, he unlocked the welter of it, let it beat in his brain and boil in his body. Where was his triumph—from what had he saved either—and how peaceful (for a little while) were men and women assuaged! He endeavored to compare the galling indignation he felt now to the vapid satisfaction he might have felt and to the jeering self-reproach that would have accompanied it. He wanted to find an advantage in his present state. There was none. In such moments the sense of ethical or aesthetic achievement becomes so attenuated that it cannot compete with coursing arteries and no sign of victory is implicit to the dilemma but only the hope of a later sign.

I'll sit up until another dawn, he thought furiously. He stalked from the porch and went around the shadowy house. By luck, the night-blooming jasmine was in full flower and he stood near an unkempt bush, breathing air that smelled as honey tastes. It exorcised the fitful beguilement Gail had left behind. His pulse slowed. The darkness became moderate and fixed again. He continued around to the rear entrance and went in. He spoke to the kitchen—to the pans that gleamed a little and the white murk that was the sink: "If she comes back. . . !"

7

ANN decided to get off and wait for the other bus at the corner under the shadow of the great, pink hotel. The vehicle upon which she had been riding discharged air and grumbled on. She immediately regretted her choice. There was a wide street beside the hotel, with a herringbone of parked cars in its middle, and now a column of men came marching down that street. They wore the insignia of officers; they carried blue notebooks; many of their khaki uniforms were store-new. As they marched, they sang. A blast of male voices roared down the hot thoroughfare, bounced from the rosy walls, soared among the trunks of the columnar palms. "Oh-oh-oh-*oh!*" The last syllable was a shout. The feet slid rhythmically. The column stopped. The song died. A crackling voice kept counting: "*One,* two, three four. *One,* two, three, four." The men marked time. She faced them—she could not look away—and they looked back at her. Hundreds of them.

A contrast shook her sense of reality, disoriented her. Limousines with chauffeurs should have been waiting in that street. Girls in summer dresses and men in slacks were the proper peopling. There should have been a little crowd around the doorman—a crowd of gentlemen in plaid tweed jackets with binoculars slung over their shoulders, and ladies in sleek sports clothes—waiting for transportation to the races. In the background, sun-dipped girls in bathing suits, girls like chocolate creams, strolling toward the cabanas.

Not soldiers. Not a khaki river.

A whistle blew. A light changed. The column moved. The voices roared again, defiantly: "From the halls of Montezuma—"

They marched past her. She knew who they were—what they were called—Officers' Training School. Swinging along. Lumber merchants from Oregon, brokers from New York, bankers from Minneapolis, salesmen from Memphis, store owners from Denver, manufacturers from Pittsburgh, lawyers from Atlanta, ranchers from Phoenix—commissioned volunteers—able Americans—specialists and businessmen—the officer nucleus of the ground force of the Air Corps. Not young—like the kids in basic training. Middle-aged—some grayheads, even, marching proudly. The volume of their voices was the answer of America. They were brave men—good men; they couldn't stand Jap-spit. They looked at her from the otherness of their new world. Their eyes remembered, longed, smiled, and went front.

Down the street they marched—into the white-hot sunshine—singing. Vigor was in the song even when it lost its thrust: "Nothing can stop the Army Air Corps!" The feet talked. March-march-march-march-march-march.

There was a furnace, far away, opening to receive them.

Bombs borne like steps in sideless ladders would fall upon them, red, loud and stinking. Jungles would cave in on them. The arctic would stiffen them. Shells would hunt them, screaming. Sharp steel would find them at night. Nameless disease. They would die. Between now and that day was nothing except this marching toward it. They were dead already. Everyone had a back like Bill. Her eyes overflowed. The violence of grief possessed her. For every one, there was a woman like herself, waiting to have what she already possessed. Compassion overwhelmed her and became a flaming sheet of hatred for war and these men marching so steadfastly and all men, everywhere, and all their wretched women. The detestable misery of it weighed her down. Such living was not to be borne. The dying to be done had made it ugly beyond dignity.

Back came the voices, softly, "You're in the Army now. You're not behind the plow. You son of a bitch, you'll never get rich. You're in the Army now!"

"You son of a bitch."

She said it to the sky.

Strong medicine. A strong prayer.

The answer shot back from the dazzling zenith. The singing and the marching were to stop all this. Some day, they would. At the price of billions upon billions of deaths and an equal number of solitudes like her own. Some day—some sunny day—it would stop forever. This reality—this beast in people, seen, recognized and cursed—would be overcome by the brown backs of marching sacrifices—and it was worth being one of the offerings, or a billion, to help do it down. Curse it and defy it and battle it and beat it. Some day—some day she would never see—some day the uttermost children imaginable would never see—it would die itself. Death to mortality! And meantime all the dying was needed to enrich the will to live.

She reached calmly into her pocketbook, took out the clipping from the newspaper, read the address again, and hailed the oncoming bus. Her nerves were steady now. Her blood was cool again, her tears dry salt her fingers erased, and she was smiling when she put her dime in the chugging box. The streets went past one by one, the vivid gardens, the winding canal, the long vistas of blue sea. She was smiling when she passed the vine-shrouded entrance to the Gracey

228

house; she counted four more street signs, rang the bell and stepped down at the roadside.

Across the way was a bungalow court, its small, neat lawns surrounded by a verdant sprawl of empty lot. Twelve cottages, cement walks between, flowers facing the sun, a sign that said "Office." She went in. A thin man with a black mustache was haggling with a man in overalls about the cost of coconut palms, transported and planted whole. She stood, listening, until the man said, "Yes, madam?"

"I'm answering the ad," Ann said. "The one for an agent on the premises."

His sharp eyes sparkled at her. "I'm Mr. Jones. The owner. Yes. I do need somebody. You're pretty young-looking."

"I think I could qualify, though."

The eyes became more businesslike in recognition of the tone she had taken. "It's not really difficult, at that. We're renting all summer—on a summer basis. The cottages are singles and doubles—rates low—and we have eight occupants at present. I'd like the development full up. It's breezy out there in the summer—as a rule. The salary is small—"

"The ad said that."

"—thirty a month—and one of the apartments free. The agent has to take charge of the office—renting, complaints, and so on—and also act as housekeeper. The bungalows are furnished, and that means linens, supplies, repairs—"

"You have inventories?"

"Of course."

"And you've made agreements with plumbers, electricians—people who do the fixing?"

"Naturally." Mr. Jones turned to the man in the overalls. "Go ahead, Vinson. Plant six of 'em and we'll see how they look. God knows, North Beach Court could stand some shade. Come on, Mrs. Gracey. I'll show you around the place."

By evening, she was settled. Her trunk had arrived. Her telephone would be connected on the following day. She had brought a taxiload of possessions from her high, mildewed cell in the Miami hotel. She was on the ground again—and if her apartment was as new as wet paint, it was also as clean as chrome plating. Bright carpets in the living room and bedroom, natural wood furniture with plain colored upholstery, framed prints of Spanish and Italian pictures on the rough gray walls, plenty of clean-smelling closet space, a galley-compact kitchen, a modernistic blue glass clock, a new little radio—and a job. She had met some member of each of the eight families: Wilsons, Bakers, Fergusons, dePaws—she couldn't remember the rest. At nine o'clock, she would go to the office in the front bungalow and stay till noon. One to five. The rest of the day was hers.

The job meant distraction—an easement of endlessness and desolation; it meant a home that earned itself and a little extra money to eke out what Bill had left and what the big house would produce—which might not always be enough for its taxes, in the long run. The job meant also that she would not be working in a crowd and under the voice of immediate, petty authority; it would not be like a store or one of the small war plants springing up in Miami. That was good.

But none of those elements explained why she had answered that advertisement and accepted the meager offer. The explanation was in her own actions, after she had left the office, prepared a light supper, and walked from her cottage to the road.

She found the coral car lane above the old house—the track two men had followed one night, ages ago (just recently), to do some fishing—the track upon which they had hastily retreated, the young man perplexed and the old man cursing softly at the Germans. She had not known about the two men, that night. She did not know now. But she could see that the weeds between the coral ruts were blackened by the passage of automobiles. So people came that way, occasionally. She walked circumspectly, dodging branches, until she came around the dunes and out on the beach.

She sat down on the sand as she had done so often before. She smelled the salty warmth of the ocean, listened, and looked cautiously through a sea grape at the house. Beige twilight softened it. The palms and Australian pines around her would conceal its shape when the newish moon surrendered to the lift of the horizon—when the only light came from stars glowing in the lush haze. For a moment she thought that she ought to go down to the house, rap on the

front door, explain to her tenant. She decided not to. Mr.
Galen would find out in the course of time. There was no
hurry. And when she told him that she did not wish to intrude and did not wish to be bothered, he would let her
alone. He was that sort of person. So she looked back at the
ocean and allowed its mood to enter her being. Her skin
tingled with subdued ecstasy.

She was close to Bill now, and this solved everything.
If he wanted something of her—if he had really spoken—
he could find her again, for she would wait here, on pleasant nights, until he expressed himself or else, by silence,
indicated there was nothing more to be said between them—
perhaps, that there was nothing more at all. She must not
think that, she told herself. Bill was Somewhere.

She poured sand through her fingers, brushed at sand
flies, listened to the surreptitious singing of mosquitoes, and
reminded herself to bring protection against them on another
night, and a flashlight, too, for going home. She felt happy.
Behind her, fireflies commenced their numberless inspection
of the night. A mockingbird sang. A drift of jasmine came
from the old house and she sat back, remembering Bill's
frank, sensuous appreciation of that perfume. It would not
have been possible for her, at that moment, to think of herself as morbid—a woman in a white dress haunting a haunted
place—a near-specter. True sorrow is unself-conscious: it
neither exhibits itself nor is it ashamed.

A long time passed. The house stayed dark, of course.
It would never show lights; that was interdicted. But finally
she heard the screen creak. Footsteps muttered on the
veranda; a barely discernible figure walked against the white
sand down to the sea, stopped, threw off a robe, and plunged
in. Ann smiled to herself: it was Mr. Galen—or Dr. Galen—
John—and he was taking a swim. Without a suit, she thought.
Her amusement was a kind of cosmic indulgence. John apparently liked to swim that way. Most people did. Only, in
that ocean, and at night, it seemed forbidding. There were
dangerous things in the sea. She could not know, of course,
that John was fully aware of them—aware, indeed, of nothing else—and that he was swimming to prove his mettle
against the heedlessness of another swimmer and to satisfy
a craving for risk and activity. By and by he came out of the
water, a pale glimmer that almost vanished when it threw

a robe around itself. He stalked to the house. The door squeaked and there was silence again.

Nothing happened for a long time. Then there were hoofbeats. Ann was puzzled. The horse cantered up the beach and was reined. A flashlight fell upon her. She stood up, frightened, ready to run.

"Beach guard," an amiable voice said. The horse snorted. "'Nobody's allowed on the beach after dark, any more."

Ann felt rage. This would cheat her whole purpose. She peered up at the vague figure. "You see—I work all day —and it's hot—and I like to sit here—evenings."

"Sorry, lady. Rule."

"Could I—maybe—sit on one of the dunes?"

"No, ma'am." The voice was young, polite.

"But the dunes are as far from the water as—that house! And surely people can sit in it."

He hesitated. "You see—if we let you sit on the dunes— pretty soon the dopes would be back here on the sand, all along the line. Necking. Swimming nekkit. And the sabotoors could get in their work."

She wondered, acidly, if they had found many saboteurs. "Of course, if you didn't see me," she said, "you wouldn't know. I love it here. I don't mean to break rules—"

There was a long pause. The flashlight was steady and she tried to smile into it. "I ain't seen you," the young voice said curtly. His heels hit the horse's flanks. The canter was resumed.

She sat down. She was trembling. But she thought tenderly of the inherent niceness of people. The young man— a coastguardman, she supposed—kicking his horse into the night. I ain't seen you. Because she was a girl and alone and probably because she was attractive—but, maybe, because he had sensed that she was harmless and needed to sit on the beach in the evening.

The different stars lifted out of the phantasmagorical east. A new smell replaced the scent of jasmine. She struggled to identify it: tarred rope—kerosene—and she knew. Oil. Oil was coming ashore in the sluggish current that moved the glassy sea. Oil from tankers. She waited through an endless period. The first acrid breath of it became a heavy and insistent reek. Tarry lumps of it were being invisibly deposited by the lazy lips of the tide. In the morning the sand would wear a black lace of it. But nothing happened.

Finally, sighing, she stood up, worked the stiffness out of her bones, and walked anxiously along the white ruts to the road. She opened her door. Ruefully she examined the bites of sand flies. She took a shower, salved the bites, and went to bed.

Some other night . . .

8

SHAWN MULLCUP was an Honorary Bloomin Boomer.

The Bloomin Boomers took its name from the Miami boom of the mid-twenties. It was a club—a men's club—and it had grown, as have so many like it in so many American cities—out of a sense of necessary self-protection and a feeling of inarticulate want. When it had been formed, in 1927, after the disaster of the '26 hurricane, its membership consisted of male citizens financially stripped by Miami's succession of catastrophes, natural and man-made. It was, as its most learned member had once called it, the "penult of passed-out prosperity—every member has one foot in his financial grave."

In those years—and the following years of national depression—the club had met monthly at the house of some member, for beer and pickles, conversation, hot dogs and poker. With the restoration of the community's financial health, the club had expanded and taken unto itself as "honorary" members a number of later-comers, like Shawn. It still met monthly. Now, however, the meetings took place in a basement dining room; a dinner was spread at eight o'clock; there was a "serious" speaker, and entertainment. Following that, members did as they pleased. There were poker games, of course, and pool and billiards in an adjacent building. And a secretary was posted perpetually at a telephone to offer plausible alibis to worried wives whose husbands subsequently came home the worse for the weather.

The club now patronized two or three local charities. It attended prize fights and football games in a bloc, wives included. Sometimes there were ladies' nights. The members were of every sort—old-timers in the real estate business,

233

bankers, polite officials, retired millionaires who appeared only in the winter, and a miscellany of others, young and old.

Shawn could not remember why he had accepted the invitation to join. His aversion to the American stag club tradition was intense. There had been reasons, he supposed. He was a stranger in Florida—in 1935—and this would be a way to meet his fellow citizens. Southern communities, even more than northern, western and midwestern, operated under the system of special privilege: to belong to the Bloomin Boomers was to enjoy a minor political distinction which would ease the red tape of citizenship and taxpaying. It was handy to have a BB membership card, moreover, in a city where malaria and hookworm had eaten away the brains of some of the cops and you were always in minor danger of being arrested for nothing and held incommunicado until you could establish your mere right to exist. A BB card was a guarantee of freedom from molestation of that sort.

Those reasons. Coupled with them, the feeling every man has for a desire to associate with his fellows—to be a man alone among men—in a world that, for the most part, looks and is a henyard. There was also—undetected by Shawn—the loneliness of all Americans who move away from "home"—generation by generation.

Nevertheless, as the monthly date of the Bloomin Boomers' dinner came near, Shawn usually found himself inextricably tied up and unable to attend. He would have work to finish—the art editor of a big magazine to dine—business-connected house guests—any excuse that would satisfy his fellows. And any excuse which had to do with the side of bread that is buttered was always accepted as adequate by the BBers.

Their food was mediocre and the waiters who served it were insolent. The "serious" speech was, as a rule, irritatingly stupid—an address on the performance of a piece of office equipment or the method of bottling soft drinks, accompanied by a badly projected talking motion picture which repeated in two reels what some perspiring oaf with glasses and a wormy mouth had just said. After that, there would be a scrawny strip teaser or a bulbous strip teaser, always with a bad voice and shabby hair, who would sing a song with some such title as "How would you like to have me all

234

alone, baby?" roll her eyes almost out of their sockets, and take off her clothes. This might have been preceded by the week's dirty jokes, two or three told by the president and the rest by some ungifted but determined member, as the meeting was "called to disorder."

There were Bloomin Boomers—plenty of them—with whom Shawn would have enjoyed talking, and, indeed, two or three of them had become his good friends. But, at the meetings, there was no chance for uninterrupted discussion. The communal singing embarrassed him, the talks were a bore suitable for purgatory, the long succession of strip teasers which inflamed so many eyes left Shawn's artist's sensibilities appalled, and the jokes humiliated him. So he attended rarely.

On a stifling July afternoon, when he had been telephoned three times by urgent members, Shawn gave in. He had been working steadily for many days and he was tired. It was the weakness of ennui, Shawn decided, that made him consent to go. While he was putting away his paints and brushes, it occurred to him to invite Galen, whom he hadn't seen for a week or more.

"Are you famiilar," he asked over the telephone, "with the great American phenomenon of the men's club meeting?"

"Consider that I have hung up," John answered.

Shawn chortled. "You are going—tonight—if you haven't a date. Every man owes it to his fellow citizens to participate in their bonhomie. It's a custom—like sulphur and molasses."

"If you can stand it, I can. Though I didn't know they let bearded men into those societies."

"I'm the only one," Shawn answered. "A concession to art. I've been solemnly asked to shave it by at least twenty members. Complaints run all the way from undignified, to a sort of insult to ordinary guys. I'll come up and get you, if you want—and we can go over the 79th Street Causeway. A guy gave me some gas."

"I'll take the bus. Plenty of seats this far up the line."

"Wear a slack suit—jumpers—jodhpurs—anything but normal clothes. People do, in summer. You can at least be comfortable."

Thalia was knitting when John sounded the door chimes.

The living room was cool. "Shawn's changing. Sit down. How are you—and how's Ann? We don't see her much— since gas rationing—and since she moved way up there."

"Ann's fine. I am. The last month or so, I've gone in for a steady diet of reading."

"And sitting in the sun. You've got a tan like Emperor Jones." She picked up her yarn and her fingers moved. "I'm glad she's fine. Shawn said—a week ago—that you were worried about her."

"I was. Did he say why?"

Her luminous eyes lifted. She smiled and shook her head.

"I found out that she'd been going out on the edge of the beach—and just sitting there—night after night—ever since she took the job at North Beach Court."

"Didn't you expect that?"

"No, I didn't. I suppose I realized when I found she'd moved up there that she wanted to be—well—near. It made me feel like supercargo, for a while. Even though I knew she wouldn't wish to be alone in the big house. I was upstairs one moonlit night and I saw her come through the vacant lot. For a minute, I believed that I was seeing another one. Then, all of a sudden, I knew—and I knew she'd been doing it, a long time. I went over and told her I'd seen her." John was embarrassed. "I thought I better offer to let her—sit on my porch, or something. It has screens."

"What were you doing upstairs in the moonlight?" She looked at him.

"Listening. Hanging around."

"Like Ann." Thalia slowly shook her head. "You haven't —? Either of you—?"

"Not anything since the flowers. No."

Thalia knitted—her piled hair shining and her face peaceful. "You know, Ann would never have moved back to that vicinity if you hadn't been there."

"On the contrary, Thalia. I'm in her way."

"No. She'd have gone up, but never stayed up there. She told me. She went to talk to a minister one day—and he was stuffy about her questions. It dawned on her that she was supposed to explore—these things—herself. Alone. That everybody is. So she began to wonder how to do it. What to do. She saw the North Beach Court ad for an agent on the

236

premises—and that suited her perfectly. But I think she took the job because she knew you were not far away. Maybe because she knew that she could find human company if it got too tough for her. And she likes you."

"She's a pretty swell person."

Thalia nodded with slow, repeated emphasis. "Bill wasn't right for her, Johnny. Bill was wonderful like sunshine and fresh air—but Ann's a thinker and a brooder. Still—she'd never had much—and he was something alive and immense—and she's as loyal as a person's own heart. You see each other a good deal."

"I guess we do. Sometimes she comes over for lunch. On rainy nights, for supper—or—she cooks at her place. You know. She's a good cook, isn't she?"

"You in love with her, Johnny?"

"Good Lord, no."

"Have you ever thought you might get to be?"

"Just as definitely—yes. Still—I live like a hermit—an emotional miser. Maybe I've always lived like that. But for different reasons both of us share two different sorts of permanent dejection—and that makes us just about merry— together—sometimes. I've had the feeling, lately, that if she could settle this business of Bill's survival—one way or the other—"

"You don't believe it, do you?"

"No. I've decided I don't. Not now, this minute, anyway."

"Shawn does."

"Do you?"

She looked up. "Only the people who know, know, Johnny. I've never had occasion to do more than—suspect." Her face was thoughtful; presently it became illuminated by another smile. "Shawn practically raves, once in a while, about the whole business. He thinks you and Ann are predestined naturals. He thinks you ought to take charge of Ann's emotions and shake her awake. He would." She laughed. "Shawn's very forceful about—love. Of course, he's also too impulsive to make much sense until you've boiled down and examined thousands of his impulses. You and Ann are sort of psychological shut-ins." She exhaled lightly. "I'm glad you can share it together. She—haunted by poor Bill. You—by—something."

"Shawn never said?"

"No." She looked at him. "I'll ask him—now, shall I?" She lifted her eyes and waited for his nod. "He's coming. That light tread is not a falling piano. We're fond of you, Johnny."

"Thanks."

Shawn burst in. "On to the world of men and merriment! What needling has my wife been doing, John? You look positively transfigured. Smug is another word for the same thing!"

Thalia stared. "What colors do you call those clothes?"

Shawn beamed and looked down. "The shoes are Alice blue, I think. The strap idea is comfortable. The trousers are ocher. The shirt—the pearl gray of a Negro gentleman's spats. The belt is shocking pink—formerly magenta. Rather chic and nifty, eh?"

She giggled. "I hope they take it in the spirit it is meant."

"Fashion?" He was scornful. "Look at John's shabby ensemble! The tan trousers—the matching shirt—and the matching skin at the open neck. Is that imaginative?"

"It isn't caricature, either," his wife said firmly. "Now —go on out and have a wonderful, vulgar time!"

Shawn made a face, kissed her, and jerked his thumb. They entered the club dining room. Shawn's assurance began to wane. He introduced John to a dozen men who stood in the ranks around the bar. John seemed at ease. He began telling people, in answer to questions, that he was a biologist —here for a quiet summer vacation—and that, yes, he thought Miami Beach was swell in summer.

The tables were set—napkins like tepees, salads in place, plates on, flowers at regular intervals. Over the tables stretched jaded spirals of crepe paper; wherever they were gathered up, a Japanese lantern hung, with a colored electric light bulb inside it. On close inspection—and Shawn's eye always saw closely—the paper showed a bilious bleach at every turn and each lantern held a handful of dead insects. The members—including himself—wore ludicrously large badges on which were printed their first names. As more and more of them arrived, the heat of the room intensified, tobacco smoke befogged the place, and voices rose in pitch and volume. Soon every forehead was dabbled with sweat and every cheek reddened from warmth, conversational effort, and alcohol.

Shawn sank into a hypnogogic state that was not characteristic of him. He grew embarrassed—overembarrassed—for his friend. He wished he had not asked John. When the bell rang and the men went to their places, he introduced his guest around the table, forcing gaiety, smiling, remembering names, laughing emptily when the rest laughed for reasons he had not noticed—and settling deeper into an angry bemusement. He looked at John, uncertain of his mood. He stared at the talking faces. He felt caged, phobiacal, a man in a zooful of brash, uneasy animals. He spooned a melting gelatin soup. Voices fragmentally assaulted his ears:

An energetic thin man—

—by what right—what legal or moral right—does the United States Navy presume to throw us out of the best offices in the city—offices we've occupied for a considerable time—air-conditioned—offices we've paid up on for the next five months—some of us? It's Hitlerism!

A man with kindly, brown eyes—

"—you're probably going to be drafted," I said to my boy, "because of the pure indecency of being healthy and normal. You better learn to shoot." So I took him out on the Trail. Fixed both of us up with .22 rifles and we went after those birds. Heron and cranes, mostly—and a few white ones with crests. Man! Did we give 'em fits! Not shooting at the bird, mind you. Oh, no! Nothing about that to teach you anything. We'd stalk a standing bird and let him have it in the leg. If you miss—that way—your bird flies off. If you hit—boy!—what a conniption! Must have got a dozen—

A fierce, fat man—

—and I'll buy a bond the day they put every laboring man in a uniform, order him to work ten hours a day—and lock him up if he squeals—and not before. We're too damned soft about war—

A doctor in pince-nez—

—it isn't any secret, down here, that eighty per cent of the men doing surgery have no more right to open up a peritoneum than they have to charge street crowds with bayonets and I'll be doggoned if it isn't just about the same thing. Butchery? Why, I've seen—

A man in a white suit and a black bow tie—

—so I said to him, "Colonel, you close the red-light district and you'll be writing the sentence of doom across the flower of southern womanhood. The red-light district is the natural barrier to the spread of natural passions. And as far as all this talk about stopping venereal disease is concerned, you might as well try and make water run uphill. It's part of the burden of human living, no more and no less," I said.

A man in the uniform of a naval officer—

—and this civilian said he thought we ought to tell the American people just exactly what's happening off the coast. Isn't that like one of those Washington bureaucrats? Tell 'em the subs are running through us like a dose of salts! They'd get mad and work harder, this civilian said. So I told him what they would do—they'd just holler like hell at the Navy and say where was it and why wasn't it fighting. Well, it's no secret to you Floridians—and you can take it all right —but the rest of the country is about as gutty as a wet dishrag—

A man with a large, cube-shaped head—

—I can tell you what'll happen, all right. The country isn't going to stand much more war from F.D.R. Fool Deal Roosevelt, I call him. First, he strangled the Japs to death and the poor rats had to fight. Then he lend-leased so much war goods to the "allies" that the Germans had to either declare war on us or else lose every single thing they'd been struggling for the last century and a half! There's your international statesman! Well, pretty soon the American people are going to get wise. Pretty soon they're going to stand up on their hind legs and demand their rights again. Lay off Europe and may the best man win. Give those Japs hellroom in the Pacific—who wants it, anyhow?—and give 'em a chance to do business. They paid us. Now—we're giving it away. I'm ready to bet that by Christmas the people will have seen the light and called off this damned foolishness—

A man in shirt sleeves—

—if any more argument against the Jews was needed, this is it. The U.S.A. is in the war. Who did it? The only people that could have done it. Jews. But this time, at last, they've overstepped the bounds. This war's going to hurt us enough so that we'll take care of the people that brought it on. Hitler did have one good idea. And the craziest part of it is that there's two types of Jews—the international banker type who is making millions hand in glove with Hitler today —and the common, ordinary kike, or scum, type who is strictly a communist, even when he pretends to be something else. But you scrape both those types to the bone and what have you got? You've got the international-banker-communist-Zionist axis that's set up secretly to destroy every country and everybody in the world but Jews. We've been too honest and decent and trusting to see through this line-up so far but, mister, Uncle Sammy is no fool all the time, and he knows what the score is now—

An eternity of it for Shawn.

The meal finally reached the ice-cream stage: a slippery pink dessert set beside tepid coffee. The bell bonged and the president arose. The malevolent palaver subsided. The president cleared his throat exaggeratedly, which caused a few chuckles, a hoot, and one loud Bronx cheer. This last increased the laughter to momentary pandemonium. The president rapped for order with a spoon. "It seems—" he began

It seems. Even the jokes had no reality, but seeming only. It seems. The most miserable preface in the language. It seems there was a widow, a traveling salesman, a college freshman, a blind man, a lady no better than she should be. *It seems* was the open-sesame to this business—this continent-wide male scribble of foul words on their own fences— this adolescent guffaw—this sickly hypocrisy of good citizens, right-thinking people, community leaders, churchgoers, and even of those whose insides curled like indignant snakes at the humiliation of being included in the travesty but who could not fail to shout and snicker for fear of being thought of as less than good sports.

Half the men here—a third, anyway, Shawn thought with fury—would not dare lie down with other women than their wives. They would fly into righteous protest at the suggestion. They would be afraid to do it. Afraid of being found out. Afraid of their wives' persecution. Afraid of physical and social consequences. And yet they, even more than the rest, doted upon this odious substitute, this mental onanism, this snide chance to pretend that they were brave, wild animals.

It seems. Far, far too much sexuality was seeming

241

among these people. They had soiled it—they and the crude purity of their churches and their spider-brained politicians and their sickly schoolteachers. In smutting sex they had made all life and living, and most of being a man, a nasty business. Women were in the sullen business, too. For these stories went home and were exchanged—and ran through the ladies' clubs—until, everywhere, nowadays, they were becoming coeducational. At formal dinners, parties, dances, in bars and night clubs, men and women gleefully swapped these stupid, salacious infantilisms. Not even stag folklore, any more. They were becoming the small talk of Mr. and Mrs. America.

Maybe, Shawn thought, this was a final and purgative step. Because indecency can exist only where there are pigeonholes for it. By becoming universal it might translate back to action, which would strip it of uncleanliness, since it has no being in the body, despite current belief. Only in the mind. These, therefore, were perhaps rifts forced by frantic instinct—instinct willing to become obscene to save a nation from the subnormal infamy of puritanism. People might finally learn by doing—which would end this poisonous ignorance. Maybe. Maybe they still had instincts strong enough to achieve that. But certainly they did not have the brains.

The president and toastmaster—

"It seems there was a girl—a blonde—young and pretty—walking past a sailor on guard in front of a Miami hotel. Now this girl had one of those deep-cut V-neck dresses on. So the sailor said to her, 'Sister, what's the V for—Victory?' And the girl said, 'On your way, sailor. This V stands for virginity.'"

The room rocked with laughter.

Shawn pushed a bread crumb along the tablecloth. He had heard it before. It wasn't even remotely amusing. There wasn't a point—not any conceivable point—except that the anecdote permitted the speaker to employ the word "virginity." And it paralyzed ninety adult males. The next one, more shoddy and more familiar, was for the same purpose; to permit the writing on the fence of another word—in this instance, "ass." There was ass the donkey and ass the fool. Polite terminology. But ass the buttocks, Shawn thought, had always been regarded as one of the most hilarious syllables in English. He stole a glance at John. The biologist was grinning. Shawn looked closer. His perspiration was increasing—around his lips was a narrow line of white. The grin was costing an effort.

"What can a duck do," the president jubilantly inquired, "that a doctor ought to do and can't do?"

An irrepressible extravert bellowed the answer.

The doctors laughed the hardest, Shawn noticed. They made their faces red, they whacked their thighs, they turned their heads this way and that, nodding the news to their fellows that it was really rich and that they, above all others, enjoyed its rare merit. Shawn knew their patients had told it to every one of them a hundred times. But the medicos were roaring with extravagant new laughter now. And the president, beaming acceptance of the flattery implicit in the noise, waited happily for a chance to tell another.

"It seems there was a countess traveling in a day coach and it seems this countess had herself a case of piles."

He was not allowed to go on until that exquisite predicament, that monumentally risible affliction, had been signalized by another blast of mirth. The joke was finished at last. Men wiped tears from their eyes. Joy, as they would have said themselves, was unrefined.

Shawn pushed his crumb.

John Galen still laughed and nodded.

The announcements were haltingly read. A man with a voice like bad brakes then arose and for thirty sweltering minutes described how crackers and cookies were made in a great bakery. Imagine, gentlemen, these shaped, rolled pellets of pure dough, dough composed of the freshest and finest flours, powdered milks, invert sugars, dried eggs— streaming by belt conveyer into ovens the size of this room!

After him, came the strip teaser.

And after her, a chance to leave. Shawn hauled John through the crowd toward the door.

He went as fast as he could, but, even so, he was stopped three or four times:

—Shawn, why in hell don't you shave? We'll buy you a razor! You look like a wop duke.

—Shawn, old man. Meet B. C. Griggs from Detroit. He makes axles—our axles will take the Axis for a ride. Pretty good, eh?

—Hey, Shawn! I liked those last pictures in that Urman

Wallen story! Boy! If you use live models—you're the luckiest guy in Miami! But where do you find 'em—they're either too fat or too lean—the ones I see!

Outside, Shawn hurried to his car. His hands were trembling so that it took him some seconds to unlock the ignition. He drove several blocks before he spoke. "Made in the image of God, John. The image."

John politely said nothing.

Shawn shoved his hand between his broad back and the seat, drew forth a large purple silk handkerchief, and wiped his face. "That's the last time. I haven't been there since the war really got under way. I didn't realize what was happening to them. The jokes—that cracker man—the dancer—yes. But they're angry about the war and they're taking it out on anything handy. Thalia's always telling me I ought to get around more in the circles of common mankind. She thinks I need contacts to keep my work up to date. What I need is some other kind of work! Clean, useful work. For instance, homicide."

"They're shaken. Jittery."

"They're just plain shaky. Great God! They can't stand the Navy taking the best offices! Why not? Isn't it war? Aren't we fighting? They shoot birds for target practice! They reneg on buying bonds because they're sore at labor. And nobody protests it! There are Rooseevlt men in that gang—most of 'em are. But they don't defend the President from a damned imbecile libel. There are men with kids in the Army and Navy—but they're not in it with the kids. Drooling the straight Nazi anti-Semitic line. In fact, a version fancier than I've ever heard! Nobody denies that, either! Nobody. That's what gets you. 'Good fellowship' and business privilege have got them so softheaded that they won't even try any more. Why didn't somebody pull a gun and shoot the whole bloody weakling mess of them?"

"They aren't weak, perhaps. Just misinformed. Uninformed. Uneducated."

"Half of them are college graduates!"

John chuckled. "Sure."

"And the jokes. I wish I hadn't taken you. We shouldn't have gone. I won't get the taste out of my mouth for months."

"It was pretty bad," John finally agreed. He pondered. "The only thing is—you see it everywhere. I'm used to it.

I've gone through the same thing, occasionally, even at scientific banquets. Well—the same sort of thing." He grinned at Shawn in the dark. "I had the idea that you took me for moral support. It's peculiar—but humanity in that mood takes quite a lot of moral courage to face."

"The memory of it grows dim, if you stay away a few months," Shawn answered slowly. "You recollect how many of those guys are good eggs—and what decent, self-sacrificing, honestly noble things they've done. So you go back. And you get that—that—sleighride on the streets of our new national slum."

"I dunno. It's part and parcel of so much, these days. They get the same feeling from the radio—from the movies —from those infinite comic strips. I don't ever read them. I don't know a human being who does, I suppose, or maybe I should say I don't remember anybody ever talking about them to me. People must read 'em, though. And the comic books. And all those magazines—the pictures of girls in pants and brassières—and the pulp stories about sex. They went to school—five—twenty—forty years ago. Ever since that, they've had nothing else but the deluge of garbage. The sleighride in the slum, as you call it. You've got art. I have science and classes. You bust up your radio. I almost never turn mine on. I can't imagine having so much time with nothing to do that I would choose to fill it listening to people saying, 'I dood it'—"

Shawn interrupted. "Do you think they can win this war?"

"Yes."

"So do I." Shawn shook his head. "But they don't know what they're in for. And maybe, if they knew now, they'd surrender to the Germans. On the same theory that, if you knew what was going to happen to you from the beginning to the end of life, you'd smother yourself in your cradle. Except for the fact that they lack the nerve to smother themselves. But they'll win the war one way or another and more or less. It's afterward—"

John said, "Exactly. Afterward we're going to be precisely where we were—spiritually and intellectually—in 1920 and 1930. We haven't grown any. We haven't learned much. If anything, we've decayed a little bit. We've grown more infantile; that's what has compelled the government to be

245

more paternal. Businessmen—the ones who kick about that the most—are the ones who are the most childish of all. Yep. When the war ends, we'll be facing 1920 all over again." He locked his hands behind his head and shut his eyes. "All over again. Plus a wrecked world. An unknown number of dead. Starving hundreds of millions. The greatest gang of trained criminals in the history of man. A probably inflated currency and a goods-thirsty public. An august debt. World-wide hatred of various peoples by various others unequaled in our whole evolution. Millions of returning soldiers who will have paid whatever the price of victory is going to be and who will want and need the jobs that civilians are going to try to keep. What may yet turn out to be a very strong Soviet Union disagreeing with Britain and us on every hand —disagreeing plausibly and realistically. New diseases we will import in this war. The necessity of competing with nation after nation that has learned ruthlessness from Japs and Germans and will be violent for generations. The likely problem of having far more women in America and in the world than men. Our present great spread of vulgarity and irresponsibility and slap-happiness, drunkenness, dishonesty, and what not. Plus the very same gang of corrupt and self-seeking politicians—the men who made yesterday, and who let today happen, and who will try to take charge of tomorrow. I don't know how many other pluses there will be— but those are some."

"I'm glad you don't know," Shawn said. "That's plenty."

"You agree?"

"Of course. After all, you're stating factual possibilities —not talking nonsense. But the crushing thought is that those gents we just left behind are the gents who will have to tackle your list."

"I know."

"What'll they do?"

"Duck every bit they can. Compromise with the rest. Maybe the soldiers who come back will have learned something this time. Maybe they'll get the basic idea that you can't go on kidding yourself in this world and keep your place. About one more generation of the big banana split is all America can stand. Then it'll have to take a brace or take a beating.

"In a world where physical science offers so much, you

can't cheat. You don't dare kid yourself any more, or rob the other guy. If you do, you replace morals with force and honesty with tools. If you do—you're Germany overnight. Or Italy. Or Russia. What those men were saying and doing, men were saying and doing in fascist countries a decade ago. Every circumstance had suddenly been attributed to some other individual or group—and they were out to get that person or those people. Not to shoulder the responsibility. France got like that a few years before it rotted out. The last time I saw Paris, it was far from bright and gay. People pushed you off the sidewalk. Taxi drivers spit on you. Green-shirts gathered in the squares at night. They were breaking Jewish shop windows. The analogy between that and some of the men's club dinner conversations here today is pretty painful. Not to say appalling."

Shawn turned right, between the white balustrades of the causeway. Beyond, on both sides, the bay lay quiet as quicksilver. A few men and women with long poles were fishing—leaning over to look, swinging back to cast.

"Common man," Shawn murmured thoughtfully. "Common man. I've got faith in him. I've got faith in common man because I have faith in nature. In evolution. What I have no faith in is common man's brand of faith in himself. Because that is always temporal. It always applies to this day, this age, this nation, this church, this code, this dogma, this government, this new official, this new bishop, this new encyclical, this new invention, this war, this peace that is to come. Common man's too smug about himself. Too short-ranged. Too bullheaded. He thinks he lives by his intelligence but he doesn't. He is saved and restored, through a thousand civilizations, by his instinct alone. Everybody sane, from Confucius to Einstein, has tried to point out that intelligence consists of knowing what instincts are and using them cognatively. But common man forever denies he's instinctual and keeps demanding that the pattern of the moment be accepted by everybody as true and final salvation. Common man suspects strangers and change more than anything else —fears them most—and yet strangers alone keep him from going stale and only change will lift him out of—this."

John gazed ahead, through the dimout, at the pale, palm-fronded silhouette of Miami Beach. "Which looks like Paradise."

"And is all frosting with no cake underneath. Fifty Nazi subs could come up tonight and paste it to pieces. They won't, though. They're too smart. They know that common man realizes he's in danger only when he feels the hot-foot bite. So they keep that day far off, in this war. It's Armageddon—but too many Americans still think it's merely a nuisance thrown across the parade of their good times. We're in for it, John, as I think I said once before."

"I know what you mean. Still, maybe the war will last long enough and be severe enough to explain to the Americans what is happening to the world, and so to them also."

"What I keep thinking is—" Shawn turned into his street—"we're a fatuous nation, now. And everybody hates us. And we don't know it. When we advise, we insult. When we assist, we patronize. We offer materials—we avoid sharing emotions. That's not adult. Our sins of omission—our insolence—have sown the whirlwind—and we're just beginning to reap it out here on the Atlantic coast. Before we're through—we'll have to take in the whole crop. Now—or in the next century. We may live through it. But nothing will ever be the same again. The old days are already history. I suppose my fellow Bloomin Boomers suspect as much—and don't want to admit it because it promises intense and long-lasting pain—so they are taking out their guilt in childish nastiness. And meanness. A sort of revenge against what they know is to come—and would like to fancy as a wrong. And the rest of their behavior is a hangover from the good old days when a grown man didn't need to be more mature than fifteen, or smarter than twelve, to make a woman or a million or a reputation or his mark."

The car rolled into the Mullcup garage. John climbed out. "It'll take a whole lot of generations to bring together the level of common man and the level of science."

"These," Shawn said, "are lousy times."

"And lousier lie ahead."

The artist looked back at the shrubs greenly growing in the tenuous street light and at the star-filled sky above. "A man ought to get moving. God help us all. I'm glad we went to the BBs, at that. Negative inspiration, kind of."

John nodded—although Shawn had pronounced the words with a solemnity which he thought extravagant.

9

Ann had walked over the beach that evening early enough to witness John's departure.

She sat down with a sense of frustration at his going away. The long reaches of sand were the emptier for it and her vigil would be the more barren. She realized that she thought of it now as an occasional vigil and she examined the conditioning word. Week after week, she had gone less often to wait for Bill. And she did not stay long, now. An hour or two. Usually it was hot and still. Usually the sunset and its tinted effects on the blue water were worth the trip for themselves. Sometimes it was windy. Occasionally she had sat in a tense and foetid atmosphere under a gunmetal sky, watching a storm foment on the horizon. It would curse, menace, and at last roar down upon her so that she would be compelled to run through the vacant lots to escape the streaming contents of the fire-lanced clouds. But Bill had never in any way signaled his presence or his wishes. Never.

Now, like uncounted other widows who had wept much at uncounted other graves (the sea was all the grave Bill had), she was beginning to withdraw herself from the ritual. Her New England teaching—the hard school that insisted upon the immortality of man and insisted also upon the black folly of superstition—was reasserting itself at corners of her mind and in the interstices of her daily hours. There was in her, still, a plumbless capacity for desolation. She still experienced fits of fury at the fact that Bill had been struck down. She still spent hours going over in detail journeys together, meals, parties, conversations held, and the recollection of physical love—now ended, forever. She still took out her frocks, one by one, looking at them and remembering where she had worn them with Bill—what they had done—what he had said about them—how his eyes had been when first he had seen each one. She could still cry quietly at a button torn irreplaceably from a nostalgic skirt—or at a favorite sweater accidentally shrunk beyond wearing again. He still possessed the largest part of Ann.

But, bit by bit, as she knew she must, she was building up a wall to contain sad memory and she was establishing more and more of her consciousness outside it. The most casual inadvertencies of life assisted oddly in that process: the sight of another gold star in a window of a cottage she passed on a bus; two little boys throwing sticks for an ardent cocker spaniel; news of the war and a feeling that the country was turning slowly but relentlessly to face it; pictures of Army nurses and Waacs which assuaged her by reminding her that women were going to face fire and that there would be, somewhere, widowers—men—sharing her sorrow unfamiliarly. All these strengthened her resolution against personal defeat; even the petty complaint and bickering of the bungalow tenants contributed: at first it merely tempted her to say, "There's a war. What can it matter?" but ultimately it taught her new uses of tact and it consumed her energy and time so that there was less of both with which to study despair.

She was healing.

That night, on the beach, she admitted it for the first time.

She was interested in the comings and goings of another man. She missed him because he had driven away.

Sitting there that evening, she let the thought of him through certain hitherto closed doors, where she could examine it more intimately.

Handsome—she had noticed that long ago. But handsomeness, like homeliness, vanishes upon close acquaintanceship; one looks beyond, at other criteria. He had the body of an athlete; he liked to swim hard and far and to lie in the sun. He was very brilliant. Even famous. But he spent most of his days reading or painting gaudy, sloppy seascapes, or fishing—although he never seemed to catch anything. He ate up books, read them in stacks, quoted them, picked them up and spoke their pages aloud—not to prove anything—but in the manner of one adding data to an endless puzzle.

Then—he made money. Ann did not know many men who had made money. She expected them to be different but this one was not different in the way she had anticipated. He had rented her big house; he had hired a cook; otherwise, he lived as simply as she did.

He looked, and even talked, like a man of various urgencies and constant action—and yet he did not act at all. He merely thought. When they were together at her house, he sometimes peeled vegetables, set plates, or washed dishes—

always placidly, always with introspective eyes, always with a friendly smile, but never in a manner that was attentive or confiding. Sometimes, she thought, he behaved as though he were beyond much emotion—as though he had been weaned from it by an untold bitterness or tragedy. Yet he was kind. He would let her talk about Bill through a long evening—let her tears fall and not seem to notice—and, when it was late—he would nod at the door and leave genially, taking all of himself and returning the tidy apartment entirely to her. " 'Night, Ann. Be seeing you."

" 'Night, John. Thanks for coming over. I'm a pest, though."

He did not seem to know—in all that time he seemed not to have noticed—that she was a woman. A pretty woman. She flushed slightly at that idea—not because it was disloyal to Bill but because it bespoke an irritating quality in John Galen. Scientists were like that, perhaps: in love with work, and knowledge, and the discipline needed to push back frontiers of knowledge. If they noticed a woman was a woman it would be only as they noticed that their own hands and feet were desirable parts of nature without which they would be unhappy and less effective. And if that were true, then, someday—years from now, she told herself quickly—a man like John Galen would perhaps make it possible for her to finish out the function of life without losing her primordial attachment to Bill. What little emotional support John needed would be easy to supply—and the giving would not compromise her heart. Relationships like that, she thought, were what people meant by marriages of convenience and arranged marriages. She might—eventually—be permitted by this world to keep her romance intact and yet not to die childless—sterile—a biological failure because of not trying hard enough to succeed even in that.

With muted, inner shock she became conscious of what she was thinking, or daydreaming. She instantly classified it as wretched rationalization. A moment later, she smiled a fraction of it back into acceptance: she was alone and a widow and even if this were her instinct talking and not her heart or her good senses, it was genuine. Life, for her, from now on, would have to be lived on some such plane—perhaps.

Then she heard the motor of a car coming up the long drive to the Gracey house. It was not John's car. She was tempted to scramble up the far side of a dune and see who it was. But she checked herself. She heard the motor fuddle into silence. The back door slammed. It had not occurred to Ann that John would leave the big house unlocked—but he had evidently done so. Soon, the front screen squeaked. Ann drew back behind a sea grape, but now she let herself look.

Gail.

Gail walked a little way on the path, stared up and down the beach, and returned to the porch. She lighted a cigarette, stretched, shook herself impatiently, and sat down. For a long time Ann could see the shining back of her sister's head and the thin, rising curl of smoke as Gail lit one cigarette from another. Nervous. Ann did not budge. John had mentioned Gail. She'd been there with Maddox on that spring evening when he had hurt his ankle. It had been a very casual mention: your sister showed up with the doctor—beautiful girl—that doctor's stuck on her, isn't he? No more than that. Nothing afterward. And Ann had seldom seen Gail since she had moved north on the beach.

She had discovered long ago that the less she saw of Gail the better the opinion she held of her. Gail would deliberately torment her with accounts of the "good times" she had had and with slanderous tales of the behavior of local citizens, servicemen and tourists. To Ann, Gail had always seemed a sadist—undisciplined, willful, selfish—a person who acted out the raging components of woman's nature—hid none—and scorned compassion, modesty, mercy, and all sense of necessary chastity. In spite of that, Ann liked Gail—or wanted to like her—but with every attempt at expressing affection she invariably acted so that her sister could view herself as being patronized. That gave Gail a basis for further shocking discourse, additional bad temper, and harsher malice. Ann longed for a state of sisterhood which her best efforts only frustrated. Gail did not appear even to want a sister. She had reduced life to an endless succession of adventures in physical romance. Ann was not disgusted by that, as most women with her background might have been, but she looked upon it as pitiful—as a search for happiness forever doomed—a half-gay, half-nasty effort to blot out an unhappy childhood and a tragic marriage—and as the uncritical result of being in love with being loved.

It was better not to see Gail, not to stir up her quick

reproachfulness—better just to keep her in the mind as a lovely, errant sister, good for nothing, perhaps, but not very harmful, either.

Now, watching Gail, Ann doubted her long-accepted definitions. The thought that perhaps Gail and John Galen had seen much of each other slowly invaded her mind. It made her bitter and weak—the latter because she could do nothing about the former. She had not allowed herself to dwell upon Gail's conduct in the light in which she now saw it—the light of its possible effect upon men, and, indirectly, upon other women who were interested in those men. Suddenly John's kindness, and the abstraction that accompanied it, were subject to Ann's suspicion. Was he being nice to her because she was Gail's sister? Or—was he merely beguiling the time between dates with Gail by listening to her, by taking an occasional meal with her, going to the movies, washing dishes, laughing lightly? Was she "a friend" and Gail something other—something more possessed and possessing, more real and rewarding?

Gail began pacing on the big veranda.

Ann forced her judgment into action. This was jealousy —or akin to jealousy—and she had always detested that emotion. Besides, she had no right to be jealous of John Galen—no moral right, no right on account of her own loyalty, no right as a widow, no right even as a woman to whom he had meant—more than she had appreciated. And yet, for a few more minutes—as she watched her sister walk from shadow into sunlight, long, blonde hair shining like new metal, like summer, like a thought of love—as she assayed with changed eyes the probable effects of the arpeggio of her figure—Ann trembled with helpless indignation. John should know better. If he did not, he was still too fine and sensitive a man to fall victim to wayward glamour.

Gail suddenly stalked through the front door. She soon appeared at the rear of the house. Ann thought, with relief, that she was going. But she did not go. She looked off toward the driveway for a moment. Then she went inside again. There was silence.

This frenetic activity gave a new turn to Ann's speculations. It was uncertain and without poise. Unnatural to Gail. It could not be mere disappointment because John was not at home. Ann knew her sister well enough to predict her reactions in any such case: she would be cold and haughty even when she was alone—for her own benefit. She might search the house, but she would not wait. Not Gail. No man would ever find her anxiously sitting on his doorstep, smoking a chain of cigarettes, tapping her foot, annoyed but persistent. So she had not been expected and this was not a date broken or forgotten. She had come unannounced and of her own accord. She was not angry. She seemed, rather, to be *afraid*.

The idea of Gail afraid had a contagion for Ann. What sort of circumstance would it require to upset her to that degree? Ann could not imagine. That very inability was alarming in itself. Why had she gone into the house? What was she doing there? Ann wanted urgently to steal through the crimson twilight and peer into one of the tall, old-fashioned windows. But she could not. Deliberate eavesdropping was repugnant to her.

She did not feel, however, that her present situation involved eavesdropping in the sense she despised. On the contrary, she had felt from the very first that Gail had intruded upon her. Upon her vigil, her privacy, her sacred little stretch of beach. She had a right to be there—and Gail had no right to enter John's house, even though he had left it unlocked. Moreover, she felt that she was not in a position to approach the house openly and find out what Gail was doing. She could recite accurately the sarcastic flash of Gail's words: What brought you here? Spying on J.G.? Tryst? Cheating so soon? It's in the Chapman blood, isn't it, my pretty, hypocritical sister? Go ahead. Don't mind me. I'll share him with you. I'm big about these things. You take the alternate days—starting now. Maybe he'll appreciate me more because of you—in the long run. Or vice versa. *You'd* get hurt—but I wouldn't, darling—because I'm honest and a realist about life and you're such a stuffy damned sentimentalist.

Ann knew. No, she couldn't walk up and ask.

Gail came out on the front porch again, finally. The light had diminished and Ann could hardly see her, but she guessed that Gail was picking up her cigarette stubs—emptying out the ashes when she opened the screen—removing traces of an unannounced visit. Soon afterward the back door slapped. Gail ran down the steps, started her motor,

254

and took off as if the devil were behind her. Scared, now—of the night and the old house. Gail was scared.

Stars emerged from the filmy blues overhead. It would soon be time for the mounted patrol to pass. John Galen was staying away for dinner. He would be absent, probably, for several hours.

The house stood out in the late light—grim and oddly alluring. In it was most of her happiness—compressed forever—laid away—death spiced with memory. It was, indeed, legally her house. And it was here—not on the tedious beach—that Bill had whispered to her, called her, tried to tell her something she did not understand.

The hour, this history, the emptiness of the house, and Gail's visit conspired swiftly within her. She rose, hesitated, and presently began to walk down the beach—white-faced, determined, nearly hypnotized. The warm sand hushed her steps. A yellow crab scuttled into a hole beside a running vine. The tide was coming in strongly. Bugs sang. She stepped over the familiar, low, winding wall of conch shells and went up the path. Her feet trod the steps. The front door creaked knowingly as she pushed it back. She peered across the dark foyer at the stairs that wound upward and out of sight. She went ahead to the Navajo rug, lifted it aside, and felt her way into the blackout room. A sound then—the accidental fall of a book—would have turned her to stone. But the room was a silence. She found a light, at last, and switched it on. Relief swept over her.

There was nothing awful here—and besides, this was the very place where she and Bill had sat, night after night, reading and talking and holding hands—laughing before they went upstairs in the dark or out onto the sand in the moonlight. The room was a comfort. A boon. She wished that she had been able to be alone in it, before. She sat down on one of the leather chairs.

Nothing was changed. John hadn't even moved the racks of Uncle Paul's canes. He'd left the little electric stove in the same place. There were more pillows on the divan—golf clubs in the corner, but, somehow, when she had seen it with John there she had looked at it with her eyes closed. Now, alone, she could open them as wide as she wanted—to nostalgia, to memory, to the otherness of this present inspection.

She was very near to Bill and yet she felt differently about him. What would have happened if he had not—died? They would be right here, together, now. But—would he have loved her, always? Would they have had children? Would he have been faithful—and what would she have done if he hadn't been? Would the children have been exceptional —or just ordinary, so that you pretended they were unique and everybody was amused at the pretense? And would they have been rich or poor? And happy, always?

"Ann."

She sat very still. It was his voice but a voiceless voice, a knowing in the mind that a voice had spoken. She was unafraid this time—relaxed, almost—as if she had come for this, aware it would happen here and only here. *Ann.* Tranquil in tone—a perfectly quiet speaking.

She thought it was necessary to move her lips enough for a whisper. "Yes, Bill?" He was somewhere, there, behind her.

"Don't look around," he said. It was just advice— friendly—light—not very much concerned—but meant, nevertheless.

Why not? Because there would be no one to see? Because it would break the spell? Or because he was in some ugly condition—some condition necessary to this errand— or some gruesome state that would show the way in which he had died? She was filled with pity—but she sat still. "Of course not, Bill."

"Ann. You're—alive. Remember that. You're you. Be you. I'm all right, Ann. All right."

"Yes, I'll remember. All right?"

"All right. Everything's—all right. Always."

"Always."

"Forever." There was a pause. His voice had receded. "It's here, Ann."

"But—what is?" She whispered more loudly. "What, Bill?"

"Here—" It was a faraway sound. And, from farther away still, he said what he always used to say: "Good-bye, now."

For a long time she answered nothing. Then, frantically, she whispered, "Bill! Bill! *Bill!*"

The pause was measured; at the end she heard a single, chiming note.

It was not like any sound she had ever heard before. It swelled softly, soared, rang sweetly and unutterably true. Notes in the same register joined it. The whole of space around her sang with a strange, unearthly chord that was not music but the stuff of all ancient melody and all the harmony of the future. Pure sound. Pure ecstasy. She closed her eyes and her heart burst from knowing it. So she sat, listening until the last, inexpressible beat of it had diminished into the kind of distance that contained it.

Then she wrung tears for her cheeks with her eyelids. She looked at the room again. Radiance, and an undertone, not of sadness such as she had known but of a sadness of present unattainability, slowly mingled within her. She clutched at the feeling that she must remember the chord as she had heard it. Even while she tried to do so, she knew that it was slipping away from her. Her exalted but hopeless awareness was replaced by a slow, inward settling of the radiance and the sorrow to silence. For another short moment, she understood perfectly every feeling and every emotion: her own and those that were universal. But that glimpse, that insight, also, swirled, blurred and disappeared.

For one mere instant, she thought, I have known the peace that passeth all understanding and I shall surely know it again—somehow—sometime.

The room existed quietly around her—and quietly she inspected it.

Be you. He had told her. *It's here.*

And another thing:

Good-bye, now.

She felt more relaxed than she had been since the long, sunlit, amorous days preceding the night when she had sat on the beach and worried because Bill's boat was overdue. I ought to look around, she said to herself, and find out what Gail was doing here. But Gail's secret anxiety did not worry her any more. I should leave, she told herself; it would be humiliating to be found here by John. But she did not rise. I was angry, she remembered, at the bold, familiar way Gail came in here. But that did not matter, either. The lusts of people, their passions and conflicts, seemed like tiny points receding toward zero—almost funny because of the grandiose character given to them by the actors and because of their actual triviality. She closed her eyes and heard the memory of the chiming notes—a blessed, mystical memory that was not the music itself but a knowledge of the existence, somewhere, of such music. *It is so different from what we think,* she said to herself.

She slept. . . .

The stutter of a hand brake wakened her. She stood quickly, overcome with embarrassment. What would she say to him? And suppose it was Gail, returning? She remembered what had happened before she had fallen asleep and the memory quieted her anxiousness. The feet on the porch were a man's.

John came in, smiling. He knew immediately that something had happened to her—that she was different—that she was happier. Her gray-green eyes were bright; her expressive mouth smiled; her hands stirred and became calm.

"Hello, Ann. This is a darned pleasant visitation."

"Is it late?"

He looked at his wrist watch. "Twelve-fifteen. Early."

"Late. It doesn't matter. John. I came in here—hours ago. I—Bill talked to me. I think he did, anyway. I know it. Though it wasn't talk, exactly. He said, 'Good-bye.' Then I heard something. Something wonderful!"

John bustled about the room—busily, casually, to make it easier for her to go on talking unconcernedly. He emptied an ash tray. He ripped open two new packages of cigarettes. He straightened the pillows on the couch. "What did you hear, Ann?"

"Music."

The unexpectedness of the word caused his flesh to prickle. He turned his face away and kicked flat a corner of the rug. "Music?"

"Do you think there's such a thing as music of the spheres? Or celestial music?"

"I don't know." He smiled at her. "I don't know what I think—really. Who does?"

"I heard something wonderful, John. Whatever it was. And if it was just in me—I'm wonderful. Because I'll never forget how it made me feel. Never. No matter how lonely I am, or how miserable, or how sick, or if I'm broke—I can always remember—*that* happened to me."

"I'm glad, Ann. I honestly swear you look different."

"I am. I know now that it's another kind of world from the kind I'd believed in. That's enough to know, isn't it? I mean—that it's so much more than we think?"

He glanced at her intently. "Yeah. That's enough for anybody with sense. Plenty."

"You aren't going to be all scientific about it, are you?"

"No, Ann." He grinned. "That's Maddox's department." He sat down, lighted her cigarette and his own, and shook his head. "Poor old Maddox! And yet—so darn like all the rest of us. So objective about the world outside. So incapable of being objective about the inside world!" His eyes twinkled. "You don't mind my being scientific about Maddox, do you? After all, he's not involved in your celestial music."

She shook her head. "Not a bit. In fact, on the contrary. It's made me remember about Gail. She came up here around seven o'clock."

"Gail did?" He was surprised.

Ann then told the story of her evening in sequence and she tried, as she described each event, to convey her own emotions. Her voice was often puzzled—at times she flushed delicately—but she went ahead from the beginning to the end. "You see," she finished, "I found out a lot. I found out I could be quite—jealous of you—in a very mean, superficial way. I found out how—other women—must often feel about Gail. But the most important thing was, I found out that Gail is scared—frantic. I think I ought to try to learn what has frightened her, and help her."

John said, "Did you ever consider that Gail was frightened—all the time? That her behavior was like that of somebody running away from something? Escapist?"

"I never did. But now that you say it—"

"People who are cruel—or wanton—or angry—always, Ann, are frightened people. That much I do know. It can be genuine, honest fear. Or it can be deep and irrational fear. But it's fear. All those words—cruelty, wantonness, viciousness, violence, irritation, rage—are names for different reactions to different kinds of fear. And then, of course, everybody's afraid of many things—or nearly everybody. People are afraid of people and afraid of themselves—afraid of getting hurt and getting killed and getting trapped—a billion things."

"But Gail seemed so abnormally afraid! It gave me the shivers! It showed extra plainly, I think, because she believed she was alone and nobody could watch."

"Of course."

"What was she doing here? Looking for something? Did she leave something? Do you know?"

"No, I don't, Ann." He started to speak and changed the subject in his mind. "But I do feel that we ought to let her keep it to herself as long as she likes. If she knew you'd watched her, she'd either be furious or horrified. Then she'd never confide in you—or anybody. Don't you agree?"

"It's awful to be like that!"

"Yeah."

A silence fell between them. She broke it. "Gail was only here that one time—so far as you know?"

He laughed. "Aren't you being feminine as hell? However—no."

He told her about Gail's second visit. She listened the long while, nodding sometimes, smiling, understanding the man who talked earnestly, often self-consciously.

"Still, Ann, I can't think of anything—" he paused, searching back in his mind—"anything at all she said that would throw light on her reasons for being here tonight." He remembered, again, how alarmed Gail had been when she had first heard of Bill's "ghost"—and how carefully nonchalant she had been when she had brought up the same subject on the evening of their date. But she'd said nothing then to explain her original alarm and nothing ever that would account for the frenzy Ann had witnessed. There were shapeless inklings of agitation in Gail's conduct—there were no facts to read from. "You want me to make some coffee?"

"No, thanks, Bill." She started, and smiled up at him. "John, I mean." She was unembarrassed—surprised that she was not phrasing quick apologies for the slip. But, after all, it was a simple, explicable thing—and John understood. "I would like to go home now, though."

"I'll walk with you."

"Would you mind terribly if I walked alone? You see, I want to. It's perfectly safe."

He followed her to the back door. He watched her white dress merge with the shadows of the silently toiling vegetation. " 'Night, John," she called back cheerfully.

" 'Night, Ann."

10

LATELY, John had been engaged in another and different experiment from the one by which he had attempted to communicate (or had communicated) with Bill Gracey's "ghost." This experiment had occurred to him in the midst of maundering over problems relative to himself, his present, his new adventures, and his future. It was necessary, he felt, for him to know more about the nature of his own brain —its suggestibility—and the extent to which he could be influenced by it. From that, the extent to which he could be influenced by not known processes might at least be guessed at. A lifelong empiricist, he was unused to the idea of aberration—of affect—of changes causable in himself by unconscious or subconscious factors. He consequently tried a series of repetitions of one simple experiment—the handiest that came to mind—in order to test that characteristic.

Each night, when he was not too sleepy for it, he lay on the couch and stared at the ceiling of the room. He had fallen into the habit of pulling back the blackout curtains and opening his windows after switching off his lights—and from the outdoors—now from moonlight, now starlight, and again from the dim halation of sea- and earth-shine, there came a variable quantity of light, faint but steady, and always sufficient so that the ceiling was visible—not as a yellowed, musty paper but as a mere pale expanse above him. At this, he gazed. It was his determination from the first to hypnotize, command or "prejudice" his vision in such a way that the hazy area overhead would lose its negative quality and take on a color. Red, he decided.

So, frequently and for a long period, he would gaze upward, thinking that the space at which he peered would soon seem red. He had tried that for many nights unsuccessfully when it occurred to him that a proper preconditioning of his own mind was perhaps necessary. If he went ahead endlessly peering and wondering whether or not he would eventually "see" a red ceiling instead of a white one, nothing might ever happen. Certainly nothing had come of the attempt in several nights, except tedium, impatience, eyestrain, and a growing impression that he was acting like a fool. But what if he tried to convince himself before the attempt of its certain success? Would that achieve a different result?

Autohypnosis, after all, was a documented fact. Millions had performed it. There was nothing mysterious about it. Yoga was partly founded upon it. Coué had once made a sensational vogue of it. Doctors saw minor examples of it every day, in patients who had worked themselves into believing they were worse or better than was the case, or sick when well, and vice versa. Prejudices, from the technical standpoint, were often mere autohypnoses. And so, for that matter, was religious faith.

John therefore changed his technique. Determinedly, he read the lesson to himself. And at last, one night, when he lay down, he did so with assurance: others had hypnotized themselves into endless convictions different from fact; he could, and he was going to. The difference in result was immediate.

Now, he stared at the ceiling and thought it certainly would turn red. He did not wonder if it might. He had accepted the idea that he could make it do so and that it would. It did, of course. He saw, not without a remote spark of astonishment, that a pale pink bled into the blank pallor so boresomely familiar to him. The whole surface was presently suffused with a pinkness that deepened through rose and magenta to scarlet. The "color" at which he gazed seemed more luminous than was possible in the actual light volume above him. By an act of "will" he had created, above his own head, a glowing, scarlet roof. The commenting part of his mind observed that, having done it, he now realized how anybody could: this was the mechanism of all self-deception. Here he lay, a good scientist, looking at a purely subjective phenomenon but one so seemingly real that, were he unaware of the exact steps leading up to it, and had he merely glanced aloft to see this scarlet ceiling, he would have assuredly assumed that there was an indirect lighting system, red in color, hidden by the molding.

This demonstration was so vivid that it held his attention for many subsequent nights. He found that, by deciding his ceiling would be green—or so appear—he could achieve a green ceiling, also. Or yellow. Or blue. And, finally, having thoroughly established his "conviction," he could apply it at will, just as the operator of a light-organ might—causing the imagined and projected "colors" to swirl, merge, take sunset patterns, arrange themselves in stripes or polka dots and submit in every conceivable degree to his caprice. He realized, of course, that his will in the broad sense of the word—his will to see reality as it was—had first to be made subject to a premise: the premise, in this case, that there was such a phenomenon as self-hypnosis and that he could practice it. Within that premise, however, his "will" operated as freely as before and he had power to change the colors as he pleased. He retained also the power to waken the hypnotized part of his brain out of the experiment at any time and, once again, to see the ceiling as it was—a wan, white glow overhead.

It was a rewarding experiment, but also puzzling. He felt certain that others could readily repeat it. Indeed, he knew from the study of psychology that many persons had made far more imposing experiments with the technique. But the fact that the combination of conviction and imagination could make such manifest unrealities seem so vividly factual disturbed John about himself and about all other people.

From it, one had to suppose that much of consciousness consisted not in the real seeing of actual ceilings, but of fancied colors, put there by wrong education, by gossip, by superstition, by social custom, and a thousand other agents. In the light of what he had been able to demonstrate in a mere dozen evenings of effort, it seemed certain that some unguessably large part of his daily life was occupied with the attentive acceptance of qualities and concepts that did not really exist at all, but had been manufactured.

By the same token, he abruptly thought one night, he or anybody could become "convinced" of negatives. That is to say, if he (or anybody, or everybody, or, say, everybody like himself) accepted as a certainty that such-and-such did not exist—or that so-and-so was impossible—then for him or for them—those things would not be perceptible or could not be accomplished. A person who did not "believe" in ghosts thus might never see or hear one—even if the ghost were there. On the other hand, one who "believed" would observe that which was not. The thought was interesting on the supernatural plane. But on more mundane planes, it was fascinating. It made clear how an attitude could arise—a belief—a custom—a code—a dogma—anything—and gain immense credence. It explained why such attitudes and beliefs persisted in the face of disproof: the "convinced" individual could not extricate himself from his position even when confronted by a demonstration of his error, until he first understood thoroughly the technique underlying his particular persuasion.

John could also appreciate the process of falling unconsciously into the thing. All those who became aware of what was happening only at the moment when the ceiling appeared as red, would believe the ceiling to be colored. Furthermore, they could never find out otherwise. Not understanding the process by which they had gotten into the conviction, they could not shake their heads, blink their eyes, banish the "artificial belief"—and look up into normal reality —or truth.

It was at this point that he reached Gaunt's chapter on "Conviction" in *De Rebus Incognitis*. He was glad of his experiment when he read the chapter. Without it, he would not have followed Gaunt so understandingly. He read it twice in one night.

And he read much of it again, later, to Ann:

DE REBUS INCOGNITIS

SEVEN LECTURES
TO AN IMAGINARY AUDIENCE

BY

WILLIAM PERCIVAL GAUNT

FARRAR & RINEHART

INCORPORATED

ON MURRAY HILL   NEW YORK

CHAPTER VI

CONVICTION

It is amusing to contemplate the related and former meanings of words from the standpoint of racial slips-of-the-tongue and lapses of old wisdom. A portion of semantics is dedicated to the process. But the average man will hardly bear with the semanticist, whose efforts will only remind him that all his sturdy present conclusions are tinged with his chronoid nature and that much of what he says today is expressed in the opposite or the complement of its intended usage. A study of the evolution of the word at the head of this chapter, for example, would lead one into a study of how man fell to thinking about his thoughts. Disparities relevant to the word have sprung up, since the Roman era, and they are illuminating in a most essential manner, but I shall point out only one as a come-hither to the embryo etymologist, the literary philosopher. That man who has *convictions* is regarded as a deep and earnest thinker, but that man who is *convicted* lands in jail.

We are, of course, convicted by our convictions. The boundaries of the latter mark the scale of the former. No man can think or evaluate, dream consciously, or even guess, beyond the limits of his convictions, whether they have been imposed upon him by parents, preachers and the classroom, or deliberately taken up for one "reason" or another. And most of us, of course, live so vigorously in the ego that we have neither the time nor the energy to set aside the miniscule "I" and find out what manner of convictions sustain it. The "I" floats upon somebody else's ocean, in consequence of that. It accepts the mere opinion that bodies of true conviction exist outside itself—in churches, in national constitutions, in the Bible, in secret societies and civic clubs, and in books on etiquette, hygiene and the like. To a large extent, it allows itself to be indoctrinated with such external opinion. It is redeemed or it becomes agnostic; it is patriotic—and a liberal or a conservative; it is a Mason of certain degree; and it tips its hat to ladies just as it brushes its teeth. If its accidental or chosen convictions occur within the vast latitude of human adaptability, such an ego will adjust in fair harmony to its like-minded fellows. Confronted with an unfamiliar problem, or with criticism, it will refer to the body of conviction for proper response—to a priest or to Emily Post, to a book on baby care or to the law. However, when a question arises for which the parent body had no appropriate answer, the "little I" is suddenly frustrate. Lack of convictions now convicts him. He can no longer act subjectively. He becomes perforce hysterical or melancholic, owing to unresolvable conflict. And if this quandary occurs to similarly confined multitudes, a group, or even a whole nation, may grow, on the one hand, into destroying paranoids or, on the other, into vegetative self-destroyers. Violence will blow the prison out or collapse it in; and the "little I" will be burst or crushed by the catastrophe. . . .

I need not point out upon how many occasions this has proven to be the mechanism of war. The phenomenon may be most plainly observed in modern Germany where Hitler (the most surpassing example of the "little I" afforded in history) articulated in loudly repeated detail all the points of frustration for the collective egos in Germany. These were, all, the frustrations of one general conviction which had been vigorously implanted, generation after generation: the conviction of superiority—superiority of the race and its kultur, of the nation and so of each unit therein. Such a conviction of superiority is scientifically a false attitude—an acceptance of a concept about one's self and one's neighbors which lies wholly outside fact. The danger of it is not in the mere holding of the notion, but in the effects upon the holder which arise from the constant counter-action of fact. Of truth, that is. The prison of conviction closes; external reality becomes inaccessible; its presence is felt as mere pressures, sounds, smells—which take on unwholesome meaning to the incarcerated ego. Eventually, the "little I" becomes obsessed by the only possible solution of his frustration which can have a logical seeming to him: since he is superior, but somehow hemmed in, the world outside is in error. His mission now is either to draw the world into prison with himself or to destroy it—in either case, from the action-point of his convictional cell. He therefore becomes a messiah—a paranoid messiah or a suicidal messiah—but a messiah in so far as his mission is concerned. This is the mechanism which explains, on a national scale, the fall connoted by pride.

Hitler and his insectile sycophants stressed the central conviction of superiority. This defined the size of the prison. The invention of such terms as "Aryan," "Nordic," "super-race" and so on height-ened the sense of "unjust" compression together with a feeling of lack of world-wide appreciation. It also inflated the missionary compulsion. It gave the national conviction a set of measurements by which the German people were levered into activity. It was then necessary for the ambitious Nazis to take only one further step: i.e., to name which walls were to be pushed out or pulled in first, second, third, and so on. Hitler, with simplicity and suitability for his unconscious purposes, selected a scale graduated from the standpoint of risk: internal Jews, Rhineland Germans, Sudeten Germans, internal Protestants and Catholics, Poles, Frenchmen, and finally, the world. Thus, in correct perspective, it becomes clear that the vaunted Hitlerian "intuition" was no majestic capacity for statesmanship and no military genius but merely the crudest of actuarial faculties: the ability to assay physical risks on an ascending scale.

The foregoing will serve as one example of a generalized description of conviction and as an illustration of the process in collective action. As such, it is mere analogue—a fairly superficial and limited portrayal of one momentary consequence in history of one single facet of activated, joint conviction. I have chosen it deliberately, however, to hint at the importance of a new understanding of conviction in daily life and in political activity.

The German acceptance of essential Germanic superiority has many past parallels. All have ended in catastrophic downfall of one sort or another wherein the ruin of each stands as an exact monument to the nature of the conviction that brought it about. For, of course, conviction of racial, national or cultural superiority itself is a mere group exaggeration of various protective individual rationalizations familiar to everybody as the private vanities and excesses of friends and neighbors. It is a sort of federated prejudice, a codified compensation reflex, and a form of community bravado not unknown in this country, where separate states are guilty of it on one level and the whole nation is guilty on another.

However, the reader will be able best to explore the workings of the psyche in the field of conviction by an act of introspection. The more august examination of whole nations befuddled will serve as mere incentive. So I shall draw attention mainly to the convicted situation of the human unit in respect to a more commonplace form of personal conviction and particularly to fixed attitudes concerning religion.

Religious convictions of every sort have always complicated the integrity and assiduity of persons along lines outside those of the parochial. Such individuals, converted to or convinced by a church creed, have often radically altered their behavior from the antisocial to the beneficial. They have often so augmented passive behavior with acts of public welfare as to leave an indelible impression concerning at least the special or limited worth of religious conviction, even in the minds of the nonreligious. This fact is large-looming in the unsorted mass of data which the general person considers to be of a sound, informational nature. So far as I am aware or can discover, no statistician has yet been forward enough to make a tabulated cross section through various church-member groups in order to discover how widespread and efficacious the over-all benefits may be, or may not be. Indeed, no criteria of human behavior standards have been established which are acceptable enough to lend validity to such a survey even as an order-of-magnitude demonstration. But the very *absence* of criteria, after some two thousand years of the Christian religion, and many more thousands of others, distinctly suggests that the hypothesized survey, if practicable, would show that nothing had been added to the statistical character of mankind either by church dogma or by church-implanted conviction. That, however, is an observation rather than an argument.

For an appraisal of religious result, one might more likely look at a historic phenomenon, such as the church since the inception of the era of science. Here, after the church had held man steadfast in medievalism for a millennium and a half—after, that is, the power of religious conviction had been given an undisputed opportunity to express itself in a variety of societies for the entirety of that awful epoch—the discovery of the scientific method occurred. Faith had failed to budge man for fifteen hundred years. However, roughly commensurate with the new step in human thinking came the rise of rebellion *against* the motionless ancient church. Protestantism, then, was born along with modern scientific method—and was greatly stimulated by the discovery of the fruitfulness of that method. The subsequent increase in general knowledge, the rise of democratic states, and the proliferation of goods and machinery took place coincidentally with the division and spread of the various Protestant sects.

These sects have uniformly claimed that the benefits of the new era were due to "Christianity"—and that opinion is, also, part of the body of collective data.

There are reasons to suspect the assumption, even on a historical basis. For, if the Protestant churches undid to some degree the absolute dogma of the Roman church and so permitted their members a broader franchise in the fields of realistic knowledge, they did not, with the passage of time, keep pace with scientific advancement. Instead, they continued to divide and subdivide through quarrels over theological minutiae, until, at present, there are some hundreds of kinds of "Christian" churches with some hundreds of diverse creeds which must be accepted upon "faith" (by voluntary blind conviction). Thus it may be seen that the protest of the "protestants" was only in some small degree away from authoritarianism and only in some very small measure toward a willingness to accept and assimilate new truths as they were discovered. Only one church would have been necessary for the purpose of continuously adapting the fundamental precepts of Christ to new learning in the realm of physics, psychology and what not. There is no such one church, but only, as I have said, a multitude of sects, all of them set by convictions against a variety of the findings and hypotheses of more learned and detached members of the community as a whole.

This is the picture which currently confronts the individual without a "religious" conviction. It is remarkable, in view of the chaotic absurdity of the Protestant churches, that there are any Protestants at all. Manifestly, the joining of a church by an adult, or the continuing affiliation with a church of a person grown adult, can have nothing basically to do with pure intellectual conviction. It is—it must be in every case—the response to one or more other motives. And so, upon inspection, it proves to be. The motive may be tradition—which is part habit and part uncritical prejudice. It may be a simple response to the herd instinct. It may be the product of the compulsion of a conscience formed out of the instinctual urges present in every human being and the miscellaneous concepts and superstitions about conduct which infect present society. It may even be something yet more superficial—a liking for the members of a certain congregation, or for a minister, or the mere proximity of the church edifice. All such "convictions" are lightly held in detail —and people change about from sect to sect without severe moral compunction or intellectual distress. Indeed, in some instances, mere social rank plays a part in determining the sect in which an individual will feel comfortable. Variations of the creeds of these casually chosen and carelessly changed churches are considerable; their common denominator can be said to consist of hardly more than these three postutales: that an anthropomorphic god exists, that a philosopher named Jesus existed, and that there is an anthropoid life hereafter.

The Roman church, however, although persisting in exactly its medieval form, to this day manages to maintain a large membership—an occasion for even more amazement. As an organization, this church is possessed of several peculiar aspects which the Protestant sects lack. It is world-wide; it is politically compact; it is ordered like an army, and it is provided with absolute authority at the top. It permits its members to believe in freedom of action within limits but it takes over in its entirety all responsibility for the psychology of guilt and punishment. Thus the Roman church acts as the *conscience* of every member. The Roman Catholics also do not make distinctions between the spiritual and material worlds, which are absolute in Protestant sects. Even a prayer may be bought, in this intellectual oligarchy; and the price is regarded as a measure of value, not only to the living but to the dead.

Moreover, in the Roman church there is no room for dissent or debate—excepting only as an exercise. Convictions cannot be challenged. All moral, ethical and spiritual matters have been determined; a member cannot resist or deny those determinations and still retain his standing. Finally, this church reserves for itself the power to brand heresy, and also to excommunicate—in a manner inclined to intimidate any persons with even a vestigial faith in the doctrine.

By such devices it has stabilized the human mind. By ruling out individualism, it has made it necessary for its erudite members literally to split their minds into two parts, one of which is loyal to antique and untrustworthy dogmas and the other of which must proceed separately in the pursuit of science or commerce or truth as it is known in this era. As one would expect, it is a further policy of this particular church to indoctrinate prospective members and all the offspring of members while very young, and for this purpose the church has managed to cause a separation of the school system— here and in many nations—a most astonishing breach in the real principle that underlies religious freedom as a human right, for it denies to its members the very freedom of instruction which is the common property of all other citizens.

It may be seen that, while affiliation with a Protestant sect is a matter of conviction, or something even less—affiliation with the Roman church is the additional product of powerful psychic and social devices, some of which lie entirely outside the realm of faith, or even the realm of religion, properly considered. Indeed, the absolutism and mental regimentation of Romanism runs parallel to that of fascism in politics and economics. The "soul" prepared for total church authority possesses only a residue of mind, automatically conditioned for temporal absolutism. The truth of that is shown by the official and unofficial relationships of Catholicism with fascism during the last fifteen years. It would be difficult, one might guess, for the Roman-conditioned mind to see the flaws in fascism just as it is doubtless impossible for a truly convinced Catholic to understand in full the principle of democracy. Democracy cannot exist for one presubscribed to limitless church authority. By that very token, it grows increasingly difficult for the Roman church to retain its members in modern democratic societies and completely impossible to retain all of them in the medieval frame of mind. Thus the church itself is being slowly forced to change its dogma and one may expect an acceleration of the process in the future.

Because of such reductions to absurdity, such schism, such rigidity, and many other flaws, the Protestant sects and the Catholic church *suggest* that their effect upon the so-called progress of the so-called Christian world must have been nil, or small—or, even that the net effect may have been adverse. There is no way of proving any relative historic value in these organized convictions to the world; the existence of so many codified systems for resigning personal autonomy may have seriously interfered with the normal growth and spread of intelligence. I, myself, believe this to be the case, and it is my hope eventually to make a separate elaboration of the reasons for my belief. Here, I merely suggest a line of inquiry. . . .

We have every right to ask ourselves today in what ways man in the aggregate is any better off than he was a hundred years ago, a thousand, and ten thousand. When war, mass murder, pestilence and slavery are included in the assay (as they must be), it might be found that, after two thousand years of Christianity, more men die sooner and harder, the average city has a shorter life and is more thoroughly destroyed, there is more famine per capita, more disease per capita, and more misery. Certainly, at the time of Christ, a smaller number of human beings were in slavery than at present. We are too prone to consider ourselves, even now, as enjoying the fruits of knowledge that is only hypothetically available to us—and far too reluctant to compare ourselves with the past on the basis of a death for a death, a slave for a slave, a sickness for a sickness, and torture for torture. We feel that if the current death could have been avoided by known means, or the slave freed, or the disease cured—it represents advancement. That is a most extraordinary illusion. . . .

One more aspect of bodies-of-conviction is worthy of inspection as a prelude to the individual's enigma. That is, the relationship with past and discarded bodies of conviction—with pre-Christian faiths—with paganism. I need not allude, I trust, to the fact that both the Roman and Protestant forms of Christianity are still essentially pagan in so far as their rituals, symbols, housing, etc., are concerned. This is common knowledge, although it is seldom dwelt on. But, what major difference is there, even in the matter of central conviction?

We can hardly speak of monotheism here. There are three gods in the Trinity. The Catholics enjoy the reverence of a goddess, besides: the Virgin. And, by the simple expedient of saying that God (the gods) made man in his own image, these religions have successfully rationalized the obvious anthropomorphism practiced by savages, who are naïve and foolish enough to take the opposite position and make gods and goddesses more or less resembling themselves. Nothing is really achieved by the reversal. It is a mere device which has stamped half of mankind as most credulous, for upward of two thousand years. If there are matters in the universe worthy of the reverence of modern man (and I do not doubt there are), they can certainly not be such.

Between Zeus and Jehovah there is no marked difference in so far as conceptual characteristics are concerned. An afternoon with Bulfinch and an afternoon with the Saints multiplies this sense of identity, or at least of mutual parenthood in mass thought processes. The Throne of God is scarcely an improvement on Mount Olympus. It is somewhat more universal, somewhat more congruent to the planetary hypothesis—but in essence it is the same lofted platform. A study of the sacred works of all the contemporary religions, together with an examination of paganism, will endlessly multiply the similarities of concept and even of detail in anecdote and fable. The honest scholar finally must conclude that if one is to be regarded as a myth they are all myths and that if one is in any sense true they are all true in the sense that man has a perpetual, universal tendency to translate his earthly experience into heroic-sized characters which he then names, worships and serves. It thus becomes manifest that man permanently exhibits the tendency in some form or forms even though he begin without a godhead and subordinate gods supplied by a religion or a church.

Some such conclusion as this was reached by Carl Gustav Jung in his theory of the relationship of legends to instinct. The former, he suggests, are the inevitable product of the latter—its expression in man, and, incidentally, a sign of man's evolution beyond the beasts. Religion, then, may be regarded as instinctual: it is a natural attempt to express man's inner patterns in terms comprehensible enough so that a solution of his problems will be made mechanically available.

Why the average scientist does not discern this truth, I cannot understand. He accepts, readily enough, the phylogenic pattern described by the development and the growth of an individual human being. He points to the ear of a grown man and thereby exhibits the gill of a fish. But that there may be a parallel psychical phylogeny he usually will not even consider. He indicates the presence of all manner of tropism and instinct in lower animals. But when asked the function and whereabouts of instinct in himself—he flatly denies that it exists. He prefers to consider his psyche a tabula rasa, or a production of his own effort—a parthenogenic entity in space and time, a conscious ego without a past and with, in consequence, no future, either. This insistence, of course, greatly delimits his own function—for it is in itself a preconviction of the precise sort I am discussing.

These various hypotheses concerning religious conviction might be carried a step toward the future. One could prophesy the rise, through knowledge of instinct, of a scientific church—a church which, on the physical plane, not only accepted each new forward step in knowledge, but abetted the taking of such steps. One could imagine such a church using not blasted and barbaric dogma, but the most enlightened theories of psychology, for its creed. This church would pay less noisy lip service to Christ, God, the Virgin, and the Holy Ghost—but it would be able to make an eternal application of those truths which are implicit to the various archetypal qualities reposing now in each god. The plain and extraordinarily cogent wisdom of all the thinkers and philosophers from Lao-tse to Jesus Christ—and it is the same wisdom—could be winnowed of paganism and sifted of theological chaff, in such a church. Worship would then become not loud fearful praise and gloating broken pledge but action taken by the members as individuals, inasmuch as nothing save action could be accounted either as worship or as reverence.

Only a single quasi-dogmatic statement could be made in such a church: truth lies equally within and without each man in forms that are relative and that change with man's changing perceptions. Such a church, founded on subjective struggling toward all truth and every truth and on the objective enactment of a life in harmony with as much truth as the individual could grasp, would, once again, occupy in our society a place outside of and above the "physical" sciences. For this church could afford to apperceive that even Einsteinian relativity is temporal and that someday members of it would look back upon the uttermost mathematic of this century as quaint—an advancement, to be sure, and a great feat of reason, but not quite correct and not quite adequate—just as the earlier theories of Newton were not quite adequate and correct. A church literally dedicated to truth—to the conscious study and understanding of instinct as well as to the acceptance of the outer world as it is discovered—would gradually put an end to all other religions, dogmas, creeds, sects, arbitrary convictions, and emasculating faiths —because it would *be* living truth. Nobody has yet successfully founded such a church.

Until it is evolved, or until individuals commence to evolve it for themselves, whether in the name of religion or of integrity, common man will continue to rot accursed in every cell of the world-wide penitentiary of conviction. Even agnosticism or skepticism is a confining prison, for what is a greater paradox than that a man should believe so much he is able to discover he believes nothing! Such a person, had he a rim of perspective from which to look into himself, would find he is lagging behind Descartes. He thinks—therefore nothing is for anything.

The gospel that demands "faith," that insists on the acceptance of conviction before it accepts the one convinced, makes a mockery of half of man's freedom—the subjective half. Those who eschew it and go no further—most of the self-styled "intelligent" men of these times—have lifted their foot in a laudable step, but refused to find where to set it down in order to move forward.

It is pagan to require the human psyche to accept first on faith that there is a god or that one will be taken to heaven for leading a good life. Such acceptance leaves the accepter his own victim. If he succeeds in its autohypnosis, he will be the dupe of it forever after, or for as long as conviction lasts—the happy dupe, the fanatic dupe, the holy dupe, the bigoted dupe, even the socially more useful dupe—but always the dupe. And that man who once deludes himself, who once betrays his integrity, cannot again trust the convictions even of his physical senses unless and until he undoes his basic self-deceit. He is in an induced sleep and not alive at all. His living is consecrated to his death. He rewards and punishes himself (or his church does) according to the most perfidious premise man has yet devised—a premise which would be frantically eschewed by all the teachers of truth including Jesus Christ himself, who advocated truth as a way and an end, and who constantly attacked dogma.

The invention of hell and heaven is no longer necessary to the modern thinker. He sees the polarizations of all such opposites take place within himself through the exercise of integrity. A family of gods is not necessary, or a godlike man—for his problem has become other: to discover and re-create truth within and around himself. He will follow that purpose to the ends of time, find those ends in it, lose his ego in the continual pursuit, and so, in living without fear, destroy the very existence of the fear of death.

From the oldest epoch, man has secretly known that wisdom and truth are one and that neither is wholly external but each is half within himself. So far, however, except in the case of individuals, he has not dared or cared or had the courage or perhaps the evolved intelligence to examine the subjective realities with the elaborate candor he applies to the physical sciences. All our ruined civilizations are, in a sense, examples of the failures of a one-sided search. The other side has been deposited in a creed, bound over to a church, or buried in a political, national, racial, economic or hysterical conviction. This must now be done away with.

For the only conviction a man can begin with is conviction in his existence, and the reality of it, and the reality known around him. From there, the way back into his own consciousness, and the way thence to understanding of what is eternal, is difficult and endless. But the reward is inexpressible. . . .

The concept of what I have called "preconviction"—or faith—the empty syllogism whereby the subject agrees to agree first, and afterward turns upon himself with exultation because he finds he agrees—is the great masterpiece of superstition. Indeed, *faith*, as it is commonly accepted, *is superstition* and the father of superstition. For, whether it is faith in the notion that a rabbi of great insight, half lost in history, was the "son of the living God," or faith in the "immaculate conception" of that rabbi's mother, or in an amulet, a witch doctor, a quack remedy, or a bit of folklore, it is all, in a very large sense, of one piece. The conclusion is a portion of the hypothesis and the conclusion itself conditions behavior in relation to the hypothesis. The power of the process lies in the power of suggestibility—which is very great.

That man who accepts without challenge the idea of the son of God or of immaculate conception will very likely feel and act "reborn." He can do no otherwise, for that would be a patent (and intimidating) form of self-betrayal. His "rebirth" is what he had been told will happen and what he expects after he has put himself through the mechanics of "faith." That man, also, who believes the quack, will surely heal specifically and temporarily if his trouble is functional rather than organic—and most trouble is. That man who notices a misfortune, however small, after breaking a mirror, crossing the path of a black cat, or walking under a ladder, becomes a lifelong missionary of the "omen" and a culture center for superstition—which is the same process in reverse. The *same* process, to labor analogue for those feeble in logic, is the alarmed *expectation* of that man who has accepted the sinister quality of black cats, ladders and broken mirrors; nervous expectation is as powerful a causal agent of disaster as is holy confirmation of reform.

The process is a closed circle. It seems to have boundless dimension because it is susceptible of perpetual motion along its round curve. In the matter of the rabbi—which is to say, the matter of Christianity—the original admonition, if I interpret it correctly, was to have "faith" in the truth. The truth was delimited by the knowledge and intuitions of a man who lived two thousand years ago. Much of this truth has changed during the interval, but the followers of Christ have not undertaken to examine it properly and bring themselves up to date. I hazard the guess that Christ himself would have done so. He would not be quarreling with the theory of evolution today, or the planetary hypothesis, or Einsteinian relativity. As I interpret the sense of what he was trying to convey, all of it was directed toward individual subjectivity. He seems to have been endlessly impatient with old superstition, old dogma, and the pursuit of the letter of the old law. He would decry its present equivalents. And that quality—that very integrity—cost him his life. The appeal which he repeated in as many figures and parables as he could invent was an appeal to eschew the rusty irrationalisms of the past and to act individually according to the highest level of inner honesty.

There is not, today, a church that would last long if it openly advocated the adherence to intellectual deceit. Therefore every church has found it essential to retain and to magnify the technique of preconviction, the "sacred" myth, the dogmatic blood-oath. Such a process is not necessary for the genuine following of Christ, as I understand it—and, indeed, is so far from what must have been the intentions of Christ as to be most dismaying. The central soundness of his philosophical and psychological teaching has long since vanished in ritualist thought forms.

That there must still be maintained a set of symbols for the average man, rather than a lucid brief on the matter of subjective integrity, I do not doubt. A level of knowledge and consciousness may someday be reached at which all symbols are unnecessary. At that time, knowledge and wisdom will be directed toward the absolute; but we are many millions of years away from that time. At that time, what might be described as a "scientific understanding of the nature of consciousness and the purpose of evolution" automatically would be the compelling motive of each individual common man. Only a moment's thought is needed to show how measurelessly far we are from such a situation, as a species. But the time shall surely arrive, if universal circumstances permit our tenure of the planet during the necessary interval: a time when there would be no need to translate the phenomena of life and death, of awareness and of inward struggle, into symbological terms. Useful "explanations" of these facts, in that imaginable, far-off era, would not be necessary in the sense they are today because people, through inward consciousness of the nature of their own selves, would then have truer explanations and understandings of existence than our minds are likely to formulate at this hour.

But even before we shall be able to discard wholly obsolete symbols and think in as yet undiscovered realities, we must progress, as a species, through changing symbols. Those which Christ offered in parables would serve common man well, I daresay, for millennia to come. Unfortunately, their meaning has been lost to view in "Western" society. They are commonly "translated" into mundane terms, while, in their original context, they were mundane analogues for subjective entities and activities. The "religions" that stemmed from Christ ignored, from the first, his central thesis of honesty of inward awareness and embraced, one by one, the symbols of paganisms predating Christ. Thus the story of crucifixion and resurrection, while in the grand sense a symbolically revelatory legend, has been so channelized, so commingled with barbarisms, so heavily suffused with fleshiness, with agony, vinegar, earthquake, thorns and blood, that in repeating it every Christian church practices unwittingly a form of penitentism, of public masochism, which is in no sense and no way suitable or comprehensible to an educated and oriented honest modern consciousness.

(When one considers the children who are exposed to this heathenish business, on the one hand, and to enlightened justice, humanity, good taste, and kindness, on the other—when one knows as we now do their normal affinity with barbarism and their psychological inability to understand resurrection as a symbol—when one contemplates teaching democratic philosophy to young persons who are learning at the same time that their god was nailed, stabbed, bled and bashed to death—one can only be amazed that instinct is powerful enough to have saved the "Christian" world from any disaster worse than the present one. Of course, the present disaster is by no means the possible limit of catastrophe which may yet befall the Western, Christian nations owing to their paroxysmal and schizoid behavior in this trap of faith—so damaging to the integrities of most children and so deceptive to all adults.)

Such "Christianity" and such methodologies will vanish, or they will be revised symbologically, or else they will continue until the discrepancy between their superstitious bases and the scientific method grows so enormous that either mass mania will destroy these "Christians" or some other nation will take advantage of their debilitating dilemma and subdue them.

Revision would be the most desirable. A religion of inner truth, through, of, and for truth, so long as it used the correct symbols, would furnish common man with the means of speedy spiritual progress. At present, he is attempting to find in economic and sociological systems a solution for those problems which neither science nor modern religion attempts to solve—problems which concern his own inner self. He will discover no surcease, no noble and enlarging future in any such thought designs—for none of them is concerned with the source of man's present woe: the psyche of man. Man alone is concerned—his actual nature—his soul, if you will. . . .

The most burdensome of common convictions is the set that refers to death. These are, in a sense, more distortive than convictions which interfere with wholly known truth (churchly, dogmatic, and so on), for such material can be dispelled by reason and sensible evidence. Death, however, is not like a Roman Catholic worship of images, or an elaborate Presbyterian anthropomorphology, or a Christian Scientist insistence upon the observation of nonsense.

All men die.

The theories of "immortality" which have persistently sprung into being throughout history can easily be accounted for by a study of the ego, or "little I," as it has been called here. Since most human beings devote the bulk of their energy to the maintenance of the identity, orientation and pleasures of the "little I," it follows that they will not detachedly anticipate its utter disappearance. Wherefore they invent imaginary realms in which they assume the "little I" will repose during Eternity.

The urge of so many persons to imagine paradises for themselves is not a gauge of the nature of the universe but of the meagerness of the ego. All Valhallas are "little I" regions; the pleasures (rewards!) of most are physical; a few hypothesize nebulous emotional advantages such as the aeonlong adoration of a deity. None is more than an extension of or enlargement upon some function already enjoyed on earth. And none of these everlasting joys, as has been noted by many observers, could possibly serve the spirit of a man for more than a few hours—let alone for millennia. So the psychic vacuum of the devotee (or convinced man) is plainly shown.

Not having intelligence or imagination enough to look forward to an interesting heaven, he looks forward to one he would find insupportable and he fitfully strives for it, or performs rites for it.

or spends money to be prayed into it. His weakness, indeed, is the reason that makes him build such big churches, install such loud organs in them, and costume his pompous capers so gaudily: he tries by objective enlargement to shout down what is really so small and so weak subjectively. How obvious! How silly his course in relation to it!

All formal heavens have been surpassed in perfectness and appeal by a multitude of earthly pursuits, intellectual achievements, and even physical establishments. This very fact shows how suspicious man is of every religion's heaven, how unwilling he is to invest much psychic energy in its design, and in what literally trivial opinion he unthinkingly holds his "surviving" ego. As a matter of subjective fact, an ego that is merely putting up with this world in the hope of dull rewards for patience in another is already so unalive that one might naturally predicate for it no real chance of long-range survival.

It would be well to consider the actual teachings of Christ and other philosophers in respect to the matter. In them is discerned a different theme from either hell-fearing or heaven-chasing. Their teachings suggest that the object of individual life is to clear away and dismiss all ego-attached values, all temporal pleasure and distress, all "selfish" thought—and so to create a state of higher purpose, or transcendent and understanding awareness, wherein the wants of the "little I" no longer exist. It is interesting to note that, where such a selfless condition is achieved, the necessity of a heaven no longer exists: i.e., there remains in the individual no ego demanding a heaven. Such a person lives for the sake of nature—his own—that of his fellows—and the nature of nature itself. He is aware that he is so doing; he can neither dread nor dote upon the various fruits of his instincts.

In a certain logical way, that individual is already immortal. Consciousness itself, correctly functioning, produces states of knowing that beggar the work of all heaven-architects. It would pay people to make the attempt even as an experiment—and if the effort became general, the world-wide result would be something very much resembling life after the Biblical Judgment. It would not be an inconsiderable achievement. There would be no wars, for example, no poverty, no races, and no injustice. It would be a happy, democratic world.

But most men—most Western men, at least—are so tightly affixed to the idea that the little ego of the individual is the alpha and omega of consciousness that they are unwilling even to attempt to surrender any of it that they have. Scientists, for example, will

argue flatly against the existence of "personal immortality"—as
though that were the only phrase besides "dissolution" which would
suitably describe the nature of man and cosmos. Such persons
merely demand a reverence for the boundaries of their own awareness; and they make the demand in kindergarten terms—in the
terms of egoistic restriction—inasmuch as they have not, for the
most part, entertained any state of consciousness other than that
of thought and direct sensation, after the age of five or ten—at
which period the accepted Western, American, British, Texan or
Parisian attitude of the mind toward the mind was taken to be
mandatory.

It is very easy—and quite fascinating—to make certain elementary experiments with personal consciousness in order to demonstrate the unreliability of the acceptance of the ego as one's entire
self. For example, people, like domestic animals, think of their "selves"
and their names as one. They are not, of course. The names are
pure chance. A James or a Helen might have been a Frank or a
Genevieve. To consider that—to consider one's personal consciousness as being differently or variously named—is to take a small step
in assaying ego. The next step is to consider it with no name at
all, which produces certain enlightening though minor degrees of
fresh thought. A third step might be to consider one's ego as somebody else—not the person for whom it has taken itself—and material
for that speculation may be supplied by the fact that one's ego is
not the same to different friends or the same to any particular
friend that it is to the inner self. One may also experiment with
the idea that identity is its own illusion—or that one is the only
awareness and the world is illusion: i.e., solipsism. Next, one may
turn to the readily discernible fact that the ego changes—that one
is not one's same self today or that one behaved like another yesterday. From myriads of such simple observations—which resemble
those a good chemist would make straightaway on a new substance—
the psyche can learn about the chameleon nature of its ego and can
perceive that the condition of its ego is the product of other and
different forces from those which maintain, say, a brick as a
permanent entity. A detached observer would normally undertake
a search into those different forces and components.

I submit that, if he did so, he would presently begin to compile
a mass of "moral" data. He would see, from the evolutionary standpoint, that awareness is a means of survival and that survival has
tended to increase awareness. He would see that when consciousness
becomes conscious of itself, the subjective balances, or opposites,
are perceived, and the function of *choice* among them becomes more

and more voluntary. In the face of the existence of such choice, he would see that further survival depends upon appraisal—appraisal by man of himself and his needs as well as of his naked environment. And he would see that by appraising the human (and human-relationship) values to be chosen, he would always set up a *moral* attitude toward himself and others.

At the end of such a logical process, he would discover that the ego which rationalizes in order to augment or exploit itself is destructive of all consciousness by acts both physically direct and mentally indirect, to the exact degree of dishonesty involved in the rationalization. Thus the moral nature of consciousness in nature would bloom as a flower of pure logic for him, without the need of dogma, messiah, or preconviction. So long as his symbols were germane to his logic, he could use any, for himself. But to others, with other symbologies, he could reasonably apply only the principle of integrity and reason. To teach them subjective logic, he would have to learn their symbols. This should be the central meaning in truly religious teaching—a meaning generally honored by meticulous avoidance.

(It might here be noted that "insanity" comes more from the reluctance of mankind to concern itself with the aspects of the psyche which lie outside the ego than from the devastation wrought upon the ego by the external world. Not locomotives, not prison walls, not poverty, not tall buildings or battle sounds drive people crazy so much as the attitudes of others, and, especially, their lacks of attitude. The schizoid is not the victim of a personality split by the harsh action of environment; he is, simply, one who cannot assemble a personality—or can no longer maintain a personality—in a world where people have insufficient consciousness to understand the psychical components which he is endeavoring to become or to go on being. The paranoid escapes reality, certainly, and the maniac and the melancholic—but all of them escape by a reflex exaggeration of some portion of a valid psychic entity which the general public did or would not admit the existence of. What society said was not so, these persons knew was somehow real, and by a concentrated exaggeration of it they tried first to offer proof and were finally carried away in the effort or escaped responsibility through making it. Insanity is therefore the big church, the loud music, and the costuming of an ego-religion—the unit expression of escape through misshapen conviction and, again, a demonstration of ego-smallness—this time, the smallness of collective ego. In that sense, the world, not the madman, is mad first.)

I am always amazed that a nation of people so materially venturesome as the Americans are so ventureless in the other half of nature and life. It is eccentric of them to take one of only two attitudes toward death: the skeptical, which merely denies the survival of consciousness, and the preconvicted, which accepts one heaven or another. These two positions are rather like "optimism" and "pessimism"—both of which, of course, are utter superstition, consciously chosen to satisfy an inner orientation which bears no truly needful, finally useful, or ever genuine relation to fact. Thus, to say that one is an optimist or a pessimist is equivalent to saying that one is a crystal-gazer, because either state involves the *future*. Such positions are, again, attitudes like faith, and share superstition with faith. To argue about death from such postures is sophistry. There are other and better attitudes; attitudes more natural and more vital—particularly, since the whole nature of the relation of awareness to cosmos will never be completely understood by men, who can have only certain numbers and levels of consciousness under any given conditions.

Indeed, scientific proof of the immortal existence of the ego after death would certainly bring about the end of living man. For how many would go on here if there were a better world handy—and how many men would keep their appetite for trying if it were proved that they were in continuous peril of being burned alive for quintillions of years? Some religions, of course, do produce a modified replica of the foregoing states. Their devotees walk through life as living death, awaiting resurrection—or they shiver through it in a multiplicity of nervous fears and compulsions. Again, were mundane life to be stretched out for a mere million years and were every man of us to become a Wandering Jew, what new life would be allowed to persist—what new forms could nature try—and what progress would the individual make, if he had a thousand thousand years in which to accomplish it? What would love be to ever-living lovers? There may have been people faithful to each other for eighty years—but who would remain consistently so enamored for eighty thousand?

It has been sadly said that there is death in life everywhere. But is this not, rather, the very life of living? Is not the inscrutability of extinction the true subjective drive of every outward event in daily existence and its conscious understandability the drive of inward life? Is not the unknown number of our days their justest and most potent incentive? And if consciousness is not aware of itself before birth or after death, is it not immortal all the while it lives—because it is unable to know death as it knows life? Finally, for one single different pair of illustrations, could not death be accompanied by

that flash of understanding (fitted into its own negligible segment
of what we call time) which would bridge the gap between our
insatieties and infinite content? Or could not the insight be achieved
deliberately? Have we the right to deny the possibility of such
speculations to those who make them? Even scientifically, we have
not: for awareness is, or is accompanied by, an electrical phenomenon; the death of every man might be his constellation of it. Or his
utterly honest thinking might arrange it in its true pattern. There
are inklings for that very sort of theory; there are endless intimations in subjective report; and we are only at the beginning of
them—we who have nothing to "accept" or "deny."

For death, like living, has its planetary solitude for each man.
But the functions of that solitude have atrophied among us and
we have lost our inward understanding of the meanings of death
because of it. In that, we have lost half the meaning of life. Did
we not know we were to die, we would be children; by knowing it,
we are given our opportunity to mature in spirit. Life is only the
father of wisdom; *death is the mother*.

11

SOMETIMES, now in the long summer, they sat together for hours on the Gracey veranda and she listened while he read —quietly and with just enough emphasis to give rhythm and significance to the words. Sometimes they went fishing together, or sightseeing, or dining out.

By boat on the Miami River—the "great, gray-green, greasy" Miami River, Ann called it—to the Seminole Indian village. They walked among the platform huts and watched the women in their bright clothes run sewing machines in the thatched shade and they watched the black-eyed boy wrestle with an alligator.

By bus to the wooden trestles that strung the Keys like beads. They fished all day with hand lines and ate a picnic lunch and came back in sunsets that displayed all the colors of the Seminole women's skirts.

By sightseeing boat on a tour of the artificial islands in Biscayne Bay, the pumped-up, million-dollar islands of the boom, symmetrical as cakes and frosted with the semi-precious palaces of the rich.

By bus to the Everglades. They cast plugs in the sweet-water canals—canals that ran as straight as map lines through the yellow-brown prairie and bisected jungle patches called hammocks.

By their own car on linear roads to restaurants near the sea, or inland, under the soft night sky, where there would be food and music and murmurous other people—men in uniforms and girls with down-flowing hair, with eyes that gleamed over table lights, with scarlet smiles.

Florida in the south is low and level. Ann said God's bulldozer had gone over it. Coral was its hardest rock; in contour and substance it lent itself to the reticulation of roadways and geometrical sculpture by steam shovels. Ann believed that the people who missed hills and mountains in Florida were literal-minded; there was plenty of topography, she said, but it was upside-down: the clouds.

Often, when her workday was ended, she would come over to the Gracey house for a swim—bringing her bathing suit and taking it back, wet, to her cottage. She never left it; that would have made it a symbol of possession, an interference with his original wish for solitude, a small, shaped intrusion on his clothesline. Such afternoons were all alike.

This one was in August . . .

John and Ann lay back against the dunes—accepting them—as though the slant of sand had been carved for human comfort into a long seat facing the arena of the sea. The sun leaned above them. It cast the shadow of Ann's chin on her neck, of her breasts on her satin-clad ribs and of her feet upon the beach. They watched seven airplanes in the high blue overhead—seemingly fixed there, like collected dragonflies. They watched a torpedo boat make practice forays upon a passing tanker.

People passed. It was a cooler day than usual—a day for walking—and these human beings came along from the populous regions a mile to the south.

A boy and a girl with a wet-eared spaniel. The two children carried paper sacks for gathering shells; their dog galloped in a zigzag, daring the waves that rubbed out his little tracks as fast as he made them. The children spoke cheerfully.

So did the old man with white hair who passed by next. He held a surf-casting rod, eyed them with curiosity, and said, "Beautiful day. Breezy." They agreed.

But another man, who went past quickly, did not speak. His mouth was fixed in the expression of the memory that urged him on; his muscles worked leanly; he seemed trying to knead that recollection into a different form or to stamp it into the sand so that it would be buried, or, perhaps, to cast it away in the savage glance that he threw from them to the ocean.

"I wonder what's wrong with him?" Ann turned her head to follow the angrily plodding man.

"Woman."

"How do you know? Could be money."

"Nope. In the case of money, he'd be pale and scared—or red and furious—but—"

"But exactly what, Mr. Bones?"

"He'd have his mouth shut. He wouldn't have that hangdog look. That sharp, unconscious expectancy of more frustration to come."

Ann thought that over. "I believe you're right. He's married to her. She's an unnatural blonde."

"He gave her the rent money. She spent it in a dress shop."

"He invited his best friends to dinner and she bawled him out."

"Because he protested when she trumped his ace."

"She broke his favorite putter," Ann said, "trying to pry open a window."

"She went out with salesmen while he was working his fingers to the bone."

"She used his old-fashioned razor to scrape the labels off last year's jelly jars."

"She sold his shotgun. She pawned his fishing tackle. She traded his waders for secondhand lace curtains. She sent his hunting clothes to the church rummage sale."

"She had his poker table cut down and repainted and surprised him with the new coffee table in the living room."

"Golly!" John was awed. "She lost the gas ration tickets."

"Or gave them away to con a social superior. And she put his dressing gown into the border of her rag rug."

"She tried to cheat the tax collector—and didn't tell him first."

"She eats popcorn in bed. Her Doberman pinscher sleeps with her. And doesn't like him. She wears hair curlers at night and snoods in the daytime. She has asthma."

"The poor son of a gun."

"Oh, I don't know."

"You don't know!" He rolled slightly and stared at her. "Haven't you a drop of compassion in your veins?"

Ann shook her head. "He greased the car with her cold cream, remember? And he worse than snores: he rumbles. He has a secretary who can't do shorthand—and he doesn't know she knows it. He broke the platter she won when she graduated—trying to show the Ellises how to juggle. When he has three drinks, he stands on his head and recites. He's a card, you know. And he bobbed her hair when she was asleep. That was the year they got married. He puts sulphur ointment on his pimples. And he's always teaching her how to defend herself just in case—the old one-two—and every time he shows her, he gets through her guard and slaps her. Then—year before last—he tanned that mink in his den—"

"I yield," John said. "Let him walk."

The boy and girl returned. They were arguing shrilly about how long Superman could stay underwater.

"You must have been a lovely child," John said. "Vengeful."

"I was pious."

"I doubt that."

"I sang."

"Sang what? Battle songs?"

"Hymns."

"Where?"

"Club meetings. Parties. In church. Mother was proud of me."

"I'll bet you flirted with your audience. Rolled those large, custom-built eyes."

"Certainly. And I found out I got more applause if I almost forgot the words and let my treble fade down to a worried whisper."

"You were an apple-polisher."

"The teacher's pet," she agreed. "It was easier that way. I always got A, you know."

"Spent recess in the library."

"That kept the little boys from throwing salamanders at me."

"Made neat notes and were careful to leave them around."

"I was efficient in such matters. It gave me more freedom and spare time—in the end."

"For what?"

"Various things. One year, I was in danger, mostly."

He frowned. "Danger?"

"Railroad trains bore down on me. I was tied to the tracks. I slid over cliffs and hung on roots. Houses I was in always caught fire at night. There were explosions. I was in submarines—and things like that. People saved me. Movie stars."

"I see. What did you do other years?"

"I was a vampire—for several."

"You mean you went around drinking human blood? Normal—for you—I should imagine."

"Not that kind of vampire. I broke men's hearts like skeets."

"Oh."

"What about you? Did you do a good turn every day?"

289

He lay back and stared at the sky. "I was an eagle scout, if that's what you mean."

"Honestly?"

"Honestly."

"Then you can tie knots and make a fire without matches and set bones?"

"I can read semaphore," he answered portentously. "I can make bannock. Name trees. Track bears. Shoot the sun. Build canoes. Breed guppies. Box compasses. There is very little I cannot do."

She looked at him critically. "You are in pretty good shape. Hiking?"

"Natural strength."

"What's—natural strength, if anything?"

"When I was a small boy we lived for a while in Buffalo. Down the street lived the Oeppel family. Mr. O. was lazy."

"Never did a tap of work in his life."

"Never a lick. Just sat on his porch in the spring and summer and in his parlor in the winter. His wife was a washerwoman."

"His children fetched and delivered the laundries in a little wagon."

"Precisely. For years, he hardly budged from his rocker. He weighed more than two hundred pounds. Many an afternoon, I used to lie in the privet hedge and watch Mr. Oeppel just sit and breathe—"

"Occasionally letting go with your beanshooter—"

"I frown on the thought. One day the people across the street moved away. I forget their name. The van came. The moving men got the upright piano out on the walk and somehow tipped it over. It pinned one of the men on his back in the grass. Mr. Oeppel rushed over and lifted it up all alone. The other two moving men had run for help. It was very impressive."

"Let me see now. Where are we?"

"Natural strength," he said with some asperity. "Mr. Oeppel had natural strength. Like me."

She was silent for a moment. "You do have a rather good figure—for a professor. A marked lack of round shoulders and flat chest."

He raised up on one elbow and peered at her. "Your own figure is worth passing comment, Mrs. G. I've always intended to mention it. It takes the eye. A second-rate lady author could do things with it. Lemme see." He squinted. " 'She lay in the eloquent downflap of the setting sun—her firm chin up—the lithe contours of her limbs extended in shadow that meandered with a darkling attenuation on the sand where it fell from the ruby-crested apogee of her big toe—' "

"Go on. That's very good."

" 'Gilda-Mae's raven hair was not quite Stygian but fell back from her brow in a casual part—curling heavily—musky—shot with reddish glints from the eloquent downflap of the setting sun—like the tendrils and curling wisps of the first delicate smoke that rise under the proud attentions of the arsonist—' "

"I give you a semicolon."

"Don't stop me. 'Long days of idling at his side on this far-flung, paradisal stretch of wonderland had tanned her the color of a filbert.' "

"A truffle."

" 'She was as tan as topaz. Her eyes—what eyes she had! Ordinary men called them hazel—' "

"Filbert, that is, isn't it?"

" 'Hazel. They could change with each delicious fancy through the woodland ranges—the grays, greens, mysterious olives—' "

"Shoe size, five double-A. Gloves—"

" 'Her nubile, purple lips—' "

"This is Countess Crimson. Seaproof."

" 'Her waterproof lips—' " He started to laugh, and she laughed.

"Johnny," she said, "you ought to try writing. Under a woman's name. You'd be better at it than painting. The female readers in the grain belt would positively devour your stuff."

"What's the matter with my painting? It's improving. You can tell the landscapes from the portraits."

"I didn't know you'd tried any portraits."

"Crabs. Pelicans. Shawn said they were astonishing." He lay back on the dune and gazed at the sky. "Wonderful guy, Shawn."

"He was always a wonderful guy. Everybody loved him. He was a young man when I was just a little girl. For two or three summers, he drove the ice wagon. I practically worshiped him. You see—he kept a box of fig bars up in front and every time he brought a cake of ice he gave me one. Then he went away—to college and to art school. Word finally got around that he had even gone to Paris—and the dogs. Practically everybody who leaves New Lancaster is presumed to have gone to the dogs—as though there weren't any other place outside the town limits. It's fairly spiteful."

"I must remember," he said lazily, "to stock up on fig bars. An odious confection."

She laughed again.

But he did not laugh in response. He fell to thinking.

She turned so she could look at him. His brows knit. On his studious face came an expression like fear. This, she knew, was concern with his trouble—with whatever trouble it was that had taken him from his work and deposited him on this beach. She examined the thought. With his country at war— with so much to be done—he was one of the last men to relax like this, to sit alone, to stretch his vacation from month to month. Maybe he was planning some intricate experiment or investigation. No doubt he was. And yet—that would hardly explain his moods and his attitude. It would not explain why he sometimes almost made love to her—and always altered the words into mocking and always sheered away even from mockery. It would explain nothing—really. He was sick.

She could not believe that, either. . . .

I'll have to get it over with sometime, he thought. Sometime soon. She has recovered from Bill and all about Bill. Surely she has. Otherwise, she wouldn't be able to choose this very beach as her favorite place to sit and sun and swim and talk. This very spot on this very beach. No. She's all right. It's me. *If I only knew.*

"A last dip?" he asked.

She nodded gravely. "If you want, Johnny."

They waded into the warm water. She teetered and he took her hand. They went on together, not looking at each other.

PART IV

THE TIDE

1

JOHN GALEN found his answer on a night in September.

It was one of the endlessly hot nights—the heat moist—not a burning, arid heat, but sweating—the air fragrant with jasmine and frangipani—the moon full—the clouds low and rounded—an arranged sky that rolled overhead like a stage effect—the dark sea shattering into gold.

He had first taken Ann to the movies.

They sat with a couple of thousand soldiers in the air-conditioned auditorium, laughing at Donald Duck, staring grimly at the bomb-raveled news reels, and pursuing the pursued blonde star along nine whirling spools of celluloid. Afterward, they bought a newspaper and read headlines: Russians falling back, Japs advancing. They crossed the street and ate ice cream in a drugstore that played drugstore music on a loudspeaker in the wall. When they returned to the damp, furry night, they drove home along the beach.

Ann was fairly content. She knew John well enough now to follow the expressions on his face by mere glances—as a child follows the picture narrative of a favorite storybook. In April or May or June she had merely said to herself, Bill would like him, or, He and Bill would make good company. By and by she had changed those phrases: Bill could have learned much from him, or, I wonder if Bill would ever have had that kind of poise, or even, *would* they have liked each other? Finally she had surrendered to the facts. She had sought out John because she had secretly known that his companionship, his learning, his assured bearing, and the mere masculinity of him would help return her from wherever Bill was to wherever she had to be. Bill would approve of that, she had said, during the transition. Now she could think. It does not matter what Bill would say because I am me. Bill said so. I am young and alive. I must decide.

Bill is gone, she could say. There was a time when I wished more to have gone with him than to be here. That time is over. I am a woman. I must remember to be one—always. Not a woman eternally mourning, though not one who forgets. Not a woman escaping from grief but a woman who can contain grief like a diminishing child that never vanishes altogether but that is never born into an autonomous life, either. I shall have to go on being a woman all the years of my life.

And John, she thought, is beginning really to love me. She could see it at the corners of his mouth, in his eyes, in the steadiness of his head when he looked at some small part of her. The beat of her heart was as slow but evener, painful, sometimes, still, but with purpose—warmer, gentler. Much of me died with Bill, she thought; but there is so much left to live! Someday, when the appropriate moment came, they would speak about it. They would do what John thought best. And in a year—more—less—it would not matter, when the time came—they would be married. This is the way it was for widows—young widows—lucky ones.

To John, as he drove in the pearly, perfumed night, the crescendo of this relationship seemed to have reached necessary expression. He could not decide what kind. He had tried to sit it out—to stretch time—to copy carefully in September the attitudes and emotional mannerisms that had been natural for him months before. It was wise under any circumstances to stay here—and his necessity seemed for a while to match hers. Now, though, the end of summer had come—in this land where summer was only a hot winter and winter a cooler June.

He was in no doubt about Ann. Their felicity was and would be a quality more profound than the affections, customs and common interests which held most men and women together. He had not been a bachelor on principle but through default of knowing any such girl. If the weather of his constitution remained clear a while longer, he would ask her to marry him. She would do so, and they could go back to Chicago to add to his business and his teaching the new career of family-making.

Altheim and Poole would surely assent, John thought, under such circumstances. His inner conflict was waged over an ethical and psychological problem: whether to tell Ann about himself now, or to wait until he surely knew and tell her then. A very human feeling, common to men even younger than himself, urged him to take all the steps that would hasten the hour of final understanding: many of his so-called best years as a potential husband and father were already lost to work, to study, and to restless, unproductive search for entertainment, for diversion, for seemly appearances. Many years lay ahead—good years—but he was no longer a youth. Only Ann was young. Both he and she seemed to realize that, half consciously, they were compressing the conventions—that their very concentration upon the need of lingering represented an unexpressed sense of hurry—a fateful sense of it—a prescient urgency.

They wound their way along the sweet-scented avenues. Big houses, pale-colored by day and now white in the moonlight, lined both sides of the route. Lamps shone in a few of them; the windows of many were boarded up against rains and the possibility of hurricane. These houses were set well back from the streets, shaded by the dark, glittering foliage of royal palms, coconuts, petticoat palms, traveler's palms, Melaleucas, gumbo limbos, Florida almonds, sea grapes, citruses, tung trees, royal poincianas, Parkinsonias, mahoganies, spathodias, Australian pines, bauhinia and golden shower trees, banyans and other ficuses—garnished with ligustrum, bamboo, oleander, hibiscus, yuccas, Surinam cherry, pandanus, yellow elder, house-high poinsettia, carissa, night-blooming cereus, Ixora, sea lavender, sun-baked rosebushes and gardenias—and draped to the apices of their tile roofs by Mexican flame vines, tecoma, stephanotis, thunbergia, solanum and, everywhere, bougainvillaea. When they made soft zooms onto the bridges that crossed the many shimmering canals, they slowed to look along the water thoroughfares winding through the dimmed-out city, toward great houses where yachts were tied up at sea walls. The trees and the flowers and the grass shone greenly; the gray-blue water was riffled here by the quiet passage of a canoe and elsewhere by the splash of a fish.

"It is so beautiful, day or night," Ann said, "that you can hardly believe any of it was built by greedy people—or for anything else but beauty. The idea of speculation seems crazy. And the thought of ugly places, like Colored Town—three miles away in the same moonlight—makes you feel as though either you were out of your mind or everybody else was."

"It could be," John answered. "About everybody else, I mean."

" 'All the world but thee and me—' "

297

When he reached North Beach Court, she did not invite him to come in. She asked, "Coming in?"

He shook his head. "Guess not. See you tomorrow."

"It was a lovely evening." She sat there beside him, quiet, looking at the silver beatitude.

Then he kissed her. " 'Night, Ann."

Her completed consent was in her reply: "Good night, John."

She went to her house—walking through the rapturous satisfaction of the moon-slaked city.

John stopped his car, switched off the engine, and strolled around the old mansion past the parallel rulings of the clapboards and on down between the pallid conches. The tepid sea swirled and chortled. Overhead, three night trainers carried red wing lights and low monody toward the horizon. Silence pursued them. He stood looking at the water.

Through his brain ran a montage of his life—backwards. It commenced with the day at the armory when Poole had discovered his condition. He felt that day again. He could see, presently, a thousand classes laughing at his academic quips. Another thousand days spent amid the tinctured stinking of laboratory apparatus. And a thousand in the business offices he had occupied—offices which descended in elegance from the beige and chocolate quarters of this present to a single room with an oak gate, two desks, gold leaf on the glass door and one acrid stenographer. College—and the duckboard walks around the campus—books, the proms he couldn't afford to go to, the football games he saw on autumn afternoons—sun-shot, pungent, knee-deep in leaves. High school—somewhere, a saxophone band playing sweet, absurd music: *you've got hot lips—Swanee, how I love you, how I love you—'way down in Missouri where I heard the melody.* Boy Scouts chopping the ends of dead chestnut logs to build a cabin in rolling, wooded eastern hills. Church and Sunday school. The feel of a Buster Brown collar and a Windsor tie. *Glory be to the Father, and to the Son, and to the Holy Ghost. Amen.* And amen to that . . . He was a little child with the too-big clothes that little children wear, squatting in the middle of a privet hedge, trying anxiously to get his pants down.

Slowly, the night in front of him braked to a stop. Time came to an end. The moonpath drew back—as though he were the seeing lens of a motion-picture camera pulled away from it. The thrum of the returning planes changed into a musical note. A few, and then many luminous snowflakes gathered between him and the sea, swirled fast and faster and cut out the view. Exaltation rose within him to such a pitch that he began examining himself to discover how he could bear it. The firefly snow coalesced as a sheet of light. Voices spoke in his ears—faintly—then loudly—saying nothing with manifold imperatives. In another instant, the glory of this situation vanished. For a reason he did not know, he was afraid. His terror grew and beat upon him, shaking his brain, driving him into the last, stiff extremity of alarm. He gathered his will to name the horror or to denounce what had no name. But he could not find out, by then, who he was—so he knew he could not give identity to any other thing. He foresaw, as the light burst and left darkness, that the very planet upon which he stood would now shoot away and abandon him to Panic.

A while afterward, his thoughts reappeared in discordant fragments. He knew that his mind was preparing to think again as a tuning orchestra prepares to play. The air smelled salty. It tasted of warm salt. There was somebody called Ann, and he remembered her. He could see the constellations, make them out, name them, presently. His head ached. Suddenly he knew where he was.

He rose slowly, shakily. He put his hand to his mouth and looked at what was smeared upon it. Sickness came in his stomach. He walked a little way—a yard—before sitting down again. The sea-smoothed sand where he had lain was now furrowed, scarred, scraped, piled, tossed and kicked about. He was panting deeply, quietly. The moon had moved a certain distance. He turned back and stared at the great house; all down its side was a sepulchral glow. One by one unknown tears wrung themselves from his eyes. At last he rose and walked painfully up the path and the steps.

The biggest mirror was on the back of the bathroom door.

Blood had run down his shirt front. He had torn open one shirt sleeve and burst his leather belt. His stained trousers, sprinkling sand, were caught at his hips and pleated loosely over his ankles. He stuck out his tongue and shuddered. He took off his garments and stayed awhile, quivering, under the shower. He toweled himself mechanically. The pain in his head was quieting. He thought of Maddox with cold impotence—but he was still spitting—and it would have to be Maddox. He went to the telephone—naked, dark with bruises. He moved the dial three times—three only; he said thickly and without conscious prefatory thought, "I want to make a call to Chicago. Person to person. The number is . . ."

2

SHAWN MULLCUP walked into his studio and shut the door. He stared vituperatively at a large painting of a girl in a green dress being kissed by a man in an Air Force uniform. The picture had been holed, a little to one side of the center. A four-pointed tear extended from the hole. The painting looked as though it had been hit violently by a fist—which was true—and the fist had been Shawn's. There was a letter thumbtacked on one corner of the frame. He approached the letter, his beard aggressively elevated. He read it:

"FOR HER MAGAZINE

"Dear Shawnie:
"You know how dearly we love your work and how much I hate to return this one. It is something of a shock to realize that the great Shawn can slip, occasionally. Darling, the girl simply hasn't the je ne sais quoi you, oh, always! somehow have managed to give your girls! Besides—and I hate to point it out—your girl is a fudge blonde and the story depends on the fact that Harlopa Seean is platinum blonde! War nerves, darling, or what? If it's just or what, why don't you run up to little old Gotham and let us shake the sand out of your shoes for a little while? We miss you so! Now, don't get sore, and be a good boy, and please turn her into a metal blonde and pretty please put on those highlights or whatever it is that makes the women readers practically *feel* the naughty approach of a hand and the gentlemen start to reach. Admiringly and hastily,
"Quinna Bunnus
Editor"

300

A facetious gleam came in Shawn's eye. He picked up his palette and brushes. He puddled color. He changed the high-lights and the gentleman's hold on the girl. He altered the hair to a high heap of shattering blondness which had an artificial look and a telltale suggestion of mouse brunette at the cowlick and part. He stepped back, cocked his head, contemplated the transformation, and then, putting down his palette and brushes, picked a dry spot on the canvas and slugged it again, making a second hole.

After that, he began to whistle.

He took a five-cent copybook from a shelf and sat down with a pencil. In the book he wrote, whistling the while:

"School children are taught that civilization has been achieved. That is a basic error. Willa and Willie must be undeceived about it. Humanity is still part barbaric, part medieval, and at best only part civilized. That is what should be taught in every school. Teaching civilization as a fait accompli makes kids accept the world in its current state as a properly finished product. It renders them unable to fight against their own local barbarisms because they cannot discern them. It makes smug, stultified citizens. Whatever else is allowed to kids, they are entitled to learn that America to date is a rank bust in many departments, as are all other countries. That we are hard-trying, slowly succeeding barbarians. Talk to Thalia re this."

He closed the notebook and put it back on the shelf.

Now, from a drawer, he lifted a portable typewriter. He turned his drawing board flat, screwed it tight, set the machine on it, rolled in a sheet of paper, and began to type:

THE CYFER PHENOMENON

Pericles Cyfer, quondam mule-skinner, erstwhile pitchman, and currently a gigolo in some demand among certain ladies of the Park Avenue haut monde in the city of New York—a trade, mission, profession, art, job, avocation, or hobby in which his natural proficiency made up somewhat for a lack of the little elegancies—woke one morning in the puff-covered swan bed of an establishment situated on a setback high above the aforementioned thoroughfare and stared at the gilded foot of the plaster bird, in the presumed visceral portion of which he had obviously spent the night. He soon recalled the name of the lady. Then he transferred his gaze to his own foot.

A plashing and hissing ushered itself fragrantly from beyond a half-open door. A telephone rang. The lady, clothed in adherent bubble-masses, answered the phone. Her chirrup was expectant: "Hello?" Her contrapuntal lacked verve: "Wrong number."

Pericles had closed his eyes during this brief scene—which is a cogent commentary on the trade of gigoloism, for not one man in ten thousand would have closed his eyes: the girl had long, curly hair the color of the inside skins on peanuts, a figure which, in a de luxe musical show, would have been lightly frothed with gauze and carried around by Nubians on a big platter, and the over-all complexion of soap statuary. In addition, after she hung up the phone, she cast a hopeful eye toward Pericles, stopping strategically for a moment, and detaching two or three Victorian bubble-masses. But his lids did not so much as bat.

When she had gone, he looked at his foot again. He did not know why. People often do not know why they look at their feet. In this case, it was simply an impression—tenuous, nebulous, diaphanous— that he was not through looking at his foot. The bath sounds were resumed. Little by little, indeed, they became explicit. Pericles smiled to himself indulgently, gave a small, internal start, opened his mouth to say something—and, instead said nothing at all.

He sat up rather violently and hooked his left foot over his right knee. The veins at his temples swelled delicately. His hands contracted. Now, quickly, he set his feet side by side on the rug, which was made of polar-bear skins sewn together and thickly padded underneath—a tender trampolin designed by the young woman both as an emergency and a safety measure. Pericles, however, was not in any way concerned with the rug. His attention was wholly occupied by the discovery that his feet no longer matched.

Of course, nobody's feet match. There are discrepancies in size and minor distinctions in shape. But the foot at which Pericles gazed—his left—was an altogether new and different foot. His right was the same right that had hoisted him aboard ranch wagons, sustained him on the pavements of winter-bitten and summer-stung streets, and taken him to such places as the one in which he now agitatedly sat. His new foot was smaller than its mate—the basic model. It was paler. It had a higher arch. Its toenails were perfectly formed and exquisitely manicured, as contradistinguished from the blunt, masculine nails on his right foot. He lay back, setting sole to sole, heel to heel. An inch shorter. He peered in the mirrors: it was he, all right—somewhat pale, but hopefully recognizable still.

Quickly he rose and quickly dressed, tying the red bow that went with his dinner jacket somewhat unevenly, because his fingers shook—and all the while regretting the necessity of making an appearance on the street at the pedestrian hour of ten in such clothing. Alas, he had not been prepared, on the previous night, for being stolen from a dowager by this titian and virtueless virtuoso of lucubricious larceny. Dressed, he crept to the door. He opened and closed it noiselessly. He crossed a large, circular foyer. He punched for the private elevator. He then descended to the street and so proceeded up it— hardly noticing the passers-by or how they noticed him. His eyes were on apartment numbers and presently he turned into the office of a fashionable medical man who had treated him on one unhappy occasion. A matter of occupational hazard.

The nurse recognized Pericles with an expression that was a mixture of ribald hauteur and fatuous availability. "Dr. Poontolly is busy," she said. "But I'm not."

If she only knew, Pericles thought, giving her a little buffet and concentrating again upon his more pressing problem. "Tell him it's life and death."

"But it never is," the girl said.

"But this is. Hurry up."

She then perceived that the clammy dew on his lip was not overatomized cologne; she shrugged and left the room.

Some twenty minutes later, Pericles—again minus his habiliments—stood before Poontolly, who hemmed a good deal, crepitated his eyes, bent, squinted, and shook his head. "Bilateral asymmetry of the most marked sort," he murmured, "involving the foot—" he gripped his patient—"tibia—scapula — Curious I overlooked it."

Pericles shakily peered down. "Holy jee-whistling-hamus," he said. "It's coming up my leg."

"There is nothing," replied Poontolly, "coming up your leg."

"The littleness and the fanciness," Pericles answered in a desperate tone. "Look." He walked—walked with a limp. "That's since Sixty-ninth Street!"

"Amazing," said Poontolly, "I didn't notice you had that anomaly. Didn't observe you limped, as a matter of fact. But, then, I was hardly concerned with—"

"I didn't limp! I went to sleep with matching feet!" Pericles sat down. "Look, doc. This is a disease or something. I had two dogs like my right as late as four A.M. this morning and I could get a witness to prove it, if necessary. That is—I think I could. That is—it was witnessed, but I'm not sure I could produce—"

"Quite so," said the physician, who was a bit of a bouleversed boulevardier himself. "I understand. But you are mistaken about the onslaught aspect of your case. A thing like this is permanent. It begins in early childhood and develops as the individual matures—"

"Give me," said Pericles firmly, "my shorts and my pants."

"Quite." The physician smiled and shrugged. "There is nothing, naturally, that medicine can do for you. Nothing. You are, after all, entirely normal in other respects. I might even say—abnormal. You should congratulate yourself upon such reputed advantages as you enjoy—"

Pericles stopped with one foot in a pantleg. His face went chalk-white. "By noon," he said rather thickly, "at this rate—"

"Abandon the thought that it is progressive. Such notions are pure superstition. Old wives' tales. Go out and practice life as you are—"

Pericles went out. He ran out, not even bothering to badger the nurse.

His steps took him downtown—he did not know why. As he walked—or lopingly limped—he kept gripping his left thigh and he was sure beyond doubt that it was shrinking slightly, softening, losing the long strength of its muscles—eroding into the air in order to match the leg and foot below. He passed a flower shop—and a pair of girls who smiled at him and at his costume with a mixture of sad understanding and aptitudinal boast. He scarcely tipped his hat to them. He did, however, observe the discreet sign of a bar and hurried inside, where he hoisted himself onto a stool and commanded a double rye whisky.

While he was waiting for another, a mechanical event slowly announced to him the further advance of his extraordinary malady. This state of affairs—

Shawn pulled out of his typewriter the unfinished fifth sheet of his fable. He threw all five into a wastebasket. He weeded at his beard. He lighted a pipe. He walked over to the crossbar on the contrivance that opened his skylight and chinned himself. He took two telegrams from his hip pocket. There was a light knock on his door. He put back the telegrams and opened the door.

John Galen was standing outside, smiling so that Shawn did not at first pay much attention to the grayness of his face. "Hello, Shawn. Hope I'm not interrupting anything non-interruptible?" His voice was garbled slightly; his tongue evidently impeded his speech.

"The very guy I wanted most to see! Come in. Never say that telepathy doesn't exist. I summoned you!"

"I daresay you did. Had an errand to do—started

early—and made the usual detour here. How are the kids? Thalia?" He waited, still smiling, for Shawn's comfortable response. Then he walked over to the wounded canvas and chuckled. He touched the wet paint with his forefinger. "Self-criticism?"

The artist also laughed. "I'm not sure. Was I criticizing myself? Or that lovely magazine? Or the American public? Editors? Or the state of art? Or all of them? I'll refer the question to myself someday soon. Who knows everything? Nobody. So everybody is always partly wrong and sometimes altogether wrong. The fact should condition a man toward striving for accuracy. I will make the struggle—but right now I think that maybe it was self-criticism."

John turned, thought a moment, and said quietly, "You're upset, pal."

"Yeah." Shawn's eyes brooded. He made a motion toward his hip pocket and arrested it. He squinted at his friend. "What's the matter with you, too—may I ask?"

"Me? Oh." John shrugged. "Burnt hell out of my tongue."

"Ann all right?"

The dark eyes became worried. "Far as I know. I took her to the movies last night. You haven't heard from her today?"

"No." The artist pondered again; they sat there, respecting a mutual silence. "Japs killed my brother," Shawn finally said. "Flier."

"I didn't know you had one who was a flier."

"Oaf. We never got along. Salesman. Kind of guy who rides a motorcycle with his cap on backwards. Life-of-the-party species. Devil with women—the variety you can be a devil with. Kicked out of college for prankery. I didn't even know he was overseas. We don't write. He barnstormed a bit a few years ago. The Aussies pushed back in some damned jungle recently and found him tied to a tree—with the regular Japanese trimmings."

Again, John's eyes spoke for him.

Shawn sighed. "I think—maybe now—I'll buy me a cap and start to wear it backwards, myself."

"Buy two."

Shawn walked to his friend, reached an arm around his shoulder, and gave him a hug. He moved away again, grinning. "Okay. Two." He rubbed his hands over his broad face. "The times we've fallen on are so damn evil! And so few people know!"

"Ever read a book called *De Rebus Incognitis?*"

"Gaunt?" Shawn closed one eye in a grimace like a fixed, satirical wink. "Lemme see." He quoted: "'. . . and this, then, is the scientific proof of ethics, for ethics derive from within man—and not without, as John Stuart Mill would have it; but until humanity discovers the fact—until humanity puts the fact in conscious practice—man dealing with man from inward moral knowledge and not by "economic law" or for some sociologic "reason"—man behaving toward man according to his discovered nature and not according to the prejudice of blind, instinctual religion or vacuous nationalism—he will continue to be the author of his agonies and the artist of his Armageddons.' "

"That's the last sentence in the book, isn't it?"

"Yeah."

John rose and walked about in the studio. He saw the sheets of typewriter paper in the wastebasket, took them out, and commenced to read. Shawn sat down, staring at him keenly.

John finally said, "How in the world do you find the time and energy to do these things? And everything else?"

The artist's voice was light. "You ask a great secret, there, John. Of course—it doesn't take much time. Or much energy. And that one, like its hero, wasn't going anywhere. Besides, I suddenly began to feel an abysmal ass—sitting here batting out nonsense—"

"Why don't you print these things?"

"Oh—the time has passed, once. It won't roll round again for a while. Look. You know how to produce or to summon time and energy. I do. Most people don't. You ought to persuade some of the wizards at Langer to make a study of the thing. I've been brooding about it, lately. We talk about how bad these days are—and how few people realize how bad they are—and we never wonder why. Why don't Americans see and know and understand and do? Why?"

John's eyes were skipping over the typed lines and his lips curved in a smile. He was only half-listening. "Why?"

For a while, then, Shawn held John's attention. "Here we are—well into the greatest and most horrible affair that has ever involved us—the one that's going to change our complexion and our social skeleton for good—and almost nobody realizes it. We're as unprepared, psychologically, for the fight as we were for last December seventh. And we're going to be as unready for peace as we were for war. A diverted and doodling population is going to have to go through a hell of a lot of false and erroneous and obsolete states of mind in order not even to catch up, but to keep tagging along. Everybody who can't trail the facts of the history ahead will fall out and become a dead weight, or a mental case who will try to halt the procession.

"And I can tell you why. It was time, long ago, to quit doodling. To throw away the all-day suckers. But we didn't. We won't. We'll call our diversion, our wasteful gestures the substance of our morale—our 'American way'—and we'll cling to crap, forsaking all spiritual hardship, till the last gun of heartbreaking reality is fired—and afterward, too, no doubt."

"Doodling?" John repeated.

"What America needs now and at least until the fate of the future is reasonably secure, is a course in not-doodling and in how to avoid psychological waste. How to read a magazine or a newspaper without seeing the advertisements. How to listen to the radio—if you must—without hearing the commercials. How not to waste too much time peering at spectator sports. How to get over the comic-strip vice. Current events are dynamite; why pour maple syrup over them? Stop the soap operas. Ration inanity, slop, garbage, waste cerebration, everything that tends to create the unconscious impression that the same old world is dawdling along in the same old fashion.

"Start it in schools. I was just making a note about that. Legends and myths and fairy stories have a purpose—but their purpose isn't what the schoolmarms think. It's to implant in the psyche the idea of good and evil, of justice and injustice, of the struggle of man. Beginning in the boy and girl phase, it's to get into the state of mind of the giant-killer instead of the giant, of Red Ridinghood instead of the wolf, of Theseus instead of the king who tossed him into the labyrinth or of the Minotaur that inhabited the place. The Columbia University scholars have recently made the great discovery that the old legends are not literally true; so, in a benighted and half-witted attempt to approach their own dreary concepts of reality, they have thrown out the old legends. They never understood their function. They don't know that the legends are the parables of instinct—the prereligious format of human aspiration and ethic—the natural man's picture of his own inner nature. Every progressive school in the land bravely taught the kids that there was no Santa Claus and no Pandora. All the tradition in time which tended to arrange and regulate childish instincts was tossed overboard. What happened? Did the kids become paragons of reason? I ought to know—I've got two. They became parrots of reason. They also became Pandoras and Christmaslovers, themselves. And they went out and demanded legends anyway. For that demand, a new and meaningless—or, rather, morally corrupt—set of legends was immediately devised. These endlessly sentimental radio plays. The trash about the sure-shot ranger. And the supersafe superhero who doesn't belong to anything related to god or devil, nature or moral truth—who has no Achilles' heel—who never quarrels with his fellow gods or himself—who always gets his man and whose operations leave no possible explanation for the present situation of a world in hell—as do the older, time-tested myths. The little boys and girls kiss inward conflict goodbye, nowadays, at an early age. They thereby move into an unreal world where all the struggle is physical—and tremendous—and where, on the plane of awareness—everybody knows what to do and the bad breaks are all just bad luck. It is a world where the forces of evil have no force. It is a world where right always triumphs—setting up in the minds of the youth of the nation the fancy idea that right carries within itself the quality of triumph—rather than the truth, which is different. The truth, I mean, that right sometimes triumphs, owing to high human principles and hard human struggles which include not only external conquest of evil but preliminary conquest of the evil within each hero.

"This is doodling. This is mass schizophrenia. You wait. Wait until we get further into this war. Wait until you see great hunks of the American people fail to react—stay asleep—go on dreaming—assume that they're all right as is and without effort because right triumphs, and Superman, who is somebody else, will do the job for them. Wait till you see the shock when Americans find out that their boys are having a hard time winning. Wait for the follies in the peace to come! The distress of the doodlers is going to pile up apathy and make an unpretty picture on this beloved American scene. On a vulgar and infantile scale, we've become a nation of compulsive lotos-eaters. The thing is habit-forming. It spreads into all categories of thought. You can't raise realists—intellectual realists—on the stuff that has passed for intellect in this nation for the past quarter century. The intellectuals became materialists and thought it was smart instead of the damnedest blunder—the most overt act of mental asininity—in the history of thought. I'm talking too much."

"Go ahead," John smiled. "I enjoy it. Besides, I've got a sore tongue."

"We the sweet-thinking, sweet-sucking people! Our sins of omission are getting to be as big as the continent—the globe." Shawn shook his head. "We've doodled so long that we haven't any proper values. We think what happens to us is something so different from what happens to everybody else that we may never even realize our enemies are all of one piece—or that the very name of it is merely an Idea. A familiar, recurrent idea. An idea we ought to hate intensely enough to send us charging against every homicidal maniac who accepts it and practices it. An idea that crops up at home, too—as it must, since it's a fundamental one. Pearl Harbor and Bataan weren't very important—in that sense. They were mere incidents in the everlasting attempt of the idea to spread itself. They—and all that will ensue from them—are just our first American taste of what has been poured upon China and Poland and Russia and Norway and Holland—and what will go on being poured so long as there are tyrant rulers, tyrannical nations, and even tyrannical individuals within a country.

"We are at war. But our soldiers fight to come home, only. Home to mom. Home to chocolate sodas. Home to the ideas and the products sold to them by twenty solid years of soap opera. It's not enough!"

John's eyes were remote. When Shawn stopped talking, he focused them. "I see what you mean. You love America and you believe in America and you—and I, too—have faith in America—"

"But it's faith as Gaunt described it. A superstition, unless you work at it yourself—from a self-started urge that's based on what is real and true, not upon what you are 'convinced of.' Have you talked to the soldiers around here?"

"Some."

"And what?"

John shook his head. "Good-natured—like all our youngsters. A little startled at being soldiers. Maybe a little sullen about it. Want to get the war over in a hurry and get back to Main Street and—to all the lollypops in your list."

"You think they know what they're fighting about? Because I don't."

"I don't, either. They were never taught history as it really went—other people's, or our own. And they don't want to be told what it's all about, now, either. I got in an argument with three of them in a bar the other day. They think everything's propaganda—including the truth."

Shawn nodded. "That's what they think. Because why? Because everything they have known, pretty much, has been propaganda. All advertising is propaganda, for instance. So all art—" he looked at his picture—"of the kind these kids know—art paid for by advertising—follows the line of the propaganda of business. All the history they ever learned—as you say—was propaganda. Propaganda neatly arranged by school boards to produce not the truth, but the idea that America is the greatest, noblest, most perfect, kindliest, most loved, and most enviable nation on earth. That is propaganda to keep the school boards in the saddle. Hell of a way to teach history. And they've listened to the propaganda of the Germans—and to whatever colored or biased news the Allies have given out—which is less in bulk, but is regarded as similar bilge by millions—tens of millions—even when it's God's truth. Poor kids!" Shawn looked out through the door. "Miami Beach, for instance, manufactures reams of crooked history. Not news. Not the whole truth. But a report of something, hoked up to make people believe this is heaven. And every chamber of commerce in the country does it. Every civic club."

"The principle of Hitler's big lie operates against these kids, too," John said. "I mean to say, the facts of this war—every bit of it on every front—are so enormously hideous that it takes a pretty capacious imagination to accept them. The small mind just can't. Can't believe reality—says it isn't so."

"Exactly. Then—there's so much German and fascist propaganda here. The anti-Semitic stuff, for instance. People don't realize, any more, that if it's talked up beyond a certain point it'll lead to little acts—and if the talk isn't dealt with and the little acts begin—if the people who understand the meaning and the laws of democracy don't quench it—anti-Semitism alone could grow big enough to distort and finally to destroy the democratic concept here. That's happened before in other countries. Once any group gets chasing five million Americans around the map—you're done for. Every prejudice boils up. Pretty soon you'll have martial law, a strong man, concentration camps—the principle of liberty dead, law abandoned, sanity lost. We're going to be the last nation to go through that peril. Everybody's had to, all over again, in this century. It's a regressive business—another spasm in the doctrine of the survival of the momentarily ensconced. Germany fell under it and grabbed Europe. Italy fell. Japan was never anything else.

"Propaganda. German propaganda in America. We wouldn't let them emplace guns here—but we let them slip their anti-Semitic virus around, and their anti-Russian bacteria, and all the rest—and nobody knew enough to call them or make them ridiculous—which, on a Homeric scale, is all they are and all the Japs are. Deadly—but absurd. Cruel—but pompous. Energetic—but asinine in the face of history. It's no wonder these soldier kids try to be skeptical and cynical and unimpressed by feelings. Every civilian mile they've walked or driven took them past billboards shouting half-truths or downright lies about everything from the enjoyability of a movie to the efficacy of a tooth paste. Every other hour they've spent in class has been devoted to the study of expurgated data. Their minds have been framed—and they suspect it without knowing by whom or for what. It's a tragic frame-up—because now, when we need the guts of clear understanding, we're getting an infantile response. The response of the nice but bewildered, the brave but perplexed, the puzzled, unimpassioned people who are not unprincipled but who have put their principles in one place and their practices in another. We've fed our young generation on goo—then put them to feeding guns, overnight. Who can blame them for finding in themselves only one concrete wish—the wish to get through with the immediately visible nasty job and get back to the candy—the harmless life in a harmful world—the cradle in which we Americans have for so long rocked our own civilization. For, by God, civilization is still in its cradle!"

John cocked an eyebrow. "Amen," he said. He looked at his watch. "I've got to go."

"Stick around. I have a problem."

"Can't. Friend of mine's coming in on a plane."

"Who?"

"Fellow named Johann Altheim. A doctor. He decided to take a vacation. Out of season for here—but Johann's eccentric."

Shawn nodded several times. By and by he fished the two telegrams from his hip pocket. He set aside the one that told about the death of his brother. He handed the other to John:

UNIVERSE MAGAZINE IS ARRANGING WITH U.S. NAVY FOR THE COMMISSIONING OF SIX LEADING AMERICAN ARTISTS AS LIEUTENANT COMMANDERS STOP WILL BE STATIONED ON BOARD WARSHIPS TO MAKE SKETCHES AND PAINTINGS OF BATTLE ACTIONS STOP IF INTERESTED PHONE COLLECT

B. A. BAILEY, EDITOR IN CHIEF

John thought again of the day he had sat in Poole's office in the armory. It was a memory, he realized, that would jump back into his mind often, during the months ahead. He looked up from the telegram, his question in his eyes.

"I'm still thinking," Shawn said. "They both came this morning."

"Thalia? The kids?"

"All right. They can rent this house and make something. I'll earn something. There's a nest egg—good-sized."

John thought about the fair-haired Thalia and murmured, "Penelope—waiting for Ulysses. Lot of 'em, nowadays."

To his surprise, those words filled Shawn's eyes with tears.

"Yeah," he whispered. "Penelope. She's always there—waiting for me. That's a wife. That's what makes a marriage. I never quite knew how to put it before. Penelope."

"You said, 'I'll earn something,' Shawn. Not— 'I'd.' "

"Did I?" Suddenly his face relaxed and he smiled. His eyes shone. "Then we know—don't we?"

3

JOHANN ALTHEIM bounced out of the plane, rushed across the hot cement pavement, reached over the barrier, and shook John's hand vehemently. His dark eyes had the same amused sparkle. His nose kept pointing at the objects of his endless curiosity. He was as cheer-giving as always.

John had watched the throttled descent of the plane with misgiving: the little man from Switzerland might strike an unharmonious note here, or he might be too distressed to be himself, or he might be irritated at having been taken from his practice. Now, seeing him, John felt that he should have known better. Nothing could change Johann; he would not let it.

"I never get used to seeing so much territory that is all one country," he exclaimed as they walked to the car. "It was cool up there. Down here, we are inside a steam boiler. Right? I love to fly! Who doesn't? Yet—it makes two kinds of people—like everything else, eh? The fliers who look down at little man and grow wise through compassion and perspective and a comprehension of horizons. And those others —who become contemptuous of man. Ah! They should never be allowed to leave the earth! In their hearts—such matured abortions never do leave the earth! They are in it! John, you look wonderful! Thinner, yes. You are tanned like a—like a lifeguard. A walnut!"

And he kept up a fire of observation and comment as they drove down Twentieth Street to the boulevard and across the bay. John appreciated it.

In Colored Town he said, "This is my first glimpse of the South. Pigpens again! Man's inhumanity to himself, that he always pays for, over and over! It even has a bad smell. Why do Americans always consider themselves so superior to Europeans—in the trifling matter of plumbing? They are not, eh?"

On the boulevard, he gazed upon an old house with metal walls stamped and painted to resemble stone. "Magnificent! Here is the brownest period in the land—what? Circa Garfield. Not just badness in architecture but an iron imitation of badness! And not just in Milwaukee, where no doubt it came from, but in the tropics! The trees with their headfuls of flowers. The orchids and the palms—and Milwaukee, imported. Amazing."

When the car swept out on the Venetian Causeway he drew a breath, stared for a long while at the blue water, the serene gaudiness of the islands, and the long, low panoply of Miami Beach—green with trees—alabaster where the stark, imaginative hotels shot above them. "This—I did not expect. This is—*ravissant! Incroyable! Wunderbar!* And again—so American! It does excel the European concept. And it does have the plumbing, eh?"

When John turned up Collins Avenue and passed the hotels—some filled with soldiers—some still marked "Restricted" and "For Gentiles Only," Johann shook his head. "And that—how *very* European. Nowadays—eh? How peculiarly Middle European. We are too new in America. One generation. Two. These others have been here three. Four. So we are still foreigners. Is that it?"

"Someday," John answered, "people will know enough to allow themselves citizenship in the human race."

Johann nodded. "So. Meanwhile—" He shrugged. John steered to avoid a marching column of men, and slowed as he passed alongside it. The small man's eyes took in every face. "I wonder how many know how little is left to them? Who does know?"

"If you were going to be killed tomorrow," John said slowly, "by accident or by war or in any way—today would be half your life."

Johann laughed. "A sorry condition of thought! Today is all your life, no matter what! Today—now—this minute—this present time that does not exist, for when you anticipate it, it is not yet here, and yet when you examine what should be here, it has gone!" He looked back at the marching men. "This is a stupid state of humanity! To fight with each other because they are too weak and too lazy and too greedy and too ignorant to use that same violent urge, each one, in the struggle against himself. Or with himself. However you please. These marching boys are an essence, aren't they? They are the essence of every prejudice every individual

316

would not eradicate in himself, and of every lie each man and woman has told himself, and of their combined individual greeds, and of their willful know-nothingness. These are the sacrifices laid on the altar of weakness—each person's." He sighed. "It is curious how we try to worm away from it! How we pretend that a multitudinous individual failure is a high, collective purpose! How bitterly we discipline our armies and how mercilessly we chastise our enemies because we do not have the simple sense to discipline and chastise ourselves! How many devices we try—how many isms—to hide the fact that man is responsible for it all, and man by man—not man in the mass. How can a man exist in a mass? What an absurdity!"

When the hotels and houses gave way to an open stretch of flat, cobalt sea—hot and mirror-bright—John pointed and Johann stared, speechless. . . .

It was very late that night before John finished his story.

They were sitting on the veranda in front of the old house—which Johann had greeted with the word "Exotic!" John's tongue had swollen thick, toward the end. He had not mentioned it, and struggled on, while Johann ignored the increasing distortion of his speech. Now, at last, John stopped. "That's every bit, I think. The girl—the two girls, rather, because Gail also occupied me for a while—and Shawn—and Maddox—and the ghost. And my—fit."

Johann chuckled a little. "I have always thought, John, that you were a person to whom things would happen—if you ever got out of those classrooms and away from the Bunsen burners. You are one of those—those—psychological architects. You make interesting structures—and interesting people come to inhabit them—which causes interesting things to occur. And you have a nose for interesting places in the world of things. This house."

John's chair rocked moodily in the dark. "I didn't mean to drag you away from anything, last night. I didn't really intend to ask you here. In fact, did I ask? It's hard to remember."

Johann replied first as a doctor. "Those spells are going to give you a good many moments of perturbation, John. A good many lapses of memory. You were, last night, in a state resembling shock. I knew what was wrong when I heard you.

The first instant. Maybe I had been half-expecting that information. And you didn't exactly ask me to come. Now. I will prescribe for you, certainly. That will not cure. It may forestall. It will help. And you shouldn't be alone, eh?"

"I want to be alone more than ever," John said fiercely.

"Yes. But it is not practical, eh?"

"No."

"And you have said nothing to the girl named Ann?"

"How can I? What shall I say? Good God! All summer—she has been coming up, inch by inch—out of—out of what began when that raft floated ashore. Right down there. She is going to fall in love with me if she hasn't, already. And I love her. And now—"

"How big a love?"

"I wasn't in love before—ever. It's big enough. You must have loved somebody—"

"If it is big enough—it is big enough."

There was a long silence. "Being people sometimes gets on your nerves, doesn't it?"

Johann laughed softly. "And for that—we have what you call nerve, eh? Courage." His voice sank. "I could tell her for you."

The temptation blazed in the speed and violence of his refusal. "No! That isn't why I phoned you! I'd give my soul, nearly, to have her told. Not to be, myself, this new sickness in her life and the surgery which exposes it, besides. That's a job, eh?" His throat was husky, now. "But I gotta, don't you think?"

"Not necessarily, Johnny. I'm a doctor. Your doctor."

"Would you?"

John could feel the look in Johann's eyes as he responded. "I think I would do it myself, too. Yes. I know. Afterward—"

"My afterward—isn't. Hers—"

"Is." Johann's voice was low and steady. "Is. If she is what you said—she will find out that, also. Pain is a teacher. She can learn many new invulnerabilities, now. Not of the heart. The invulnerable heart is the dead heart. Of the soul—which cannot be slain."

"Just the same—!" His fist hit the chair arm.

"You are trying to have her sorrow for her. It is enough to have your own. If you project upon her—all this—you will only add to her burden. Suffering is a solitary business.

318

Shared suffering too easily becomes ritualistic—or perhaps a deceptive pleasure—or even a mere rationalization. If you project upon her the misery you feel for her—you will rob her that much of her spirit. It is all she has to go on."

"I know." John let time pass. "Sleepy?"

"Yes. Very."

John took Johann to the front room upstairs. Josephine had blacked it out and carried up his suitcase. The light clicked.

The little man was smiling. "This where the ghost lives?"

"One of 'em, I guess. Mind?"

His large head shook rapidly. "Oh, no. I am full of ghosts."

John looked at the bed to make sure it was properly prepared. He remembered suddenly that he had left Paul Gracey out of his recital that evening. Too late, now, to do anything about that. And no need to bring it up. It might have been a different bed. It certainly was. They couldn't have left it . . .

"What is it?" Johann asked.

"Nothing. Just checking up. It'll be stuffy as Satan's sweatshirt in here—but that can't be helped. Subs outside. Shipping—convoys—"

Johann was chuckling again. "A small enough discomfort for the privilege of confusing the Nazis!"

"Good night, Johann."

"Good night, my friend."

4

IN THE MORNING, early, John rose and dressed carefully. He spent a long time shaving. The face looking back at him was tired but the eyes were very alive. Silver glints in the stubble of his beard. He wondered if he would ever see it all turned gray. He pulled the razor; its thin blade made a rasping sound. I was an all-right looking guy, he thought. And he thought, I could have made love to a lot of women; I know many men who did; I wonder why I didn't? He thought, I could have been married—and some half-enigmatical "we" could have grown children now—or growing. He watched a frown come on his face and the lines tighten and deepen around his mouth. Thank God, he thought. There is some justice, after all. And Ann, he thought. That, too, was some measure of justice. How many children—how many generations unborn, never to be born . . . ? Thank God. And yet— he did not feel thankful. He felt sick.

He wiped the shaving cream from his ear lobes and nose and washed his face in tepid water. He tiptoed upstairs— barefooted—and looked into Johann's room. The doctor was lying on his back, snoring a little, his body curled and brown, like a gnome's. Peaceful. So much intelligence—so much compassion. There was a smell of coffee in the house. Josephine had come, then. He stopped in the kitchen for a cup. Josephine's mood was infolded and she did not even return his good morning. He walked out to meet the brassy day.

This was the hardest task he had ever attempted in his life. This being made to give to another the death of love. This execution of herself and himself. Death, he thought contemptuously, is not the worst thing in a man's life, only the last. He stopped on a dune, in the sunshine, and glared at the sun-shot sea. All the long months of hope and communicated hope—all these were falling in a winter without its autumn. Now the curtain was rung down and he was left in front of it—a public idiot—while she remained behind it, weeping. Damn the imagination that gave a man insulting entities of himself, rank excesses to suffer! Damn the false flesh! Damn the self-seeking subtlety of love! Better a thousand times he had left her to tend one sorrow! Damn sensibilities and words! Damn the sun and the sea and himself, small perpendicular defeat! He could not carry one grain or syllable of her grief even into a sought grave—and he had made it all out of the habit of arrogance. He would shout, rage, hurl his arms.

He would not. He sucked together his intestines, sneered at his apologies, slew this last of his pride, and walked down from the grassy sandpile—worse than all alone—but once more continent.

It has been given to me to do this.

Yellow flowers were blooming along the lane that led to the road. He picked a bunch of them and went on—the sky azure, the clouds white and capacious. He knocked on Ann's door. She came running from the kitchen, licking her

320

thumb. In pajamas. With her dark curls heaped by a ribbon. Morning-new and made up as though there were to be company for breakfast. Cool—as though it were a Connecticut summer day—not Florida in September. As though she were a young woman in love.

The door opened.

"Hello, darling," Ann said.

He held out the flowers. Each petal vibrated. She looked at them and her mouth pursed a little. Her head did not move but her eyes came up. "Don't be so jittery, you dope. Shawn told me."

He was staring at her. He did not know that he would have dropped the flowers—and that she took them. "S-s-s—" He assembled the pieces of his voice. "It's funny. I never stuttered before. Ever."

Ann just laughed. "I'm having waffles. I kind of thought you might come over—early. People with house guests always get up early. It's the neurosis of hospitality."

"Look—"

She laughed again, turned away from him, and hurried to the kitchen. He sank nervelessly upon the divan..

Shawn had told her.

"Waffles," she called presently.

He went into the dining alcove and began to eat the waffles, chunk by chunk. Occasionally, he glanced at her. She sat quiet. Her pajamas were satin—pale lavender and burgundy. A burgundy bow in her dark hair. *Like a bunch of lilacs.* Shawn had said that about her hair, once.

I should feel relieved, John thought bitterly. But I do not. She is being too unmoved. Too *forgiving.* No. Too *accepting* —too much a thoroughbred about a situation which lies outside character and courage. He hurt himself with that thought. Finally, because she did not speak, he said in a shaking voice, "Shawn? How did he know?"

"Johnny. That's so easy. I almost knew myself."

"You did!"

"Well, I knew something was wrong. Like—"

"Like—?"

"Oh. The things that go wrong with people. Like cancer. Do all men believe their dissembling is so effective?"

He seemed perplexed by that.

Ann laughed a little to lead him. "You aren't the sort of

man to start doing nothing, when your country commences to fight. Admit that?" Because he flushed slighty, she knew he was listening: his eyes were very far away. "Then, Shawn knew that Johann Altheim was coming—suddenly. Out of the blue. And—you'd 'burned' your tongue. All that—together with the fact that Shawn knew, anyhow, what might happen. He came right over after you'd left his place."

John looked at her, then. His eyes shimmered. "Swell guy."

She nodded. "He told me in a few words. It was the only time I ever saw him like that. He just—sat down—and said what he had to say—and then he didn't say anything more."

"I should have, a long time ago. Soon after we met. When I—"

"When you what, John?" Her voice was expectant.

"When I knew that—when you—when I—hell! When I took your house. So you'd know about your tenant."

"Is that what you were going to say?"

"You know it isn't."

She waited, but he did not go on. "Shawn knew, of course, what I was going to do." She said the words flatly but the meaning of them showed in her eyes.

"Nothing to do. Nothing you can do—in a case like mine—"

"I don't mean that."

"I know." He drew a deep breath—slowly, queasily. "Let's stop kidding, Ann. All I can possibly say in my own behalf is that I had hope. Quite a lot of hope. This business takes a thousand forms. It changes. It's different in different people. I believed I had the right to count on my hopes. Now that they've—fallen apart—I realize I never had any such right at all. To the extent that—that we've been friends— my presumption was just one more cruelty for you. One more misery that drifted up on that cursed beach. One—"

"John!" Her voice was low but peremptory.

She cupped her chin in the palm of her hand and looked at him for a moment. When she began to talk, she glanced down. But, as her words were poured out softly—accented by their several emotions—she kept gazing back into his eyes. "This much—up to now—was your business. Your part. But the part you came over here about—is mine. *Me.* Last night was quite a long night, John. Yesterday afternoon was long for me, too. I went over to the beach awhile—though it wasn't necessary and I knew that. I realized, yesterday, that I am a *certain* person—a *particular* person—"

"Of course. You're—"

Her eyes quenched that. "I am a very ordinary person, too. And I want to speak about that when I come to it. The first thing I began to think—after Shawn told me—was that it wouldn't and couldn't and didn't make any difference to me—about you. Don't talk! Shawn was sure of that, also. Don't you realize he was—or he wouldn't have come here? He wasn't trying to break bad news to me. He was trying to do you a favor. Do you know what that means? Not—how much it shows Shawn cares for you as a friend. But how well he understands *me? Us? Everything?*"

He rubbed his face. "Ann, why go on with it?"

"I realized that in my whole life I have never done much for anybody. Or given much that cost me anything. I haven't much to give. Anything I have must be inside me if it's there at all. And I realized that what I gave to Bill—he gave back to me. When he was gone—I missed what he had meant— not anything that I had done. If a woman has children—it may be enough. But all we had—"

"Ann," he interrupted desperately. "Don't you know I can't accept myself as a cause for sacrifice?"

"I know. But who's to make the interpretation of 'sacrifice'? You love me."

"I loved you. Now—"

"Now you're going to fall in love with death? Are you? Would that be worthy of you?"

"I don't know. God. I don't."

"It's been only a little while. The spring—the summer. Two seasons. What happened to Bill and me—just happened. Suddenly it was all over. For a while I thought—the way you must—that life was over, too. Everything. Sunk in the sea—out behind the sunset—gone—almost beyond remembrance. Then—there was Bill whispering to me. His ghost— I believe. If you want—a deeper understanding of Bill inside me than I knew I had. An understanding that gave itself a voice. A voice that could express the principle that underlies everybody like Bill. They can't describe it—but I explained to myself something about him I didn't seem to know when he was alive. And I didn't just wipe Bill from my mind. I didn't run from the memory of him. God knows, I ran toward it when I could. But the memory—the ghost it made, if that's what it was—turned me back. Back to me. Say I turned myself. It's still the right way." She hesitated. "And I suppose I knew all the time that I had to hurry. That every minute was precious. Because you knew. Haste is communicable. That kind."

John stood up and went to the window, shaking his head. He came back after a moment. Ann poured coffee into a blue cup and give it to him. "You can run away," she said in a lower tone. "You can go through all the things that you will have to go through—alone. You can take any satisfaction you like by saving me from sharing your—your sickness. But it won't be a very proud act. Behind it will always be the thought that it would have been more real—more honest—more alive—not to go away from me. To take me. Because—if you go—you will have robbed me of my chance to be—really to *be*—what I said I was. Somebody different. Somebody *particular*. Somebody not just like everyone else. You'll have cheated me—that way."

"Ann, don't talk like that!"

"To be myself," she said gently. "Just myself. To have had you accept the small thing that I am. To have done it and all that was necessary to accomplish it—inside myself—in the short months that existed for doing it. To have fallen in love—really—deeply—"

"*Ann!*"

She looked at him still, smiled wistfully, and pushed back her hair. "I know. I shouldn't be sitting here making love for two of us. But I have to, John. You never would have. You—" She shrugged. "There's the other part—the commonplace part. I'm a woman. Like every one that ever lived. I love you—and the time is running down—and I am impatient."

Now he whispered, "You really mean it, don't you, Ann?"

"I really do. You see—you can be a puritan about this. Spartan. All the things men love to be when living is cruel. I am talking about the *kind* part of love. The yielding part. It hasn't anything to do with discomfort or sickness or you stricken or me taking care of you. It concerns only what happens inside people. Don't you understand any of that, John?"

His eyes were steady on her eyes. Light flooded them. "Perhaps."

"Then—"

"But all my feelings go the other way, Ann. I feel as though I should protect you. Spare you. Take care of you. And now I can't—*no matter what!*"

"You should protect me. All the rest of my life.. You should protect my self-respect. You see—I have already decided. I decided, maybe, when I first saw you. How do we know *what* we really know? You were so seeking and forlorn. And I was trying to hide being unimportant from myself. We fell in love. I did with you, anyway. You have to decide the rest. I can only make you know what I believe and what I feel and what I want; then you say. How well I do it, Johnny, is how much of a woman I am—to you." Her eyes filled and she faltered. "I can't think of any more ways to explain it—and I can't go on trying forever!"

"Imagine," he answered softly, "what I've been thinking this summer. Thinking—hoping—"

"Why, though? What did it matter—either way? One hour—if it is the most cherished in your life—lasts forever. One month—one week—a year—two—what difference is there? It always comes to an end. But it is remembered to the end. It exists."

"I told myself that sometimes."

"Now—we both have said it. Can there be anything more to it? Anything? Ever?"

"No, Ann."

"Then I have made you understand!"

His eyes were shining; his throat moved painfully. "Not very well, Ann. Or—maybe I do. Both our prides are humbled—altogether. I—I won't try to figure it out any further. Not now. I just know I wouldn't—throw away—anything so precious. What you call so 'particular'—" he tried to smile—"to use your own silly name for it." The brightness in his eyes spilled over. "I'll accept that. Though why I should have it offered—now—or any time—" He could not go on.

"Johnny."

He lifted his eyes.

"It's late for us—already."

He bent his head.

"Will you—come around the table? And take me in your arms? And—?"

"Yes."

5

JOHANN was at breakfast, being attentively served by Josephine. Her Stygian humor had disappeared. She was saying, as John came into the room, "Indeed it is mysterious, doctor, indeed it is!"

"Josephine and I," Johann explained, "have been discussing the nature and behavior of the human heart. I find that Josephine has been married four times. It gives her a certain detachment." He was looking at John searchingly while he maintained amusement in his tone.

"Just the opposite of a detachment," Josephine answered uproariously. "A a-tatchment—four times over." She went into the kitchen, whooping.

John sat down. He gave back his friend's look. "Been calling."

"Yes," Johann said.

"It was a miracle. Like one."

"I thought so. Somehow, John, I didn't expect you'd make a mistake. I expected she'd—"

"Shawn had already told her."

Johann put sugar in his cup. "That doesn't surprise me, either. He—also—sounded like quite a guy."

"Quite a guy." John listened to the sound of it carefully. "Yes. He's quite a guy—Shawn is. But look. You're facing a man who's probably engaged, or about to be married, or married in the eyes of God! The technical definition doesn't seem vital—at the moment."

Johann lifted his cup and saluted delicately. "Congratulations. Why didn't you bring her over?"

John laughed. "Because she has a job. Because she sticks to it—even in this kind of weather. Oh, I don't know. Because she wanted to be alone with herself. She'll be here for dinner."

The psychiatrist turned his eyes away so that the ecstatic

326

expression of his friend would not interfere with his appreciation of the circumstance in his own fashion. He wanted to meet Ann Chapman Gracey. It wouldn't be easy for her—all this. She doubtless knew. And he could help—he would explain that. But, then, she wasn't the sort of girl who looked for easy things to do. She was married to a sailor. She dwelt alone in a formidable house. She swam out for a raft. She holed up in a hotel by herself with the earthquake of her destitution. She got her own job to be near her new man and she stuck as though she were plated on him, when the tempest broke there, too. Some girl.

"Have a good rest? Want to swim? Fish? Shoot some golf? Read a book?"

Johann came to himself. "Rest a few days. I'm very happy, John. I suppose you'll be coming back soon—and I'll see a lot of you, eh?"

"Yes. Soon. I want to work. I have notes on several ideas. Drugs to take part of the sting out of it for these guys in khaki that march and sing around here. As if they were on their way to a football game. I ought to hold out for a while —hadn't I?"

Johann answered, "Why not just—spend time with Ann? Plenty of men to work."

"Bad as that?"

"Could be. Your family—" Johann smiled gently. "Who can tell? You do what you think you should do. You've got Ann. She has you. It's all you need. And you're all she needs. You can't shop around for time—ever—anyhow."

"That's something Ann knows better than I did," John said seriously. "What about a program?"

"Let's loaf. Matter of fact, I didn't get a good rest until daylight. Overtired, I guess. I had the most haunting, damnable nightmare. It kept coming back and coming back all night. I'd sit up and switch on the light and smoke a cigarette and go to sleep—and be back in it all over again."

"What was it?"

"Not so much images—as a feeling. One of those state-of-mind things. I kept feeling that I was struggling to get out of the bed—struggling with all my might—because I knew if I stayed there long I'd never get out. I had the most tremendous determination to stand up and stagger outside— to holler—to summon help—and I couldn't figure out why.

I just knew it was so, in the dream. And I'd sort of weaken. It would get darker. I'd fall back—and try—and fall back—and then just lie there—overcome with a horror of merely being there. After a while—I'd get in that stuck phase of a nightmare. The thing where you know you're pinned down. You quit struggling. You can't budge. Sheer horror comes over you. You realize you've lost the battle and that you are going to stay there for good. Then I'd wake up—covered with perspiration—the bed in a mess. I'd smoke. Calm myself down. And do it all over." Johann had been watching John during the last part of the account. "What's the trouble with you?"

"Just that it happened to somebody else in that bed. I'd forgotten."

"What happened?"

John told him.

The psychiatrist listened with a concentration that became amazed and, at the last, eager. "By George! I've had patients tell me things like that. Dreams with roots in some other reality. Or somebody else's reality. I won't say I scoffed at them—I didn't. But I was dubious. What do you think we need to explain that?"

"I must say you're mighty calm about it. It was thoughtless of me to put you there. But I wasn't sure—"

"Thoughtless? Why should you think of anything else? It was lucky! I'm delighted, John! What man like me wouldn't be? Now—I'll be able to nod my head to patients and say, 'Of course. Go on.' But what does it? Your belated remembrance—and hospitable anxiety—plus telepathy?"

"Would you say, for instance, that time might be different from what we think? Or space? Or both? Do you want to consider, Johann, that the personality is an electrical entity which obeys laws like those of quanta math? Or do you prefer the simpler and more naïve hypothesis of ghosts? It happened, after all."

Johann shrugged exaggeratedly. "You have got me."

"It's a matter that has caused me considerable speculation lately."

"Last night—I thought you were being dramatic. I see now that you mean serious thought."

"I certainly do. There is, at the least, what we will call an 'influence' here. Whether or not it is a projection that we

328

living people make from the past behavior of Paul Gracey and his nephew—I just don't know. But here it is. There must be a cause and there must be a reason. It must be natural and it certainly isn't readily explained. Maddox made a bust of it—I thought. I haven't heard you on the subject."

Johann laughed. "After last night—I'll need a new brief. You'll have to give me time."

"I'll move you, too."

"Move me! And spoil my fun? You will not!"

John saluted amiably. "Okay, pal. But this old edifice is no place for the fitful-minded."

"Speaking of which—" Johann paused and went on because he knew his friend would understand—"you've been fairly hardy to stay here, yourself."

"This is the morning for people to be hardy, I guess," John answered lightly. "Just the same. Thanks for coming. Though I'm sure now that wasn't what I'd intended."

The psychiatrist grinned. "No?"

"Not consciously."

"Unconsciously, then—put it this way. You knew that if I knew, I would be here at once, if I could. And you are aware that, sometimes, not to impose upon a true friend is to make the greater imposition."

"Through how many levels of reversal could you tag an idea like that and keep track of yourself?"

"Nine. I've tried."

John was amused. "And how many levels are there?"

"Maybe hundreds."

"Then let's just say—thanks for coming and let it go at that." John bent to pass the Navajo rug. "I suggest putting on a bathing suit. You'll perspire all day, anyhow. You can dunk yourself from time to time in the ocean. Or take showers. Both of 'em lukewarm—the sea must be ninety. And flat. It's forgotten how to make waves."

As John began to change his clothes in the front room, he pursed his lips. He was a good whistler and he whistled Schubert's Serenade. Johann listened, his luminous brown eyes sad and far away; by and by he began to move his head in rhythm to the liquid notes.

DINNER was merry. When it ended and the night hung steaming over the isolated house, John and Ann urged Johann to accompany them to the movies. Air-conditioning, they insisted, would revive him of travel fatigue. Paternally, he urged them to go alone and denied that he needed to be cooled. They argued next that they would not think of going without him. He sketched, with scathing humor, the presumptive plot of the picture they would probably see. They wanted to be together alone—which he knew and which they did not wish him to know. And he wanted to be alone, also—which they did not know. The interchange played itself out in amiable chaffing. John drove Ann away.

Josephine had gone.

As soon as the car had followed its headlights into the green tunnel of the road, Johann hastened back into the empty house. He began the search.

He began it with a feeling of wonderment. The task seemed self-evident to him—one that should have been undertaken months before. The voice of the ghost sounded in his mind—or the voice of whatever a "ghost" might be. *It's here*. The refrain. *Here, Ann. Here.*

What?

Had Gail looked for it—whatever it might be? He should have asked John more about her visit.

What?

Old Paul's relics? Bill's? A fortune or a will? Nothing of that sort, Johann thought. But surely something. The impression dwelt deep in Ann's subconscious. No doubt it had been transferred there from Bill's hidden, living thoughts. Or perhaps entities—the very arrangement of atoms—produced a delicate emanation—a continual announcement of mere presence. There was a line from Kipling: "Something lost beyond the ranges. Lost and waiting for you. Go!" You knew it was something and—almost—where it was.

Somebody should have looked.

He could search that evening in two rooms only—his own, upstairs, and the blackout room where he now sat. No light could be shown in the others because of that which moved and that which lay in wait outside beneath the quiet sea. If there were nothing in either of the two rooms, he could talk to John and they could go through the rest of the house in the days that followed.

Johann walked around the four walls, scrutinizing and rapping with the utmost care. He then rolled up the scattered rugs and examined the boards in the floor and their joinings. Next he inspected each piece of furniture—taking the seats out, methodically squeezing the cushions, turning over the divan and the chairs and looking at their bottoms. He took off his shirt, presently. Perspiration shone on his trunk; old dust settled there, also, and ran in streaks. His hands turned gray and then black. He went to the kitchen, unrolled a length of paper towels, and brought them back to wipe away the worst of the smudge.

Paul Gracey's walking sticks next occupied him. One by one he took them from their moldered rack and held them under a bridge lamp, twisting, pulling, unscrewing. He discovered a compartment in a ferrule; inside was a metal box lined with yellowed paper which contained a once-white powder. He shook it out under the light, touched his finger to it, tasted gingerly, and spat. Cocaine. A collector's item, to be sure—but not what he was seeking. In another stick was a dirk. A light bamboo cane held a long, rusted poniard; the stick was the type which, when grasped, allowed the blade to be pulled free by the assailant and so driven into the victim. There were several more conventional sword canes—the blades rusted by this hot, salty atmosphere. No place for such a collection. On some of the sticks were dusty tags and Johann read them: John Pierpont Morgan, Theodore Roosevelt, Eli Whitney, Alexander Graham Bell, Edward. That would be the king. One stick was dimly autographed: Alfred Tennyson.

Johann rested, and smoked a cigarette, holding it daintily in his soiled hand. This was the end of a hobby. The hobby of an odd old man who had met a peculiar death. There were, no doubt, other cane collectors who would relish this curious galaxy—who might even pay a high price for it. Where would one go to find them? Hobby magazines? The newspapers of Philadelphia or Boston? No doubt. All manner of men from all parts of the world had been presented with these walking sticks, or purchased them, and had leaned upon them or hung them somewhere in closets or halls to be forgotten. It was a strangely undecorative collection—and peculiarly futile.

He began next with the books. There were Paul's old volumes in glass-fronted cases and the new books Ann and Bill had purchased. He shook them out, one at a time, and leafed through them. The night wore on—hot—tomblike. The movies had closed—their dimmed-out lobbies going altogether black—the last customer stepping from the sharp, cool air into the amniotic darkness. John and Ann had not gone to see a movie, then. He smiled.

There was nothing in the books. He went upstairs—pausing at their broad, invisible commencement to wonder if the ghost would speak to him, and taking each riser with a slow, uneasy foot. He switched on his own light, inspected the blankets that covered the windows, and pulled the bed apart. Still nothing. He tried the walls and the floor and the furniture without success. He had encountered only dust—a scurry of it under the bed and time-smelling clouds of it as he had disturbed the furnshings.

He was very tired, now. He remade his bed and sat on its edge, smoking. Into his mind he allowed the old fears and the superstitions of his species to trickle—exploring them as they seized hold upon him—trying to share what John had felt, and Ann, and perhaps Gail also. Looking down at the place beneath his right hand he could envisage the ghastly accident to which his nightmare had referred. Soon, he found it necessary to exert his will in the opposite direction.

I, Johann Altheim, he thought intently, will not be panicked. I will not be driven to run from here into the infected night. I do not know all that is, and all that can happen; but I do know that I can witness all, whatever it may be.

He rose.

In the stained mirror, his face stared streaked and pale. His eyes burned. He peered at the reflection of the area of room behind him and winked grotesquely at himself. He extinguished his cigarette in a china dish on the bureau. There were books in this room also—a stack of them in a corner and, at the bottom of it, a big family Bible. He shook the dust out, book by book, and at last carried the Bible over to the bed where the light was a little stronger and his eyes would strain less than they had in the gloomy corner.

Tucked in the back of the Bible was a letter—written in a man's flowing hand—with purplish ink that had not faded, upon paper that was not brown or yellow or gray with the decades. Johann sighed very softly and held the paper close to the low-powered light bulb. His hand shook.

"Dear Bill," the letter commenced. This, Johann thought, was surely what was "here." Bill would think of the family Bible as a proper hiding place. And he would hide nothing— unless it was something very secret, or important, or personal, or troublesome. He turned to the last page, shrugged at the signature, and began again at the salutation:

"Dear Bill:

"You probably will have a hard time remembering me— Howie Evans. I sat next to you in Sophomore Chemistry lectures, though—and I was a cheer leader, one year. I used to admire you a lot—remember the off-tackle slice that you made that beat Dartmouth? But I never got to know you much and I quit in my Junior year. Before you throw this away—it isn't any appeal for funds. It's something I think you ought to know about—or somebody ought to—that has been worrying me for a long time. It's about Gail Chapman." Johann's right eyebrow lifted. He glanced through the endless purple ink. The letter had no paragraphs. "Last fall I happened to run into old Westie Elvers and he told me you were going around with Ann Chapman. Then I heard you were married to her. Maybe I should have written you all this sooner—though I don't know if Ann is like her sister. I hope not. Because Gail is some kind of a fiend, in my opinion, and I think you ought to know about it, anyway, and maybe her family. How I happened to get to know Gail is a long story and I'll try to make it short. After quitting in my Junior year, I bummed around a lot in a lot of jobs and I was working with a mining outfit that was starting operations on some copper-silver ore in the Shotgun Mountains. There were three or four settlements around the region and some dude ranches and a few little ranches that people were trying to work seriously, on account of the fact that a water supply came out of the hills and ran a few miles before the desert dried it up. This was used for irrigation. Bleak country. Not many women except the hustling kind who hung out in a town named Hobe. Well, I got to know most of the people, including a guy named Todd who was trying to start a ranch. He lived in a trailer on the flats with his wife and baby—Gail was the wife, as you realize. She was the best-looking woman for a hundred miles around there—and she was the kind that isn't exactly flirtatious but that gives you one of those sizing-up looks right away. The kind of look that makes you want things. She had started out all right in those parts, I guess, but it wasn't any life for her kind—you could see that—and she was fed up to the eyebrows. Not that it matters how she felt—but that's her side. Anyhow, this Todd was a pretty elegant guy, I thought—and people did. The ranchers were doing what they could to help him along and he might have made out. Of course, some of the dude ranchers had the Todds around on account of Gail mainly, and you know how that is. You could see that Todd was worried about Gail and the baby and dough and the crop of zucchini he had put in that year, and you could see he was jealous but not the kind to come out with it. It was one of those things. The frost got his crop. Then some desert rat and his old woman moved into a caved-in prospector's shack up in the high country on the creek. The old woman was a typhoid carrier and in a little while there were about forty cases in the area—including Todd and his kid. Gail didn't get it—it would have been the mercy of God if she had, I guess, but those people always miss. I will say this. Gail had been trained as a nurse somewhere and she stepped in and gave everybody advice and help and worked day and night. She went from ranch to ranch and house to house and stayed with it like nobody's business for weeks. Work stopped up at the minehead—a lot of us were sick, too—and I came down and tried to do my part. A doc came in from someplace and worked hard, too. I used to sit with Todd and the baby, sometimes, while Gail had unhooked the car from their trailer to go around making calls. It was a rotten little old trailer for three people and wearing out by then. They used to run the car engine evenings to charge up the battery so they could have lights inside at night—but the exhaust leaked into the trailer and they had to quit that, so sometimes I'd sit around in the dark with just a flashlight, half the night, with the baby bawling and Todd just lying there, taking it. Then when Gail came back I'd go over to the Willis place and sleep in the hogan. I didn't get typhoid, either, for some reason. Then one night they an-

nounced over at Hobe that they were going to have the big
annual dance anyway and Gail asked me to take her in my
car and I said I wouldn't but after a while I said I would. She
said she had to have a little recreation or go nuts—and
maybe it was half true, at that, because she'd been skimming
along on mighty little sleep. Anyhow, she put the bee on me
and I finally gave in. Who wouldn't? So late that afternoon
she drove the trailer up to a different spot—it had been out
by their land—she decided Todd and the baby would be
better off in the shadow of the mountains which came down
early in the afternoon. It was hot weather. So she parked
the trailer up there and walked back to the road all dressed
up and said Todd was better and could get around a little for
the baby if he had to—and what the hell, anyhow. I drove
her to Hobe. Well, it was a terrific shindy and everybody
got pretty boiled and some got really cockeyed. It was in a
grain and feed store with a hillbilly band and the boards
swept clean and polished the way they are from the bags
dragging over them. All the no-good dames were there and
as many of the rest that were well and cared to be. I got
high and fooled around with all of the babes and then along
about two A.M. I decided to get Gail and take her home if
she'd come. Well—I didn't spot her right away and when I
did I saw her just breaking away from a guy named Stevens
in a corner. She chased him off and she looked at her wrist
watch and then, so help me God, she turned as white as a
sheet. Her face got terrible. She started for the door and she
looked at her watch again and she came back and she saw
me and she pulled herself together so fast it sobered me up
entirely. I asked her if anything was wrong and she said the
heat had got to her for a minute and would I take her outside. So I did. I was all out of the mood—whatever the mood
was—and we had a drink from a bottle and came back. She
wouldn't leave till four A.M. then—and I took her back. This
time I drove her right to the trailer and shut off the engine
and coasted the last hundred yards in case Todd and the kid
were sleeping. Well, she thanked me and got out and opened
the trailer and I turned my ignition switch and then she hol-
lered to me. Todd and the baby were dead. The engine on
the car hooked to the trailer had run out all the gas—and the
carbon monoxide had asphyxiated them both. She was pretty
frantic and I roared after the doctor and we worked on them

but they were dead. The funny thing is, I didn't think of her getting pale and looking at her watch at the time. In fact, I didn't think of it for weeks. They had a coroner, naturally, and Gail said that Todd must have got up and started the engine to charge the batteries to get some light and had fallen asleep before he thought to turn it off. That was all there was to it. But I'm damned sure she left that engine running and left Todd and the baby sleeping when she came to meet me at the road—and I think there isn't any doubt she looked at her watch when I saw her and realized they were dead and out of her way by then. Anyhow, she had 'em buried in a cemetery that didn't cost anything—with a couple of natural stones for markers—and she scrammed out of there in a hurry afterwards. I've seen her picture in magazines a couple of times since then and I've also read her name quite a few times in columns, so I know she has been raising merry blue hell. I quit the company and the mountains before I remembered about her looking at her watch. When I did, there wasn't anything I could do. I can't prove all this. Neither can anybody else. But it haunts me, Bill, and I thought since you had become sort of the head of the family, you ought to know. That girl is a killer and she hadn't ought to be loose. Yours as ever, Howie Evans."

Johann folded the letter along its creases. He put it in the pocket of a coat in his closet. He undressed, took a shower, walked slowly up the stairs again, turned back the dank sheet, switched out the light, and lay for a while, smiling thoughtfully into the close, inky atmosphere of the room.

7

THE MORNING shone like new metal. A haze overhung the glittering landscape, suffusing its aureate quality. The sun's own gold had seemingly been vaporized on earth. The sea was dark blue—the water near shore clearer than the air—and every grain of the coarse brown sand could be separately discerned. The eye followed the lineaments of half-sunken shells and coral rocks as though there were no boundary between air and water. Baking heat was reflected by the dunes. Gulls sat motionless on the ocean surface. But the vegetation was not wilted like northern growth; it held itself stiffly in the blazing light, searching with exposed leaf and frond, and with every tendril that crept through its own black shadows, for more and ever more of the dazzling deluge.

Johann took breakfast in the kitchen alcove, and walked a ways on the shimmering sand. Turning left, he cut between the dunes and across the green puzzle of the empty lots. Ann sat in the office—wearing a crisp, white dress. There were headlines on her newspaper about other jungles, and about men moving gigantically upon the age-bloodied steppes. She put down the paper. Her eyes were unsecretive, vivid with the green and gold outdoors.

"Good morning, Johann. Sit. It's fairly ferocious outside."

"The salt and the dampness. Still—I've seen it worse in hotter countries. Curiously stifling today, though. John's still asleep, so I ambled over on the chance you might not be."

She laughed. "I'm very dutiful. But there's not much likelihood anybody will come by today to rent a bungalow. Or even that the tenants will complain. Too hot."

"You look marvelous. Cool, too. Want to talk? Or shall I leave you with the day's news?"

"We have quite a lot to talk about," she answered. "You and I. The sooner the better, don't you think? I'm glad you came. It's strange." She drew a deep breath and stretched herself proudly. "He is so different. So similar. So different. That probably sounds naïve to you."

"Nobody ever made a wiser expression of it."

"I don't even know if I love him. Or—rather—how much. Or in just what way. This morning, I found myself thinking that maybe he had merely made me love myself again. He has, you know."

"But then—you should. You're alive, aren't you? Capable of so much. You know what you're doing. To those who know—a deep happiness always comes. They are allowed to love themselves that way—the feeling behind your eyes—memory—anticipation—that—" he smiled slightly, impishly —"that stretch."

Ann flushed. "The New England in me resents being called physical—and wants to hide the resentment by making an objection. But the other part refuses both impulses."

"It should. All the physical connotations have been badly

bruised by your forebears, Ann. It's a shame. To make a woman grow up feeling she is not allowed to exult in being female—well. I could talk to you for months about the harm I've seen it do."

She nodded. "I know. Life's so different from what we've been led to believe. All of us. All American women. We were getters. Get a beau. Get engaged. Get married—"

"Be-get children—"

She chuckled. "Two. Three, at most. Get a home of your own. Get a car. Get ahead. Get behind your husband in business. Get good marks in school. Get a scholarship to college. Get yourself the right sort of friends. Get into the proper clubs. Get everything."

"Which is why so many of you have no give left in you. Then—when the push comes—you snap. And come to me."

There was a pause. "I tried like the devil to cheat," she said. "To tell myself Bill sent him—things like that."

"A hundred million consciences founded on unnatural values." He thought that over. "Fifty million, anyway. And fifty million more people in this great and wondrous nation trying as hard as they can to erase all trace of conscience— by one method or another—so that conscience cannot bother them again. Trying to escape from it. And it is all so simple. Admit the real laws of life. Admit what really goes on within yourself. Tell the truth to yourself about yourself—always. And bear in mind the laws—the punishments to the individual and the responsibilities which, if dodged, will devolve upon all the rest of the people in the world and make them hate. It is too simple for most people, these days. Besides, the doing of it is as difficult as birth and death and everything in between—because that is what it is."

Ann had listened—her eyes earnest. " 'To thine own self be true, and it must follow, as the night the day, thou canst not then be false to any man.' "

"Only—" his eyes twinkled—"to find people's own selves, I have to peel off so much, nowadays. The dirty little truisms of school. The absurd prejudices of whatever town or state or country they're brought up in. The traditions of whatever class they belong to. The mass of barbaric nonsense stuffed into them by some religion or other. And an ignorance that is as extensive as their misinformation. A peculiar condition for people to let themselves get into—when you think what a complex world they're trying to run."

"As long as you are living with all your heart and mind and energy—with your self-control, and with your body too—you don't worry so much about what other ignoramuses and fools can do. Or whether they can hurt you. Or even about what's going to happen to you. I suppose, though—" she frowned—"that's easy for somebody like me to say. In love—"

"On the contrary. It's what that phrase about 'not being your brother's keeper' means. And the one about the mote and the beam. When people start to get—and stop giving out—they have to mind other people's business. In order to get—your attention is diverted necessarily to what the other person possesses. It's when you give that you are able to concentrate correctly on yourself. You're built for production—creation. Everyone is. But the idea is just opposite to what most of my patients believe—and they'll argue it for weeks with me."

"But I feel almost guilty. Not quite. I've got so much—in such a short time—"

"—for giving what? Everything you are and have. And to what?"

"That part doesn't matter! Excepting—"

"Excepting—?" he asked quickly.

"You could talk to me about it a little. I'm no doctor."

"Oh." He smiled. "I shall. I'd rather talk about you a minute longer, though. Mind?"

"No."

"You've got to remember that I'm an old and very good friend of John's. I don't need to say that nothing in his life has made me happier—or meant more to me—than the way you entered it. The way you are." He stopped—but she made no sign of dissent, no motion of false denial—and he had known that she would not. His chin lifted a little. "On the other hand, I'm a doctor. A specialist in the human personality. I'm apt to be blunt."

"Of course."

"What do you think—now—about Bill?"

"I wouldn't be able to do—what I am doing now—if I hadn't known about Bill before this. Before any of this dawned on me."

"What did you know?"

"I knew the only thing—I guess—that any woman needs to know about her—dead husband. All that matters. All that I have a right to know. I guess it's all that one person can know about any other person they care about, really." She hesitated.

"Yes?"

"What happened to him was what he wanted."

His head assented and his eyes softened.

"I mean—" she said—"he was doing what he wanted. If he had known that he was going to die doing it—he would have gone on doing it with all his might. Anyway."

"Suppose he hadn't wanted to do it?"

"Then," she answered quickly, "I wouldn't have had to grieve much over him, would I? And I wouldn't have anything much left to carry in my heart."

"Yes, Ann."

"And that's the thing every widow has to find out about herself—that she *can* carry it." She spoke softly. "A gold star isn't much, on a flag, in a window. Only the people behind the window can add any luster to the giving that put it there."

He couldn't look at her any longer. He walked, rather jerkily, almost professionally, to the window; he stared hard at the hard stare of sunlight, at the same zinnias which John had braced his eyes against the day before. "Do you think Bill's—around?"

"No. I think he was. I believe, now, he went wherever he had to go."

"Why?" he asked.

"Don't ask me. I couldn't tell you. I just think so. You can say it's preconviction—I guess John believes that. The kind of knowing Gaunt argues against in that book. You can say it's imagination and hysteria and subconscious things and the biggest wishful thought in the world. But I guess I know, and no one—"

"No one in the whole world has the slightest right to interfere with that sort of knowing, Ann. But—another thing. Why do you believe your Bill—tried to express something to you?"

She was smiling gravely. "You must still want to believe, for yourself, that whatever happened was an activity of my subconscious memory. An effect on me Bill had when he was alive—that I didn't notice consciously."

"I didn't say that. I never will. I know that much about what makes living people tick, even if nobody knows all."

"I've considered. There was something on his mind. Something about the house—or in the house—and it may even have impressed me while he was alive. Bill and I hadn't been married long enough—or maybe not in the exact way—to share every confidence. And he had a great sense of responsibility. He worried about others. It was swell of him, I thought. He worried about Gail, for instance."

"Ah."

"John's told you about my sister?"

"Yes. He's told me pretty much everything that's happened to him this summer. Everybody he got to know—and so on."

"Well, Bill worried about Gail and tried to talk her out of being the way she is. And he worried about poor old Hank Maddox falling so hard for Gail. Things like that. He used to worry—even—about Shawn's temper—which is a waste of time. But, then, Bill didn't understand people like Shawn."

"You think, then, that Bill might have died troubled about some sort of unfinished business not his own?"

"Bill's own business was finished. He kept it up to date—always."

"I see."

"I suppose Bill felt that if I stayed around here I'd find out what was troubling him—and maybe I could help. Then—the last time—maybe he changed his mind. I don't know. He went away and whatever was 'here' will have to work itself out. I heard that music. What do you think about it?"

Johann shook his head. "Nobody can tell you what to think about a transcendental experience, either. That's also your assignment."

"It doesn't make you think things. It makes you feel things and do things. I heard a little echo of it—again—last—" She shrugged and smiled. "That's my department. You're right."

He had come back to the chair and seated himself. His

341

face was fatherly. "I really haven't so much to say about John, Ann. I'll send you a book that'll tell you how to take care of him and what to expect and what to do when the things you expect, happen. It isn't nice—it's horrible. It'll be a lot harder watching a man go to pieces slowly—and lose his mind—than it was to find out a man had been killed in battle."

She smiled and said nothing.

"He has a couple of near relatives who—went rather quickly. A few years—after the first attack. And the last months—in both cases—were awful."

"Then there'll be a time when he'll need me even more than now," she said. "There isn't anything to stop it?"

"We don't know anything."

"He's brilliant, isn't he? He doesn't talk about his work."

Johann understood that, and so, for a while, he recited John's accomplishments in the field of biochemistry. He made for her little tables of the presumed numbers of lives John had saved by his research and discoveries. "And those saved lives will go on," he said, "generation after generation. And then—there are all the youngsters he's taught— and what they achieve—every bit of which will be at least in part due to the inspiration and the intelligence of Johnny Galen. Yeah. He's wonderful. Lot of 'em in this world. Never enough, though. And we'll miss that guy—someday —as few men are ever missed. You—and I—and some others you don't know."

"Girls?"

He looked at her acutely. "No, Ann. No girls. He was too elaborate a proposition for most women. Most of the sort he knew in Chicago. I don't mean John was a saint. But he was never deeply in love before. I know that. And I realize why you asked about girls. It's odd." He hesitated a moment. "I can't recall any woman ever reaching that degree of freedom from jealousy. Not any I've ever known intimately, anyhow. I'll remember that, child."

"You forget it," Ann answered quickly. "He's something different."

"You may not think so—after—after. You see—they sometimes retrogress through all the descending levels of manhood and civilization. You won't be licked. I know that

342

now. But you'll lose a lot more of what you've thought of as yourself—getting that much wisdom—that way. You know you'll go back to Chicago together?"

"He said so last night."

"And you know you can call on me—day or night—always?"

"Yes. Yes, I shall."

He had turned toward the window again. He thought about epilepsy. His guts shivered and he had to use all his will to keep his shoulders steadfast. He saw with studied clarity that he would gladly have given his life to save either this girl or his friend from that future. But, then, he also knew that someday she would be on the other side of this, too—alone and sure and quietly splendid. She had found out what was inside women. People. And he had found out about her discovery. In a minute, or an hour, he could again be happy with them. This, too, was living—packed and potent—terrible and ecstatic—no getting, no security—but no fear and a measureless sense of participation.

"Just this one more thing, Ann. A thing you and John and I have to take steps about. I've found out what was 'here'—in the Paul Gracey house. I'm sure I have."

Her face slowly lost color. "Is it about Bill—or me?" She shook her head. "It couldn't be!"

"No. It's about Gail." He reached into his pocket. "A letter. I found it—because I hunted for it."

She took the pages with the flow of purple ink. "I meant to look," she said softly as she started to read. "I might have. It kept coming back to me."

He sat in the chair, concentrating on the white coral edges of the roadway and the stiff, still, colored flowers, until she had finished. Now her pallor had returned and her eyes were barren. "That's hideous."

"No, Ann."

"But, good God! a thing like that!"

"Wait a minute. Listen. We've got work to do."

8

GAIL's gaudy little apartment was cool. An installed air-conditioning machine—a present—hummed loudly at the window through which it sucked the hot, moist, outdoor air. But Gail could not hear the mechanical sound. She kept the radio at a higher volume. A dance band beat about among the mirrors and cosmetics and Venetian blinds. *My mammy done tole me.* This eloquent, defeated dirge, which ushered in the first war months, drowned the humming machine and carried into the bathroom where Gail's passionate body lay under a sheet of scented water. She sang the last words hoarsely: *Blues—in the night!* The breath to lift the phrase from her throat also lifted her breasts above-water; as she sang they sank again, firm, white islands, perfumed, rounded, phrased by exquisite functioning.

Her face was as blank and pallid as a statue's.

But you must come, Ann had said.

But you must come.

Somehow, Ann had never said it like that before and Gail knew that she must come. She knew it and she lived in an hours-long world of dread about it. Her past, as attached as a shadow, might now be thrown ahead of her by a new light; she might topple into it.

She tried to excuse her clinging history by concentrating on the more immediate past. There was Hank Maddox. Hadn't she given him up? Had she not turned him over to Martha? Hadn't she deliberately picked Martha because she had realized Martha would make a less tormenting companion for the doctor than herself? Of course, Martha was a dope and a sly dope at that—but Hank would never find it out. Hank would probably marry her. Because she was sexy and obvious and a little bit creepy about loving—just as Hank was. She liked to get drunk and scramble, just the way Hank did; together they would find plenty of company.

Wasn't that a sacrifice? Wasn't she really—decent?

Wearily, ineluctably as always, Gail decided she was not. She'd grown so sick of Maddox that she had transferred his cravings just to be rid of him.

The Blood Bank, then? Wasn't that something? Three hours, three times a week. Her. Gail Chapman. In white again. Helping the volunteer physicians. Being ordered again. "Nurse. Tourniquet, please. Sponge." An officer had talked her into that. A dandy guy—back from the South Pacific. He'd lain there—in the next room—and talked her into what she had sworn she would never do again. "If you ever were a nurse, Gail, you gotta put out now. No kidding. What the hell kind of woman are you? In fact, who in hell do you think you are?"

So she had volunteered. Three hours—three afternoons a week. Except once in a while, of course, when hangovers made getting up out of the question.

Damn the officer.

If he'd known that she'd offered three hours only and on three days out of seven, what would he have said?

She knew.

He would have laughed.

He wasn't there to know, of course. He had gone back to the Pacific.

Pictures kept coming in the newspapers. Those endless pictures of men lying face down on sand and face up on stretchers. Pictures of nurses, even—in GI shoes and coveralls.

Damn the luck for having to know a trade that would somehow manage to give her a sense of guilt other girls didn't have to put up with. Damn her life—it was always like that.

She stirred the water and sighed.

Sense of guilt. She'd pushed that away long ago. It was gone, dead, executed, done for. If they wanted her for a nurse—let them draft nurses. That was it. She'd quit at the Blood Bank and wait for a draft. If no draft came— well, she would continue to support military morale.

She sighed again and touched herself with invitation. *You must come up tonight, Gail.*

She'd have to break the date with Lieutenant Commander Porter. And he was shoving off tomorrow. Well, he would have to shove off without anything better than a pinup. At least, war made men appreciate women.

There was even something haywire with that, she realized. Something wrong with all her thoughts. There always had been. She'd never had the start in life—the opportunity—that a normal girl required. And she had been dogged by atrocious bad luck. Her present way of living—

345

the heedless having of fun—was the only method by which she could honestly fight back against a dishonest fate. For life, if you really looked at it, was crooked. Nobody got a fair break. And that was why people were crooked. They only patterned themselves after reality. If the way things happened were honest—people would be more honest. Honest the way she was.

She lowered her hands slowly into the water and commenced to cry. For no reason. For no reason, long tears slid onto her cheeks—stopped to be refilled—and ran on again, until they joined the water in the tub. She was jittery. Drinking too much. But everybody was jittery these days. Who wouldn't be?

An extra man at dinner. At John's—at Ann's—at the old Gracey house. And what had been in Ann's voice? What compulsion? What sweetness? What change? What knowledge? Or what treachery?

You couldn't trust Ann. You couldn't trust anybody who, as a mere child, would let you almost drown them— and then not tell. Not protest. Not do anything. That was more unreasonable, more undependable, more inhuman than every accusation and every punishment could have been. Was that why Ann had chosen it?

Gail sat up straight and took a washcloth. She soaped it and began to scrub her face. The tears stopped.

But it was getting her. All inside herself she burned and shook. She was afraid. She was afraid because she did not know what frightened her. The adhesive shadow of her past? I don't have any past, she told herself, except a practically endless sob story. Nobody on earth could be blamed for reacting to misery.

Nobody could. But she went on blaming herself.

Two crimson faces came into her mind—a grown one and the face of an infant. Crimson and rigid. That happens to me, she thought, hiding her face under the cool, sweet-smelling washcloth, at least ten times a day. That's more than three thousand times a year. Maybe I'll live long enough to get up to a hundred thousand times. She laughed aloud and for a small, horrid piece of a second she thought that somebody else was standing in her bathroom laughing at her. She took the cloth away and peered around, knowing it was her own voice, but acting, still, with muscular instinct

346

—acting like an animal to whose nostrils has come the smell of alarm. A hundred thousand red faces. God! And she didn't know—she couldn't tell—she wasn't sure. She had tried and tried but it wasn't possible. The mind wasn't a mind—it was a down-curling labyrinth, a spiral tunnel, and you didn't think, if you ever happened to hit that particular skid—you just went down and down it, grabbing at smooth sides and spreading your legs to stop yourself and never even knowing how fast you were going.

For a long time after Todd and the baby died, she'd been relieved.

Not exactly glad. But relieved. At first she'd been afraid to admit that, even to herself. But at last she had made the confession and felt better for it. She was not meant to be a wife or a mother. She had made love to too many men before she had met Todd to stay in love with one constantly or to be satisfied by one man continuously. It wasn't nymphomania—because the books said nymphomania was the result of frigidity and anybody who could feel the well and overflow of loving so often and so variously and from so many causes—and so satisfyingly, for a little while—was not frigid. And it also wasn't nymphomania because she could take them or leave them alone. Like Hank. She could give them away. It was just—what she had said to John Galen. Someday everybody would be like her—and then she wouldn't be regarded by so many people with such disapproval. Or did she imagine the disapproval? Or was it envy?

She climbed from the tub and rubbed herself hard with the towel. It was work and it made her muscles tremble. She opened a little refrigerator, took out a cold split of champagne, and drank it while she dressed in pale lavender and gold. When she drove away in the roadster, the wine had brought relief. She felt bright and disembodied. The sun was melting into a late afternoon haze. A fitful breeze had at last sprung up—papers and dust rose ahead of her, spun, and collapsed in the street again. Soldiers were working on the hotels. When she had to wait for a green light, she waved at them.

She stopped her motor after she had turned into the cave that led to the Gracey house. She sat in the silent car, thinking—remembering. She was remembering the afternoon of her search in the old mansion. And she was thinking hotly about turning her car around and dodging the command invitation to dinner. Overhead, the branches gushed as though rain were being poured upon them in brief torrents. It was only the wind. Between gusts, the tangle was as still as the grave, and hotter, stuffier than ever before. When you need air in this country, she thought, you can't get it; you get practically smothered, instead.

If she went on, dinner would be an ordeal. If she went back to her apartment and made a date, dinner would still be an ordeal—because she would wonder and worry about not keeping her appointment with Ann. She stared into the tall, twisted thicket. It made her nervous. You couldn't see five yards into it, in some places, and wherever the eye penetrated the irregular interstices, the effect was more ominous still. Holes. Mouths. No person could walk through such stuff. Only ghosts. And the green things were all alive, all imperceptibly moving, growing; they fed upon themselves and they choked and killed everything which they reached: bodies, graves, houses, cities—everything.

She pressed the starter button and raced up the drive.

They were waiting for her. Ann and John and the little new man who looked something like an over-age kewpie. But the minute you thought that, you knew it was a wrong thought. He was some kind of dynamo. And he wasn't on the make—whatever else he was. He had looked at her in the most friendly and the most unsexy way imaginable.

They went out on the front veranda, with cocktails.

Gail dismissed Johann and concentrated on Ann. Something had happened. Something Gail could name. Something Gail could always recognize—the way animals recognized things. Gail looked from her radiant sister to John and caught his eyes, frank and shining, upon her. Well, he was turning it into a proclamation. Suddenly Gail felt weak with rage and hatred and envy and despair. Ann had done it again—with Bill hardly dead! Gail knew she was pale— knew her inner sickness was visible—but she also knew how to hold her face and even move it so that what was going on inside her would appear to be caused by her body and not her mind. A moment of oppression—of dizziness—the heat. Hangover, they would always think.

John handed a cocktail to her. She spilled it. She made a laugh—too high, but adequate. "I'm about dead. The heat.

348

And I'm katzenjammerish." That little man was staring at her. She brought the glass to her lips and downed a martini. In a minute, she would be better.

Johann, his name was. He stood up and began peering over the dunes at the oily, toiling sea. "Funny. We've all been praying for a breeze—but this one doesn't do much good. Like a furnace. Can't make up its mind to get organized. Pushes the water around without kicking up a surf. Well, maybe it'll cool off later."

That gave Gail a chance to finish her thought and to recover. Damn Ann for the hypocrite she had always been. Sly cat. Cheat. And how could she possibly be such a hypocrite and look so angelic? An echo answered that question— an echo that told Gail the same thing applied to herself. Not that she ever looked angelic. But that she could be as Babylonian or as Pompeiian as she pleased one night and on the next morning she could look as fresh and untouched as the morning's rose. She had practiced that and reveled in it. She was sure it proved that sex was not sin. Some inexorable fragment of her mind insisted that she apply that same definition now to Ann. If it was not sin for Gail, it was not sin for Ann—and Ann had a right to her present appearance.

John was refilling her glass. Small seas were breaking on the beach at irregular intervals. Ann was smiling at her.

I'm wrong somewhere, Gail thought desperately. Wrong again. It isn't love that's guilty or anything about love—but why do I have to be tormented now, on account of Ann? Am I jealous for John? She thought that she was very jealous. But, still, not that jealous. If Ann had decided to live the way I have lived, she thought furiously, she could have done it with the same assurance she has now. She wouldn't bite herself day and night, the way I do. That's why I get so enraged.

Now Ann was going into the house. "I'm the cook," she explained. "It's Josephine's night off."

"I'll help you." Gail said it harshly. She felt too weak and weary to budge. But she knew that the offer would be unexpected, so she made it.

"You certainly won't, darling. You're our guest of honor. You stay out and talk to John and Johann. Everything's nearly set, anyway."

349

The reddened sun fell against the windshield of a pa-
trolling boat out on the restive, darkling water and came
back to them as a spot of color, a danger flare, far off, small,
distinguished by its isolation. Gail saw that they were all
relaxed but consciously kindly and that their eyes rested upon
her with a significant expression. Patronizing, she tried to
tell herself. It was not that. Perceiving. It galled and rankled
her to be the object of any such attitude. But she was growing
more afraid, now, and she could not rise to a formed, de-
fensive act of disavowal or of rebuttal in advance.

They were being terribly nice to her.

She appreciated that during dinner. She ate the madri-
lene and the chops, the peas and the au gratin potatoes, the
salad and the crackers and cheese—ate them effortfully
and consciously, as though she were counting money. She
made automatic responses. But she knew also that they were
closing in upon her, that this hour had a purpose different
from the unspoken revelation about John Galen and her
sister. They were closing in on her like the night. It was
deliberate and it was beginning to unnerve her.

Talk withered.

"We'll have coffee and brandy back on the porch," Ann
said. "It's all ready on a tray. You carry it, John." Her voice
throbbed, softened itself.

A half hour of twilight was left. The wind had died.
Johann killed a mosquito inside the screen. John said he'd
had them repaired but that bugs still got in. Ann poured the
coffee and added cognac.

Then Gail said in parched syllables, "Look. What's it
all about?"

There was silence. The two men squeaked their chairs.

"You." Ann spoke softly. "We want to talk to you.
Maybe it was mean to drag you through dinner. But what
we want to say will take time. And it's important."

"I've had a growing, sneaking suspicion that some sort
of family soul-struggle over me was in the air. Well, I don't
want any part of it! We can go ahead with the act that all
of you adore me—or I can scram now and save a lot of
nonsense. If you tried to torment me—all right. You did."

Johann spoke. He had put down his demitasse. "Not torment you. Condition you—perhaps." His words were tran-

quil. "You came up here one day when John was out, Gail. You spent quite a lot of time in here—alone."

Gail's response was delayed. "Are you going to tell me that somebody robbed the place? Good God! I—"

"Not at all. Just that—we know what you were looking for. We think you were pretty courageous. And we think we can help you find out what you want to know."

Gail felt her insides scatter like giblets in an explosion. She clutched at them and recovered sufficiently to make a sensible response. "I was waiting for John. I wanted to finish a—a conversation we'd had. He owed it to me. I guess I was too late to collect, though, even then."

Ann flushed and looked at the sea.

John said, "Why did you wait inside, then? Why didn't you stay on the porch here? It was pleasanter."

Gail spoke bitterly to her sister. "You were spying."

"I saw you."

Johann was shaking his head negatively at John.

Gail stood up. "If that's what this sugar-coated inquisition is for—you'll all excuse me."

Johann's words were gentle. "No, Gail. You sit down. You thought the ghost up here—the ghost John talked about —was Todd's ghost, didn't you? It was very brave of you to come here and face that—deliberately."

Gail did sit down then. She felt utterly hopeless. They had something on her.

Johann handed a letter to her.

While she was reading, darkness began to invest the veranda.

She held herself rigidly and she read slowly. When she came near to the end, she had to shift her position and tilt the pages in order to see. After she had finished, she handed the letter back to Johann. He took it. She could feel her body going to ruins. She knew that she was now without hope or purpose or escape. That lousy little Howie had called her number. He had seen her when she had looked at the time. He had remembered. He had written. And Bill had known about it before his death. Bill had been the first to regard her the way the whole world would now regard her. Bill had wanted the world to know. Bill had haunted this house— where the letter must have lain in some hiding place, radiating her guilt like phosphorus at night and emanating the odor of it in the gloomy daytime. Her voice was a whisper that barely brushed away the silence: "Who can prove I was guilty—when I wasn't?"

She had framed that thought through the long interval. It was ready in its frame—for this slim possibility. She was facing it now—here—in the unreal murk of her own sister's porch.

Nobody said anything.

Gail felt her voice commence to cry and she had to use it that way. "Did you have to bring me up here and tell me that all the rest of your lives you are going to believe I murdered my own child and my husband? That Bill Gracey died believing I was a murderess? That he has been dragging his ghost around here to get you to find it out and pin it on me? You know that nobody can stand a thing like that. I can't. So you've done it. Or he did it. And you've shown me. And that's that." She tried to stand.

"You didn't kill your husband and your child," Johann said. "We wanted you to come up here to tell you that."

"I didn't?" The sound of it was blank.

"Listen, child. Listen. Don't speak. Just listen. You've spent a long and horrible time trying to escape from the shock of that night when you looked at your watch and turned pale—and remembered you'd left the motor running. You were a nurse—once. The shock of remembering was so great—remembering the oversight and its probable consequences—realizing that it was too late, when you did remember—that you've never since been able to think of anything but your own culpability."

"Why should I have? Not that I—!"

"You knew you were so sick of life on that desert—the way you had lived it and the way you were going to live it—that you were almost crazy. You feared that you might, some-day, have actually done such a thing. All people can have fears like that. And when you were dancing—when you remembered the running engine—when you realized that by that time the gasoline would all be gone—you began to believe what you have been fighting with yourself about ever since. To believe that you left the engine running on purpose—subconsciously. You've studied enough psychology to know about things like that. You hated your life enough

352

to know that such an escape was possible. You accused yourself on the spot. Then—because it was too late anyway—however it turned out—you went on dancing. You decided you had committed a subconscious murder and that you had a perfect alibi—and you probably thought you'd prepared that subconsciously, too—and that was the end of it."

"What makes you think I decided all that?"

"The way you lived. The way you live. Nobody I ever knew of has run from himself any faster or harder or farther. But you weren't right, you know. You were terribly wrong about your diagnosis. You see, Gail, you've always been afraid of yourself. You've been destructive and you know it. Think back to the time you tried to drown your sister. Maybe that began the whole thing. You've given in to destructiveness many, many times. It scares you. You assumed you'd destroyed your own child and husband—to escape misery. You went on escaping with all your might, afterward."

"It's easy to say that." Her voice was dull. "You're a doctor—I suppose. A psychiatrist?"

"Yes."

"I'll be going along—"

"You won't be, Gail. There are a couple of things you overlooked. You've got to know them, don't you think? After all, it's your conscience that's blinded you. You've got ten times as much as Ann. The warped kind of conscience, I mean."

"I suppose," she murmured acidly, "you can prove that I never had an evil thought in my life and that I was just careless. You can prove I was as innocent as—" she strangled—"little Todd."

"Yes. I can."

She didn't reply.

Johann's voice was low and rapid. "You should have talked to somebody about it—long ago. Anybody. Ann would have been perfect. Look, child. We're going to put an end to your self-torment. That's why we asked you here. Why we made such a ritual of it. It's so simple. Did your husband know you were going to the dance?"

"Of course."

"Did he want you to?"

"He said so. He was a kind guy. Too kind. He urged

353

me to, in fact. I'd been working a long time. A lot of cases. I was pretty shot."

"Could he get out of bed?"

"He was weak. But he could, yes."

"Then—if you went off in a hurry and left the engine running—why didn't he shut it off? He knew the exhaust leaked into the trailer. Was he awake when you left?"

"He said good-bye."

Johann halted. "He said good-bye." He let her think over that phrase. "Are you sure you left the motor running?"

"No. I just suddenly didn't remember turning it off. I think I left it on. The batteries were low—and I was dressing—and late—"

"I see."

"But—Todd wouldn't do that. Not Todd. He was weak in some ways—and all that—but he wouldn't have got up and started the motor and killed the baby and himself. See? I've thought of that."

"But if you had left it on. And he'd just lain there—doing nothing."

Gail's reply was sharp. "But it would still have been me! Leaving it on—on purpose but without admitting it."

"Still, he might have let it run."

"I don't know."

"You didn't leave it on—subconsciously. You see, Gail, if you had wanted to do a thing like that—however unconsciously—you wouldn't have picked something that he could have stopped. And even if the most hidden part of your mind had planned something that he could finish—it would have been different. Even if you'd left it running—hoping a hidden hope that he would lie there with his misery and a knowledge of yours, until he and the baby died—*you would have behaved differently*. What actually happened was that suddenly—in the midst of the dance—you got the horrible thought that you might have left the engine on. Right? You automatically looked at your watch. You then knew it would have been running long enough—if Todd hadn't turned it off—to kill them both. You accused your inner, secret motives, instantly. And that is why you decided to brazen it out with Howie Evans. You began to hide things, from *then* on."

Her head nodded in the shadows.

His voice was low and very firm. "The subconscious

mind—is my field, Gail. I know something of how it works. If all that happened had been a concealed scheme of yours— you would never have had that instant of realization. That horrible recollection. That glance at the watch. That sickness. That quick recovery. You missed realizing that. Do you see? Your subconscious would have prepared your behavior at the party along with the preparation of the deed. You'd have danced serenely all evening. You could have got drunk safely —without giving anything away. You would have been all innocence from the beginning to the end. You would have armed yourself against the slightest chance of having any queasy moment—such as you did have. It isn't compatible with the rest of it. What really happened, Gail, was an honest mistake—if, indeed, you left the engine running at all. You're a nurse—trained in responsibility for detail. You were taking a night off. In the midst of it—you recalled a detail—a dangerous detail—you'd overlooked; or that you couldn't remember having cared for. Your first thought was of the time elapsed. You checked that and saw it was too much time for any saving action. So you then grew pale. If you had grown pale and scared first, and kept peeping at your watch—one could put a different construction on the situation. But you didn't. It went the other way. You were not a subconscious murderess who caught herself in the act. Impossible. You were, at worst, a nurse who had made a slip—such as any nurse can make. And do you know why you have put the wrong construction on it?"

Again her head shook.

"Because you have always thought incorrectly about yourself. All your life. It's a mistaken process, Gail, and I think you won't be able to keep it up any more, after tonight. Billions of people do it. You see—you're a puritan at heart. And puritanism is a monstrous thing. It's wrong because there is no perfection in nature. The notion of an original sin comes from the perfection idea; it, too, is monstrous. The idea we are born guilty is a hideous idea. You're the end product of all such superstitions. You married Todd to escape the hospital. That was your only mistake. You tried to keep him— and the baby—alive. He killed both—to free you—and that was his sin. Nobody can judge either. You and Todd just began wrong. He ended wrong. You're not ended—yet. Not if you give up thinking you're fundamentally wicked—and give

355

up, also, forever running away from that thought. You see, you don't have to pay for Todd's guilt, just because your act of marrying him was dishonest."

The darkness was now close to absolute. The sky had thickened beneath the stars. The wind was more restless; it pushed treetops and poured through the unnumbered leaves. The insects were not audible. Time passed on the breathless veranda. Gail's shoulders drew together and the sound of a sob overrode the uneasy night. From the distance came a sudden noise of hammering—muted, fast, incongruous. Gail's sobs grew longer and the pain in her clenched throat was perceptible to them. Ann slipped across the porch and her figure merged with the figure of the weeping girl.

Johann and John left them.

They blinked in the blackout room and became accustomed again to illumination. John looked at his old friend with his heart in his eyes. He didn't say anything.

"Cigarette?" Johann was smiling with good cheer. But his face was slick with the sweat of night heat and calm effort. "Spiritual suffering," he sighed, "is so often just conceit."

John took a cigarette. Those were hard words, for Johann. Hard—and meant—and merited.

The psychiatrist frowned. "What's that hammering about? Sounds as if it were over where Ann lives."

"Search me." John paced the familiar chamber. "Is there anything we ought to do for Gail?"

"Nothing that Ann can't do better." Johann's eyes shone again. "Get to the right log and you break the jam. I hope— and I think—that we did." He pursed his lips in a silent shape of whistling, walked across the room, and patted the heavy curtains until they were flat against the window frame. "The blackout rules have been made stricter. I noticed today they were actually boarding up the hotels. I suppose the subs have got so tough we aren't allowed to risk even a crack of light. Strange sensation—this living in the dark. After Chicago. Do the home town good to be blacked out a while. What's the matter?"

John was standing stock still. "Did you say they were boarding up the windows?"

"Sure. Even those that faced west. It'll be hot indoors for the soldiers, won't it?"

John strode to the portable radio and switched it on.

356

Johann stared uncomprehendingly. The voice came—flat, and yet excited:

". . . at present about twelve miles offshore. Communication with the British West Indies has not yet been restored. Coast Guard vessels proceeding ahead of the storm report it to be of full hurricane intensity. Owing to the fact that information concerning weather has been a military secret, the approach of this disturbance was not announced until the last possible moment. Local authorities feel that, as a result, there may be many unwarned persons in the area and all residents of sparsely settled, outlying districts are urged to make sure that the warning has been carried to every person in their neighborhoods. . . . I will now repeat the last bulletin. It was announced at three P.M. today that a storm of tropical intensity was rapidly approaching the Florida coast . . ."

The two men looked at each other for a moment. "I'll tell the girls," John said. "We better get out of here."

9

WITH ANN and Gail, they shut doors, raised windows a few inches, turned out lights, and hurried into Gail's car. They had to wait at the main road for the passage of a procession of swiftly driven military trucks. Then they ran the car north and turned into the lawn around which the bungalows were built. Ann and her sister raced into the cottage for Ann's clothes. Wind whipped them as they crossed the grass. The door crashed behind them. There were lights in only one bungalow. John and Johann ran up to it. They found a middle-aged woman hammering furiously at her storm shutters. Three youngsters, white-faced and shrill, were helping her.

"You'd better get away from here," John said. "The storm will hit pretty soon. We can squeeze you in—"

" 'Tisn't too much of a blow, according to the radio," the woman replied. "I've been through several. We're all right."

"We'll take you to a hotel in Miami—"

The woman turned. Light from inside her house streamed upon her determined face, her flying gray hair. "All the rest of the tenants ran away. But it's too late, now.

Road below'll be jammed solid with trucks and fools running around in cars. You give me a good, solid little house—and I'll prefer it to a hotel. It's noisy and you may get wet—but that's about all. We're several feet up, here. Ten, I figure."

John hesitated. "Can we give you a hand?"

"I'm about finished." Her voice was indignant. "Imagine trying to keep a hurricane a military secret! If that don't beat the Dutch! Come on, small fry. Around to the back door!"

She went away in the boisterous dark. Her children followed her.

The men stood irresolutely. "You suppose it's a fact—about the roads being clogged up?" the doctor asked.

"What?"

Johann repeated it in a shout.

"Search me. Doesn't it strike you that it's blowing harder all the time?"

"Yeah. Let's go help the girls."

Inside Ann's bungalow the lights burned brightly. Gail was closing a suitcase. Ann was hurrying about in the bedroom. The little building vibrated. Ann leaned through the door. "Everybody out all right?"

"There's a woman with three kids who's staying—"

"Mrs. Pole. She would. Should we evacuate her by force?"

"She said," John answered, "that the road will be jammed below here. I guess a lot of traffic has been rolling past. She thinks she's safe. Been through others."

Gail spoke quietly. "We can look—and turn around before we get caught in any traffic mess—if there is one. After all, the Gracey house has been through several, too—and it's still there."

They piled Ann's suitcases into the luggage compartment. They drove south. Hard gusts hit the car; Gail had to wrench the wheel fiercely to keep from going onto the shoulder. Cars moving at a faster clip began to pass them—headlights streaming up from behind, glaring on the road alongside, and shooting ahead, licking up puddles of darkness in the pitted pavement. Presently they rounded a bend and saw in the distance a line of red taillights that stretched out of sight—crimson eyes in a blur of headlamps reflected by the rear ends of trucks and passenger cars. They overtook the procession rapidly, even though Gail slowed so as to judge its pace. Here, the road ran close to the beach. The sea, on their left, was black, deeply crested in white. It boomed on the sand. The wind pressed them, swaying the car on its spring suspension.

It began to rain. The windshield was heavily splashed—there was a momentary remission—and then a deluge. Road, cars, sea and inland vegetation vanished in the silver-white torrent. Another car swished past them, skidded savagely, found traction again, and swept its red lamp into the downpour. Gail stopped. Rain drummed on the top of the car. From time to time a wet rumble against the side made a sound different from that of the downpour.

"It's the sea hitting us," John said. "Look. We better turn around. We aren't in any parade that we can follow. The damned waves may cut the road ahead, anywhere along here. I'll take your place, Gail—"

"I can make it." Gail had the car in gear. She executed a U-turn swiftly—lest another car bear down upon them from the opaque world of the rain. "It's about a mile and a quarter, I guess."

When, finally, the rain diminished and they had found the entrance to the Gracey house, the wind was blowing with force enough to make itself felt as an obstacle in the green tunnel. Gail drove in second gear. She parked close up against a wall of the house.

They went in—running—carrying Ann's luggage. The back door slammed. John switched on the kitchen light; the dimout would not matter at such a moment. They set down the bags and looked at one another. The house still contained its own silence: the incomprehensible thunder of the sea was outside of it and apart from it. Shutters flapped. Joists and rafters creaked. Loosened scrollwork batted against the weathered clapboards. But all of this did not seem to affect the pent, enormous stillness within the house.

"Perhaps," Johann said slowly, "I should try to find my way over to that woman and the children and stay with them."

Ann replied anxiously, "You wouldn't make it. We barely got back here."

Gail touched his sleeve. "Don't try. What could you do if you got there? And she's been through them. She felt safe."

"There are kerosene lamps in the closet," Ann said. "And there should be kerosene around for them. I vaguely recall a can, someplace."

"Smart," John said. "I'll rustle the grub and some mattresses. Probably'll last all night. We'll hole up in the black-out room. Let's go."

Ann took a flashlight, led them in, came back, and began to hunt among old boxes and barrels in the big closet off the kitchen. She found the dusty lamps. She uncovered a rusty five-gallon can, rocked it, heard the gurgle of kerosene, and began to polish the glass chimneys, putting the flashlight on a barrel and rubbing with an old rag. Closet cobwebs gathered in her hair. Now and then she could feel the house shake, as though it were in jaws. She whistled a note to herself— and could not hear it—and knew then how loud the wind was. She was aware of what might happen to all of them and she considered that awareness. Johann, she thought, has lived much; it would make no difference to him. Gail had the consolation of understanding herself at last. John. He would almost choose it.

She thought of herself and she smiled in the penumbra of the single flashlight ray: it could be now, or tomorrow, or in fifty years. She was happy within herself. A gift, she thought, and she did not think in terms of sacrifice or of courage or of unselfishness.

She filled the lamps.

Gail walked alone with another flashlight to the second story of the house. She stripped blankets from the beds and carried them to the stairhead. She threw them down to John. When he called, "Enough," she went back to the front room and yanked down the quilts that had blacked it out. She turned off her light and pressed her face again to the vibrating windowpane. Presently her eyes could see through the spouting rain and churning salt water to the gathering far mountains on the open ocean; she watched them shoulder toward the beach; ten or fifteen feet high; they toppled, crashed and bellowed up to the low dunes. She stared at this vague scene awhile, smiling. *It's okay,* she thought. *Okay.*

Johann carried the lighted lamps for Ann. He set them on tables. He did not say anything at all—or think anything, perhaps. He had been in battles; one did what was necessary.

For the rest—one looked at one's fellows with attention. As always.

John piled the folded blankets. He made a neat arrangement of the canned goods and kitchen utensils. If the current failed—they might be able to cook eggs and coffee over the lamps.

Now, they were together again.

They moved four chairs close.

When the electric lights quietly went out, the lamps took over their function—dimly.

Somewhere, down the road, a pole had gone over. Somewhere, the wires had spat sparks in the sightless deluge and somewhere else a fuse had blown, pale lavender in the tumultuous night. The sea moved ashore. It gnawed and boiled under the pavement, sucked it upon itself, and turned it over and over, pulverizing it. Where there had been a highway was now a socket in the road—a cavity through which each black and terrible wave swept inland upon sea grape, sand, trailing vine and frail weed. Leaves abandoned their branches. Bare stalks in the tangled jungles ceased hissing and commenced to shriek. Here a tree bent down and flagellated the underbrush until its roots yielded and it toppled over. Here the top was snapped out of a wracked Australian pine or a compressed palm and sent flying over the dark and beaten earth.

In front of the Gracey house the dunes were being dissolved. The sea carried its racing hills higher and higher upon them and presently the wind, having scoured the fresh rain off the land ahead of the ocean, pressed tongues of salt water up paths and around the sides of the house into the crushed coral where Gail's car was parked.

The lights were off everywhere, now. Throughout the vast region, people sat inside their hot homes, around radios, beside candles, looking at each other. The great hotels screamed, caterwauled, shook and shuddered. Soldiers sat silent by the tens of thousands in their quarters, sweating out a barrage they could not answer. Electric wires lashed and snarled in the streets. Wood ripped. Metal snapped. Ropes sang. Here and there, an ambulance staggered through the horizontal pandemonium. Doors and coconuts, branches, tree trunks, boards and brickbats attacked across the pouring night. Windows broke. Signs winged to the Everglades. A windrow of royal palms lay down in a main thoroughfare, machine-gunned by the wind. Boats hidden far up the river yanked at their multiple hawsers. An incautious gull was dashed to death on the streaming wall of a skyscraper. Beach cabanas were flung loose by the encroaching mass of the sea, chopped into kindling, and fed to the wind and the darkness. Tents were stripped away from an orderly formation; denuded men scurried like ants in a hill ripped by a hose.

The four people in the Gracey house were silent. They smiled and sweat. The sea was beating the doorstep—no doubt of it—although it was a change in the feel of the house that made them know, rather than a sound—because they could hear no sound now, except the wind. When the water came into the blackout room, sluicing under the front door and down the hall, John tasted it with his finger to be certain, snatched up the blankets, and went out. After he returned and nodded reassurance, they relaxed a little.

A piece of the roof went. They heard that: a berry box crushed by somebody far away. But the house budged with the sound—jumped on its foundations. A nameless hammer beat like Thor's on the walls overhead until it, too, was hurled into the storm. But now the wind had a hole to speak across. The room was full of a hollow, huge jug sound and the Navajo rug rocked back and forth, back and forth, like a valve; the oil lamps smoked in the wind and the room became cooler. The storm was getting at them piecemeal. They knew it. And the sea was rising toward them.

John went to the kitchen. He opened the back door, which was in the lee. He switched on his flashlight. The rain fell horizontally. The only visible portion of the thicket was so tossed and smashed that it made no comprehensible pattern. In the far murk, a few still standing treetops flailed against the streaked horizon. He pointed the light down. The water was hip-deep and running like a river—inland—into the jungle. The wind had tipped over Gail's car and the sea was cascading about it viciously. He returned. They looked at him questioningly and he shrugged.

Johann made the rounds of the room with a bottle of cognac and glasses. John and Ann took a little. Gail shook her head and leaned close to the physician. "I'm all right the way I am," she said clearly. "I like it this way."

He nodded slowly at her.

362

The storm broke in like lightning. They had been sitting very close together, Ann bending over the radio, listening. Now and again, she made a report. *At its height along the coast. Moving toward Homestead.* Then, suddenly, the windows crashed. No glass flew because the curtains and comforters caught it. A shape took out the window frames and fell heavily in the room. A table went over. The lamps dropped to the floor and shattered. Kerosene blazed up. John saw the blackout blankets whipped aside by the invading wind. A plank, hurtling through the night, had speared their windows. Now, as he took Ann by the hand, the flames of the burning oil licked up the draperies. Wind from the hole blew upon the fire, fanned it high, and spread the kerosene. Johann, with Gail, ran around it, toward the kitchen. Within seconds, there was too much blaze to extinguish.

They went down the back steps, jumped into the water—and stood there, huddled together. The Gracey house began to glow. Wind bent the four people—salt stung them—sand bit their skin. They backed up, across the open space, toward the mouth of the drive. John used his light. The road was packed with vegetation; the sea spilled through and over it but they plowed among the trees, lashed by a thousand whips. John tried to shield Ann with his arms. He felt her push back against him, and saw in the light of his flash, a snake swimming frantically in the running water. He stopped and waited until it had disappeared. Johann and Gail were behind, floundering toward the light. The water became shallow as they penetrated the vegetation that had been piled on the road. He could see that Ann's arms had been cut. His shirt was in tatters.

Then the wind stopped.

It stopped as though it had been turned off at some celestial vent. They straightened up. A furious assault bent them again—and again stopped. The trees dripped. The water roared. Behind them, the sea played its continental tympanum. The earth still shook. But there was no wind, and the rain slackened.

"It's the lull," Ann shouted—and her voice was loud. She lowered it. "We'll have a chance, now, to get to the bungalows for the rest of it."

But they stood, with the water rushing around their feet and the wet branches hanging everywhere in the desecrated night. They looked back. Flames were bursting from the Gracey house. And yet, it burned softly, like a picture of fire; consuming orange arms rose embracingly around it. The sea sounds drowned all roar or crackling, so the conflagration seemed utterly silent. The house was silhouetted by its cremation. Another segment of roof slowly collapsed. Sparks rose a little distance and swarmed down on the surrounding earth. What remained of the scrollwork now hung like lace in the sheets of fire; black ribs were serially exposed as the wallwork peeled away from them. The entering wind had spread and fed this silent consummation; now, in the dead air, it ate at every portion of the old, dry mansion. They could not go on for some time—in spite of their need for haste. This abnormal destruction, this unexpected and gaudy incineration, was necromancy—unhallowed and yet satisfying.

Johann said to Gail, "You know, I left that letter in there."

She turned and he saw her face plainly. "All of us left something that's better off for being there."

Ann said, "We must hurry. When the wind comes back the other way, it won't bring the sea ashore—but it'll be wicked walking through."

John led them out of that place.

10

THE MORNING that followed was halcyon. Its clouds were as white as mountain snow; the sun was gentler than it had been for a month; every fallen leaf was droplet-jeweled; and all the air was perfumed by crushed flowers. This is the climate of forgetfulness that follows the storm; it is lulling and lovely weather and it continues, always, until nature can no longer bear too much beauty too easily produced—and destroys some little of it to balance good and evil and to make necessary room for the future.

That function, Shawn thought, as he looked down from the window of an airplane, is half the explanation of living and dying. He could see mist rolling like cotton across the 'Glades and the jade glitter of water holes but, from the plane's height, there was no sign of the hurricane that had passed on the night before . . . Clearing away the present for the sake of the future was a manifest main process of nature. It was the glory of humanity. But it had to be understood. The individual had to stand under it, literally, with his soul—support it, and know it, and not be swept away in it, uncomprehending.

Materialists—people who no longer associated themselves with nature, who thought that the tentative cities and the fugitive civilizations were all of nature—people who lived in the madness of absolute objectivity—Americans, Shawn thought—reinterpreted that august principle to fit concepts narrowed by their point of view. They still paid lip service to the sacrifice of the present generation for the next. But they spent a thousand times as much money and effort in the maintenance of the living as they spent to assure the favorable birth and prospects of newcomers. They gave ten thousand times as much energy and thought to the enjoyment of superficial pleasures in the present as they gave to a consideration of how that present might be organized in the behalf of those to come. So they were traitors to nature—to law: to God, if God was the name they gave to living.

The plane descended in the washed world. Shawn stepped into the warmth, waited for his luggage, and took a cab. The people were already mending the damage—men stripped to the waist, women in bright slacks and blouses. It had not been a bad blow. From the taxi he could see that only a few things had suffered—shrubs and flowers, glass and trees. The leaves would grow back. The trees could be stood up. The glass could be replaced . . . Sailors marched with a new tempo—the tempo of threat survived and balmy morning. Soldiers drove buzzing truck convoys in that same fresh rhythm.

Thalia came out to meet him, first. She kissed him and stood away from him a little, smiling. "Well, commander. You look wonderful. Do you realize I never saw you without a beard before?"

His eyes gleamed. "Don't underestimate me without it. There was only one difficulty. It left a bleached area around the firm, relentless mouth. A barber stained it to match— till I get it sunburned."

Thalia took his arm and laughed and held him still. "Ann and John are here."

"Wonderful!"

She told him quickly about the night on the seaboard and the blazing death of the Gracey house. He turned his hat over and over in his hands, looking at it. "There's so much more to tell," she said. "But I'll leave that to them. Imagine! After what they went through—the first thing they did when they could move, was to walk five miles and then hitchhike—to find out if I was okay! The phones weren't working—early this morning."

"Like 'em, isn't it?" Shawn blew his big nose and went into the house and through it and out to the patio.

Ann and John were jubilantly assisting Willie and Willa in the preliminary policing of the lawn. It was a small wilderness of heaped leaves, fallen branches, palm fronds, coconuts, boards, boxes, other people's porch furniture, wet paper, garbage cans, a strip of a wooden fence, and a car fender—a wind-borne miscellany. The children saw their father, yelled, ran up to him, saluted, and then jumped on him as though he were a tree to be climbed.

The tableau was short: sunshine, the shouting kids, the oaklike man.

"I'll get you some breakfast," Thalia said. "Then you can unpack. John and Ann are staying here for the time being. You won't mind if they keep your room?"

Shawn didn't answer for an instant. He let the little girl slide easily to the lawn. "No, Thalia. You see—" he looked at her—"I'm shoving off again tomorrow morning."

"Oh." Her eyes rested upon him and journeyed beyond him. She smiled. "I'm so glad it isn't—this afternoon. Or tonight. Something really rushed."

After lunch, John watched Shawn assemble the art materials he would require on his mission. He sat for a long time while the big man concentrated on the vivid minutiae. He could see Shawn in his mind's eye—somewhere behind steel barricades on a ship's deck—these very pencils in his hand, that very pad braced against a stanchion. All around would be the Pacific—cobalt, violet, lavender, green. In the distance, a flat island like Florida, here across the bay. Overhead, this same blue, water-color sky—this sky that looked as though it had been painted with a dilution of the Gulf Stream. In Shawn's sky there would be Jap planes—a hornet's nest of them. Their iron motors would come screaming down.

They would eject their steel defecation. Here and there planes would blaze vermilion—burst—fall as smoke and sticks. Yonder, one would meteor into the level ocean, dying in cloud-sized live steam. Behind the ship, a crooked wake would boil. All the guns would be firing. A thousand instantaneous tracer lines would rule the air above it. The intent, slack-faced men would crane their necks and lunge their guns about. The deck would tremble and undulate. Eardrums would burst. Rent metal would howl and ricochet. Blood would squirt and spatter. Shawn would stand there, sketching.

When, someday, the men roared onto a foreign beach, Shawn would be with them. He would have a carbine in his hands and his brushes on his back, then, and these khaki pockets would bulge with grenades. In the exotic ecstasy of battle, the light burning in his eyes would be a light kindled by Thalia and by the two kids and by America—which he had excoriated with such skill and which he so passionately loved.

"What you thinking of?"

"You."

"I was thinking of you, son. Going to get married soon?"

"Right soon. Real soon."

"I wish—"

"What?" John asked. He looked at the mixed mischief and embarrassment in the artist's eyes—and at the hidden affection. "Doggone, I'll ask the bride. But Johann'll have to be best man. You can give her away. Okay?"

"Suits me." Shawn smacked him mightily on the back. . . .

Later in the afternoon, before they drove to Miami for what Shawn called "legal adjustment," the artist walked along the sea wall with Ann. "Something tribal in this business, gal. And, Lord, what a cozy wench you look! I'm down-right proud of you. God!"

She laughed—and sobered.

"I know."

"Damn if you don't." He paused and watched the mullet an exact inch below the surface. "Wonder how they stay on that course? Look, Ann. You making any long plans?"

"I sort of have to."

"Good girl." He didn't ask what they were.

So she told him. "Johann wants me to read a lot of books. He's going to have a clinic of soldiers and sailors—the ones that get mentally damaged. When the time comes—I'll be able to work there."

"I'm going to kiss you."

She looked up, and laughed again.

"It's going to be one hell of a kiss, you know. The post-ceremonial peck will never suffice for your old uncle Shawn."

11

IT WAS a day in October. Johann Altheim had sent from his office—smiling—a soldier who had not smiled since an afternoon in the early spring when he had leaped from behind a fallen palm to carry his bayonet forward. Now, Johann peered over the park with a faint impress of the soldier's expression on his own face. The leaves were turning. Lake Michigan had a frosty-blue look. The sun had cooled without losing its glitter, a strange, inevitable phenomenon of autumn. Someone knocked on his door. It was not the next patient, but a hospital messenger. "Telegram, Dr. Altheim."

The little man fished under his white coat for a quarter. He read the message:

> WE ARE LEAVING TOMORROW FOR CHICAGO.
> JOHN IS WORSE BUT DON'T LET ON YOU KNOW WHEN
> YOU SEE HIM. WE ARE INCREDIBLY HAPPY. THALIA
> AND KIDS FINE AND SEND LOVE. I SOLD THE GRACEY
> LAND. WANTED TO KEEP JOHN DOWN HERE BUT HE
> IS DETERMINED TO TRY TO WORK IF HE CAN. LOVE
> FROM US BOTH.
>
> ANN

12

THE GREAT, new battleship with the undisclosable name came about, behind a bow-hill of cobalt sea, and the torpedoes shot past her stern. Every antiaircraft gun aboard her opened up and the commander of a distant cruiser said with admiration that she looked like a burning fireworks factory. On board her, helmeted, relaxed, his eyes gleaming, Shawn sketched. A sailor halted and yelled, "Sure is yorking up her red-hot guts!"

Shawn winked.

13

GAIL stood in line. She had always hated queues and she still did. But she knew that she was going to stand in many now, and the knowledge did not precipitate her customary wrath: her face was as tranquil as a nun's. When her turn came, she flushed with eagerness and bent toward the middle-aged interviewer, resting one hand on the desk. It was not blood-tipped, as it had been for so many years. And Gail's poured gold hair was in a bun. She gave her name in an impersonal, efficient tone. Her pale-blue eyes rested upon a sign above and behind the woman's desk, danced once, and became matter-of-fact. The sign said: "Army Nurse Volunteers Register Here."

14

JOHN walked along the boulevard at a steady pace. He liked to walk—enjoyed the thrust and pull of his muscles. He took pleasure from the ring of his heels.

Cooler in Miami. The northwest breeze had in it the smoke of burning vegetation. Not burning oak and maple leaves, but a fair approximation of that aroma, for the tropics. No clouds. Gulls and pelicans. But not a cloud.

Pick up the tickets. Stop for the bag that was being repaired. Then back to Ann—and to Chicago—and to work. Ann wouldn't like it if she knew he was running errands alone. But she was busy packing.

His feet slowed with a certain misgiving. No use kidding about it. The thing struck like a fist—again and again—and every time you felt a little bit weaker. Not physically weaker, exactly—but weaker because you were growing different. You felt like Alice eating the part of the mushroom that diminished her, or like the Cheshire cat dwindling to a smile, or like somebody a Gorgon had looked at. Weaker mentally?

369

He ran equations through his head—and stumbled on one of them. His pace lagged. He frowned in an effort to recover the exact detail and arrangement of the mathematical symbols.

That mood submerged itself and he looked outward again. The world sparkled. The illumination of Florida was more unreal than ever. He came to an iron lamppost and waited for traffic to flow at the right angle.

How I love Ann.

And he thought, A year. Two. Every time I open my eyes—she'll be bending angellike above me, smiling. Like a mother. Like the mother of all mothers. And when I die—

The light hopped up—orange—and up—green. He could hardly make it out against the bright blue sky.

Still, he lingered.

When I die—will there be that flash of understanding? That moment of knowing just how infinity means eternity to me? Do I know now?

A little of the spirit of the scientist asserted itself. It was good—all good—if you made it good—no matter who you were. Because everybody was part of everybody else— and, being part of everybody, you were as indestructible— as what? As electrons. Because you were an electron. How vain—how idiotic—to waste time wondering about afterward when you were destined to discover anyway. When afterward was always now. No matter what.

Lovely Ann. Poor Ann. No. Lovely Ann.

How long, too long, have we, the living, considered our lives as sacrifices to death! Surely, it goes the other way: we ought to think of death only in relation to our endless aliveness!

The lights clicked once again.

He stood still and quietude came into his mind. The world of sound and angles, of smells, shapes and vibrations commingled, melted, and flowed away from him. He was alone with himself. This, he thought, is not vision but the withdrawal of earthly vision. He waited patiently for more to happen. He had a sense of movement—not in one direction but in all the directions of expansion; he was gradually enabled to perceive the comfort of his shining, gray nothingness—both from the center of it and from its ever-widening peripheries. The light increased and became blinding—a classic white light and, presently, the whiteness beyond passion. All at once the brightness took on every hue. He knew that he was what he was observing and what he was experiencing.

I am this, he thought. This perfect awareness. This sentient geometry. This polychromatic infinitude. I must halt here and discover what it is, then, that I am. He studied to do so. He could feel phrases trying themselves in response to his endeavor. Here is the heart of me and the heart of the universe—time viewed without emotion—the changing shape of space, and its colors. Out of this comes art, music, knowledge. This is the mathematical seed of living. Beyond good and evil, pain and pleasure, thought and matter, lies this construction—this becalmed ecstasy—this crystallized forever.

He lost, suddenly, his identification with the expansion of the figure and was merely contained by it for a brief moment. Then, as he strove to recapture the whole experience, he found the external half of it growing white around him again. His temporal sensibilities were restored. It means, he thought—it meant, he amended—so much more than I could gather in that little moment. I shall have to find it again—to find it by search—by recollection and study—for I belong there.

I came from there.

He was unsurprised when the surrounding world materialized. Here was the iron post of the lamp, the street, the passing crowd. Now, he thought, I belong here. I have come back from the journey within. Ann is waiting for me. The tickets. The suitcase. My work.

He tried again the equation over which he had stumbled and he could not only recall it with clarity but it seemed, for a few fading seconds, to be a simple thing—the homework of a small child. That shows, he thought, how much more work there is to do—how great is the oncoming range of men's minds. Such is the future, whereof I have seen the completion and the beginning also.

What was it? The experience of the primordial atom which had exploded into the universe? Its equivalent in consciousness? The Veddas had foretold as much. Abbe Le-Maître had hypothesized it. *Philosophers and physicists.* The full course of the phylogeny of memory runs back to the start

371

and forward to the end. He began to walk, in lucid bemusement. His foot stepped down from the curb. He was smiling.

A truck horn sounded, loud as a trumpet. The vehicle loomed beside him, its chrome plate shining, its voice like Gabriel's. He scarcely noticed. I am life, he thought. I know what my experience means because I am that experience.

It means